If I
Never
Met
You

Sunda *:mes* bestselling author, Mhairi McFarlane, was born i ꞏland in 1976 and her unnecessarily confusing name s onounced Vah-Ree. After some efforts at jour-nalism, started writing novels and her first book, *You Had M it Hello*, was an instant success. *If I Never Met You* is sixth book. She lives in Nottingham with a man a cat.

Also by Mhairi McFarlane

If I Never Met You

Mhairi McFarlane

HarperCollins*Publishers*

HarperCollins*Publishers* Ltd
1 London Bridge Street
London SE1 9GF

www.harpercollins.co.uk

Published by HarperCollins*Publishers* 2020
6

Copyright © Mhairi McFarlane 2020

Mhairi McFarlane asserts the moral right to
be identified as the author of this work

A catalogue record for this book
is available from the British Library

ISBN: 978-0-00-816948-0

This novel is entirely a work of fiction.
The names, characters and incidents portrayed in it are
the work of the author's imagination. Any resemblance to
actual persons, living or dead, events or localities is
entirely coincidental.

Typeset in Bembo by Palimpsest Book Production Ltd, Falkirk, Stirlingshire

Printed and bound in Great Britain by
CPI Group (UK) Ltd, Croydon CR0 4YY

MIX
Paper from
responsible sources
FSC™ C007454

This book is produced from independently certified FSC™ paper
to ensure responsible forest management.

For more information visit: www.harpercollins.co.uk/green

For my sister, Laura
the human Lisa Simpson

1

Dan

What time you think you'll be back tonight? Roughly?

Laurie

Dunno. SOON I HOPE.

Dan

You hope?

Laurie

Everyone has raspberries in Proseccos 😊

Dan

I thought you liked Prosecco. And raspberries

Laurie

I do! I've got one. 😊 *But denotes a certain type of Girls Night Out that's not very me. They're calling them 'cheeky bubbles'* 😑

1

Dan
Your problem is other people like it too? Can't imagine my criticism of a night out being 'people ordered the same drink' 😊

Laurie
. . . Except when you said you hate stag dos that 'start with getting ten pints of wife beater in at 7am in Gatwick Spoons'.

Dan
You can't take a moment off being a lawyer, can you?

Laurie
HAH. You misspelt 'you got me bang to rights, Loz' 😊

Dan is typing

. . .

Dan is typing

. . .

Last seen today at 9.18pm

Dan must've thought better of his reply. Laurie clicked her phone off and pushed it back into her bag.

Obviously she didn't really mind the cliché, booze was booze, that was *trying to be wittily acerbic* bravado. It was a distress signal. Laurie was at sea and her phone felt like a connection back to shore. Tonight was an unwelcome flashback to the emotions of lunch breaks at secondary school, when you had a single-parent mum and no money and no cool.

So far, the girls had discussed the benefits of eyebrow

microblading ('Ashley from Stag Communications looks like Eddie Munster') whether or not Marcus Fairbright-Page at KPMG was a bad arsehole who'd break hearts and bed frames (Laurie thought on what she'd gleaned, that was an emphatic yes, but also gathered that a verdict wasn't desired). And how many burpees you could manage in HIIT class at Virgin Active (no idea there, none).

They were all so glamorous and feminine, so carefully groomed and produced for public display. Laurie felt like a dishwater-feathered pigeon in an enclosure full of chirruping tropical birds.

Emily really owed her. Tonight was the product of something that happened roughly once every three months – her best friend, and owner of a PR company, begged Laurie to join their team night out and make it 'less bloody boring, or we'll spend the whole time discussing the new accounts.' Emily, as CEO and hostess, was at the head of the table putting everything on the company credit card and handing round the Nocellara olives and salted almonds. Laurie, late arrival, was at the far end.

'Who was that, then?' said Suzanne, to her right. Suzanne had a beautiful shoulder-length sheet of custard-coloured hair and the gaze of a customs officer.

Laurie turned and concealed her irritation with a ventriloquist's dummy smile. 'Who was what?'

'On your phone! You looked well intense,' Suzanne rolled her doe eyes upwards and mimed a sort of chimpanzee-like, vacant trance state, her hands moving across an imaginary handset. She whooped with girlish, alcohol-fuelled laughter, the sort that could sound cruel.

Laurie said: 'My boyfriend.'

The word 'boyfriend' had started to sound a trifle silly, Laurie supposed, but 'partner' was so dry and stiff. She had a feeling her present company already thought she was those things.

'Awww . . . is it early days?' Suzanne combed her fairytale princess hair over her ears with her fingers, and put her flute to her lips.

'Haha! Hardly. We've been going out since were eighteen. We met at university.'

'Oh my *GOD*,' Suzanne said, 'And you're *how old*?'

Laurie tensed her stomach muscles and said: 'Thirty-six.'

'Oh my GOD!' Suzanne squawked again, loudly enough that they had the attention of a few others. 'And you've been together all this time? No flings or breaks? Like, he's your first boyfriend?'

'Yeah.'

'I could *not* have done that. Oh my God. Wow. Was he your . . .' she lowered her voice, '*First*-first?'

Laurie cringed inwardly.

'Bit personal after two drinks, hah?'

Suzanne was not to be deterred.

'Oh my giddy aunt! Oh *no!? Je-SUS!*' she said gaily, as if she was being fun and not judgemental and prurient and generally awful. 'But you're not married?'

'No.'

'Do you want to be?'

'Not really,' Laurie said, shrugging. 'I'm not madly pro or anti marriage.'

'Maybe when you have kids?' Suzanne supplied. Oh, subtle. *Piss the piss off.*

4

'Are you married?' Laurie said.

'No!' Suzanne shook her head and the lovely hair rippled. 'I want to be married by thirty, for sure. I've got four years to find Mr Right.'

'Why by thirty?'

'I just kinda feel that I don't want to be on the shelf.' She paused. 'No offence.'

'Sure.'

Laurie briefly debated saying: *you know that this is really rude, right? I mean you know you can't stick 'no offence' on the end like it takes the curse off?* And then made the usual British calculations about the ten seconds of triumph not being worth the hours of embarrassment and hostility afterwards.

'Where are you from, Laurie?' said Carly in the animal print top, sitting on the other side of Suzanne, and a familiar heavy lead settled in Laurie's gut.

'Yorkshire,' she said, with a bright *aw-hell-please-can-we-not* smile, which she knew would be lost on the recipient. 'You can probably tell from the accent.'

'No, I meant where are you *from?*' she said, vaguely gesturing at her own face. *Of course you did.*

The usual fork in the road opened up: answer the question she knew they were asking, or pretend not to understand and prolong the agony. If you didn't pander to it you were being ungracious, chippy, *making a thing of it.* You were the problem.

'Yorkshire, seriously. I was born at Huddersfield Royal.'

A moment ticked past and Suzanne, to no surprise whatsover, pitched in: 'She means where are your mum and dad from?'

'My dad's from Oldham . . .'

A fresh tray of cocktails arrived, cucumber curls inside like ribbons, and Laurie's genealogy was abruptly demoted in interest.

'. . . My Mum is from Martinique,' she said, but a distracted Carly and Suzanne had already forgotten they'd asked.

'Y'what?'

'Martinique! My Mum is from Martinique!' Laurie said shrilly, above the music, pointing at her face.

'Your mum's called MARTINE EEK?'

Fuck it.

'I'm getting an Old Fashioned,' Laurie said, standing up abruptly. Make of that name what you will.

Then she saw them, a chance glimpse through the shifting throng. Laurie involuntarily grinned at the ignoble thrill of unexpectedly seeing something she definitely wasn't supposed to see, huddled in a banquette, twenty feet away.

Her colleague Jamie Carter was out with a gorgeous young woman. So far, so predictable. But, rather than an unknown lovely, Laurie was ninety-nine per cent sure that the woman he was cosying up to was the boss's niece, Eve, who he was specifically warned off going anywhere near, the day before she arrived. Office gossip dynamite. Possibly employment contract terminating dynamite, depending on just how protective Mr Salter was.

The warning had been the source of much mirth at the office: Jamie really was a 'Lock Up Your Daughters' threat.

'Might as well fit Carter with a GoPro, from what I heard,' she'd guffawed, 'The secret life of the neighbourhood tom.'

Laurie was picking at a bag of crimson seedless grapes at the time, and the office junior, Jasmine, unintentionally outed herself as yet another with a crush by blushing the same shade as the fruit.

Well, whatever had been said by his superiors, it obviously had a devastating impact. Jamie had the legal undergraduate and twenty-four-year-old babe out on her own after hours and sipping Havana Club within a week.

Laurie had to admire his balls. And no doubt she wouldn't be the only one.

The risky choice of companion aside, The Refuge was exactly where she'd expect to see a man like Jamie on a Friday night. Chic's 'Good Times' was blaring and an artwork directly above their heads, a factory chimney skyline picked out in black and white tiles, declared THE GLAMOUR OF MANCHESTER. He and Eve were suited to their subtitles.

A glittering cathedral of a bar inside a nineteenth-century hotel, it was only about fifteen minutes' walk from their office on Deansgate. It wasn't as if Jamie was in deep cover. Why take such a risk?

Perhaps he'd simply gambled he wouldn't be caught here by any of the old sticks or suburban snipes among their colleagues. Yes, that would be it, as what little Laurie knew of Jamie suggested he'd enjoy playing the odds. It was unlikely he'd notice her, for more than one reason, in her vantage point among a gaggle of women at the other end of the room.

She could see Jamie was in his element, handsome face animated in storytelling, a palm theatrically clapped over forehead at one point to emphasise dismay or shame. Eve was visibly falling for him by another degree with each passing moment, her eyes practically star-shaped, like an emoji. (And didn't he wear glasses, usually? Hah, the vanity.)

Jamie was clearly an expert at this, a completely practised hunter in his natural habitat. Whether Eve knew that she was this weekend's antelope was another matter.

His hair was short and dark with a curl to it, his cheekbones like shoe moulds. They'd come straight from the office, him still in white shirt sleeves. And Eve . . . hmmm, Eve knew they'd be doing this, as she was in a navy pinstripe trouser suit, jacket discarded, with a red silk camisole, swinging earrings, matching spiky ketchup-coloured heels. No doubt her nine-to-five practical flats were crushed into that capacious bag (was that a Birkin? Oh to have rich uncles).

Laurie felt a shiver of awe at how well Jamie and Eve fitted in, amid the din and the crush of all these bright young things, their mating rituals, taut stomachs and brash confidence.

Imagine being single, she thought. Imagine being expected to go home and take your clothes off with someone you'd never met before. Horror. Doing it for a hobby, the way Jamie Carter did, felt alien to her. Thank God for Dan. Thank God for going home to someone who *was* home.

As Laurie waited in the four-person deep rabble at the bar, she pondered The Jamie Carter Phenomenon.

Jamie's arrival had caused a stir from his first week at her law firm in the way conspicuously good-looking men were wont to do, and in the way anyone was wont to do in offices where people spent a lot of time in zoo captivity, feeding on distraction. The death of the fag break in the modern age,

Laurie noticed, had been replaced by snouting round social media profiles for material for discussion. Laurie was constantly thankful her life was far too boring to make a sideshow.

At first there were excitable whispers at the water dispensers in Salter & Rowson solicitors that someone as fine as Jamie was single, wondering if he was an eligible bachelor, as if they were in an Austen novel. And, as Diana said, he was 'without any baggage', which Laurie always thought was a harsh way to refer to ex-spouses and children.

Then in time, the excitable whispers were about the fact he wasn't apparently interested in dating anyone in particular, but that he'd disappeared off into the night with X or Y. (X or Y tended to be, like Eve, a beautiful intern, or a friend of an employee.) Laurie thought this was only a surprising turn of events if you'd never met a man with lots of options and nothing at stake before.

How old was he, thirty? And hungry for not just a plethora of dates but also professional advancement, if the second layer of whispers about him was to be believed.

The only unusual aspect to Jamie's reputation as a stealth shagger was that he picked his targets cleverly. The interns had always finished their interning, the friend of a friend was never a close friend and what Russians called *kompromat* was scant. Therefore, while it was known he was a *ladies' man*, he never got blamed for ladykilling, or suffered a poor testimonial about his sexual prowess from a scorned woman. Jamie Carter never got into any trouble. Until now, perhaps.

2

'Hello?' said a male voice at her elbow.

'Hi,' Laurie said, starting as the subject of her reverie appeared, as if she'd summoned him. She felt a stab of irrational guilt, having been thinking about Jamie, spying on him.

'You out for the night?' Jamie said. He disguised it well, but Laurie could see he was apprehensive. They'd never spoken at work, knew each other by sight only. He had no measure of her and no goodwill to exploit.

They were both lawyers: she could work backwards through his thought process in approaching her. He'd seen her, therefore there was a fair chance she'd seen him, with Eve. Better to brazen it out and act like he was doing nothing wrong than leave Laurie unattended with a tale to tell.

'Yeah. Tagging along with my mate's firm. You?'

'Just a couple after work.'

Heh heh oh really. She toyed with asking 'who with?' but was a shade too drunk to judge whether it'd clang as obvious.

'What're you having? In case I get served first,' he said.

Bribery now, was it.

'Old Fashioned.'

'That's it? You're queuing for one drink? Where are you sitting?'

Laurie pointed into the dining area.

'There's table service through there, you know?'

'I wanted the change of scenery,' Laurie said. 'Where are you sitting?'

Yes, she could play mind games too. Knight to your Rook!

'Same,' Jamie said. 'Last time, the waitress took too long. Mind you, this is carnage.'

Hmmm. He'd spotted her, panicked and made an excuse to follow her out here.

Laurie noticed when he spoke that his incisor teeth were tilted slightly inward, like an uncommitted vampire. She suspected this was the true secret of his incredible appeal, the deliberate flaw in the Navajo rug. Otherwise he was a little too wholesomely, straightforwardly good looking. Somehow, the teeth made you think carnal thoughts.

They suspended conversation to stake elbow space on the bar and catch the barman's eye. Laurie got served first and volunteered to buy Jamie's, but he wouldn't let her.

She was less convinced this was chivalry than unwillingness for her to discover his order of a lager and a Prosecco with a raspberry bobbing in it, which made it clear he was on a date. She heard him tell the barman anyway. Her cocktail took long enough to make that they returned to their seats at the same time, having traded awkwardly shouted staccato remarks about how it was *heaving in here*. As they neared

Laurie's destination he stopped and leaned in to speak to her, over the Motown decibels.

'Could I ask a favour?'

Laurie got a waft of light male sweat and classy aftershave. She fought to keep her face straight and look like she didn't know what was coming.

'What?'

'Could you not mention – *this* – at work. Who I'm with?' he gestured at Eve at their table, who was studying herself in a compact mirror. She had a feline sort of beauty, hair slicked into a long high ponytail. Like a sexy assassin. Laurie squinted and pretended it had dawned who it was.

'Oh, why not?' Laurie said, faux innocent.

'It would be very much frowned upon by Statler and Waldorf.'

Statler and Waldorf was a longstanding nickname for Misters Salter and Rowson. Laurie knew why he was using matey we're-in-this-together shop floor nicknames.

'Why?'

'I don't think Salter wants his niece socialising with any of us.'

Laurie smiled. If she wasn't miserable, wanting to further delay returning to Suzanne, and several drinks to the good, she might not wind him up. As it was . . .

'By "socialising", you mean shagging, and by "any of us", you mean you?'

'Well,' Jamie shrugged, slightly taken aback and evidently at a momentary loss. 'Who knows what goes through the old goat's mind. You'd have to ask him.'

'OK,' Laurie said.

'Thank you,' Jamie exhaled.

'. . . I'll ask him!'

She waited for the punchline to land and enjoyed Jamie's aghast expression when it did.

'Hahaha!'

'For fu—' Jamie performed a mixture of bashful and still edgy. He was being winsome and acting vulnerable because right now she could choose to do him damage, of that she was sure.

'I'm not a fan of the office gossip,' Laurie said. 'I won't say anything. Don't muck her around, OK?'

'It's not like that, I promise,' Jamie said. 'It's career talk.'

'Uh huh,' Laurie said, casting her eyes back to where Eve was tilting her chin, pouting at her own reflection.

Laurie returned with heavy dread to her seat, only to see with joy that Emily was in it, and everyone else had clustered round the other side of the table to screech at something on one of the girl's phones. Blessed release. Given the volume of the music, at this distance, they might as well have gone to Iran.

'I am flying a humanitarian mission. Did you get Suzanne-ed?' Emily said, as Laurie took Suzanne's former position next to her.

'Yep.'

'She's a complete fucking twat, isn't she?'

Laurie's Old Fashioned went down the wrong way as she coughed in delighted surprise and Emily slapped her heartily on the back.

When Laurie had her voice back, she said: 'She let me know I was an old maid and weird nun for my uneventful romantic history.'

'What a bleak cow. Last I heard she was hopping on Marcus from KPMG and he has a community dick, so no one's taking her advice.'

Laurie coughed on her drink again. 'A what?'

'You know, used freely by everyone. Open access. A civic resource.'

Laurie managed to stop laughing long enough to add: 'And she and Carly asked me where I was from.'

Emily did a grit-teeth face.

'I said Yorkshire and they said . . .'

Emily put a hand on Laurie's arm and tilted her head. 'No, I meant where are you *from*?'

Emily had been spectator to this enough times to know how it went. In lairy younger years, it was usually Emily who jumped in with a: 'First of all, how dare you . . .' while Laurie shushed her.

'Oh Loz, I am sorry. Clients love them, so I'm scunnered. Why do bad people have to be good at their jobs?'

Laurie laughed, and remembered why she so often said yes to Emily. She thought there was a lot of truth in the closest friendships being unconsummated romances. Emily was a high-flying executive, Tinder adventuress and queen of the casual hook up, Laurie was serious and settled and steady, yet their differences only made them endlessly fascinated with the other.

They still had a sense of humour, and a bullshit detector, and priorities in common.

Emily opened a Rizla paper and put it on the table, dainty fingers sprinkling out a slim sausage of tobacco. Emily had smoked roll-ups ever since they met, when she hung out of Laurie's bedroom window in halls, bottle of Smirnoff Moscow Mule in the other hand.

'She asked me who did my work,' Emily said.

'Work?' Laurie said.

'Work,' Emily took her hands off the cigarette in progress and pulled her cheeks up, while making a pursed-lips trout mouth.

'What the . . .? You don't look like you've had anything done!'

This was true, although Emily had always been physically extraordinary to Laurie. She was tiny, golden limbed (which *was* due to a professional painting) with the face of a Blythe doll, or manga cartoon: eyes floating miles apart, tiny nose, wide full mouth. It all misled you, so you didn't expect her to have the language of a docker and the appetites of a pirate. Men fell in doomed passions on a near-weekly basis.

'Mmm, hmm. About a month after she arrived. Was tempted to sack her then and there. Except she'd have gone round the other agencies saying Emily Clarke sacked me for pointing out her cosmetic work and the fact I'd sacked her would seem to prove it and I'm too fucking vain for that sort of mockery.'

'What a bitch!'

'Right? She says "oh no, I mean I thought it was very tasteful, very discreet". At first I thought it was bad manners but I'm coming to suspect she's a straight-up sociopath.'

'They walk among us,' Laurie nodded, twitching at her

phone screen. Dan had never replied. He was the one always telling her to go out more and yet he was doing the antsy 'when you home' routine? In long-term couple code that was a *don't be late and smashed* hint, without wanting the argument that might ensue from actually saying as much.

'You know that better than anyone, with your job.'

'Ah well, maybe she's right and I have missed out. How would I know? That's what missing out means,' Laurie said, feeling philosophical in the way you could after five units of alcohol.

'Trust me, you haven't. I'm taking a rest from dating apps,' Emily said, tugging at her hemline where it cut into her thighs. 'Too many mis-sold PPIs. The last guy I met was Jason Statham in his photos, and I turn up for the date and it's more like *Upstart Crow*.'

Laurie roared at this. 'Are you still Tilda on there? Has anyone figured it out? Do you really never tell them your real name?'

'Yep. I make sure there's no bills left out if we go to mine. You don't want Clive, thirty-seven, personal trainer from Loughborough, who's into creative bum-plug play, tracking you down on LinkedIn.'

'Groooooo.'

'Ignore Suzanne. Everyone here,' Emily waved her arm at the general bar-dining area, 'Wants what you have. *Everyone*.'

Hah, Laurie thought. She was fairly sure she knew at least one person here who didn't want what she had, but she appreciated the sentiment.

'You don't!' Laurie said.

Emily's utilitarian approach to sex bewildered Laurie. Perhaps Emily needed to meet Jamie Carter, and they'd explode on contact.

'I do, though. I'm just realistic it's probably not out there, so I make do in the meanwhile. It's not common, what you have, you know. Not every Laurie finds her Dan, and vice versa,' Emily said. 'You two were hit by lightning, that night in Bar CaVa.'

'And there I was thinking it was baked bean flavoured tequila shots.'

As she left, Laurie noticed the now-empty table where Jamie and Eve had sat. No doubt he'd sidled past when she was deep in conversation with Emily, keen for her not to see them leaving together.

Career talk, arf. Like he'd chance a sacking for telling her about his LPC course in Chester. Like he'd chance a sacking if the prize was *anything* less than taking her home.

He must think Laurie was naïve, or stupid. The trouble with liars, Laurie had decided from much research in the professional field, is they always thought everyone else was less smart than them.

3

Laurie clambered out of the cab into the heavy smog of late summer air and the nice-postcode-quiet of the street, aware that while her senses were muffled by inebriation, neighbours with families would be lying in their beds cursing the cacophony that was someone exiting a hackney.

The throbbing engine, sing-song conversation, slamming of a heavy door, the clattering of your big night out heels on the pavement.

Two weeks back, the sisters next door had managed to have such an involved back and forth for ten minutes about whose puke it was, Laurie had been tempted to march out in her pyjamas and pay the soiling charge herself.

Ah, middle age beckoned. Hah, who was she kidding, Dan called her 'Mrs Tiggywinkle'. She was the girl in halls who kept a row of basil plants alive in the shared kitchen.

Loud-whispering 'keep the change,' to the driver, she ducked under the thick canopy of clematis that hung over the tiled porch, grabbing blindly for her keys in the depths of her handbag, and once again thought: *we need a light out here*.

She'd been infatuated with this solid bay-fronted Edwardian semi from the first viewing, and knackered their chances of driving a hard bargain by walking around with the estate agent gibbering on about how much she adored it. They bought at the top of what they could afford at the time, and in Laurie's opinion it was worth every cent.

Their front room, she liked to point out, was the spit of the one on the sleeve of Oasis' *Definitely Maybe*, right down to the stained glass, potted palm and half-drunk red wines usually strewn around.

There was a honey-yellow glow from under the blinds, so either Dan had left the lamp on for her or he was having another bout of insomnia, passed out on the sofa in front of BBC News 24 with the sound on low, feet twitching.

Laurie felt a small rush of love for him, and hoped he was up. As much as it was authentic, she knew it was also in some part due to spending a trying evening surrounded by strangers, feeling homesick and out of place. Not belonging.

As a 'person of ethnic origin' who grew up in Hebden Bridge, she didn't care to revisit that feeling often. Even in a cosmopolitan city she got the OH I LOVE YOUR ACCENT? EE BAH GUM jokes. 'You don't often hear a black girl sound that northern, except for that one out of the Spice Girls,' a forthright client had said to her once.

She thought Dan might have waited up for her, but the moment she saw him, she knew something was badly off. He was still dressed, sat on the sofa, feet apart, head bowed, hands clasped. The TV screen was a blank and there wasn't any music on, no detritus of a takeaway.

'Hi,' he said, in an unnatural voice, as Laurie entered the room.

Laurie was an empathetic person. When she was small she once told her mum she thought she might be telepathic, and her amused mother had explained that she was just very intuitive about emotions. Laurie was, as her dad said, born aged forty. Better than being born aged nineteen and staying there, she never said in reply.

The air was thick with a Terrible Unsaid and her antennae picked it up easily enough to feel completely nauseous.

Laurie clutched the jangle of her keys to her chest, with their silly fob of Bagpuss, and said: 'Oh God, what? Which of our parents is it? Please say it now. Say it quickly.'

'What?'

'I know it's bad news. Please don't do any build up whatsoever.'

Laurie was about six or seven drinks in the hole and yet in an instant, completely, pin-sharp sober with adrenaline.

Dan looked perturbed. 'Nothing has happened to anyone?'

'Oh? Oh! Fuck, you scared me.'

In relief, Laurie flumped down onto the sofa, arms flung out by her sides like a kid.

She looked at Dan as her heart rate slowed to normal. He was regarding her with a strange expression.

Not for the first time, she felt appreciation, a bump of pride in ownership, admiring how much early middle age suited him. He'd been a kind of jolly-looking chubby lad in their youth, puppyish cute but not handsome, as her gran had helpfully noted. And with a slight lisp that he hated, but oddly enough, always had women swooning. Laurie always loved it, right from the first moment he had spoken to her. Now he had a few lines and silver threaded in his light brown hair, the bones of his face had sharpened, he'd grown into himself. He was what the girls at work called a Hot Dad. Or, he would be.

'You couldn't sleep again?' she asked. His insomnia was a recent thing, due to him being made head of department. Three a.m. night sweat terrors.

'No,' he said, and she didn't know if he was saying no, I couldn't sleep or no, that's not it.

Laurie peered at him. 'You alright?'

'About you coming off the pill next month. I've been thinking about it. It's made me think about a lot of things.'

'Has it . . . ?' Laurie suppressed a knowing smile. The atmosphere and anxiety now made sense. *Here we go*, she thought. This was a clichéd moment in the passage to parenthood. It belonged in a scripted drama, shortly after a couple had seen two blue lines on the wee stick.

Should he trade in the car for something bigger? Would he be a good father? Would they still be the same?

1. Nah. There's no room out there to park a people carrier anyway.
2. Of course! He could try to be less sulky, perhaps, but that was about it. Kids had a way of automatically curing excess self-pity, from what Laurie could tell. At least for the initial five years.
3. Yes. The same, but better! (Actually, Laurie had no idea about the last answer. If they procreated, it would be the

best part of two decades before this household belonged
to the two of them again, and inviting a tyrannically needy
midget intruder to disturb their privacy and contented
status quo was scary.)

But the done thing in a couple was to pretend to be sure
about the imponderable things, whenever the other person
needed comfort. If necessary, deploy outright lying. Dan could
pay her back when she asked tearfully after returning from a
failed shopping trip, whether her body would ever look like
it did before.

'I don't know how to say any of this. I've been sitting here
since you left trying to think of the right words and I still
can't.'

This was hyperbole, because Laurie left him having a shower
with the Roberts radio broadcasting the football game, but
she didn't say so.

'Look,' Dan said. 'I've realised. I don't want kids. At all.
Ever.'

The silence lengthened.

Laurie sat up, with some effort, given her foolish shoes –
strappy silver slingbacks she fell for in Selfridges, that 'look
good with plum toenails' according to the sales girl – weren't
anchoring her to the floor very steadily.

'Dan,' she said gently. 'This doubt is totally normal, you
know. I feel the same. It's frightening, when it's about to
become real. But we can do it. We've got this. With having
a kid, you hold hands, and jump.'

She smiled at him, hoping he'd snap out of it soon. It felt

like a role reversal, him demanding a deep talk, her wanting to do enough to make him feel taken seriously so she could go to bed. Dan was flexing his fingers, steepled in his lap, not looking at her.

'And it's me who has to push it out,' Laurie added. 'Don't think I haven't googled "third-degree tearing".'

He wouldn't be easily joked out of this, she realised, looking at the depth of his frown lines.

She felt them running at different speeds, her carrying the noise and trivia of the night out with her like a swarm of bees, him evidently having spent a pensive period staring at the shadows in the sombre Edward Hopper print they hung over the fireplace, worrying about the future.

'It's not just having kids. I don't want anything that you want. I don't want . . . this.'

He glanced around the room, accusingly.

Stripped floorboards?

'What do you mean?'

Dan breathed in and out, as if limbering up for a feat of exertion. But no words followed.

'. . . You want to put it off for a few years? We talked about this. I'm thirty-six and it could take a while. We don't want to be mucking about with interventions and wishing we'd got on with it . . . you know what Claire says. If she knew how great it would be, she'd have started at twenty.'

Invoking this particular member of their social circle was a stupid misstep, and Laurie immediately regretted it.

Claire was both a massive bore about her offspring and a general pain in the hoop. Ironically, if they hadn't suffered

23

her, they might've have reproduced already. Occasions with her often concluded with one or other of them muttering: *you'd tell me if I ever got like that, right?*

'You know what they say. There's never a perfect time to have a baby,' Laurie added. 'If you—'

'Laurie,' Dan said, interrupting her. 'I'm trying to tell you that we don't want the same things and so we can't be together.'

She gasped. He'd say such an ugly, ridiculous thing to get his point across? Then she did a small empty laugh, as it dawned on her: this was how much men could fear maturity. It ought not to be a revelation to her, given her dad, and yet she was badly disappointed in Dan.

'Come on, are you really going to turn this into a full-blown emergency and make me say having a family is a deal breaker, or something? So it can all be my fault when it's had us up five times in a row?'

Dan looked at her.

'I don't know how else I can say this. I'm not happy, Laurie.'

Laurie breathed in and out: Dan wasn't bluffing, he wanted a direct assurance from her she'd not come off the pill. She'd have to hope they revisited the idea in a year. She was aware that it could mean their window of opportunity closed completely. And she could end up resenting Dan. There'd be no playing tricks, pretending to take the pill when she wasn't and *whoops-a-daisy*. That was how Laurie was conceived and she knew the consequences were lifelong.

'Is this purely because I want kids?'

She would take it off the table to stay with him, she knew that in a split second's consultation with herself. It was unthinkable to do anything else. You didn't lose someone you loved, over hypothetical love for someone who didn't yet exist. Who might never exist.

'That, other things. I'm not . . . this is not where I want to be any more.'

'OK,' she said, rubbing her tired face, feeling appalled by how extreme he'd been prepared to be, in order to get his way.

She felt like she might cry, in fact. They'd had fights before where very occasionally one or the other of them had vaguely threatened to leave, usually when drunk and in their dickhead twenties, and whichever of them had said it felt sick with guilt the next day.

Pulling this now, at their age, was beneath Dan, however much he was bricking it over the responsibilities of fatherhood. It was really unkind.

'. . . OK, you win. Regular pill-taking for the time being. Christ, Dan.'

Dan looked at her with a stunned expression and Laurie froze, because again, she could read it.

He wasn't stunned she'd agreed. It wasn't a gambit. He wanted to split up.

She finally understood. Understood that he meant it, that this was it.

Absolutely everything else was completely beyond her comprehension.

4

When people did monumentally awful things to you, it seemed they didn't even have the courtesy of being original, of inflicting some unique war wound, a lightning-bolt-shaped scar. These reasons were prosaic, dull. They were true of people all the time, but they weren't applicable to Dan and Laurie. They were going to be together forever. They agreed that openly as daft lovestruck teenagers and implicitly confirmed it in every choice they'd made since. No commitment needed checking or second thinking, it was just: *of course*. You are mine and I am yours.

'But nothing's changed?' Laurie said. 'We're like we've always been.'

'I think that's part of the problem.'

Laurie's mind was occupying two time zones at once: this surreal nightmare where her partner of eighteen years, her first and only love, her best friend, her 'other half', was sitting here, saying things about how he'd sleep in the spare room for the time being and move out to a flat as soon as possible. She had to play along with it, because he was so convinced.

It was like colluding with someone who'd become delusional about a dream world. Follow the rabbit.

Then there was the other time zone, where she was desperately trying to make sense of the situation, to manage it and defuse it. He was only using words – no tangible, irreversible change had occurred. Therefore words could change it back again.

She'd always had a special power over Dan, and vice versa, that's why they fell for each other. If she wanted to pull him back from this brink, she must be able. She only needed to try hard enough, to find the way to persuade him.

But to fix it, she had to grasp what was going on. Laurie prided herself on cold reading people like she was a stage magician, and yet the person closest to her sounded like a stranger.

'How long have you felt this way?' she asked.

'A while,' Dan said, and although his body showed tension, she could already tell he had relaxed several notches. Announcement made, the worst was over for him. She hated him, for a second. 'I think I knew for sure at Tom and Pri's wedding.'

'Oh, that was why you spent the whole night in a strop, was it?' Laurie spat. And realised the lunacy of that sort of point scoring, when the whole game had been cancelled. He wouldn't go through with this. Surely.

Her stomach lurched. It was utterly ridiculous to take him seriously, and wildly reckless not to.

Dan made a hissing noise, shook his head. Whether he was dismayed at Laurie or himself wasn't clear.

'I knew none of that wedding fuss was for me. I knew that's not where I was at, mentally.'

A painful memory came back to Laurie, because it turned out her senses hadn't entirely failed her.

She recalled that the couples present had been corralled by the DJ for the first-dance-after-the-first-dance. She and a half-cut, sullen Dan were forced into a waltz hold to Adele. She felt a sudden total absence of anything between them, not even a comfortable ease with each other's touch, in place of a spark. It was like their battery was dead and if you pressed the accelerator it'd only make an empty phut-phut-phut. They shuffled round the floor awkwardly, like brother and sister, not meeting each other's gaze. Then as soon as the song was over she forgot about it, and put it down to Dan not liking 'Someone Like You', or being told to do things.

He'd made a passive-aggressive show of going to sleep in the cab on the way back. Laurie felt she'd committed an unspecified crime all day, but when asked 'What's up with you?' she'd got a belligerent '. . . NOTHING?'

But crap days in a long-term relationship were a given. You no more thought they might spell the end than you feared every cold could be cancer.

'Is there someone else?' Laurie said, not because she thought it possible but you were supposed to ask this, weren't you? In this weird theatre they were playing out, at Dan's insistence. They worked together – on a practical level alone, this seemed improbable.

'No, of course not,' Dan said, sounding genuinely affronted.

'I don't think you get to OF COURSE NOT me, do

you?' Laurie shrieked, anger breaking, causing Dan to flinch. 'I think OF COURSE NOT is pretty much fucking unavailable to you right now, don't you? We've stopped having any shared reality from what I can see so fuck off with your patronising OF COURSE NOTS.'

Dan was completely unused to seeing her this incandescently angry. In fact, the last time she hit these heights, they were twenty-five and he'd lost her car keys in the healing field at Glastonbury. They'd been able to laugh about it later, though, alchemise it as an anecdote. Comedy was tragedy plus time, but there'd never be enough distance to make this amusing.

'Sorry,' he said quietly. 'But no. Like we always said. No cheating, ever.'

'Ever?' she said, with a knowing intonation.

'You know what we agreed. I'd tell you.'

Laurie fumed, her chest tight, and tried to breathe through it. The tactlessness and the tastelessness of Dan using things they'd sincerely pledged to each other a lifetime ago. He was currently trashing that memory, and every other memory for that matter, while asking Laurie to treat it as sacred covenant. What an arsehole.

Was he an arsehole? Had he turned into one, somewhere along the line, and she hadn't noticed? She studied him, as he stared morosely at his hairy knees in his shorts, face like a baleful Moomin.

It didn't matter. She loved him. They'd long ago passed the point where her love was negotiable; it wasn't contingent on him not being an arsehole. He was her arsehole.

Laurie had passed that point, anyway. Dan had reached a

parallel one where he could abandon her. That's what it felt like: desolate abandonment. He wouldn't care about Laurie, from now on? No, no, he did want her. She knew in her guts that he did, which is why this had to be stopped before he did any more damage.

'But we've got to stay at the same company together? How's that going to fucking work?'

Dan and Laurie managed a few degrees of separation at Salter & Rowson by being in different departments, but once they were exes that would hardly be enough.

'I can start looking for other positions. I might jack it all in. I'm not sure yet.'

'Honestly, Dan, it still sounds like you're freaked out by having a baby and have decided to go full nuke from orbit to fix it,' Laurie said, in a final stab at returning them to any sort of normality. 'You don't want to go travelling, for fuck's sake. They wouldn't let you stay head of the department, either. And you hated a week in Santorini, last year.'

As Laurie said it, she wondered if the missing element in that analysis was that he hated it *with her.*

'Having children is only one part of it. The reason it's made me do something about how I feel is because you can't go back on that decision, you can't un-have a baby. It made me decide. I don't want this life, Laurie, I'm sorry. I know it's a shock after all this time. It shocks me too. That's why it took me so long to face up to it. But I don't. Want it.'

'You don't want me?'

A heavy pause, where Laurie felt Dan steel himself to say it.

30

'Not like this.'

'Then how?'

Dan shrugged and blinked through tears.

'The word you're looking for is no,' Laurie said.

Tears flash flooded down her face now and he made to get up and she frantically gestured: *don't come near me.*

'Erm . . . just you know, one minor objection on my part,' she said, voice thick and distorted by crying. It was ambitious to try to put on a sarcastic tone. 'How am I going to have kids with anyone now, Dan? I'm thirty-six.'

'You still can!' he said, imploringly, nodding. 'That's not old, these days.'

'With who? When? Am I going to meet someone next week? Get things moving on conceiving a few months after that?'

'C'mon. You're *you*. You're a massive catch, always have been. You won't be short of offers. You'll be inundated.'

Laurie finally accepted in that moment, that this was real, they really might be over.

Dan had always had the healthy, normal amount of male jealousy. If anything, more than average: he'd always been sure if one of them would be stolen away by a rival, it was Laurie. Male friends who complimented her in his presence always got a 'hey now . . .' from Dan that was entirely joking but also not. Male hires at her firm always got an early warning that she might not have a wedding ring but she wasn't single and also the guy was here on premises, so *watch yourself,* and she assumed this was by Dan or briefed by his representatives. (She'd never had to tell anyone she was 'spoken for', anyway, they always mentioned *oh you're Dan Price's girlfriend.* Funny phrase, that. Why was someone speaking *for* you?)

If the idea of her having kids with someone else got this shrug of a response, this mediocre *auto-response,* something had flown.

'Such a massive catch, you'll pass me up?'

'We've been together all our lives, Laurie, you're my only serious girlfriend. It's not like I'm walking away lightly, or that I never cared.'

Laurie was on the back foot. He'd planned for this. He was a politician who had notes; she'd been ambushed.

She still couldn't believe he wasn't exaggerating somehow, but there was a dreadful binary: if he could say all this and not mean it utterly sincerely, that would make it even worse.

There was a huge, bewildering gap in all of this for Laurie. An untold mystery in how Dan had gone from unpacking the Ocado delivery, and complaining about the plain digestives they got as substitutions for Jaffa Cakes, going for musty pints of stout in their local and laughing at dogs with overbites in Beech Road Park on a Sunday morning, to this final, total departure, with nothing in between.

It was as if one minute she'd been running for a bus, and the next she'd woken up in a hospital bed, the quilt flat where her legs used to be, with a doctor explaining they were ever so sorry but there was no saving them.

'Good to know you used to care,' she said, hearing how plaintive and bitter her voice sounded, in the darkened sitting room. 'Small mercies? Or is that meant to be a big mercy?'

'I do care.'

'Just not enough to stay.'

Dan stared blankly.

'Say it,' Laurie said, with force.

'No.'

It was the logical conclusion of everything he'd said; and yet that hard monosyllable surprised her so much, he might as well have slapped her.

5

At three in the morning, having been wide awake for hours, Laurie got up, marched into the spare room and stamped on the button to turn the big floor lamp on.

'Dan? Wake up.'

The human-sized sausage shape under the duvet stirred and Dan's head emerged, hair askew.

At first he frowned in sleepy confusion. When he focused on Laurie's face, and visibly remembered the specifics of his existence, his expression changed to a man woken by an FBI flashlight who knew exactly what he had hidden in his crawl space.

'I need to know why.'

'What?'

'I need to know why this is happening. I know you think you've given me reasons but you haven't. Only vague bullshit about us wanting different things. We've wanted all kinds of different things in the past but we never had to split up over it. We would've talked about it. I offered to hold off on kids, even put it aside, same with getting married. So it's not that we want different things. That's like a line you heard in *Cold*

Feet or something.' Laurie paused. 'Just tell me the whole truth, however hard it is. This not knowing is worse, Dan. Look at what you're doing to us, after our whole lives together. You owe me that.'

Dan stared at her and pushed himself up on his elbows. A silence stretched between them and Laurie sensed he was readying himself for honesty. This return ambush had worked, he'd not had time to rehearse.

Dan cleared his throat. Laurie was breaking out in a flop sweat but she still didn't regret asking.

'. . . I started waking up early. While you were still asleep,' he said. '. . . And I'd see life as a tunnel. I could mark off everything along the way. The wedding at Manchester Town Hall. The honeymoon in Italy. Kid one, kid two. Sunday barbecues, DIY, saving up for an extension. Still hating work, but having to go for partnership because there were mouths to feed.' His voice was hoarse with sleep and sounded strange. 'And it was like there was nothing between here and death that left the script. It was planned out for me, every step. I was expected to do it. And I kept asking myself, like a nagging voice, a whisper that got louder and louder: did I want to do it?'

Laurie could interject here that clearly, he wasn't expected to do several things on that list. She held herself back.

'. . . I felt trapped. I'd built this box I didn't want to live inside any more, but I wasn't allowed to leave it. I didn't want to leave it, as I knew how much I'd hurt you. I started being a wanker to you all the time, because I was miserable, but I didn't want to say so.'

He drew breath. 'That's the thing. I kept thinking I had to

stay to be kind to you but I wasn't being kind, so what was the point?'

'You've always been quite grumpy, to be fair,' Laurie said, with a small smile.

Dan didn't appear to listen.

'You know how people always said how could we do it, how could we "settle down" so young?'

'Yes,' said Laurie, voice tight.

'We both said it was the easiest thing we'd ever done, we never even thought of it that way. And I always meant it, Laurie, always. But maybe now, at thirty-six, it's caught up with me. I don't feel I've lived enough.'

Laurie took a deep breath and tried to get past how much this hurt. She'd stifled him, stopped him from going on expeditions, with his fascinating penis as travel companion. However, she had asked for straight answers.

'If I'd never met you – if you'd slept around at university, and we'd got together at twenty-five, or thirty, this wouldn't be happening?' Laurie deliberately didn't say this in an accusatory way, she wanted to know.

'I don't know. I can't go back and live a different timeline until I get here again, and do you know what, I promise you, I wouldn't want to. And it's not about sex. It's about . . . Oh God, I don't want to say "finding myself". But life's big decisions are mainly instinct, right? The same way we both just knew, back at university. Now I know this isn't right for me anymore. I've lost myself.'

'Is it me, I'm not enough? Or too much? You're looking at other women or . . . our friends or their wives, or our colleagues, thinking, "I wish Laurie was more like that"?' Her throat was tight and she felt as if she was stood here, stark naked. To ask these questions: it was the hardest, most exposing thing. *Tell me how you fell out of love with me. Describe it.*

'No! God no. It's not about you. I know that sounds insulting, but it isn't.'

A pause.

'OK. Thanks for being honest,' Laurie said dully.

She meant it. She didn't hate this situation any less, but she grasped it a little better. Dan being this open with her reminded her how they used to be able to talk, and the pain hit her stomach again with a physical force. She would never be able to forget how easily you could lose someone's love. She hadn't felt it slipping away.

'Won't you miss me?' she said.

This was it, the biggest question. The one that left her feeling ridiculous, pitiable, even, but she knew she had to. The idea Dan would no longer be on the 'people to contact in an emergency' space on her passport felt impossible. She needed him to explain how he could do this and not feel how she'd feel, if she did this.

'The thought of it is brutal, Laurie. Like missing a limb,' Dan said, tears starting. 'I love you. I don't love our relationship anymore.'

'We could stay together and make the relationship different,' Laurie said, eyes welling up.

They both sobbed, heads bowed, because Dan didn't want to say it and she didn't want to hear it. The sound of it was strange, in the darkened room.

'Why would you leave me like this? Why would you do this to us?' Laurie said, and she sounded like someone else. Who was this mournful, begging woman? And who was this merciless person who'd taken Dan's place? How could eighteen years end in just a few hours?

'I'm sorry . . . I'm really sorry . . .' Dan gasped.

'If you were that sorry you wouldn't do it,' Laurie said thickly, not even caring how she sounded, almost pleading. This was like a catapult back to the powerlessness of childhood, wondering why grown-ups did the completely arse-about-face cruel things they did.

'I can't not do it.' He looked like he was going to say something else and then thought better of it. Like when they told a client to go No Comment. The more you say, the more you'll incriminate yourself.

Laurie suspected what he wouldn't say, was: there came a point where feelings weren't there to be resuscitated, they had died. That dance, at that wedding. That's what she'd picked up on. Flatlining.

'And I want you to be happy. You deserve more than someone who . . .'

'OK. Spare me that stuff, Dan,' Laurie said, briskly, wiping her eyes, squeezing her already folded arms tighter. 'You're like the climber who can't carry their injured mate, so leaves them to die. Do what you need to do but don't pretend it's about anything other than your survival.'

'Hah,' Dan rubbed his face tiredly. 'You're so bloody clever, you are.'

She wasn't sure, in the tone of his voice, that it was a

compliment. It even sounded like a hint at some other part of this. Laurie was too tired and raw to judge.

'I don't know who or what I'm meant to trust in,' Laurie said, tremulous. 'We spend our whole lives together and one day it's – nah, not for me? What do I do with that? What's the lesson I have to learn here?'

'There isn't a lesson for you, you haven't done anything wrong.'

She could feel it now, the grief and enormity of what had been abruptly taken from her. A future. The rest of their lives. A promise, broken. 'Then how am I going to ever believe this won't happen again?'

'I don't know what to say. It's taken me . . . so long to work up the courage because . . .'

'Woah, you're now saying you weren't happy for *so long?*'

'No! Or not in a serious way. Just an underlying doubt. Fuck, Laurie. Working out how to do this without hurting you even more . . . it's awful. It's my mess and confusion but there was no way of it not ending up all over you.'

He was sat up in bed, head hangdog, bare chested, and Laurie couldn't help but wonder who the next person to see him like this would be, who he was going to find that he wanted more with. Who didn't make life feel like a tunnel.

'OK. There's nothing left to say. It's happening because it's happening. Thanks for everything, I guess?'

'Laurie . . .'

'I mean it. Thank you. The fact you're going doesn't mean everything before it didn't matter. Not wanting to be with someone anymore, and admitting it, isn't doing anything wrong.'

Dan looked taken aback and Laurie surprised herself with this Christian forgiveness that she hadn't known she was going to dispense, until this moment. It felt unexpectedly powerful. Was it a ploy? She wasn't sure. She didn't feel the same way, one moment to the next. Maybe, once again, it was the advocate in her. She only had this left, to make him change his mind. *Remember the woman you fell in love with. Well, the girl.*

Laurie hesitated, because she didn't want to issue ultimatums or bluffs, they were pointless. But she still had to say it.

'One thing, though, Dan. If you think you can do this, and spend three months living in some flat in Ancoats being lonely, with your "man cave" sofa from Gumtree and your Sky Sports package, and then come back to me saying it was some massive midlife crisis . . . you know you can't, right? This damage you're doing, it's permanent. If you go, that's it.'

Dan nodded. 'Yes. I wouldn't presume to think I could ever ask that of you.'

Laurie left the room, knowing that she'd lied, and he probably did too.

6

Dad

Hello princess. How's my beautiful clever daughter? Well guess what, me & Nic tied the knot!!! Just because of tax reasons, Visas, all that jazz. Did it out here in Beefa with a couple of witnesses but we're going to have a proper tear-up in Manchester in a month or so, I'll give you the details when I have them. Going to spend a few quid on it, need somewhere fancy, no fleapits. Get yourself a nice dress and send me the bill, you're one of the bridesmaids, as it were. Love you loads my darling. Austin xxx

Laurie blinked at the WhatsApp through the fug of receding sleep on Sunday morning: you could dissect this in a lab as a perfect study of her relationship with her father. All of him was in there, like a nucleus containing the DNA information.

1. Lavish praise, blandishments.
2. Surprise news, the sort that makes it clear his life is, in fact, nothing much to do with her.
3. Material spoiling, bribes.

4. More protestations of how important she is to him. A bridesmaid 'as it were'. *I want you to feel you're important without going to the trouble of actually treating you that way.*

5. Not, despite the performative paternalism, referring to himself 'Dad'. On the rare occasions she'd seen him when she was little, she'd loved the novelty of having someone to call Dad, but he always used to correct her: 'You're making me sound old.' She was baffled: thirty *was* old, and he *was* her dad?

And not forgetting 6. The worst possible timing, as always.

Laurie
Hi, congratulations to you and Nic! Will come to the celebration, just let me know. I have less fun news, Dan and I have separated. I'm keeping the house on and he's moving out. His decision, no third parties involved. Ah well. Maybe I'll meet someone at your tear-up. 😊 *xx*

Two blue ticks, immediately. So he'd read it. No reply. More Classic Austin Watkinson.

And to round it all off – and this part she couldn't blame her dad for, although it felt as if she *should* be able to – he'd now unwittingly made her phone call to her mum, breaking the news about her and Dan, even more onerous. Her parents didn't speak, so it was down to Laurie if she was going to be informed, and she should be, really. Laurie knew if she put it off, she'd end up avoiding it altogether; she wouldn't keep secrets for her dad. Still, her mum wouldn't thank her for it, and it'd feel like it was Laurie's fault.

Laurie and Dan had spent all day Saturday slowly and painfully going through it all again, and now Dan was out on a run and Laurie was actually relieved not to have to face him for a few hours, endlessly wondering if she could have said or done something different to change this outcome.

Having told one person, it had started to become real. She could call her mum and practise doing it vocally – and now, in a Dan-less house, was better than later. She sat on the third step of the stairs, heaving the plastic rotary red and blue phone onto her lap. When she bought it a year ago from a website that did 'vintage things with a modern twist', Dan had said, 'More bourgeoise knick-knacks. Behold our thirty-something pile of affluent middle-class tat!'

Did he hate all this stuff? In this home they'd made? Could she not even look at a sodding retro hipster landline in the same way? His belongings were piled into tragic bin bags in the dining room. She'd heard him, before she got up, quietly calling a local restaurant to cancel their reservation. This afternoon, they had been meant to be eating Sunday lunch at a pretentious new place nearby full of squirrel cage light bulbs and 'Nordic-inspired small plates'.

'Look at this,' Dan had said barely a week ago, in another space-time dimension, waving his phone with the website open. 'This place isn't a restaurant, it's a *dining space prioritising a thoughtful eating menu with an emphasis on provenance and a curated repertoire of low intervention wines.* Fucks saaake.'

'You wanted to try it!' Laurie had said, and Dan eye-rolled, shrugged. Back when Dan's 'rejection of things he'd nevertheless willingly chosen' was confined to where they had meals out.

43

In the cold light of morning, Laurie couldn't believe he was keeping on with this charade, that he wasn't going to be standing in some unloved, unfurnished two bed that smelled of plug-in air fresheners with a greasy estate agent and think: 'what the hell am I doing?'

Not that love or happiness was stuff, but Laurie had made them a great home and it still wasn't enough. Or, she wasn't. She felt so foolish: the whole time he'd been growing colder, quietly horrified, hemmed in and alienated by it. It was such a shallow thing, but Laurie felt so damn *uncool* for being satisfied by a life that Dan wasn't.

She listened to the ringing on the other end, replaced the receiver, and tried again. Her mum would be in the garden, and thought the first phone call was merely to alert you to the fact someone was trying to call you. She rarely answered until they'd made a second or even third attempt. It was a quirk that used to drive Laurie mad in her teenage years; they had flaming rows about Laurie always having to answer.

Her mum was 'out of the normal,' as a plumber once said, surveying the kitsch art collage of Elvis on their pink bathroom wall in the 1990s.

Her mother had very strict, controlling and conventional parents herself, and was determined to do things differently. Laurie admired this, while sometimes feeling she'd overcorrected to the other extreme.

If you'd wanted a mother who was chill with you being out until all hours and your friends accidentally dropping the F-word, Mrs Peggy Watkinson of Cannock Road was the one. Plus, she looked and dressed like Supremes-era Diana Ross.

Both Conventional and Unconventional Dads of the neighbourhood were fans. And she wasn't Mrs Watkinson, either, because she'd never been wed to Laurie's dad. Laurie chose it as her surname because at the time, her mum was using her stage moniker, Peggy Sunshine. And Laurie was no way going to have a wacky surname on top of being the only black girl in her year.

When Laurie's mum was addressed as Mrs Watkinson by a teenager, she smiled and did her characteristic hand wave. 'In a past life, maybe.' And mentioned there was wine open in the kitchen.

Your mum is the best, her friends said, as they trudged up the stairs, glasses in hand, promises extracted – by Laurie – not to tell their mums.

There were times when Laurie craved mums like everyone else had, who replaced lost PE kits, made chicken nuggets with beans and chips for tea instead of aubergine and pineapple curry, and didn't have Egyptian birthing stools on display in reception rooms.

She tried ringing her mum again, but was unsuccessful. She'd give it a last try and then give up.

Whenever anything awful happened, no one ever considered the difficulty of the admin, Laurie thought. Someone had to broadcast it, manage the fall-out. How come there were so many services in modern society, and not this one? 'Relationship Over? Let Us Round Robin!'

'Working out how to tell everyone' was a part of her and Dan's separation that was going to be almost as gruelling a prospect as being left in the first place. It felt so unnecessarily cruel that you didn't just have to go through the thing, you had to have a dozen conversations with people of varying closeness about the fact you were going through the thing.

Dan did this, Dan should deal with all of it. But he couldn't, even if she wanted him to.

Some hip friends, a few years back, had posted up a witty archive photo on social media of themselves and made an official announcement to everyone they were divorcing.

Laurie considered it, lying in bed last night, but it only really worked as a 'ripping the plaster off in one go' technique if you said it was fine, you were both OK, no hard feelings, *no bombshell story to uncover here, move along*. Essentially, hinted it was a joint decision. Those euphemisms that publicists deployed when famous people parted: 'leading different lives', 'grown apart' and Laurie's favourite, 'conflicting schedules'.

Dan once said that mutual only ever meant: 'one person has given up, and the other person concedes they can't persuade them not to,' and now that felt astute. Turns out, he was plot foreshadowing their own end. Where did he go, that Dan?

The phone finally connected, third time lucky, ha ha.

'Hi, Mum . . . yeah I thought you'd be in the garden. OK to talk? I've got some bits of news . . . No, not that.' It really did put the tin hat on this that everyone would think she was about to announce the baby. She took a breath to gird her loins.

'Dan and I have split up. It's his decision.'

She couldn't bear to say 'left me', with all its sense of passive victimhood but she had to make it clear she wasn't going to have answers. She recounted Dan's reasons for going.

'Oh dear, my darling. Sorry to hear this.' Her mum had kept the strong Caribbean inflection from the island of her own childhood. 'I know you will be very hurt but sometimes, paths diverge. He obviously has to do this next part of his journey on his own. Which is very painful for you, but it must be what his heart is telling him.'

Laurie gritted her teeth. Maddening calm was one of her mother's attributes, that could also feel like a weapon.

She knew her mum, who lived outside society's conventions in Upper Calder Valley with a fabulous kitchen garden and incense burners, wasn't going to do the 'what a bastard' response, and in many ways, Laurie liked that her mum was an independent thinker.

But right now she didn't want this stuff about *how nothing was good or bad, it was just a different choice*. Hippyishness could feel heartless. She wanted her distress to be recognised.

Laurie remembered her mum saying of her cousin Ray, who was in a serious motorbike smash, 'That which doesn't kill you makes you stronger,' and Laurie asking how someone subsequently living in an adapted bungalow held together with metal pins was stronger. 'Mentally stronger,' came the answer. Tenuous, at best. It was uncomfortably close to telling Ray to see the upside. Here was her version of that. Laurie was often struck by how the arc of history was long, but bent towards nothing really changing.

'Dan will be on his own on his "journey" for a while, and then he'll be with someone else. I think that's how this works? He's not going to become a nomadic shaman monk, Mum. He's on a good salary at a provincial law firm.'

Unless you bought Dan's blather about jacking it all in, which Laurie didn't. Maybe her scathing cynicism was adding fuel to Dan's theory they were no longer aligned, but still, file it under Believe It When I See It. She'd heard him kvetching about the state of Ryanair's delays enough times, she couldn't see him floating in tranquility down the Mekong Delta.

'Well. So are you.' *That's alright then.* Jeez.

Peggy sort of tutted, in a 'there there' way, and Laurie sucked air into her painful rib cage. She'd not eaten more than a few pieces of toast with peanut butter for days. She didn't expect her mum to be upset on her behalf, and she had feared her mum would insist this was an opportunity in disguise. Not least because Peggy thought Laurie had settled down too young, and her feelings towards Dan had always been polite rather than enthusiastic. Laurie got the feeling that Dan had presented to her as a stereotypical Nice Young Man, but her mum had found him a little dull. Peggy liked characters, eccentrics and oddballs. Speaking of which . . . her dad's news.

'Is there anything I can do?' her mum said, after listening to the practical arrangements of the dissolution of Dan and Laurie Inc.

'No. Thanks though,' Laurie said, refusing to bite at such a lacklustre offer. 'Oh, also.' Deep breath. 'Dad's got married to Nicola. In Ibiza, but they're going to have a do back here in Manchester too.'

Her mum was silent for a second. 'Nicola? Is that the one from before?'

'The Scouser, yeah.'

Laurie had only met Nicola a few times before but she liked her: a garrulous, handsome woman with her own jewellery business, who wore a lot of animal print and liked a party as much as her dad, which was saying something.

'He always said marriage was a rotten institution, a place people went to die!'

'Yeah. Well this is his journey, I guess. What his heart is telling him.'

Laurie was being sarcastic but it evidently didn't register. She could hear her mum fidgeting on the other end of the phone, and pictured the frown that usually accompanied mentions of her father.

'I shouldn't be surprised at your father being a shit by now, and yet somehow I always am.'

'He says they did it for tax breaks.'

'Ever the romantic,' she sniffed.

Of course, had Laurie said he'd done it for love, her mum would've scorned that too.

'Please warn me when he's having his reception because I do not want any chance of running into him and this woman. Wanda and I were going to come over for an exhibition at the Whitworth.'

'Mum, I don't mean to sound mean-spirited . . .' Laurie knew she was about to start a fight, even while she intellectually, rationally, wanted a fight with her mum like she wanted a hole in the head. Yet emotionally, it was somehow an inevitability. 'I tell you my boyfriend of eighteen years dumped me and it was, *oh well Dan must have his reasons to follow his lodestar* and I've told you Dad's got married, and he left you thirty-seven years ago, and you're now pissed off and angry. Why can't I be pissed off and angry at Dan?'

'You can! When did I say you couldn't be?'

'The whole "he must be doing the next part on his own and listening to his heart" stuff wasn't exactly saying I had a right to be upset.'

'Of course you do, but he's not cheating on you, he's not lied to you? What do you want me to say, Laurie? Do you want me to criticise him?'

'No!' She didn't. Infuriatingly, she still felt defensive of him. 'It'd just be nice if . . .' she trailed off, as what came next was harsh.

'What?'

'. . . As if you sounded like you cared about my break-up anything like as much as you care about Dad's rubbish.'

'That's a dreadful thing to say, I care much more about you than I do about him!'

Hmmm yeah, not what Laurie was saying, but how did Laurie think it would go, pointing out her mum's hypocrisy in the sting of her dad's news?

Her mother and father were opposite perils, Laurie realised: her dad said the right things and didn't mean them and her mum might feel it, but she never said so.

They finished the call with terse politeness so they could go away and boil resentfully on the things the other had said.

As Laurie replaced the receiver she thought: *well that was ironic, wasn't that the ultimate moment to be bonding over similar experiences? You wouldn't get this on the bloody* Gilmore Girls.

Her mum was still heavily marked by what her dad did

almost four decades ago; Laurie felt the tremor his name caused. Was that going to be Laurie's fate where Dan was concerned, too?

'At some point, you have to give up wishing for your parents to be who you wanted them to be and accept them as they are,' Dan once said.

Easy for him to say, with his kind, dependable mum and dad who thought he was a prince among men and would drop anything and do anything for him.

As Laurie sat on the stairs, hugging her knees and nursing her bruised emotions, there was muttered cursing in the distance as someone tripped over a step, the scrape of a key in the lock, and Dan came in the door.

'Hi,' he said. He was pink from running, and wore the look of apprehensive guilt he always did around Laurie now.

'Hi. I told my mum.'

'Ah.' Dan was obviously at a loss over what to say. 'I've not told mine yet.'

Laurie had guessed that from the lack of call from Dan's mum, Barbara. They got on very well and Barbara had always, in a benign way, treated Laurie as Dan's PA and hotline to his psyche, as well as his diary. Yeah, good luck with that from now on.

'I've found a flat,' he said. 'Quite central. I can move in next week.' He gulped and rushed on. 'I know this sounds really soon and that I'd had it lined up but I honestly didn't. I was on Rightmove yesterday afternoon and it just came up and when I called the agent they said I could pop round this morning. It's not great but it'll do for now.' He trailed off, his cheeks flushed with the exercise and – hopefully – mortification at being so evidently eager to see the back of her.

'Oh. Good?' Laurie said. She didn't know what note to strike, in the teeth of total rejection. She'd always had this knack with Dan, she could joke him out of any temper, persuade him when no one else could. 'He's proper silly for you,' a friend of his once said.

Now she felt as if anything she said would be either pathetic or annoying; she could hear it become one or the other to him as soon as it left her mouth. All the usual doors, her ways in, had been bricked up.

'I'm going to keep paying the mortgage here for the time being. Give you a grace period so you can decide . . . what you want to do.'

'Thanks,' Laurie said, flatly, because no way was she going to be more fulsome than that. Dan's larger salary came with a ton of stress at times, but had its uses. She'd have to remortgage herself up to her eyeballs and eBay everything that wasn't nailed to the floor. Losing Dan *and* her home felt insurmountable.

'I'm going to get fish and chips for dinner tonight, want some?' Dan added, and Laurie shook her head. The rest of the bottle of red in the kitchen would be more effective on an empty stomach. She noticed Dan's appetite was fine.

'When do we tell everyone at work?' she said. They'd mutually avoided this pressing question yesterday, but Laurie knew her office mate, Bharat, would sniff it out in days.

They'd be a week-long scandal, with the news cycle moving into a different phase day by day. 'Have you heard?' on Monday,

'Was he playing away?' on Tuesday, 'Was she playing away?' on Wednesday, 'I saw them arguing outside the Arndale last Christmas, the writing was on the wall' fib dropped in as a lump of red meat to keep it going on Thursday. 'When is it OK to ask either one on a date?' nailed on by Friday, because Salter & Rowson was an absolute sin bin. There was a lot of adrenaline involved in their work at times, which was dampened by after hours booze. Add a steady influx of people aged twenty to forty joining or interning, and you had a recipe for a lot of flirting and more.

It was a shame this had happened now, just when the Jamie-Eve gossip could have been a useful distraction. But there was no way a furtive bunk-up, even a specifically verboten one, was going to trump the break-up of the firm's most prominent couple. And Laurie wouldn't have dobbed Jamie in either. She wasn't ruthless.

Dan leaned on the wall and sighed. 'Shall we not? For the time being? I can't face all the bullshit. I can't see how they'd find out otherwise. It's not like I'm going to put it on Facebook and you're hardly ever on there.'

'Yeah. OK,' Laurie said. They both wanted to wait for a time it'd matter less, though right now Laurie couldn't imagine when that might be.

'And my Dad's got married.'

'No way!' Dan's eyes lit up. He officially disapproved of Laurie's dad in order to stay on the right side of history – and of Laurie and her mum – but she'd always sensed Dan had a soft spot. 'To, what was her name, Nicola?'

'Yeah. Some party happening here. I'm a bridesmaid.'

Barely true, but she wanted Dan to picture her in a dress, in a spotlight, in a glamorous context with scallywag dad, whom he sneakingly admired.

'Ah. Nice.' Dan looked briefly sad and ashamed as obviously, he'd not be there. 'Never thought your dad would settle down.'

'People surprise you,' Laurie shrugged, and Dan looked awkward and then blank at this, muttering he needed a shower.

As Dan passed her on the stairs and his bathroom-puttering noises started, Laurie leaned her head against the bannisters, too spent to imagine moving for the moment. When they passed thirty, as far as their peer group were concerned, Dan and Laurie tying the knot was a done deal. If they weren't thinking about it themselves, they weren't allowed to forget it.

From acquaintances who'd drunkenly exhort, 'You next! You next!' at one of the scores of weddings they attended a year, to the open pleas from Dan's mum to give her an excuse to go to Cardiff for a day of outfit shopping (the best reason for lifetime commitment: a mint lace Phase Eight shift dress and pheasant feather fascinator), to friends who told them, once they'd seen off bottles of wine over dinner, that Dan and Laurie would have *the best wedding ever, come on come ON do it, you selfish sods.*

Laurie always deflected with a joke about her not being keen what with being a lawyer, and seeing a lot of divorce paperwork, but eventually that dodge wore thin. Dan referred to Laurie as 'the missus' and 'the wife', leading newer friends to think they were married.

It had always seemed a case of *when*, not if. Laurie had

vaguely expected a ring box to appear, but it never did: should she have been pushing the issue?

The *where's the wedding??!!!* noise hit a peak around thirty-three. Having skirted around it, after news of another friend's engagement, they discussed it directly over hangover cure fried egg sandwiches of a Saturday morning.

'Do you not think it's much more romantic to not be married?' Dan said. 'If you're together when there's no practical ties, it's really real.' He was indistinct through a mouthful of Hovis. 'Realer than when you've locked yourself into a governmental contract. We of all people know that legal stuff means nowt in terms of how much you love each other.'

Laurie made a sceptical face.

'We have no "ties" . . . except the joint mortgage, every stick of the furniture, and the car?'

'I'm saying, married people stay when it's rough because they made this solemn promise in front of everyone they know, and they don't want to feel stupid, and divorce is a big deal. A big, expensive, arduous deal. As you say, you end up having the wagon wheel coffee table arguments over stuff for the sake of it, like in *When Harry Met Sally*. There's the social shame and failure factor. People like us stay together when it's rough out of pure love. Our commitment doesn't need no vicar, baby.'

With his scruffy hair, sweet expression and expensive striped T-shirt, Dan looked the very advertiser's image of the twenty-first century Guy You Settle Down With. Laurie grinned back.

'So . . . what you're saying is, there will be no weddings

for you, Dan Price? Or, by extension, me? The Price-Watkinsons will never be. The Pratkinsons.'

He wiped his mouth with a piece of kitchen towel. 'Ugh we'd never double barrel no matter what, right?'

Laurie mock wailed. 'No huge dress for me!'

'I dunno. Never say never? But not a priority right now?'

Laurie thought on it. She sensed it was there for her if she demanded it. She was neither wedding wild nor wedding averse. They'd been together since they were eighteen, they'd never needed a rush in them. Plus, it'd be nice not to have to find fifteen grand down the back of the sofa, there was plenty needing doing in the house. She smiled, shrugged, nodded.

'Yeah, see how it goes.'

Emily always told Dan he was lucky to have such an easygoing, un-nagging girlfriend and Dan would roll his eyes and say: 'You should see her with the pencil dobber in IKEA,' but at that moment Laurie felt Emily's praise was justified and she thought, looking at his warm *that's my girl* smile, so did Dan.

And it was only now, listening to the shower thundering upstairs, that Laurie realised that she'd missed the giant glaring warning sign in what Dan had said.

Yes, staying together out of love, not paperwork, was romantic. But if you flipped it round, he was also saying marrying made it too difficult to leave.

Three days later, Laurie got a packet of seedlings for colourful hollyhocks in a card with a Renoir painting, and her mum's unusual sloping script inside, read: 'To new beginnings. Love, Mum.' Laurie cried: this meant her mum had fretted on their conversation, it was her way of making amends. Maybe her mum hadn't trashed Dan, had been upbeat on purpose – to make it clear this wasn't history repeating, that Dan wasn't her father and Laurie wouldn't go through what she did.

Laurie had no faith anymore. As a lifelong believer in The One, in monogamous fidelity to the person who your heart told you was right for you, she was suddenly an atheist. If Dan wasn't to be trusted, who could be?

In the years ahead, she knew plenty of people would tell her to be open to commitment again, to true love: that fresh starts were possible and it would be different this time. She knew she would smile and nod, and not agree with a word of it.

7

Two months and two weeks later

'Can I come round?'

Laurie answered Dan's call while she was walking to the tram after work, as Manchester's late autumn, early winter temperature felt like it was stripping the skin from her face. She loved her city, but it wasn't so hospitable in November.

It had not been an easy time. Ten weeks since the split, and Laurie felt almost as distraught as she did the day Dan left. Whenever their paths crossed at work, they had to chat vaguely normally so as not to arouse suspicion, because no one had figured it out yet. And as Laurie couldn't bear the idea of their relationship being picked apart, she hadn't done anything about it. It wasn't a sensible thing to be doing, as grown-ups, not now they were living apart: they needed to face it. They'd also managed to keep it a secret from the rest of their Chorlton friendship group by pleading prior commitments to a few events, or in a couple of cases, attending singularly and lying through their teeth. But she couldn't

– wouldn't – be the one to break the deadlock, as she hoped against hope they'd simply never need to tell everyone about this blip. She hoped the fact Dan didn't want it known was a sign.

Laurie was no closer to understanding what the hell had happened. What did she do wrong? She couldn't stop asking that.

Tracing the steps by which Dan fell out of love with her was excruciating and yet she guessed she had to do it, or be fated to repeat it.

Her only conclusion was that a distance must have developed between them, so slowly as to be imperceptible, so small as to be overlooked. And it had gradually lengthened.

Of course, the one person she had told, next to her mum, was Emily, ten days after the fact, who'd unexpectedly burst into tears for her. They'd been sitting in a cheapo basement dim sum bar under harsh strip lighting, a place that was usually quiet midweek. Laurie had asked for a table right at the back so she could heave and whimper without too many curious looks.

After hearing the details of Emily's most recent work trip, a jaunt to Miami for a tooth-whitening brand with soulless corporate wonks, Laurie steeled herself and cleared her throat.

'Em, I have something to tell you.'

Emily's gaze snapped up from raking over the noodles section. Her hand immediately shot out and grabbed Laurie's wrist tightly. Then her eyes moved to Laurie's wine and her expression was more quizzical.

'Oh God! Not that,' Laurie said. 'Nope. I'm safe to drink.'

She took a deep breath. 'Dan and I have split up. He's left me. Not really sure why.'

Emily didn't react. She almost shrugged, and did a small double-take. 'You're kidding? This is a wind-up. Why would you do that?'

'No. One hundred per cent true. It's over. We're over.'

'What? You're serious?'

'I'm serious. Over. I am single.'

Laurie was trying that phrase out. It sounded a crazy reach, while being hard fact.

'He's finished with you?'

'Yes. He has finished with me. We are separated.'

Laurie noticed that someone 'finishing' with someone else was such savage language. They cancelled you. You are over. Your use has been exhausted.

'Laurie, are you being serious? Not a break? You've split up?'

'Yes.'

Laurie was holding it together better than she expected. Then Emily's eyes filled up and Laurie said, 'oh God, don't cry,' her voice cracking, as beige lines streaked rivers through Emily's foundation.

'Sorry, sorry,' Emily gasped, 'I— can't believe it. It can't be real? He's having a moment or something.'

That immediate understanding from her closest friend had been the straw to break the stoic camel's back, and Laurie and Emily had wept together until the waitress slapped two large glasses of wine down on their table, muttering, 'On the house,' before hastily beating a retreat. Here's to sisterhood.

'*Why*? Has he had some sort of stroke?' Emily said, when she got her breath back.

Laurie put both palms up in a 'fuck knows' gesture and felt what a comfort her best friend was. She'd been there from the start, since Laurie and Dan's Fresher's Week meet-cute. She was completely invested; Laurie didn't have to explain the preceding eight seasons for her to be blown away at the finale. Finale, or mid-season hiatus?

'He says he doesn't feel it, us, anymore. The night we'd been out in The Refuge, afterwards he was waiting up for me, and it came out. He'd been thinking about leaving for a while. Which you know, is fantastic to hear.' She paused. 'We'd been talking about coming off the pill.'

Emily winced.

'*Ohhhh* so it's fear of fatherhood? Growing up, responsibility?'

'I asked that, and also said that we could rethink having kids, but no. He's decided our life makes him feel like he's on a fast track to death and has to go rediscover himself.'

'Could it be a trial separation? Putting you two on pause, while he twats about off the grid in Goa, like he's Jason Bourne? God, whenever I forget why I hate men, one of them reminds me.'

Laurie laughed hollowly.

'Nope, I doubt it.' She couldn't admit to any lingering hope she felt, it was too tragic. Other parties needed to fully accept it, on her behalf. 'He's found a flat. We're going to work out the money in the next few weeks. Then that's us done, I guess. He's offered to trade the car for furniture so there will be no wagon wheel coffee table haggling.' Laurie's throat seized up again.

'I don't know what to say, Loz. He loves you to bits, I know he does. He worships the ground you walk on, he always has done. This is madness. This is an *episode*.'

Laurie nodded. 'Yeah. It doesn't make sense. The Didn't See It Coming, At All, factor is fucking with my head really badly.' She lapsed into silence to staunch the tears.

'Well, tonight just got even drunker,' Emily said eventually, catching the waitress's eye to signal another round.

In the end they'd finished the night in an even grottier bar down the street, two bottles of wine down and one heavy tip for the poor waitress who'd had to clear up their snotty tissues. The memory of the morning after still made Laurie wince today. Anyone who moaned about hangovers in their twenties should be forced to suffer a hangover from your late thirties.

The worst of it was, after the fireworks of Dan's declaration that he was leaving and that first shock of grief, the awful banality of 'getting on with it' was its own horror.

'Never mind the fact I'll be expected to do monkey sex in swings, like they have in Nine Inch Nails songs, who will I text boring couple stuff to, ever again? Like what shall we have for tea, pre-pay day? Who will I ask if they want "baked potatoes and picky bits" on a cheap Monday?' Laurie had demanded of Emily. ('Lots of people like baked potatoes!' she had promised.)

It was the end of another night of boozy mourning, and as they waited on the corner for their Ubers to appear, Emily had nudged Laurie (probably slightly harder than intended).

'Laurie, you know you're going to get the Sad Dads sliding into your DMs any day now.'

Laurie barked a laugh. 'Doubt it. Don't assume that how men are with you, is how they are with me.'

'Seriously, they're shameless. Absolutely no idea of respectful pause, straight in there: *hey I hear you're back on the market, allow me to place the initial bid.* I've heard this lament from the girls at work so many times. They all think they're catches and they're often still with their wives. They think you'll be desperately grateful for any cheer up cock they can offer.' Emily cupped her hands into a bowl shape: 'Please, sir, can I have some more?'

When they'd finished sniggering, Laurie had said, 'I don't get that sort of attention. The attention you do.'

She felt so wholly unprepared to be back out there. As Emily pointed out, she'd never really been there.

'Because a huge part of getting that sort of attention is signalling you're up for that sort of attention.'

'Hah. I can't even think about it. I can't imagine ever being any good for anyone ever again. I think Dan's ruined me.'

'OK, but don't rule out the healing power of a purely physical fling. Sometimes, you don't need face-holding *I Love You* intense meaningful sex. What *you* need is some hench dipshit with superior body strength to pin your wrists above your head and pound you with a virile meanness.'

Laurie groaned while Emily grinned triumphantly.

'Did you briefly forget your pain?'

'Absolutely,' Laurie said, leaning her head on Emily's tiny shoulder. She had the proportions of a malnourished Hardy heroine on a windswept moor. She was definitely a heroine though, never a victim.

This call from Dan was officially the first time he'd reached out to her to 'talk' in ten weeks though. Could it be . . . could he be . . .? No, squelch that thought.

'Yeah. What, to pick stuff up? You still have your key?' she said to Dan, hedging her bets, though she knew 'picking up some stuff' was a text, not a phone call.

'No, I'm coming round to see you.'

'What for?'

'I need to talk to you.'

Laurie breathed in and breathed out. Right. She'd known this would happen. Almost from the first moment Dan had said he was going. Yet it coming true so soon still took her aback.

'What about?'

'I think it's best said face to face. Is seven alright?'

Laurie's heartbeat sped up, because she could hear the strain behind the casual delivery. Dan was scared. She felt oddly scared herself. What did she have to be frightened about? It was for her to weigh her answer.

She already knew what her answer would be. So did he.

They would have to creak through the formalities of his grovelling apologies, his prepared explanations for how he could've got it so catastrophically wrong, his vigorous heart-felt promises that he'd never mess her around again. The pledge to live in the dog house at first, to do better, to try harder. (That's a point, there'd never be a better time to get that Lurcher she'd unsuccessfully campaigned for.) Tentatively working out how penitent he was prepared to be – did they raise the issue of Laurie being on or off the pill? Did Laurie want to proceed directly to parenthood with a man who'd left her on her own, while he worked through his fear of death in a sterile semi-furnished place near Whitworth Street?

No, absolutely not. He could move back into the spare room and they could take it slowly. Laurie was still in love with Dan but she was also realistic enough to know they would have a different relationship after this. It was a large wound. It had left her unable to trust him. It would take years to recover, fully. It would take years before, if he said *they needed to talk*, she wouldn't be expecting rejection and a mad flit again.

She got in and put the lights on, tried to figure out what outfit she could change into that would make her look attractive enough to suit her dignity but not like she'd dressed up for him. In the end she went for jeans and a hip-length jersey top she'd not worn in a while that showed off her more prominent collarbones, and a dark shade of lipstick, from a worn down nub of an Estée Lauder matte long-lasting she rummaged for in the bathroom cupboards. Then she rubbed it off with loo roll and grimaced at herself. She wasn't going to look like she'd been yearning and praying for this moment, even if she had been.

Dan knocked on the door dead on seven p.m. and Laurie felt his nerves in this uncharacteristic punctuality. When you're so far on the back foot that you don't want any other single thing counting against you.

He was in a new jacket, a sage green padded puffy thing she'd have told him not to buy, and she vaguely wondered if he'd dressed up for this, too. Him having clothes she'd not seen jangled her. It wasn't how she pictured him, in the intervening time. She'd been wondering if she could stand to turn him down, to make him spend longer in purgatory. The fact that she felt undermined by his buying winterwear without consulting her told her she didn't have anything like the strength.

Dan sat down and refused Laurie's offer a beer – 'I'm driving' – which she took to be him signalling that he didn't expect a yes, wasn't being complacent.

'Thanks for seeing me,' he said, and Laurie frowned.

'A bit formal? Are we communicating as lawyers now?'

He shifted his weight and coughed and didn't make any cautious gesture of amusement.

A tiny amount of dread entered Laurie's body. She couldn't read him.

'Was it to say something in particular?'

'Yes . . . OK. God. There's no good way of saying this.'

Using that line again? Jesus. She remained impassive. He didn't deserve the smallest amount of help and she'd hate herself if she gave it to him. It was bad enough she was taking him back.

'I wanted you to be the first to know.'

Laurie's palms were suddenly slick, and she could feel the pulse in her wrist. *I wanted you to be the first to know* was a REALLY fucking odd introduction to 'I made a mistake.' If not that, what?

Was he off to find himself in the Outback, despite her mockery over his poor globetrotter credentials? Was she going to have to grit her teeth through Christmas, desperately hoping he'd not encountered any misfortune while hiking through remote dusty areas of the planet? Desperately scanning his Facebook, hoping he'd post a proof of life photo, looking tanned and craggy?

'First to know what?' Laurie said finally, into the agonising silence, during which Dan's face was etched with grave worry.

'I've met someone.'

The phrase smashed into the living room like a meteorite, taking out the fireplace, leaving a smoking crater. She physically recoiled. He'd come here to say he was with another woman? Already? Laurie had not, for a single second, entertained that this was what happened next. Not this fast. He'd only just moved out? How was this possible?

'Met someone?' she repeated incredulously, staring at the pre-faded, pretend-worn knees on his indigo jeans, clothes which she realised she'd not seen before either.

Dan nodded.

'You're together, like a couple?'

'Yes.'

'You've *slept* with someone?'

This was patently a stupid question, a teenager's question, given he'd called them a couple. Laurie was so far beyond dealing with this that she had no process between the rapid firing in her brain, and her mouth.

Dan twisted his hands together and said:

'Yes.'

Laurie wanted to scream, or sob. Until now, his leaving was only words, a temporary absence, and a three-month lease. A few patching-up conversations with their parents, and Emily, a year that you 'put behind you' when you raised a glass at the New Year bells.

Now it was definitive, he'd done something he couldn't undo. Laurie steadied herself, with great effort, and asked, 'But – we've barely split up? It's been weeks?'

Dan didn't reply to this, but carried on. 'She's called Megan. She works at Rawlings.'

Giving her a name made it real. Laurie tried to quell her spinning stomach, and racing mind, to focus. There would be time to fall apart later. Lots of it. Rawlings, a rival firm. Someone he'd met in court.

'And you started seeing her, when?' she said, with restrained force.

Dan twisted his hands some more.

'Few weeks back. A month or so.'

'But you knew her already?'

'Yeah. A year, year and a half.'

'Did I really mean this little? That you could move on this quick?'

He was silent.

'What the FUCK, Dan? What?! Please explain this because I'm not close to understanding how you could be this ruthless?'

'It's not something I planned,' he said, eventually. 'I think . . . the end is more recent for you than for me, in that I wasn't happy for a while.'

'Oh God, so we're back to the idea you'd been miserable for ages?'

'No, not ages!'

It was over. He was with someone else. Yet Laurie was already asking herself how they came back from this. *There is no 'they'*, a voice told her. *There is 'them' now. Have you gone deaf?*

'You fucking sadist,' Laurie said, shrill but hoarse. 'Who are you? I don't even know. I really don't even know.'

Don't cry don't cry don't cry, Laurie told herself. Not yet, though it felt like she had psychically collapsed in on herself, like a dying star.

She had an enemy, a nemesis, a rival she never knew about, who had climbed into bed with her long-term partner when, somehow, Laurie wasn't looking.

Laurie hadn't for a second considered there was anyone else. When she asked Dan that question, that first night, it was more to embarrass him than anything. To point up the seriousness and the stakes of his actions to him. Laurie was braced to receive Dan back, and now this?

And when *exactly* did it start?

She held up a trembling hand and counted off on her fingers. 'You've been gone ten weeks, Dan, and you got together with her a few weeks back. And she's already important enough for you to come round and tell me about? Something's not quite adding up, is it? This is Concorde speed.'

Dan blew air out. He looked like his jaw had locked, that he was finding it difficult to speak. He couldn't look at her. 'Obviously we were friends, before. Only friends though, nothing happened.'

'But you knew that you were going to get together with her when you left me, didn't you?'

Dan was vigorously shaking his head but Laurie knew the bones of him, she'd known him half her life. She could see in his eyes that he was lying. Never mind that, she could see on the bare timeline here, he was lying. No intuition needed, that's how staggeringly obvious his cruelty was.

'Nothing happened before . . .'

'Don't try to fucking out-lawyer a lawyer, Dan. "Nothing happened" – meaning you waited to have sex until you told me you were leaving me. But she was right there, lined up. You left me for her.'

He shook his head but again Laurie could see he had no words, without completely perjuring himself.

Laurie still loved Dan, deeply, and yet with the excruciating pain he was inflicting on her, she felt the banal truism of there being a fine line between love and hate.

Laurie knew that most people were murdered by someone they knew; she'd stood up in court and argued for the killers' bail applications, while they wept not only about their fate, but about their loss.

In this moment, she understood why.

8

Laurie suppressed her homicidal impulses and tried to summon every ounce of someone who thought strategy for a living to handle this, to not let Dan off the hook by putting her feelings first.

'So you were obviously really fucking heartbroken. How long did you wait to climb into bed, after the Pickfords van left here? Days? Hours?'

'I was. I am. She has nothing to do with us, with what happened.'

'Oh what SHIT! You'd fallen for someone else, you dumped me for her, but you've convinced yourself she is *incidental*?! This is beyond insulting. It's downright fucking ludicrous.'

'Laurie, if we were right, if things had been OK, Megan wouldn't have happened. The cause and effect is the wrong way round if you think Megan split us up.'

Laurie gasped. 'These are mental gymnastics, *contortions,* so you don't have to feel guilty. Basically it's my fault, for not making you happy enough?'

'No! Relationships fail all the time, I'm not saying it's your fault. This is what has happened, that's all, and I know it's shitty for you, I know that.'

'Yeah relationships are especially likely to fail when one person has started an affair. You know, that thing we promised we'd never ever do to one another. Remember that?'

'It wasn't an affair,' Dan said, grimly, but to Laurie's ears, without the necessary conviction.

'Being on a promise with someone is an affair, Dan.'

He said nothing, because she had nailed it. The utter emptiness of this argumentative victory. In fact victory was the wrong word. Sour satisfaction at best, except she felt no satisfaction whatsoever.

'You had an affair and you won't even do the decent thing and say as much, call it what it is, in case it makes you feel bad.'

'I feel awful.'

Laurie had to tell herself to breathe before she could speak again.

'I begged you to tell me what was going on, *I begged you*. And you gave me a load of WANK about finding yourself. You had met some other woman you wanted to bang, and you spun me this line about your existential angst?!'

'All of that was true!' Dan said, more vehement now, but Laurie knew he was only vehement in the way anyone in a corner was, with a near-hyperventilating woman shouting unwanted truths at him.

'Was it too obvious, too LAMESTREAM, to admit you'd found a better option, like a million other boring ageing men who can't keep it in their pants? Is she twenty-five, this mysterious someone who doesn't make you feel trapped, and like there's nothing worthwhile between here and death?'

'Thirty-five.'

Instantly, despite her fury and humiliation at the idea some lissom ingénue had stolen Dan's affections, this was worse – Laurie hadn't been traded for a younger model. She'd lost to a woman of her own age, or thereabouts. It was a fair fight, this boxing match, they were in the same weight category with similar length of training. Laurie was simply too boring.

That fear was lurking behind it all, she knew that. Domesticated, exemplary employee, devoted to Dan, ticked so many boxes – but dull. Someone who could make you feel like life held no surprises anymore. Right now, she wanted to surprise the shit out of him, but the only ways she could think of involved petrol and matches.

'I promise you, that's not how it was. I was already unhappy, the thing with Megan came right out of the blue . . .'

'This is such bullshit!' Laurie shouted, reacting to hearing her name again like she'd been tasered. 'Your whole thing was *oh no I hate this conventional, being tied down, settled monogamy, it's not for me, maybe I will go backpacking.* And your first big gesture of freedom is getting another girlfriend?! Another lawyer, at that?'

Laurie had to pause for breath but she knew she was dying for Dan to say, *she's not my girlfriend, it's a fling.* He didn't of course – if she was a fling, why would he be here? Which meant Laurie was still gambling, even now, they could come back from this.

Being confronted with how little you could accept from someone, when your heart was on the line and you were being tortured, was awful. Laurie hated herself too, in that very moment.

'I don't know what you expect me to say, Dan. Great, crack on, hope the sex is amazing,' Laurie spat. 'Why even tell me?'

There was a pause, as this had been a rhetorical question, and yet Laurie realised she'd hit on a very good point. Why had he told her? Fear of Salter & Rowson's Stasi seeing them, perhaps? Except . . . this was a very ballsy move, nevertheless. Dan was the man who even after ten weeks had yet to tell his parents they'd separated (Laurie had stopped answering the house phone in case it was his mother calling); he didn't go looking for trouble or difficulty, to put it mildly.

Dan said, haltingly, 'Because . . .'

'Because . . .?'

Another silence. 'Because you deserved to hear from me' or some other platitude wouldn't warrant this hesitation, and the advocate in Laurie asked: why *has* he told you now? Why not wait a few months and look less of a bastard? Her whole body was coated in a thin layer of freezing sweat.

'Oh, fuck . . . I have absolutely no idea how to say this and it's still not real to me. I have no idea how to say this, no idea . . .'

He was gabbling.

Through a cascade of her tears, Laurie said, 'What the fuck? What more is there? Are you getting *married* or something?' Her heart was racing.

'She's pregnant,' Dan heaved out. He buried his face in his hands, almost as a defensive move, as if he thought Laurie might physically attack him.

Time stood still for a moment, time in this world that Laurie didn't understand or want to live in any more. Pregnant.

Pregnant. It echoed through their thoughtfully decorated, tasteful, affluent Chorltonite couldn't-stand-it-for-a-day-longer-could-you-Dan living room.

'She's . . .? What? It's yours?'

Dan nodded and Laurie couldn't absorb what he was saying.

If she'd been shocked before, it didn't compare to this state of total standstill. Laurie simply stared. She couldn't be. What? *What?*

'It was an accident, she said she was on the pill. But she wants to keep it. Fuck, Laurie, I didn't plan for this, I promise you, it's happened out of nowhere.'

'How . . .?' No not how, she knew how. Don't be sick, not yet. 'When?'

'Two months.'

'You've only been moved out a little over two months. You jumped right into her bed?'

Dan stared at her levelly, and emptily, and Laurie snorted, a watery snort of horror and disgust and disbelief.

'You're staying with her, and you're having a baby?' Laurie said. Dan nodded and she saw his tears and she wanted to punch him in the face. 'You told me you didn't want kids?'

He was grey-white. 'I didn't. I don't. It's an accident.'

Enough. Laurie stood up, grabbed Dan by the shoulders and manhandled him out of the room and into the hallway, shrieking, 'Get out! Get the fuck out!' while Dan made useless vague noises of objection.

'You do this to me, you tell me you don't want kids, and you do this?!'

She pushed Dan out of the door so hard he stumbled and

nearly fell over. Laurie didn't care if the whole street heard, or saw.

She slammed the door with much force and noisily slid the bolt. It wasn't exactly likely he'd risk his life by using his key to get back in, but it felt the right thing to do all the same. Final.

She leaned her head on the glass for just a moment and then turned and raced up to the bathroom, vomiting into the loo, retching again and again until there was nothing left, then slumped back down on the floor. She had a good view of the underside of the bowl and the whiskers that coated it – Dan was gone forever, but still here recently enough she'd still be cleaning up his mess. Mess? Devastation.

Baby. He was having a child, with someone called Megan. He had been having an affair for some time, that was certain, emotionally if not physically. He'd celebrated his first nights of freedom by impregnating someone else. Laurie was going to have to recite these utterly harrowing, bizarre facts until they sunk in for her.

He was going to be a dad. But not with her. An image sprung into her head, a pink turnip-faced newborn with froggy eyes, wrapped in a cocoon of white crochet blanket eyes, Dan cradling it, looking up at the camera with the shell shocked, Cloud Nine expression of an hours-old parent. He would do this, without her. She would not be the mother of his children. He would not be the father of hers.

Hers. Hah.

Laurie made a noise that sounded peculiar to her, in the quiet of the house, a kind of strangled whimper, shading into an animalistic howl. It echoed, unanswered, in her empty house.

9

Laurie rang in sick the next morning. It helped her voice was barely a croak as she spoke to the receptionist to claim upset stomach and the sweats.

'Ugh yeah you sound like shit, don't come in and give it to us,' said Jan on reception, who no one had ever confused with a bleeding heart liberal.

Laurie crawled back to bed and lay staring at the white star-shaped ceiling lampshade as the hours drifted past.

She felt certain Dan had gone in to the office because 1. he'd have guessed she might not, and they couldn't both be off without questions and a cover story about food poisoning or something, which was a falsehood too far now, and 2. he wasn't shattered by what was happening.

The only communication she received was an email from hyper efficient Jamie Carter: *Hey sorry to bother when you're on your sick bed but do you know anything about the adjournment in the Cheetham Hill robbery?*

Oh, go swivel. 'If ambition was hair, he'd be the Yeti,' as Bharat once said.

Laurie pretended to herself she was ill and therefore allowed herself to doze.

When she rejoined consciousness for a spell in the last afternoon, she had a text from Bharat – *WTAF, YOU ARE NEVER ILL! It was Di's baking day so I saved you a jam tart, but a fly got stuck in it xxx* – and another, from Dan.

Hi. Hope you're OK. Can't imagine how shit you feel Laurie and I'm so so so sorry, I never meant for any of this to happen. I don't know what to say. Call me if you want to, even if it's to shout at me.

When Dan dropped his initial bombshell – she couldn't think of that *partial account* of a conversation now without clutching her chest, like she might have a coronary with the rage – she'd wondered if he'd become an arsehole. She now knew the answer to that. Or if he'd not become one, maybe he'd always had this tendency, it had got worse, and somehow Laurie had blinded herself to it.

'Call me if you want to, even to shout at me' was revolting – the preening self-regard and false big-hearted performative good guyness of *go on, I know I deserve it,* once you'd swaggered clear of the blast.

He'd very likely robbed Laurie of her chance of parenthood herself with his indecision, walked out the door and immediately inseminated someone else. She hadn't even begun the work of working out how upset she was about her odds of motherhood being dramatically slashed, after a lifetime of thinking it was there for her at the time of her choosing.

Dan hadn't been sure about taking this huge step with the love of his life, but with Megan, it had happened instantly. He gave to her what he'd withheld from the woman who'd washed his socks for the last decade.

Dan had said it wasn't planned, but Laurie was at the stage where, if Dan said it was raining, she'd go outside to check.

The clock on Laurie's bedside table hit six. A whole day had floated by and she had barely registered it passing.

Six months or so ago, Dan had taken up running. Laurie had been pleased, even impressed. She was quite good at keeping fit, going to the gym, walking everywhere; Dan had been the one glued to the sofa with his hand stuck in a bag of Tangy Cheese Doritos.

She now saw that hobby for what it was – getting match fit for wrestling with an exciting new prospect. Spending hours pounding the streets, music blaring, not having to interact with his long-term girlfriend, while he plotted a fresh course. Beginning to break away.

They used to talk so openly, it was something they used to privately congratulate themselves on, even boast about to one another. *How come they don't discuss this stuff?* they'd say in wonder about friends, shaking their heads. *You're my best friend as well as my girlfriend, why would I not?* Dan used to say, at whatever laddish thing a friend had said he'd never tell *his* other half.

Dan was a great talker, Laurie was a talker and a good listener; when something had bothered one of them, it got dealt with up front.

That had subtly changed in the last couple of years, Laurie

realised. What she called Dan's moodiness – and it was moods, even sulks, certainly extended silences which she couldn't and wasn't invited to penetrate – was also a closing off and a closing down, putting up a forbidding wall around what was actually going on in his head.

At some point, he turned away from her, he made the decision that the solution to his problems didn't lie in Laurie.

That was the promise you made when you fell head over heels in love, really, she thought. Not that you wouldn't have problems, but that no problem would be the sort where you couldn't find the solution, together.

On the third day of mourning, Laurie's utter horror at the thought of knowing anything about Megan – simply saying the name in her head was like repeating a curse, hexing herself – turned on a sixpence.

Laurie suddenly had a gnawing hunger to see everything. It must be some part of the stages of grieving, or the shock receding. Your appetite returning after a sickness.

It was a Saturday, but time had ceased to have much meaning for Laurie, since the Wednesday night of the announcement. She wondered if she could get a doctor's note to not go in to work next week, too.

With shaky hands and weak body – when did she last eat? She thought she recalled finding half a squashed Twix in her gym bag, yesterday lunchtime – Laurie hauled her laptop onto her knees on the sofa. She opened her rarely used Facebook page, and searched for Megan. The first name, fairly unusual, would surely reveal the likeliest suspect.

Nothing. Not in Dan's friends, not in the friend's lists of those she knew at Rawlings. Megan must be one of those rare people who didn't use social media.

Unless . . . Laurie lay on her back and stared at the filigree of spider webs along the picture rail, the parts of a house you rarely paused long enough to inspect, when not laid prone, in the twilight land of the unwell. *Unless.*

Unless Megan had blocked her? It seemed aggressive, unfair – surely it was for Laurie to block Megan, in the proper way of things. But if you knew your new boyfriend had told his very-recent-ex long-term girlfriend you were pregnant, you'd know a very, very scorned woman was coming hurtling your way. Why would you leave any of your business open to it?

Laurie opened a browser again, but this time, set up a fresh Facebook profile using her Gmail address, instead of the old Yahoo one.

Laurie wouldn't need to add any friends or signal the existence of the second account in any way, she could use it purely as a stalking tool.

Once it was active and she launched her investigations again, Laurie didn't know what to hope for.

Confirming you'd been blocked was disconcerting enough when it was just someone you didn't rub along with brilliantly well at work, let alone the woman who stole the love of your life and was pregnant with his child. But if she wasn't blocked and Megan really was a twenty-first century Greta Garbo, Laurie's burning need to know more would go unmet.

With a dull thud, as she clicked on Dan Price's profile – his photo, a throwback picture of himself in fancy dress at university on the night he met Laurie, salt into wounds – and then again in his friends, Megan Mooney sprang up in front of her. Profile photo, a jokey one of Lucille Ball.

She was blocked. The bitch had blocked her, while camping here brazenly in Dan's friends. Laurie swallowed back bile, literal, physical bile.

She took a deep breath and braced herself before diving in. *Megan Mooney*. She sounded like a secretary in a 1940s screwball, or the quiet mouse 'by day' alter ego of a Marvel superhero.

Laurie checked herself: she could do this without sobbing or screaming, breathed again, and clicked.

Megan had shared some JustGiving links – OH YOU LIKE SUPPORTING CHARITIES, DO YOU, LIKE A GOOD PERSON? – Laurie internally spasmed: she might not be ready for this experience, like a wobbly patient on a ward trying to walk too fast and doing themselves a mischief.

Would she ever be ready?

What was publicly available on Megan's profile wasn't very informative, and when Laurie was scrolling birthday wishes from two years ago (was Dan there? Not that she could find) she moved to the photo galleries.

They were generally of groups, but Laurie clicked and clicked until she saw enough of the pictures so she could spot which was Megan, by her ubiquity.

She couldn't help it; her first response was to compare herself.

Megan was a redhead, nothing like Laurie physically, properly Lucozade ginger. Laurie remembered something about gingerism being a 'recessive gene' and couldn't remember if that meant Dan's child would be one.

Megan had close-set eyes, a strong nose, and an intimidating, rather than pretty face. Laurie was easily conventionally prettier. Laurie both knew this to be true straight away and yet simultaneously didn't trust it, doubted it, and hated herself for this being such a necessary measure. Laurie had never been someone who'd traded on her looks. But, as an acerbic female colleague once said to her regards the length of her coupledom, *you've never needed to.*

And much like Megan's age, Laurie moved from a split second of relief, to confusion and intimidation. If she wasn't a dazzling beauty, then how could a woman whose powers of attraction she couldn't immediately see do this to her? Dan wanted her more than he wanted Laurie, so any bargaining and comparing now was futile. Megan *was* clearly killer sexy to Dan, as she'd killed their relationship. Her powers of attraction had annihilated an eighteen-year history.

Further poking around revealed Megan was sporty and had an incredible figure, a near-concave stomach (that was about to change. Laurie hated herself for expanding the picture with forefinger and thumb, staring morbidly at the space where Dan's child was) and legs that went on for days.

If she needed to feel physically inferior to understand this, then Megan's physique could do it. Laurie had a twinge of political outrage – if she'd left Dan for another man, was it likely he'd spend any time studying his rival's calf muscles for clues as to why she'd strayed? Nope.

Here was Megan at the end of a 10k run for breast cancer

research, everyone pink faced in their Lycra gear, linked arms and holding their medals up to the camera. Laurie burned at the grinning women flanking her, the sense of sisterhood in their female cause – some for me would've been nice, eh, 'Megs'? (She was Megs on her tabard.) Hell hath no fury.

She came to the end of what she was able to see. The Add Friend button taunted her and she closed the window, a dampness gathering on her brow. Laurie fantasised the catastrophe of hitting it by mistake, Megan seeing the request.

Hah, Laurie was worried about that gaffe, when Megan had a foetus half made of Dan's DNA to explain?

She shut her laptop and lay down on the sofa again.

There had been a secretive alternative universe, a budding romance, alongside Laurie's normal life with Dan, the two timelines eventually to intersect in the most explosive way.

Laurie knew how it must have been steadily built, for them to be ready to leap into bed together as soon as the Getting Rid Of Laurie admin was complete. (Assuming that it was true they waited, of course.)

Shared glances, momentary, supposedly insignificant touching of hands, or knees, under tables. Innocent coffees after court, in which perhaps a little too much was said about their respective private lives. Rueful humour, that suggested maybe it wasn't a bed of roses. Tiny hints that you might be open to alternatives. Texts at the weekend, only light jokes, but making it clear you were thinking about someone out of hours. Testing responses, plausible deniability always there if you got nothing back.

Knowing this had happened felt to Laurie like thinking

you were healthy, going about your normal days, and not knowing a fatal cancer was flowering somewhere, unfelt, in an organ. Had Megan cheated on her partner, too? There was no sign of a significant other, but Laurie could only see a dozen or so images.

When did it start? How did it start? They were questions to which Laurie would very likely never know answers.

In a few short years, or even months, it would be past the point anyone would even think it was her business. A page had turned for Dan, and Laurie was now part of his past tense. Laurie was someone who'd appear fleetingly in shadowy form in dinner party anecdotes. Dan dandling an infant on his lap: *Oh Santorini? Yeah I went there with my ex.* Eighteen years, and she'd be worth a two-letter descriptor.

While Laurie did some exhausted sobbing in lieu of being willing to throw her nice crockery around the room, a clear thought solidified in her mind: *I am not only a sad woman. I am a bloody lawyer. I want to know when it started. I want to get this bastard for provable infidelity, even if not sexual. So there will be evidence. THINK.*

Megan was into running. And Dan had taken up running, which Laurie was sure wasn't a coincidence. When he ran, he listened to music. She was confident he *was* running and not off on any rendezvous, as he regularly came back a beetroot shade and showed her his route on Runkeeper, before dramatically collapsing and saying Laurie best fetch him a medicinal beer.

Laurie was rarely online, so the place he could interact with Megan was Facebook, and the topic they'd bond over was their stupid jogging. Running groups? Laurie used her old profile to check Dan's activity. Nothing. He wasn't the sort of person to be fair, the NIMBYs of Chorlton Community site drove him round the bend.

Music, though. Running. She'd glimpsed a playlist on his phone screen, as he wound the earphones round it.

A combination of her professional cunning and her instincts about Dan meant the answer came to her, in a second: they made running playlists together. She was sure of it. Dan used to give her endless 'mix tapes' when they were first going out, it was his kind of courtship. Song choices could covertly yet power-fully declare all kinds of things you'd never dare say outright.

Laurie opened her laptop, logged in to Spotify. She'd only ever had Dan's user name for that, and she betted he thought she'd never check in, and if she did, wouldn't know what she was looking at.

Well, she did now.

Laurie's skin prickled with the successful detective 'Gotcha!' sensation, coupled with horror at seeing it laid out, as if she'd torn back the covers on writhing bodies.

Among Dan's playlists, there was one made six months ago, called *I Wanna Run 2 U*. Nice wordplay, twat. There it was, halfway down: a song added by a different user, one calling herself meggymoon. Ugh, UGH.

The track was called 'When Love Takes Over'.

Dan's next was 'Go Your Own Way' by Fleetwood Mac. Another from meggymoon: 'Not Afraid'. It was straight call and response of two people panting for each other; Laurie hardly needed to be a Bletchley code breaker.

Dan's next: the Stones' 'Start Me Up'. *Puke.* Laurie was embarrassed for him.

It was a very modern way to transact cheating and yet it was an age-old dynamic – over caffeinated, adolescent excitement, egging each other on by degrees.

And hiding in plain sight, because if Laurie had queried this playlist, they would be a bunch of songs, and – DUH! – loads of songs are about sex and love, dummy. She wondered how Dan would've denied it. Or would he have broken down, used it as a chance to tell the truth? She'd never know.

Laurie picked up her phone, not in full control of herself, and texted Dan.

I know you were messing around with her six months back, I have the proof. I have no idea who you are anymore, and I don't want to know.

Then she turned onto her side and went to sleep. When she briefly awoke, she had three messages in reply, and managed to delete them without reading them.

10

'Laurie, I've had a science fiction film pitch from my cousin Munni. Listen to this . . .'

As Laurie took her seat on Monday morning, her office mates, Bharat and Di, were shriek-chortling at each other in a way that was both a reminder that life went on, and at the same time seemed to be happening behind a wall of glass.

Bharat's eccentric cousin Munni in Leamington Spa was a regular source of amusement and delight to Bharat. Munni once tried to get himself nominated for a Pride of Britain award for karate chopping a shoplifter running away with a frozen chicken in Morrisons, and according to a horrified Bharat, dried his willy in the Dyson Airblade after a shower in the gym.

'It is the year 2030 and scientists have found a cure for death. Good news, you'd think? No. Because now with no one dying, there are too many people. So there are two choices: kill old people, or sterilise the young. War breaks out between the breeders and the geriatrics. At first, thanks to better strength, bone density and joint mobility, plus understanding smart phones, the youth prevail.'

Bharat paused to hunch double, laughing over his keyboard.

'Poor Munni! Does he know you share his emails?' Laurie said.

'He's sent it to the head of Paramount film studios! He can stand for a few people in Manchester to hear it too.'

Laurie switched her computer on, slung her bag down, unwound her scarf.

Bharat, a Sikh man of thirty-two with a frenetic social life and love of disco, and Di, a fifty-something divorcee who adored her Maine Coon cats and Ed Sheeran, were unlikely banter partners, and yet they were devoted to each other. It was practically a marriage.

Today, Laurie was painfully grateful for the background hubbub they'd created, as she wanted minimal scrutiny of what she'd done at the weekend. It was easy enough to lie, but harder to keep her emotions totally steady while she did so. It was hard not to appear as she was – hollowed out.

Her mum used to play Paul Simon's *Graceland* on a loop, and Laurie kept thinking of the line about losing love being like a window into your heart. She wanted it shuttered. And she had to see him here, interact? The thought made her insides seize up.

It was with intense apprehension, aware that a longer absence would generate more interest, Laurie had come back into work today.

Only to find, thanks to a God with a sick sense of humour, Dan loitering outside at nine a.m., finishing a call with a client. It was harrowing, but better she faced him straight away, and without them being watched.

'How are you?' he said, looking, it had to be said, completely shit scared of her.

'Fine,' she replied, and marched past. Knowing her half stone weight loss, haunted baggy eyes and near palpable despair said different.

'Laurie,' Dan caught her arm, lowered his voice, 'I said you had a stomach flu. People asked me.'

She gave a curt nod in response, because this wasn't the time or place to be cutting or contemptuous, then pulled her arm away firmly and marched into the building.

Salter & Rowson was an old-fashioned law firm, a few streets away from Deansgate. It was a looming Victorian building housing criminal, civil and family departments, a brace of legal secretaries and four receptionists. Mr Salter, sixty-ish, and Rowson, fifty-something, had started the firm in the early 1980s when Salter still had hair and Rowson was still on his first wife and family.

A large portion of their business was legal aid. Laurie spent much time in the magistrates' court defending individuals who Dan categorised as 'toerags and scallies'. He was in civil, which as the name suggested, offered a slightly more stately pace. Laurie was old enough not to have to do the on call shifts, where she had to hack out at one in the morning.

The criminal department was the largest, and for reasons lost to the mists of time, when Laurie joined over ten years ago she was seated in a crappy adjunct office next to Bharat – litigation, specialising in medical negligence – and Diana, secretary to Bharat and anyone else in the vicinity.

She was eventually offered a move into criminal next door

but declined: she'd already struck up a friendship with Bharat and Di.

Climbing the stairs that morning, the idea she and Dan could convincingly feign being on friendly terms had been ambitious before, and was now worthy of cousin Munni's sci-fi. But Laurie had no fortitude for making major personal announcements. Did they leave the Other Woman and the rogue conception out of it, at first? How long would it take the office's sleuths to uncover it, once the game was afoot? Even without the weekend's trauma, it had been – count them – ten weeks now with no one getting a sniff at their break-up, but Laurie knew every day they were a day closer to inevitable discovery.

'I'm going out on a limb and saying the "cure for death" idea's probably been done, several times,' Bharat said. 'However, this could still hinge on whether Liam Neeson is prepared to play the sexy sexagenarian warrior, *Jeremiah Mastadon.*'

Laurie forced a laugh. 'I'm off to defend a Darren Dooley. You don't get many heroes called Darren Dooley, do you?'

Alliteration, like Megan Mooney.

'What's Munni calling this film?' Diana asked.

'PROLIFERATION. But with some sort of weird semi-colon between PRO LIFE and RATION,' Bharat said, scrolling his email. 'Pro Life, ration. Geddit? No? Let's hope the head of Paramount and Liam Neeson do. Oh God, he's cc-ed Liam Neeson!' Bharat collapsed in mirth again and Diana queried how Munni knew Liam Neeson's email address – 'he'll have guessed it as "Liam Dot Neeson At Hollywood Dot Com"' – while Laurie collected up her files for court. The world had gone digital but courtrooms still required reams of A4 paper.

Jamie bloody Carter appeared in one of his narrow suits that looked like he was in a menswear advert and should be photographed laughing, sat with his knees apart while holding a tumbler of malt whisky. Or walking down a cobbled street in a European city with a dickhead Rat Pack in tow.

He said, 'I don't mean to push,' – *yes you do*, Laurie thought, giving him a grit-teeth smile – 'Could you update me on the Cheetham case?'

Laurie gave him a brusque run down, off the top of her head.

'You don't need to check the file?' he said.

'No, I have this thing called a memory,' Laurie said. Patronising git, he was how old, twenty-eight?

'Ooooh summarily dismissed! Nicely done!' Bharat said, after Jamie raised his eyebrows, and departed. 'He's a self-sucking cock of a man, isn't he?' Di and Laurie chortled evilly.

This morning for Laurie held an assault on a kindly shop keeper. Laurie really didn't want to get her client a reduced sentence due to first time offending and the context of peer pressure, and yet she probably would.

A sheaf of notes had gone missing and Laurie was delayed five minutes, hunting them out. A crucial five minutes, as it turned out.

Diana came back from the loo and stared directly at Laurie, in an unnerving way.

'When were you going to tell us you and Dan had split up?!'

'What?' Laurie said, dully.

'*What*?!' Bharat shrieked.

'Dan's talking to Michael and Chris about it. He said that it happened a while back. And he's having a *baby*? With someone at Rawlings?'

Laurie suppressed a full-body shiver of despair, a fresh wave of stunned humiliation.

'Yeah it's true. All over a while back. I didn't know how to break it. There it is.' That *bastard*. He couldn't even give her a week to come to terms with it herself. To show her feelings would only inflame the office tattle, so she kept her face impassive and raised and dropped her shoulders. The seconds it took them to say anything lasted an eternity.

'Wait, how long ago was it that you separated, if he's with someone else? And having a baby?' Bharat said; it was fruitless to downplay it.

'Months back. Don't really want to discuss it. I'm due in court.'

She got up and strode out quickly, looking neither left nor right, trying to keep a poker face. She could still sense the heads snapping up and whispers from the receptionists' viewing gallery as she passed.

A WhatsApp from Bharat.

V sorry if that was an insensitive question Loz, I blurted, wasn't thinking. Are you OK? Xx

Laurie
Yep, thanks, don't worry. As much as is possible, can you reassure people I'm fine? You & I can talk in private sometime. Can't face Team Kerry's gang of lookalike raptors in Charlotte Tilbury descending on me Xx

Bharat

LOL. Perfect description 👌 Sure Xxx

Bharat was raucous and silly, but he was good people, and she was deeply grateful for his friendship at that moment. He loved drama, but he was ethical about it: not at the expense of the feelings of those he liked.

Her phone rang with a call from Dan as she neared the mags court. He was breathless and discomposed, as well he might be.

'Laurie, Laurie, I didn't decide to tell everyone. Someone at Rawlings saw Louise Hatherley from ours at the cop shop and she came straight back and blabbed it, and I had to face it down as best I could.'

'Megan's told people at her place?'

'She's got morning sickness and refused a drink at some do last week and apparently someone guessed.'

'Megan didn't have to say it was true? Or tell people you were the dad, did she? Fuck, Dan, is this why you only told me this weekend?'

'She said she panicked, it came tumbling out. I was going to talk to you about how we handled it here . . . fuck.'

'Know something about your mistress, and soon-to-be mother of your child, Dan? She's a fucking lying bitch,' Laurie said.

As she spoke, she felt a tap on her shoulder, and turned. The pasty pale, grinning face of Darren Dooley was in front of her.

'Alright, brief? Want me to sort her out for you?'

★

94

Trudging back to the office from court that afternoon was the longest walk. Darren Dooley pleaded guilty and got off with community service and a suspended sentence. By contrast to Laurie's gloom, he was cock-a-hoop.

Coming second in a happiness contest with a boy who'd thumped a newsagent in a row over a resealable pouch of mini Wispas, what even was life? Laurie offered him a wan smile as they parted.

'Don't rough up any more pensioners from now on. OK?'

Laurie had never felt the truth of the idea of work being a comfort before, and many people wouldn't have found hers a comfort. But she was good at her job, and it always felt like an absorbing, necessary thing to be doing.

And she had high standing at Salter & Rowson. Laurie was not only talented, she was diligent, and never rested on her laurels. Usually it was the plodders who were hard-working and careful, and the naturally gifted who did an Icarus. Not Laurie. She quickly learned that the scariness of standing in front of magistrates was directly proportional to how thoroughly you'd done your homework. She was often up against worse-for-wear posh lads for the prosecution, almost proud of winging it, using cut-glass vowels like a scythe. Well, Laurie thought it was way more rock'n'roll to know your case back to front and wipe the floor with them.

'Your Honour, I think you'll find that, IN FACT . . .' was the most overused phrase in her work vocabulary.

Mr Salter didn't build an empire without being able to spot talent, and he had seen something in Laurie from the start.

'You have that rare adaptability,' he'd said at a Christmas

do of years past. 'You're able to speak authoritatively in court and yet stay approachable with clients. Nor do you let the more *ribald* of your colleagues get a rise out of you, and without ever stooping to their level. You're a one-woman masterclass in how to handle this job.'

Bharat had mimed two fingers down his throat behind Salter's back, segueing into an audacious blow job mime that only Bharat would risk, an inch from his boss.

Whenever Dan admired her dedication in this way, she'd joke that as a woman of colour in a man's world you had to work three times as hard to be thought of as half as good. A joke, except it was true. And she'd never got into trouble, she never fell over at the Christmas do.

Laurie also never asked for anything, perks or pay rises. Some male colleagues muttered that this was the key reason for her popularity with the bosses. But Dan getting ahead had been the win for both of them. Laurie had coached him and supported him and urged him on to get his departmental headship. She felt vaguely daft about that now, as a self-sufficient woman – it had never occurred to her that he might leave her, and she should be looking for advancement for her own sake. She'd not exploited her professional potential because her fulfilment was in her personal life.

Though in honesty, as much as Laurie knew Salter & Rowson thought the world of her, she still doubted they wanted the ethnic bird in board meetings. Dan used to joke that you wouldn't mistake them for a Benetton poster.

God, she missed him. Or, a version of him that was now consigned to history.

When she reached Salter's, the oldest of the receptionists, Jan, came racing out from behind her desk to put an arm around Laurie, to tut and coo: 'Are you alright, love?'

'Yes, thanks. Totally fine.'

'But no, are you *alright*?'

Laurie had to find a way to peel her off without seeming ungrateful, although Jan only wanted to get close enough to make a rudimentary assessment of her alrightness, to inform the next hour's speculation.

The other three receptionists stared at her, owlishly. Laurie shrugged Jan off as gently as she could and stumped up the stairs, considering that any further statement on how she was completely chill with her life partner now procreating with some ginger slagbag at Rawlings was only likely to make them suspect the opposite.

Partly what was fuelling the fascination was the unlikeliness of her and Dan being caught up in this. The Boring Smug Marrieds, the butter wouldn't melts, the ordinary ones, the basics. The schadenfreude could power a wind farm.

Upstairs was barely better.

Michael saw her from a distance, beyond the transparent separation of the criminal department, and came dashing out on to the landing, while Laurie internally screamed: *NO, DON'T.* They'd worked together for a long time in criminal, Michael also at her level. He'd always made it clear he esteemed Laurie, treated her as one of the few sane voices.

Whenever Laurie walked into the lion's den that was the main criminal department, she'd learned to deal with any playful laddish verbals that were thrown her way with wit and unshockability, putting antagonists in their place. She'd mastered navigating the locker room without compromising herself, and she was held in a degree of special respect for it. Michael was foremost among her fans, he'd made a friend of her.

Once, at drinks in the pub after work, when a secretary was wondering aloud how a presentable man like him wasn't taken (Michael was handsome, in a forbidding, Rochestery way) he'd said: 'Laurie Watkinson's gone, so why bother? No one else will do' and thrown a knowing smile her way. She'd not much minded, more surprised to have his approval than anything: Michael was mostly bone dry and pitiless. Now she'd been stripped of her protected Mrs Dan status, she didn't know quite how to deal with him.

'Are you OK?' Michael said, squeezing her shoulder.

'I'm fine, honestly,' Laurie said, uncomfortable at the physical contact but without a way to stop it that didn't seem rude.

'I'm gobsmacked, I have to say,' Michael said, hot paw still gripping her, giving her an intense, unwavering look that said: *confide in me, I am on your side.*

'It is what it is,' Laurie said, with a brave soldier's smile, hoping if she repeated enough meaningless banalities, she could eventually kill everyone's interest with boredom. Death by cliché.

'Was he . . . was this going on while you were still together? It must've been. God. What a thing.'

Great, Michael, tactful. Laurie could already see how it was going to go: lots of prurient fishing, somehow made acceptable by first offering extravagant condolences. Claiming to care about someone or something, Laurie saw, could be highly manipulative. It was a way of ascribing yourself rights.

'I'm fine, honestly,' she said, ducking out of his line of sight as she pulled away towards her office.

Back at her desk, she saw Bharat was out, which was unfortunate as he'd have offered her protection and distraction. Diana said, after a tense silence which she spent near-audibly scheming how to raise it: 'If you need to talk, Laurie, we're here for you.'

'Thanks!' Laurie said, with a tight, bright smile.

Silence descended and Diana darted looks at Laurie every so often, while tapping rapidly at her keyboard at brief intervals. Laurie was tempted to need something from the filing cabinet behind Di, forcing Di to click away at frantic speed from the G-chat about Laurie's woes. It wasn't that Di was anti Laurie, but this was hot off the presses and it had to be discussed.

Laurie WhatsApped Emily. She'd not told her yet.

Don't call me, as I'm at work, but Dan's got an Other Woman, who he's now got pregnant. No kidding. Instantly. Mr 'I'm not ready for you to stop taking your pill'. She's a lawyer at another place here, and they were clearly good to go once he'd left me. He's trying to claim it's not an affair because they waited until then to sleep together.

Emily
HOLY SHIT? WHAT? I don't know what to say. Or do. I actually feel sick. Oh my God

Laurie felt a pinched, stinging sensation at the back of her throat that presaged tears, and waited it out before typing again.

Laurie

Be honest with me: did you think he had someone else from the start? Have I been incredibly slow and stupid?

It was strange that plain old embarrassment should play a starring role in this shit show. Next to the decimation of love and hope, who cared about foolishness? And yet.

Emily

NO! Absolutely not, L. I thought he was having a mid life, and once he'd bought Sonos surround speakers, failed to work the multi room function on them properly & maybe had a lacklustre boff with a girl from the gym with a Martini glass shaped bikini wax, he'd be crawling back. Pregnant? Seriously? Are you OK?

Laurie

I'm on my knees, to be honest. Can you believe I have to work with him?!! I must have been a genocidal warlord in a past life to deserve this. Or the kind of person who puts their bag on the seat next to them on public transport in rush hour.

Not only that, there was no way out. With a new responsibility on the way, Dan wouldn't be getting a new job, never mind his blather about rethinking his professional choices. The results were in. And if Laurie went – and why should she? – the rules on being hired within a certain radius, within a certain time period, meant she could either accept a job at a tiny firm in Buttfuck, Nowhere with a huge commute, or sell her house, and leave Manchester entirely. Hey, maybe she could sell the house back to Dan and Megan! She jutted her chin upwards in defiance of the pain at this thought, and her eyes met her reflection in the window. In uncharacteristic thinness and tiredness, she could suddenly really see her mother.

Emily
Repeat after me: You do not deserve it. I will come round as soon as I can. May I ring Dan and call him a piece of shit? I don't want us to forget the proper formalities in the middle of this

Laurie grinned at her handset. Best friends knew humour was pretty much always welcome and needed.

Laurie
With my greatest pleasure xxx

This notion pepped Laurie up slightly, until she needed to check something on the board in the criminal office and the whole room fell into an awed hush when she entered.

She forgot whatever she was supposed to be inspecting, stared blankly at marker-penned words that were mere blue squiggles to her, and went back to her desk, wondering if, despite the impossibility, she was in fact going to have to find another job.

The day, which had lasted several months by Laurie's reckoning, finally rolled to a close and Laurie got up bang on time to leave, intending to make as fast and clean an exit as possible. She was intercepted by Kerry, Salter's ferocious personal secretary. Kerry was a forty-something bottle blonde and dressed and carried herself like a matriarch from a 1960s kitchen sink film: leopard skin, fag frequently on and red pleather handbags. Laurie could've warmed to her if she didn't know her to be a total viper.

'Laurie. I want you to know. We've all agreed . . .'

Laurie tensed her stomach muscles and waited for the inevitable nonsense about solidarity. Dan would receive the same, of course.

'You're far more attractive than Megan Mooney. She looks like Prince Harry in drag.'

'Oh. Thanks,' Laurie said, completely at a loss for what she was supposed to say. Kerry was terrifying.

'Laurie! Call for you!' Di said, hanging out of the office doorway, and Laurie bit down her irritation that, strictly speaking, when someone had their coat on you should take a message.

'Hello, Mrs Watkinson?' said an accented older male voice, after she accepted the receiver from Di.

'Miss,' Laurie said. 'Or Ms.'

'This is Mr Atwal, from Atwals News. The Doolally boy who beat me, you were his lawyer today?'

Laurie's heart sank still further. It was rare she got shit-o-grams from the victims of those she defended, partly because the serious cases she dealt with got kicked up to crown court. It was uniquely unpleasant, explaining to someone why you'd done everything you could to minimise the impact of what they'd suffered, and put the best possible spin on the version of the person who'd inflicted it. Laurie didn't think she was in the wrong, but at moments like that, she couldn't feel it.

Oh God. Not today, Satan. She took a deep breath and prepared to justify her role in a fair and open legal process. 'Yes?'

'I thought you might like to know, he came in and gave me a bottle of wine and a box of chocolates! I do not drink, but the thought was very nice. He said he was very sorry and your kindness has helped him see a better way. Well done, young lady.'

In a moment, Laurie's ratty temper vanished. Not only was she very glad to hear Darren Dooley had made amends, there was something absurdly touching in him thinking Laurie doing her job in a courteous manner was some sort of inspirational tenderness. Poor lad. What a life he'd led.

'That's great to hear, I'm very pleased he has apologised, Mr Atwal. I hope this is a corner turned for Darren and that you don't get any more trouble.'

'Oh, I doubt that,' Mr Atwal said, in his lovely, musical, old fashioned cadence, 'There are some real, how do you say, dismal little cunts around these days.'

Laurie ended the conversation trying desperately not to hysterical-giggle. If life was entirely different, she'd be repeating that phrase to Dan tonight while they fell about.

Hell, maybe she would hire Darren Dooley to rough up him and Megan. It might give him a sense of purpose and a nice fee.

Laurie hated how powerless she was, the mask she had to wear that ate her face. Dan had done so much to her, and she could do nothing.

11

'Are you going to the Christmas do?' Diana asked on Friday, all innocence, though Laurie knew exactly why she was asking and Di knew she knew.

It was weeks away, but S&R always revved up for it as soon as the clocks changed.

'Oh. Hadn't thought,' Laurie said. 'Maybe.'

Diana fell quiet, as there was nothing she could do with this equivocal response.

'Rumours of karaoke,' Bharat added.

'Jesus. I long for death's sweet release.'

'Don't know that one, Shania Twain?' He paused. 'I can imagine it's the last place you want to be this year, but it's a shame for us, because you are the very finest company.'

In times of crisis, you saw the best of people and the worst of people. Another dose of the worst had arrived yesterday, a gruellingly awkward phone call from Dan's mother, Barbara, who was clearly desperate to get the formality of a goodbye to Laurie over with and get on with being excited about her first grandchild. She had no time for any negativity about her son's behaviour, simply saying primly, when Laurie ventured a comment about its brutality: 'I can't comment on that, really,' like she was an MP being grilled by Jeremy Paxman. It turned out 'adoring Dan' had been the vital shared interest, and once gone, there was nothing.

'I suppose sometimes you want what you want,' was Barbara's in summary insight on Dan's historic fuckery.

To which Laurie wanted to reply: *No shit, psychopaths want to strangle strangers with their stockings, it's possible to pass a verdict on what someone wanted, and how they went about having it.*

'Thank you,' Laurie said to Bharat. 'I've not ruled out going to the party.'

Yes, she had.

It had been a working week since the Dan and Laurie exclusive landed on front pages. Everyone was still subtly rearranging their positions around her, figuring out the altered rules of engagement.

Michael kept asking her to come out for a lunchtime sandwich, and on the day Laurie couldn't fob him off, she picked at a tuna wrap in Pret, braced for his gambit.

'How *are* you?' came before he'd got the cardboard ring off his ploughman's baguette.

Laurie said: 'Buggering on,' brightly, and 'I'd prefer not to talk about it if that's OK.' Michael nodded, in obvious disappointment, as much as she knew he liked to compare cases with her, it was the gore on Dan's messy exit that he really wanted.

Also, score to Emily: Laurie had indeed received weird messages from men. Among them, a quiet mousey husband of a couple they'd met once at Tom and Pri's, who volunteered, 'Dan must be mad!' and, without mentioning his marital status: 'Anytime you want to get it off your chest, I am available for drinks and light supper.' (Laurie wasn't going to go anywhere near someone who used the words 'light supper'.)

And a short solicitor at another firm called Richard who'd often been talkative in court, who observed on email: 'I've always had a thing for café au lait/mixed race girls. You know, you look like Whitney Houston (before she became a bit of a crack whore I hasten to add!).'

Oh, and the university friend, Adrian, who asked if she wanted to meet up given he was in town on business, and when she politely declined, replied: 'I'm in a five-star hotel room. What am I meant to do with this enormous erection in front of me?'

Laurie blinked at this message for a full minute and replied: 'Ask him politely to leave?'

She screen-grabbed the exchange and sent it to Emily, who said she wanted it framed and on her wall.

It all appealed to Laurie's sense of the ridiculous, until she remembered this was What Many Men Are Like, and these were what she was left with. She wasn't ever going to experience desire again, simple as that.

So there were two dates in the calendar to dread: first, the looming Christmas party. When she and Dan were together, they jointly invented a reason to miss it. They'd been creative: for many years, a phony anniversary worked. Then Salters moved it by a week and they had to find fresh excuses. So they tag teamed. One went one year, the other the next. As long as the event featured one of them, it gave the appearance of attendance.

It was Laurie's turn to give it a miss, by the old rules. But if Laurie ducked it, everyone would know why. And Dan was a head of department this year, so he'd have to be there. He'd dumped Salter's favourite to impregnate a woman at the much reviled Rawlings; he'd want to reaffirm his loyalty.

Laurie had a grim binary option: absenteeism, which spelled shame and cowardice and everyone feeling sorry for her. It stank of defeat. Or a party with Dan, during which everyone would get pissed enough to stare, commentate. The things people said sober were bad enough. Jan had already asked if she'd had her eggs frozen.

Laurie had considered asking Dan not to go, and all things considered, he'd probably have to oblige her. That also reeked of defeat, however. She didn't want him to know she couldn't cope.

The second date she feared: the birth. She knew whatever recovery she thought she'd managed would be destroyed that day. Laurie genuinely might accept Emily's Valium for that. Chemically coshing her way through it seemed the only way.

Oh, and not forgetting her dad's wedding. That loomed next month. Laurie felt like life contained nothing but hurdles. Hurdles, toil and sadness. Too early for a drink?

'You doing owt this weekend?' Bharat asked.

'Not really. You?'

Laurie smiled as Bharat told her what, or rather who, he was doing. ('He's called Hans, he has a beard and he is every bit as gorgeous as terrorist Alan Rickman as Hans Gruber in *Die Hard*! Grubby Hands, I'm calling him.')

She stared out at the street lights, chin propped on palm, morose. Rain streaked the fogged-up office windows, which were forbidding, ink-black panels by half four. The precious daylight was over well before the working day was.

It was the kind of wuthering, northern, wintery Friday night that was designed for being in a relationship, Laurie thought. Even your wildest nocturnal adventurers might shrink from going out buccaneering when it was this bone-marrow chilling, and saturating-damp. It was weather made for big socks, takeaway curry, Shiraz and episode four of that spy drama thing on iPlayer. Laurie would still have all those things tonight, plus a bath.

She would be in bed by midnight, trying and failing to go straight to sleep, mind churning on endless questions. Desolate in the dark, doing the kind of crying where you make heaving noises, face screwed up, childlike. She'd been doing that off and on ever since Dan left, unless she drank enough that she could go to sleep fast enough to outrun her imagination.

Laurie never thought of herself as a dependent person, not at all, but it turned out you needed things – or people – you depended on to be taken away from you to judge that.

Bharat and Diana left and Laurie did her bravest most authentic grin and wishes for them to have a good 'un, see you Monday, knowing full well that as soon as Di was out of earshot she'd be clucking her pity that Laurie wasn't at all herself.

As the clock hit six, Laurie gave a deep inward-sucking

sigh as she thrust things into her briefcase. Around her were spinning chairs, not many at Salter & Rowson played presenteeism on a Friday night. And Laurie knew if she stayed later than this, she might get nobbled by Michael, who would correctly deduce that iPlayer could wait.

She got to the lift without anyone stopping her and felt relief as the doors rolled shut. Any small talk was agony. The place was pretty much deserted now anyway, just dribs and drabs and beyond closed doors, Misters Salter and Rowson. When the doors were an inch apart, the tip of an umbrella appeared between them, whacking from side to side. The doors stopped, and tiredly trundled open again.

Laurie felt a pang of irritation at her space being thus invaded, and her journey being delayed. The fully opened doors revealed Jamie Carter, now resting the umbrella against his shoulder, as if he was Steed in *The Avengers*.

Ugh, *of course* it was him holding her up, in a self-consequential manner. *Of course* he couldn't wait the forty-five seconds it would take for the lift to take Laurie down, and come back up again. And, of course he was making the display of being last out on a Friday night.

He gave her a raffish 'forgive me' half smile, and Laurie polite-grimaced in return. *Yeah it still doesn't work on me, pretty boy.*

Were they going to attempt stilted conversation? She hoped not. She angled her mouth down into the funnel neck of her coat and stared at her prim patent Mary Jane shoes, hand gripping the bag strap on her shoulder, to signal it was certainly not expected.

When her sight flickered sideways, she saw Jamie, clad in a somehow conspicuous dark charcoal trench coat, absorbed in his phone screen, mirroring her body language.

They bumped down one floor in silence, until a loud mechanical screeching startled Laurie. Jamie Carter frowned.

After a brief silence, it happened again. *Crrrrrrbmmmmmpfff,* a metal-on-metal squealing noise that made them physically grit their teeth. The lift shuddered to a halt, with the lurching sensation of a drunk tripping over. There were a few unpromising glitching noises of clicking and whirring, as if the lift was discussing what had happened with itself.

Then, nothing.

12

Laurie and Jamie looked at each other. A quality of silence had descended that seemed quite final, in terms of the lift changing its mind. Jamie prodded his index finger against the G button, several times. Still nothing.

'Try going back up?' Laurie said.

Jamie pressed the floor 2 button and again, no response.

He shook his head and jammed his finger against the button marked HELP.

After a tense few seconds, the speaker below crackled into life. 'Hello! Who is this?'

'Hi,' Jamie said. 'It's Jamie Carter, in criminal. This lift has stopped.'

'Hold on!' Mick the security guard bellowed.

Jamie and Laurie gave each other polite eye rolls, shoulder shrugs. A minute ticked by. Then another. What felt like a small era passed, and both Jamie and Laurie muttered 'fuck's sake' under their breath in unison, as they reached what must be a gargantuan seven minutes of standing in silence with a near stranger, in a lift.

'We're in danger of evolving as a species here,' Jamie tutted, making Laurie laugh.

'Any news?' Jamie said, after pressing for attention again.

'I said hold on!' Mick said, his exasperation carrying through the tinny speaker.

Jamie looked at Laurie, checked his watch under the cuff of his coat, they both made more British tutting noises, muttered 'typical', did more shrugs, and more eye rolls.

'You in a rush?' Jamie said, eventually.

'No . . . not really,' Laurie said, feeling her lack of vibrant social life when stood opposite the Captain of Friday Night Plans. 'You?'

'Yep.' Jamie looked at an expensively solid silver watch again. 'What's he *doing*?' He pressed the buzzer again. 'Hi. Still here.'

'I just said hold on!'

'I don't know if time's moving differently down there but up here it's been ten minutes?'

Moments ago, Laurie had resented Jamie's intrusion, now she felt quite fortunate to be able to delegate this problem to the most entitled and pushy of the firm's advocates.

'Yeah, well, get used to more of that.' Mick said.

'What?' Jamie's brow furrowed as he leaned on his forearm and jabbed the intercom again. 'Speak to us, Mick.'

'Right . . . the maintenance company say it's going to be an hour. Hang tight.'

Jamie's brow furrowed further and Laurie gasped.

'Sorry, that sounded like you said an HOUR?' Jamie said.

Pause. Crackle. 'At least. Sorry. How many of you are there?'

'Two of us. Myself and . . .' Jamie looked over.

Laurie couldn't help but grin as a stricken blankness spread across his face.

'Laura?!' he said triumphantly, palms up, a *how did I do?* to play up the fact he hadn't been sure.

'Laurie,' Laurie corrected, with a smile.

'*Laurie*. I knew that! Sorry. Long week.'

'Do a crossword together,' Mick said, audibly chortling.

'Ha fuckin har,' Jamie said, after letting the button go. 'An hour?!'

He looked at his watch. 'Fuck's sake. Gone seven?' Jamie fiddled with his phone. 'No coverage at all?! Fucking HELL.'

This aspect of captivity was obviously a major sting for Jamie Carter, whereas Laurie wouldn't have thought about whether she could get online or call anyone for another five minutes at least. Maybe Dan was right, maybe she had become insular and boring. Should she be trying to Snapchat with dog-ears filters, from inside this Faraday cage?

Jamie yanked his coat sleeve up, checked the time again – although in the last minute, Laurie was guessing it had only moved forward by a minute – and jabbed at his phone again and then waggled it. 'What about you?'

Laurie rifled her own iPhone out of her bag and peered at the screen. It was covered in spidery cracks and fractures. It looked like she felt. She shook her head.

'Absolutely wonderful,' Jamie said, looking at his phone again, in disgust. He threw his umbrella and briefcase down and pressed the button.

'Hi, Mick. Would you do me a favour, would you call my date for tonight and tell her I'm trapped in a lift?'

Laurie laughed out loud, a real belly laugh.

'What?' Mick barked.

'Call her. And say I'm trapped in a lift, put our date back an hour.'

Wait, he was *serious*?

'OK, here's her number . . .' Jamie read it from his iPhone. 'O – 7 – 9 – 1 . . .'

Jamie took his coat off as he did so, shucking it over his shoulders in a manner that somehow felt showy even though he was simply taking a coat off.

'What?' he said, glancing over, unbuttoning a cuff and rolling a sleeve up.

'He's got a job to do, he's not your PA!'

Jamie rolled his eyes and ignored her.

'No one is answering that number,' Mick said over the intercom, moments later.

'I bet she thinks an unrecognised Manc landline is PPI,' Jamie sighed. 'Thanks for trying, Mick.' He rolled up his other sleeve, and sat down, sighing heavily.

Laurie realised there was no longer any reason for her to be standing up either, and followed suit.

'Are you claustrophobic?' Jamie said.

Laurie shook her head, self-conscious that the wave of panic she'd just felt was obviously visible.

She was telling the truth; she wasn't, to her knowledge, claustrophobic. But right now she'd been unexpectedly reacquainted with sensation of breaking her arm as a kid, having

114

a heavy plaster cast on it, and waking up in the dead of night freaking out: 'Get it off me, get it off me!' She'd been fine in this lift, until that very second, when the four walls pressed in and with no hope of escape, her chest tightened, and her fists clenched, nails digging into her palms.

'Breathe,' Jamie said, watching Laurie. 'Concentrate on breathing. We'll be out of here before you know it.'

Despite what she said, he was smart enough to spot she wasn't coping. Typical lawyers, she thought. We read people constantly. We don't necessarily care about what we discover, but we read them.

She breathed, and calmed.

Laurie and Jamie had exhausted polite, banal chat about Salter & Rowson's internal politics, and the gnarly attitudes of certain magistrates, and the clock had barely shifted. Twelve minutes had passed since Laurie last looked.

Out there, 6.25 p.m. would've arrived without noticing, it would've been an eye blink, a long stride in the short distance to the tram. In here, it was an eternity.

Jamie saw Laurie clicking her phone agitatedly to check the time and she remembered he knew she couldn't be picking up messages, and stopped.

'How is only twenty-five past six?' she said, mournfully.

'Yeah this feels like the film *Interstellar*,' Jamie said, 'If Matthew McConaughey came back to Earth and his daughter's an old woman, my date's probably married with three kids by now.'

'Has this taken a real crap on your plans, then?' Laurie said.

'Was it a first date?' she said, in a 'I'm not just an uptight workaholic!' way, she hoped.

'Yeah it was. And Gina, twenty-nine, from Sale, is not likely to be impressed at being stood up. We met on Tinder, actually, so she'll be on to five other standbys after half an hour. Gina twenty-nine from Sale waits for no man.'

Laurie laughed: this sounded less like dating, more like studying a menu in a specialist sauna. She wasn't made for being single in this time. A sad weight pressed on her ribs.

Tinder. Or Deliveroo for dick, as Emily called it. Laurie inwardly shuddered.

The intercom buzzed. 'Hello?'

Jamie was on his feet in one bounce, in a feat of agility: 'Mick! Hello!'

'Hello. There's good news and bad news.'

Jamie sagged. 'The bad first?'

'It's going to be another hour. Sorry.'

'Oh for fu— And the GOOD?'

'They're certain it'll only be an hour from now.'

'Mick, that's all bad news!'

'Sorry.'

Jamie turned back and slithered down the wall.

'Permission to cry, Laura?'

'Laurie!'

'Ha ha, oh God, sorry. I've got a blind spot where I'm determined to call you Laura. I'm turning into my dad. LOOK IT UP, MARJORIE!'

Laurie laughed again and decided to enjoy Jamie, when he was the only pleasure to be had.

'It's a very cool name. Is it after anyone or anything?' he added.

'Laurie Lee, who wrote *Cider With Rosie*.'

Jamie squinted. 'Wasn't he a man?'

'Very good!' Laurie said. 'Five points to Slytherin.'

'Oh wow, presumed ignorant. And I'm in Slytherin, am I?' Jamie said. Laurie grinned.

Resigned to their fate, they crossed an imaginary boundary – she felt herself relax – where making the best of limited resources for entertainment felt oddly nice. Like the final days before Christmas, where you can't wait to break out on holiday, but no one's doing anyone work and are pelting each other with Quality Street. Sometimes it's more enjoyable than the holiday itself. Must be something to do with relief of having choices removed, and expectations very low. Laurie wondered if she was a chronic over analyser.

'*Cider With Rosie* was a set text for my English Lit GCSE so I won't pretend to be better read than I am,' Jamie said.

'And you got the Harry Potter reference too, don't be hard on yourself,' Laurie said, with a smile. 'My mum didn't know Laurie Lee was a man, she just liked it. It's very much like my mum to trot off to register the name without even checking she had the gender right.'

Jamie smiled back.

'I wish I had a quirky story about my name, but nah.'

Silence fell again. Jamie hung his glossily curly head, temporarily out of conversation.

They had another hour to kill. Laurie decided to chance her luck.

'It didn't work out with Eve, then?'

'Eve?' Jamie looked up and his forehead creased in what seemed genuine rather than feigned confusion. She was probably a few conquests ago, to be fair, Laurie thought.

'Niece of Mr Salter? Long hair? I saw the two of you in Refuge back in the summer, remember?'

'Ohhhh, *Eve!*' Jamie said, in a possibly faked moment of comprehension. 'Nah. Went out for dinner and career advice chat, but that was it. More than my life's worth anyway, what with the family connections here. Like messing with a Mafioso's wife. And she's very young.'

There was a pause as Laurie intuited Jamie was doing some internal sums, in light of Laurie's knowledge.

'You didn't say anything to anyone else here about seeing us, did you?'

'Nope. Why would I? You asked me not to, if I recall right.' Although if you didn't do anything, why so edgy? Laurie thought.

'Well, thanks,' Jamie said. 'There's lots of people here who'd have it on a global email before they'd knocked the lid off their macchiato.'

'It's a very gossipy place,' Laurie said.

'You're telling me. I owe you one.'

'You don't owe me, don't worry,' Laurie said, trying not to snort at what sort of 'one' Jamie might owe her. 'I can't stand the way people here feel entitled to know others' business.'

'Hah. Agreed.'

Another silence descended and Laurie knew it was because Jamie was in a quandary: the only other possible topic was her ex, and yet that fell under category heading: other peoples' business.

'You're, er . . . separated from Dan Price in civil, is that right?'

He risked it. Probably for the same reasons Laurie mentioned Eve. If Mick had given them a timeframe of fifteen minutes, there was little chance that these hot potatoes would be gaily lobbed about the place.

'Oh yeah. As separated as you can be,' Laurie said, and tried for a satirical smirk that came off as strained.

'I don't know him that well,' Jamie said, and trailed off, obviously struggling to judge what was appropriate.

'I feel like if I say anything polite about him it'll stick in my throat and if I say anything negative, it'll make me look bitter,' Laurie said. 'Safe to say working together is fucking awful.'

Laurie thought again about the day to come, when Dan dashed out because Megan was in labour. Having to hear about it on the office grapevine, the glances, the whispers, *who's gonna tell her*. She'd be expected to put her anger aside and wish him well. A baby carries all before it, how could Laurie's feelings matter more?

How Dan would be in a floating state, partly due to sleeplessness, and briefly imagine the hatchet could be buried in the wash of love and wonder he felt. She could imagine the horrifically misjudged *Laurie, meet my son/daughter xx* text and photo already. The retraction later, which would come via mutual friends: *'He feels so stupid about that, he'd been up for twenty-seven hours straight. It was a difficult birth in the end, ventouse I think, and you're still very much a part of him/on his mind.'*

Then they'd think they could tell Laurie he'd taken naturally to fatherhood, as if that wasn't akin to driving hot nails into her hands and expecting her to say: *Oh that's nice. It's an ill wind that blows no one any good: from the ashes of us, comes the miracle of new life.* It's an ill fucking wind alright and I'll give him a ventouse.

She'd be furious and scorched by this until the end of her days. She felt delirious thinking about it.

'I bet it's a nightmare,' Jamie said. 'I actually left the last firm I was at in Liverpool over a similar, uh, complication. Not anything like as serious a relationship. But we didn't function well as colleagues, after.'

Laurie suppressed a smile and nodded. No shit, Jamie Carter had left an angry trail of women in his wake. However, he'd inadvertently hit on a rich seam of conversation – Liverpool. He and Laurie discussed the city she knew from her university years versus the one he knew from his twenties, and that launched them into student times, and the pressures of their early lawyering. Laurie was starting to feel light pressure from her bladder, too. She had visions of having to squat in the corner while Jamie Carter turned his back and whistled a Maroon 5 tune.

Eventually, like the Voice Of God, Mick interrupted in the intercom and said 'We're getting you moving! Only a couple of minutes,' and both of them whooped their relief.

The lift jolted into life and Laurie would 1. never take its movement for granted again and 2. be getting the stairs from now on anyway.

Mick was waiting for them on the ground floor, looking delighted.

'Were you about to start drinking your urine?'

'I'm certainly going to drink some imported Czech urine now,' Jamie said.

'Hell yes,' Laurie said, and wondered if she and Jamie Carter would ever speak again, outside shop talk. Sharing this ordeal was worth a 'hi' in the corridor, and a head nod if their eyes met in departmental meetings. Maybe not much more.

They said their hearty goodnights to Mick, and thanked their saviour, the man in the boiler suit with the monkey wrench.

As Jamie held the front door for Laurie, he said: 'Hey. You might very much want to get straight off, and please say so if you do. But given we've both had our Friday nights trashed, fancy a quick drink? Drown our sorrows?'

'Oh . . .? Sure.'

Laurie surprised herself by not only accepting, but wanting to. She was secretly gratified that after an hour and a half of confinement together, he didn't want to get away from her as fast as possible. And she didn't think for a second Jamie was trying it on, either. She understood what he meant, she felt it too: going home now to dinner for one was pure surrender. They couldn't let the lift win.

'Nice one,' Jamie said, with a dazzling smile, and she momentarily saw a flash of the powers that inflamed boss's nieces.

13

They went to Trof, an artfully scruffy bar for hipster youth and middle youth in the Northern Quarter, with barmen in beanies with beards, on the basis the usual pub nearby would be overrun with their own.

What if anyone saw them? Laurie wasn't worried, despite being recently uncoupled. When she asked herself why, it was because the idea she and Jamie Carter would have a dalliance was such a leap, the speculation wouldn't get off the starting blocks. She'd explain and guffaw and everyone would concede, *yeah, we were reaching, there*. Laurie didn't know whether to feel reassured or saddened by this.

In some sort of devilishly brilliant coincidence, 'You're So Vain' was playing at volume as they entered, as if they knew Jamie Carter walked into bars like he was walking onto a yacht.

Laurie loved the interior's golden glow and heaving warmth, compared to the violet-black cold of Manchester outside. She did like being around people, she realised, just not people she knew and was required to talk to.

'What're you having?'

'Big red wine please,' Laurie said.

'Right you are.'

What was his accent? It wasn't straight up northern but it definitely wasn't southern, either.

Jamie pushed his way into the scrum at the bar. He had a sort of natural swagger she'd admittedly probably loathe in a member of her own sex. Watching women watch Jamie, Laurie allowed herself a split second of feeling relevant and hip by being with him, even though she wasn't with him. She threw her scarf down and hummed along:

You gave away the things you loved
And one of them was me

Laurie wondered if in fact this song was about Dan, and her dreams had been clouds in her coffee. Dan would've been jealous of her being out with some handsome interloper, once upon a time. *You're where? What about your dinner? Why's he asked you out, might I ask?*

She'd lost Dan's interest, she didn't know when. She needed to identify the week, the day, the moment. The habits she'd got into that must've snuffed out his interest, bit by bit.

Now, Dan neither knew nor cared where she was. It was funny being in a raucous barn like this, not psychically tethered to him. Her soul concaved and she forced herself not to think about him, or his evening dispensing foot rubs and leafing through the JoJo Maman Bebe catalogue.

'Has Gina been in touch?' Laurie said, after Jamie returned

with the drinks, and she saw him surreptitiously glance at his iPhone.

'Yeah, I explained my predicament and she thinks I'm making it up, so that's that. To be fair it does sound a bit made up. What about you? Not "back out there" yet?'

'Ah. No. I'm scheduled to get "back out there" in about 2030, I think.'

'Quitters' talk! Was it a bad break-up?' He put his lips to his pint. 'Don't tell me if you don't want to.'

'You didn't hear?'

'No? People don't tell me much and I don't really ask. Only he's with someone else and no one saw it coming. Typical of our place that they'd expect to, what's it got to do with them?'

Laurie gave Jamie a precis. She shared more than she intended. Once she'd started speaking to a neutral party, it was like staring into the unjudgemental face of a counsellor.

Except he did judge it. At least Jamie Carter, man of the world, doing an authentic jaw drop at these details confirmed it was a shocking ordeal, even to a soulless womaniser.

'Fuck! Knocked up already? Oh, Laurie. That sounds torrid. Having to still share an office, beyond grim. Can't you make him find another job?'

She knew sympathy and liberal use of her name was part of Jamie Carter's repertoire, his deliberate charm, but she let herself be charmed by it anyway. Also, he was probably emphasising he knew her name now.

'Nope. He's got a kid to support soon,' Laurie said these words quickly, before she could care about them, 'I can't imagine he'll be willing to move. She's got a good job here. And I don't want to lose my house; my mortgage has got much bigger. I don't want to commute. I won't let him make me leave. I'm trapped!'

Jamie shook his head.

Laurie concluded, 'I'm probably going to spend the rest of my life figuring out what the hell happened.'

'He's not worth that much of your time,' Jamie said, knocking his glass to hers, and Laurie appreciated it, while thinking, *from the man who'd never give anyone much of his.*

'Another?' she said, making to get up, as they'd drained the first round fast. Laurie was liking being out and hoped when he said one drink he'd meant three to four, as was British tradition.

'No,' Jamie said, and Laurie concealed her pang of dismay. He gestured at Laurie rising in her seat, to sit down.

'I mean yes, but let me. You deserve table service, and I want some peanuts. Or wasabi cashews or whatever it'll be here.'

Laurie beamed.

With the second round, and then a third, Laurie must've had pretty much a bottle of red wine on an empty stomach and she was being a level of candid with Jamie she was going to regret in the morning. Yet she couldn't stop herself.

'I've never been a vengeful person, but I have fantasies of bringing Dan to his knees. I want him sobbing and begging for me to take him back, even though I know it'll never happen. It runs through my veins like lava, I can physically feel it.'

'Yeah I get that. I've been that angry at the world, in my time. How would you do it?'

She shrugged, grinned. 'Haven't figured that out yet, have I?'

'It'll come to you. You've got a look in your eye that clearly states you're not to be fucked with.'

Laurie nodded, pleased. If there was one thing she'd learned tonight, Jamie was easy company. She wouldn't trust him as far as she could throw him, but he was a good crack. Craic, whatever. Ooh, inebriation felt nice. An escape from herself. Laurie rolled a beer mat on its side, caught it in her other hand.

'Can I ask you something? Was the rumour true that Salter told you not to touch his niece? What did he *say*? I can't imagine how he phrased it.'

Jamie laughed. 'Oh, that did the rounds did it? I swear Kerry listens at the door, I can't believe he's stupid enough to tell her as much as she knows.'

'I'm sure she does. Or she's bugged the room. She's our own Wikileaks.'

'It's both true and not the whole truth. Am I speaking in confidence here?'

Laurie held up her hand and did a Scouts honour sign. 'I've been relying on that since halfway through my first wine, to be honest.'

'It *was* warning me off Eve, but more than that, a whole "get your life together if you want to get on" gruff paternal lecture.'

'Wow, seriously? Bit much?'

'I've applied to be made partner.'

Laurie did a double-take. 'Like, third wheel? Aren't you . . . quite young for that?'

'I went to see them both and said I am young, but I'm completely committed and definitely ready.'

Here was the white-hot ambition that put backs up and noses out of joint.

'Yeah. I want to take on tons more work for a stake. I pretty much pitched them my vision for the future of the firm, for half an hour. They said they'd think about it.'

Laurie swirled her wine in her glass.

'What was the life coaching about?'

'When Eve arrived, Salter had me in to say, she is off limits, but also, a major sticking point in promoting me is my' – Jamie made air quotes – '*lifestyle*. "You're someone we can't trust around the wives and girlfriends at the Christmas party."' He did a baritone imitation voice: '"That matters, young man, whether you like it or not."'

'Hahaha. Bloody hell.'

'Yeah, I mean, they're old fashioned and conventional, aren't they. They only understand long-term partners, marriage. Two by two onto the Ark.'

'It's a bit much to say they can't promote a single person! Jesus Christ, is it 1950?' Laurie would've thought this unfair anyway, but in her current predicament she wondered if a spinster would also be ruled out, and her blood heated.

'It's not single, per se, it's my kind of single. Being seen out with someone different every weekend. Playing the field. It could, and I quote this word for word, "leave the company vulnerable to blackmail." No, I have no idea what that means either.'

'Oh no,' Laurie said. Then, indiscreet in drink: 'Dick pics. They mean dick pics and revenge porn and sex tapes, surely?'

'Oh jeez . . . yeah you might be right.'

Jamie looked slightly uncomfortable and Laurie realised she'd been a trifle direct and crude. She'd indirectly referred to his . . . King and privy council, as Dan's dad called it. His junk. Argh. She'd not congratulate herself on this moment when she awoke blearily tomorrow.

'If only they'd asked, I could've told them of my strict "no making or sending grot" policy and given them access to my iCloud to prove it. I'm not a lawyer for nothing.'

Laurie laughed.

'So, either I get myself a steady, respectable girlfriend by their end of year deadline, or no name above the door for me,' Jamie concluded.

'They were that prescriptive?'

'Oh, it was coded. You know. *Unless something changes . . .*'

'Is that likely?'

'Put it this way. I'm kind of a communist, when it comes to relationships.'

'You think we should all be state owned?'

'I think whenever they fail, we focus on what specific people did wrong within the system, overlooking the fact that the whole institution's rotten and dysfunctional. I don't think it works – cohabiting, monogamy. I mean, I think it *works,* practically – halving the cost of living, getting a mortgage, raising kids. I can see why capitalist society wants us to organise ourselves that way. Then the government doesn't have to find you full-time nursing care when you have the massive stroke, because someone stood up in a church and told a God they didn't believe in, fifty years ago, they'd wipe your arse.'

'Wow,' Laurie said. 'I wish someone would write their own vows and use those exact lines. I pledge to keep your bum cleft clean. Certainly better than that "I will always make your favourite banana milkshake" BS.'

Jamie laughed, a body-shaking laugh, and she could see he was taking to her, perhaps more than he expected to. She wanted nothing from him, and she was bright, his equal and dry of humour. These things might be a novelty, given who he romanced.

'But works *emotionally*, makes you happy?' Jamie said, swirling his drink. 'Not so much. It's usually a fostered dependency on someone you slept with and felt briefly passionate feelings for in your twenties, and you feel guilty moving on once its time has passed. In fact, that guilt is often the trigger for putting the roots down, tying yourself into it, convincing yourself it's as good as it gets. I've best-manned a few weddings where that is the exact description of what's going on. It's the least romantic thing imaginable. Yoking yourself to someone you've been having the same disappointing missionary with since Fresher's Week.'

Laurie twinged hard at the direct relevance.

'Great best man!'

'Hahaha. I left the part where I think marriage is a grotesque harmful sham out of the speech. No, I mean, I don't push my controversial views on other people. Live and let live.'

'But you were in a relationship in Liverpool?'

'Ah. Nah. She wanted it to be that, and I thought a semi-regular cop off was a semi-regular cop off. I'm very . . . upfront about my priorities since that experience. Leaving any room for doubt can go badly.'

Laurie was equal parts fascinated and repelled by Jamie's cynicism.

'I think long-term relationships are the most potent demonstration of Sunk Cost Fallacy you'll ever see,' Jamie said.

Laurie picked up a small handful of dry roasted and threw them into her mouth. She only noticed, on chewing them, how wildly hungry she was. 'Meaning?'

'The definition of Sunk Cost Fallacy is a refusal to change something that makes you unhappy. You won't, because look at the time and money and effort you'll have wasted if you do. Which of course only means more waste.'

Had this been what Dan decided?

'Well. Happy weekend to me. You're as much fun as falling into a barrel of tits, aren't you!' Laurie said, and she and Jamie both burst into loud, alcohol-fuelled laughter.

Jamie paused. 'None of this is remotely personal by the way, not as if I knew you and Dan as a couple.'

'None taken,' Laurie waved her hand. 'What about falling madly in love though? Don't you make any allowances for that?'

'I do, I only hope it never happens to me. It looks from the outside to be a temporary heightened manic state during which you do yourself all kinds of damage and make reckless promises you can't keep.'

'Hahaha. I guess it's that too.'

'That's all it is, I'm sure of it.'

Laurie had no comeback that didn't seem pitiful, given her circumstances.

'Hey. I hope poor Gina, twenty-nine, from Sale isn't looking for a soulmate, if she's meeting guys like you?'

'Oh, I'm pretty confident that's not the kind of mating she's looking for,' Jamie said, with a wolfish knowing glance, and Laurie said, 'Blee.'

14

'I've had an absolutely mad idea, while at the bar,' Jamie said, and Laurie sincerely hoped it didn't – shock, horror – involve getting naked. She would feel both embarrassed for him and dismayed by him. 'It's either a fit of divine inspiration or the stupidest notion ever to spring into a human mind.'

'High stakes, here,' Laurie said, bullishly, but she cringed. Him setting it up like this meant it was potentially embarrassing if she said no. She'd not had so much as a hint of sleaze from Jamie, but, well. That might be the secret of his success.

'You want to get back at Dan Price? Realistically, unless you mean the kind of revenge that could see you getting sent to prison, that will involve making him angry, bewildered and jealous, am I right?'

'Yes . . .?' Oh God, he *was* going to try it on? *I've got a fiendish plan, it involves you sitting on top of me. What's in it for me? Oh, merely the joy of seeing you prevail over this terrible gentleman.*

'I need to show my conventional settledness to get this promotion.'

'Yeeesss . . .?'

Oh, God.

'What if we pretended we were dating? Proper whirlwind romance, stuff of fairytales. Social media nowadays is the perfect place for showing off.'

'Me and you?'

'Yes. I mean, I know I'm not as good for your brand as you'd be for mine,' Jamie said, taking a deep glug of his beer.

Laurie sensed behind the bravado, he was slightly nervous about her response. This seemed an odd reversal of power. He was the one everyone wanted to be seen with. *All the girls dreamed that they'd be your partner.*

'How would it work?'

'We could post loved-up pictures on Facebook, Instagram, whatever. Praise each other to the skies. All over by Christmas, once it's served its purpose, because they'll give me a verdict on the partnership by then. But we both go around saying we'll always care about each other or whatever. A no-fault divorce where we stay best of friends.'

'People would buy it? You and I have barely spoken before now.'

Laurie shrank from saying: no one is going to think Hermione Granger here is having it off, big style, with Draco Malfoy.

'If we sell it well enough.'

'You think Salter & Rowson would approve? Am I really impressive enough to get you your promotion?'

'Are you kidding?! You're the golden girl. The haloed one.

The *star*. Salter adores you. I struggle to think of anyone's image who could do me more good by association.'

'You say this, and you didn't know my name earlier!'

Jamie covered his eyes with his palm. 'Aaaargh. Only because Michael refers to you as Lozza. I could hardly call you Lozza and couldn't remember what it was short for.'

Laurie laughed.

'And Dan would think I'd moved on and was having an absolute ball?' Laurie toyed with the stem of her wine glass and thought, damn it if this idea doesn't have immediate appeal.

She was flattered. Might as well admit that element to herself. Jamie Carter was prepared to publicly declare himself in love with her? This Greek God was prepared to anoint her his Phony Goddess? It did feel like the most longed-for boy in school asking you to prom.

It's because you're in favour with Mr Salter and Mr Rowson, she reminded herself, *you're swot girl offsetting his louche image, remember. The whole POINT is you're not a natural choice for him, you're subverting the rock-star-and-supermodel expectation.*

'Oh, we'd make sure it was obnoxiously romantic,' Jamie said. 'We'd blow Tom Hanks and Meg Ryan out of the water. We'd make *Sleepless in Seattle* look like a Ken Loach film.'

'Hahaha. Hmmm. I mean, if I wanted to mess with Dan's head . . . it's certainly not what he's expecting . . .'

Laurie knew that this urge to hurt Dan, to get his full attention again, was beneath her, and unhealthy. So what, though? Life, she had realised fully, was extremely unfair.

'I don't know Dan Price very well but I do know male psychology,' Jamie said. 'Was he ever jealous?'

Laurie nodded vigorously. 'A lot. Very.'

She wanted this known. She had mattered, once.

'Then I promise you, he can be again. We could help each other.'

He fixed his gaze on her steadily and Laurie knew she was getting a variant of his seduction routine. Laurie had never met a proper ladies man before, only gobby lads who fancied themselves as busy scorecard shaggers and weren't worthy of the title, really.

She was anthropologically curious. To other women this must be magic, and to her it was a card trick. She'd quite enjoy doing a Penn and Teller on his act, deconstructing it.

She looked at Jamie's intense dark blue eyes and glowing skin, the light sweat on his brow, that thick dark hair you wanted to push your fingertips into, and wondered what age he was when he discovered how beautiful he was, and the power he wielded over women.

Awareness of that power, plus having a quick wit and no heart of his own – a dynamite combination. His laidback manner, his playful sense of humour, his ability to focus exclusively on you – these were the ingredients, Laurie figured, that added up to *a man who made husbands jealous*. He should ditch the law and become a high-class gigolo, working La Croisette in tennis whites for diamond-rattling divorcees.

Had fortune and fate vomited him into her lap, at precisely the right time?

'It *is* mad. And yet. It appeals,' Laurie said, hesitantly.

Jamie broke into a broad smile. He had her.

'You'd have to meet up with me every so often to create our dynamite content, but apart from that. We need to set terms and conditions for this showmance. Text me your personal email and I'll message you over the weekend.'

They agreed they were both awash with drink and needed to head home to find food, and Jamie insisted he'd see Laurie into a taxi.

As they stood on the pavement, Laurie's teeth chattering, her arms folded tightly across her body, she said, 'I have a question.'

'Yes?'

'You were told that Eve was off limits. You want this major promotion. You still took her out to talk work. Why? I mean, the risk versus reward doesn't seem to stack up.'

Laurie knew what she thought had happened, and nothing he was going to say would persuade her otherwise. She was curious at how he'd explain it away.

'She asked me out, not the other way round, and so technically she took me out. Eve's no wallflower.'

Laurie tilted her head. 'Still . . .'

'Ack, I got very annoyed with the idea her sixty-two-year-old uncle gets to choose who she's allowed to socialise with. I can be like that sometimes. An obtuse little twat. Yes, it was a risk, but if I'd given in to their rubbish I couldn't have lived with myself.'

'You were, in fact, respecting her agency and autonomy?'

'Precisely,' Jamie said, grinning. 'And, she's going places. I was networking, if you want the unvarnished version. That was the incentive.'

'With a twenty-four-year-old?' Laurie raised a sceptical eyebrow.

'I'm not kidding, she's ferocious. Photographic memory, doesn't miss a thing, would leave any of us for dead without checking for a pulse. She told me her nickname is *Eve of destruction*. One day she'll have her name above the door, of that I'm sure.'

'Yet you didn't close the deal?'

She could tease Jamie that Eve wasn't into him, but Laurie remembered the body language from the night in question.

Laurie wouldn't have dared be this personal and lairy if she wasn't hammered. But this was her professional training. Pursuing something until you felt you understood it. You couldn't advocate for someone without it.

'I know it runs contrary to what you think of me, but I'm perfectly capable of enjoying female company without it having to end in bed.'

To be fair, Laurie had felt that herself, only hours previous.

'Plus she was, as said, way too young for me.'

'How old are you?"

'Thirty-one.'

'I thought you were younger!'

'I'll take that as a compliment, though I bet you meant immature. How old are you?'

'Thirty-six.'

'I thought you were younger,' Jamie said, tip of his tongue in corner of his mouth.

'Thanks!' Laurie huffed.

'I thought it was a compliment when you said it?'

Laurie rolled her eyes.

'Here you go,' Jamie flagged a hackney. 'I'll email you over the weekend?'

'Yes! Thanks.'

It was only as the cab pulled through the streets that Laurie noticed the pitfall in this plan, the part that didn't suit her, at all – she hated being a scandal. She was an intensely private person, maybe because her parents, in different ways, were such a show.

Plus, they had some significant credibility hurdles to clear.

Which was going to be harder, persuading everyone Jamie Carter could settle down, or that Laurie Watkinson could fall for a Jilly Cooper-level cad?

15

to: LaurieLee101@gmail.com
from: jamieryancarter@gmail.com

Hi!
As discussed here's how I thought the arrangement might work.
Obviously feel very free to say either, no, these are the ravings of a
lunatic, or suggest any guidelines of your own.

As said, we'd start next weekend (how you fixed to take a photo
in a bar, early doors Saturday?) and then run it up until Christmas.
We can work out the break-up details in the New Year. God this is
civilised compared to actual relationships, huh? 😊

1) Not that I'm saying this is our professional speciality, but – the
way to make a lie work is to mix in as much truth as possible.
In terms of origins story, let's say we got trapped in a lift and hit
it off during a drink afterwards. Mick can verify. And hey that's
essentially true, right?! (Right? 😟*))*

2) We'll bung up Instagrams and Facebooks on a roughly weekly basis and generally make it clear we're having a better time and are more smitten than anyone has been since Taylor and Burton. Without the fights, drinking, giant rocks and remarriages. OK, maybe with the drinking. We'll try to keep it as tasteful as possible obviously, and no public mucky talk or anything too ripe. Neither of us want to return to the smoking wreckage of where respect for us once stood, once it's over. All posts to be pre-approved by both parties. (Oh and none of that 'Snuggling up, hashtag blissville' stuff! Brings me out in a rash)

3) No seeing anyone else during the period of the 'relationship.' No public wooing. No PDAs. Being cucked is very much not the look either of us are going for here. I'll delete my Tinder. No, no need to thank me for this extraordinary sacrifice ♥

4) This might be the sticking point, but, for this to work for me I kind of need us to go to the Christmas party, as a couple. Misters Salter and Rowson's beady eyes will be firmly on that event & it's the one major on-premises showcase for our Coupled Upness. I know you're not much of a one for the company do (Michael told me that too) (think you may have a fan there, FY to your I) (no bagging off with him until you've finished fake dating me thanks 😊*) but it's the prime opportunity to make sure this gets results – for both of us*

5) Oh, last point, but vital. The way secrets get round in good faith is everyone thinks they can tell someone they trust, and that one person trusts someone else, and so on. I propose we tell absolutely no one, not a soul, that this is fake. Zero risk of exposure, peace of mind for both participants. Consider this a Non Disclosure Agreement for afterwards, too. We never talk about this not being real.

Whaddya think?
Jx

Hi Jamie,
All sounds good, except the CHRISTMAS PARTY?? oh GOD I'd rather tour the Helmand Province in a day glo unitard. ☹
Lx

L,
Haaah, I did think you'd object. It is quite a harrowing experience. I don't mean, you know, making out while you sit in my lap. Just arrive at the same time, sit next to each other, leave at the same time.
Jx

Argh. OK, we have a deal. NO KARAOKE THOUGH
Lx

A deal, but Laurie had already decided to break the rules.

'Look at us in a garden centre on a Sunday, we're officially wholesome, middle-aged and deeply heteronormative,' Emily said.

'Don't non-hetero conforming people go to garden centres on Sunday?' Laurie said, unclicking her seatbelt.

'The cool ones don't.'

Emily had announced she wanted to do things with Laurie that weren't pubs, bars and restaurants.

'Otherwise I will have helped you out of a broken heart and into cirrhosis. What could you not do, when you were with Dan, that you wanted to do? Ring the changes. Enjoy your freedoms!'

'Erm . . . he was funny about indoor plants. And especially flowers. He said they were amputated dying things merely giving the illusion of life. Little did I know they were a metaphor for our relationship, har har. I had to fight for the potted palm in the front room. And he was heavily allergic to anything with fur obviously, so that ruled pets out.'

'OK well pick something Dan made difficult, and do it. Or get it.'

'I'm not sure I want a dog; I'm not ready. Maybe a cat. But then I'm the single cat woman cliché.'

'Plants and flowers it is then. Aim for "Ladies and gentlemen, Mr Elton John!" kind of levels of foliage.'

Inside they got a shallow trolley and Laurie filled it with bright flowers in pots and kitchen garden herbs.

'This is very therapeutic actually,' she said. 'Can we look at the Farrow & Ball tester pots now? I love them.'

'Knew it. You are a natural home maker. I am a natural home wrecker.'

This was the perfect conversational opening to outline the Jamie Carter Indecent Proposal to Emily. When Jamie said 'one person' was always the leak, he surely didn't mean loyal female best friends unconnected to their workplace. But no need to spook him by querying it.

Laurie paused, expectant for the delighted cackle.

'You're not going to do it, are you?' Emily said, pulling them to a halt in the Paints And Painting Accessories aisle.

Laurie did a small reel back.

'What? I thought you would be SO into this. It's like a public relations campaign on steroids. As a life experiment.'

'That's why you should take me seriously when I say don't do it.'

Laurie was so startled she could only blurt:

'Why not?'

'Because, for one, it's lying. I know that sounds quite superstitious and I can't be more specific. But it's lying, and lying goes wrong. Lying is just bad karma.'

'Em, you old hippy! Can Mrs "I won't travel anywhere where I get fewer than three bars on my phone or fewer than four stars on my hotel" be talking like this?!' Laurie was a mixture of amusement, incredulity and slight worry at this unexpected take. She took Emily's advice seriously. Apart from the stuff about hench dipshits.

'I know, I know,' Emily said. 'But I've got rid of anyone who's ever worked for me who has lied, immediately, and I've never regretted it. You're not a liar, which is why you shouldn't get involved with a big bout of lying. It's not you.'

She hit on something that bothered Laurie from the start of hatching the Jamie plan and still niggled her now. That everyone saw her as utterly status quo, conventional. It had never mattered before, this strait-laced identity, because she was that, and she was content. To discover no one would accept her as anything else? Unwelcome. Emily was paying

143

her a compliment, and yet it was the first time she had made her feel worse.

'That's what appeals to me. Being like me doesn't feel good right now.'

Laurie fiddled with a tiny tin of Mole's Breath and put it back again. Maybe she should repaint the whole house, from top to bottom. 'As for being fired, I can't be fired for pretending to date a colleague. I mean, how could they ever prove I wasn't dating him? The bosses have no say in what I do out of hours, if it's not illegal.'

'Hmmm. Then, what if, when you're feeling vulnerable, and this player is pretending to be into you, you start falling for him for real? A romance that is like a sugary high from cake icing calories and stardust and make believe is going to screw with you. If he doesn't.'

A harried-looking couple joined them and Emily and Laurie moved away, a tacit agreement to save the rest of the conversation for the journey home, and went to pay for Laurie's greenery.

Outside, Emily blipped the alarm on her Mini with the key fob, and threw the tiny boot open.

'All I'm saying, Loz, is I don't think some man pretending to feel things he doesn't feel and you pretending to feel those things back sounds like what you need right now. Are you sure he isn't into you, and this isn't some completely meta way of pulling you?'

Laurie hooted with laughter and Emily huffed, 'Oh yes, that's ridiculous, and what you're suggesting is completely sane. I mean, of *course*.'

'It would be funny if you knew him. He's practically fending them off with a poison-tipped umbrella, he's no need for long game scams with sad older women. Meanwhile I'm about ten years away from being able to look at another man. And if I was ready, Jamie Carter would not be that man. He's one of those preening egotists that only a twenty-four-year-old would crush on and think she's going to marry. Which is probably why he dates twenty-four-year-olds.'

'Is being his date going to bother Dan that much, if he's such a fanny rat fool? I mean, maybe it would upset Dan if you picked up with his best friend, but not this guy? I am not suggesting you do that, either.'

Emily had taken against this project, wholly, instantly and instinctively, and it seemed nothing was going to change her mind. But then, it *was* ridiculous, Emily was right. Launching a fictitious relationship for Dan's benefit was nothing like healthy moving on. It had 'end in tears' all over it. The thing was, it was starting in tears. Laurie was ninety-eight per cent tears. She suspected she'd always be part tears, now. She had nothing to lose.

Laurie shrugged, as she fitted the penultimate plant into the boot. She'd have to hold the fern on her lap.

'I don't know if Dan being bothered is achievable,' Laurie said, feeling drained and empty as she spoke. Jamie had been sure, but he hadn't been through what Laurie had. 'I don't know if he cares enough anymore. But if anyone's going to bother him, it's Jamie Carter. Great nobsman of our age, and a professional competitor. Dan already can't stand him because they all think he's pushy at work; it's perfect. If Jamie gets his promotion he'll be Dan's boss. Oh God, now I think about it, please let him get the promotion. This is a single goal win for Jamie Carter and a *double* win for me.'

Laurie felt a little grimy at saying this and yet, she could hear a little more of her old self returning too. She could be irreverent, confident and funny. Not simply some wet blanket who had smothered Dan.

'Mmm,' Emily said, mouth twisting at the word 'win'. 'Is he online? Show me a picture of this vainglorious idiot.'

Laurie pulled a glove off and swiped at her phone, stabbing at the Facebook app, searching through her friends. Jamie had added her after the lift night. It was to help the deception, though she suspected he'd smoothly send a request to any woman he'd marked interesting/useful. The twenty-first century equivalent of flipping your business card into her hand.

'Here.'

Laurie proffered her iPhone, waited for *the hmmm I don't see why he thinks he's so special* sniff, disclaimer. No one could survive this build-up, especially with a cynical woman in protective mode.

Emily was silent for a second, swiping. She turned Laurie's phone on its side, landscape mode, chewed her lip. 'Oh. *Oh.*'

She handed the phone back.

'OK. Yes. You've convinced me. Do it.'

Laurie was momentarily stunned. 'Are you joking?'

'No. No offence, but I didn't think what passed for fit at Salters & Rowson would mean someone that fit. He's got that sulky mouth, stubble, square jaw thing I love. Brrrr.'

'He's clean shaven at work. He's also got glasses that appear

146

and disappear, now I think about it. He's a Talented Mr Ripley schmuck, isn't he. He was probably known by another name, with a long story about being an orphan, at his last firm.'

'I dunno about that but he looks like a *GQ* cover. He should be on a speedboat in Rimini. And good God, he knows it. But then, would it be possible to not know it? We shouldn't place unreasonable expectations on him.'

'I won't ask what we should place on him.'

Emily pulled a one eye shut, tongue loll gurn face. Laurie started gurgling with laughter, drawing looks from a family nearby trying to cram panels of wooden trellises into the rear of a SEAT Ibiza.

'Dan will be in a tatty heap,' Emily said – God, Laurie realised, the 180-degree swing was genuine, the Jamie Carter Effect was real – 'I couldn't pass that up. I can't in all conscience tell you to pass it up. Have fun. Don't fall for ideas of fixing any lost boy fuck boys, though. Don't start to believe the love of the right woman could cure him. It's bound to cross your mind at some point.'

Laurie blanched, but was very pleased to have Emily back on board.

After they got into the car and belted up, Emily said: 'You know when you're sick, if you get up, shower, dress, put your make-up on and act human, you can feel much better?'

'Yes?'

'It has an impact on how you feel. If you play act being loved up with this man, you may well get happier. But sooner or later you're going to get mixed up in it. You're going to start wondering if you've started to mean it, or whether he has. I don't want it to make you anxious, for you to get hurt.'

'I'm not some suggestible fifteen-year-old! Seriously! You think we'll hold hands for two minutes and I'll start humming Taylor Swift songs and browsing *ELLE Wedding*? Looolll.'

'You may laugh at me, Watkinson, you often do. Doesn't make me wrong.'

'Also this man is a take no prisoners nihilist. It's not a case of his heart needing to be in it. I don't think he has one.'

'How will it work, the relationship?'

Laurie went over the M.O. again and Emily said: 'You should be done up to the nines for the first date.'

'Oh thanks, instead of old Mrs Miggins here shambling up.'

'No, you're beautiful as you are but if this is Operation Mindfuck for Dan, no stops should be left unpulled out. You don't show off, and this calls for showing off. I'll get you a hair appointment at the salon I've started going to in town.'

'Does it cater for hair like mine?'

'Yes, I'm going to send you to my hairdresser, she's done loads of courses in Afro hair and would love to get her hands on you.'

'You're sure?' Laurie said, feeling apprehensive about being gotten. 'White people salons don't often know what they're doing. And even if she's keen, I don't really want to be her guinea pig.'

'Honestly, it's her passion. She's shown me loads of photos of lots of her clients with hair like you. Trust.'

Laurie didn't trust, if she was honest, but she also wouldn't have known where to start *glamazoning* without Emily's help – she still used a hairdresser in Hebden who came to her mum's house, whenever she was back.

Laurie relaxed into listening to Emily's excited burblings about what she should wear with cheerful indifference. If only there was a way of the Issa concession at Selfridges similarly transforming her ripped-up insides.

Plants deposited, front room looking pleasingly jungly, Laurie waved Emily off outside. After she started the engine, she gestured to Laurie she wanted to say something, lowering the window.

'Loz, if you *do* do this showmance. One thing. Consequences. The law of unintended consequences.'

Laurie frowned. 'Uh?'

'This screams "consequences", all over it. You won't know what they are now but I promise you, they'll arise. Be prepared for that.'

'Oh. Yes. You're probably right. But I can't think what they'd be?'

'No. They'll happen though.'

'How do I prepare for the unknown?'

'You can't. That's my point.'

This seemed excessive caution to Laurie, and she was the queen of caution.

On paper, the crime was perfect.

16

Outwardly, Laurie went to work, she was in reasonable spirits, she was as efficient as ever. In her private life, she looked busy enough to be respectable. Not falling apart.

Laurie was coping, only in ways that made other people feel comfortable. It was a performance, going through the motions. She was as empty and as fragile as an Easter egg. The truth lay in moments like the Thursday evening where she found the box of photo albums under the bed in the spare room. She leafed through a packet of Snappy Snaps from 2005 and ended up crouching, sobbing, feeling as if she'd been stabbed.

She'd never grieved for anyone close to her, but she guessed this must be similar: times when the tide went out and she felt almost normal, and times when it came rushing in and she felt like she was drowning.

It dawned on Laurie – other than the pictures he had on his phone, Dan had taken nothing of sentimental value with him. Only a few short months ago, she'd have thought that spelled intention to return. Ha. Nope. The hard copy visual record of their near-two decades together, casually discarded.

She knew if she challenged Dan he'd weakly insist he had every intention of sorting through and asking for duplicates, but it wasn't the time/didn't want to upset her/couldn't complicate the painful business of his going, by divvying up their mementoes. HAH. As if starting a family with another woman wasn't the motherlode, no pun, of painful complications. What if wanting to take photos might've given Laurie some comfort that he still cared, and that might've mattered, and he should've taken them for that reason alone.

Don't look don't look don't look, she instructed herself, as she took the lid off. She'd glance and look away, she told herself. She opened the envelope packet on top. An Ark of the Covenant for her emotions. Laurie was probably going to do the skin-melting screaming CGI skeleton thing, as unleashing the evil spirits of the past overcame her.

The first pack was pretty much the most poignant she could've encountered. Thanks, random chance, you bitch.

Their impromptu staycation at The Midland.

They'd been getting their kitchen done, and it had taken forever thanks to inadvertently hiring the greatest cowboys in the North West to fit it. Their story ended in the small claims court, because don't fuck with two lawyers at once. Laurie had almost lost her mind after nineteen days with a room that resembled an ISIS stronghold, with bags of crisps for dinner and being fed a daily diet of lies.

While she curled foetal, Dan had gone off, made a call and surprised her by saying, 'Pack a bag for two nights away,' before bundling her into a taxi.

They'd pulled up minutes later outside the imposing

entrance of Manchester's fanciest, Grade II listed grand hotel. Laurie had always hankered after a night there.

Dan had explained the circumstances when booking, so they were upgraded to a suite, the floor space as large as a penthouse flat.

'Can we afford this?' Laurie said, bedazzled, as Dan handed her a glass from the complimentary bottle of cava.

'Yeah, ish,' Dan said, 'Worth it for the look on your face alone.'

It was an amazing forty-eight hours, after the chaos and despair of 'Sorry, love, we didn't know that was a supporting wall because you didn't warn us,' and being coated in brick dust.

Sitting in a palatial king-size bed, eating room service chips and giggling like a pair of kids at a sleepover. It was Dan at his best: spontaneous, generous and caring.

Laurie held one of the floppy rectangles depicting the episode, Dan pointing to the toilet in their colossal hotel bathroom, pulling a 'what the hell' face. They took a series of photos like this of the lavish fixtures and fittings, in poses usually seen in local papers by people upset about pot holes, which seemed hilarious when half cut.

The last in the set was Dan and Laurie checking out, stood by the ball-of-lilies flower display in the lobby, Dan holding the camera above their heads, hugging Laurie to him tightly. A team. A duo. Best friends. Turning adversity into an adventure. Dan looked so pleased with himself and Laurie looked so happy.

She limped downstairs and lay on the sofa and let the sadness and desolation wash over her for the thousandth time.

Out of the corner of her eye, she saw her phone screen ripple with a message. More cascaded down, blip – blip – blip. It was a WhatsApp group she was in, titled 'Claire's Baby Shower' for its original purpose, though that baby was now two.

Claire and Phil were successful Chorlton friends, along with Ed and Erica, and Tom and Preethi, the people they socialised with most as a couple. Laurie had expected more messages of condolences from them, she knew they knew as Dan had bumped into Tom, told him, and told Laurie he'd told him. And she'd had the creep DMs from Adrian: news travelled invisibly and fast.

She only got a text from Claire saying awful for her and was she OK and the usual things, and Laurie replied she was gutted but coping, thank you, and Claire didn't reply to that one.

Laurie didn't entirely mind, but registered it was slightly dismissive.

The messages carried on pinging at hectic speed and Laurie roused herself to pick her handset up. She lurched at the sight of her own name. It took a fraction of a second to tell it was being typed in a tone and manner that clearly wasn't meant to be seen by her, the owner of the name.

Claire
It's a funny one, at first I said to Phil I didn't believe it as they seemed so solid but the more I think about it, the more I see it. Laurie's so smart but her sense of humour can be quite cutting! Dan was always more laidback, somehow? Laurie's sharp in a way that is good in court and maybe not so great in a marriage

Pri

Yeah I said the same to Tom. I think L was very driven and Dan felt neglected a lot of the time. She must be devastated though, starting a family straight away with the other woman! 😞

Erica

I think he's been a shit to Laurie. If she wouldn't commit to having kids you don't have an affair do you? I am sure he has his side to it, but it's awful for her

Pri

Did she not want kids? I thought she was open minded but not in a hurry

Claire

If she did she's never shown much interest. You know, Dan's a good looking man with a good job, you can't take his sort for granted these days, in the baby-making years, that's the simple truth

Ugh. *Baby-making years.* Laurie felt grimly vindicated in her previous low-level grumbling dislike of Claire. She was a Stepford Wife, basically, but coated it in lots of twenty-first-century, faux feminist, socially acceptable concern trolling. So, instead of, 'Why aren't you home to make Dan's dinner?' it was, 'It must be hard on you working those hours, do you do Sunday batch cooking? I have a great dhal recipe,' looking only at Laurie.

And Laurie had also noticed men got different treatment from Claire. She claimed once as a yummy mummy, she liked polo necks so much as 'If you pause while your head is stuck inside it, putting it on, you get a few seconds' peace!' and Dan had guffawed and said: 'Smell of burning martyr!'

If Laurie had said that, *oof*. She'd get some icy response about not understanding the fatigue until you had one. Claire merely simpered and batted Dan's arm.

At Claire and Phil's, men did the jokes and women talked shop(ping).

Pri
Back out there at our age though, can you imagine? Shuddering.

Erica
Absolutely cringing at the thought. No 30s guy wants to date a woman of same age with her clock ticking, they're busy chatting up 25 year olds online

Claire
Any guy single at this age will have more issues than you can shake a stick at. Or divorce behind him, step kids. 🙁

Pri
Yeah slim to no pickings. Poor Laurie.

A minute after her gut-wrenching bewilderment at how they could be conducting this dissection of her, in front of her, Laurie sussed exactly how it had happened. She'd been included in the original Baby Shower team but it had been so long since she replied, they thought they were a trio.

Right there was the answer why she'd got such minimal sympathy: she'd not played the game properly. Laurie turned up at their houses often enough, she'd had them round to theirs. But in the digital age equivalent of nattering over the garden fence, she'd never pretended to be interested in Claire's daughter's tongue tie, or Pri's luxury shed–slash–summer house.

Not least because she had a job where she spent hours in courtrooms with her phone on silent. Not being interested in social media made you seem aloof these days, except Laurie wasn't aloof, just busy and slightly baffled by it.

Erica
Who is the other woman? Had it been going on for a while? Playing away makes my blood boil tbh

Claire
She's called Megan, she's a lawyer and IDK! Dan says not – but for them to be expecting this soon?

Pri
Dan told Tom it was one of those bolt from blue type attraction things where he met Megan and he knew straight away something was going to happen. I think Dan's riddled with guilt at hurting Laurie, didn't expect it to move this fast. Some sort of contraception bork . . . 😬

Claire
Hmmm. Would be curious to meet her! Also I have TONS of stuff of Ella's to offload if they want it. I am done with the baby

having thanks, whatever Phil thinks when he's had a few Doom Bars 😊

Classic Claire: using the fact she'd had three kids to tell everyone about her sex life (the detailed circumstances of conception of each always discussed as if she was merely telling you where she got her nails done).

Laurie had been coping, almost, with this involuntary ringside seat, but the baby chat was more than she could stand.

Laurie
RIGHT HERE GUYS 👍

She paused and checked.

Pri – Seen

Erica – Seen

Claire – Seen

Yeah you have been seen, and found wanting.

They would now be setting up a Laurieless group in record time, titled HOLY SHIT. She was sure they'd bond over this story of their terrible gaffe and take it on tour around Chorlton, once the agony of it subsided. Laurie thought, you know what: let them.

She left the group.

It was very obvious they'd chosen Dan as the survivor. After a polite interval, it would be Dan and Megan praising their Ottolenghi cauliflower dish and admiring the bifold doors on the extension. Dan had a new partner and a baby on the way, he wasn't a single, spiky anomaly. *Two by two on the Ark*, she heard Jamie say. Yep. They'd left her to the flood-waters.

Laurie opened Facebook and removed Dan from her In A Relationship With status, a task which felt teenaged and yet necessary. She forced herself to check and what a surprise: he'd done that first.

She was glad of a WhatsApp message from Jamie Carter, confirming arrangements for Saturday.

Concluding: 'Also do you have something new to wear? All helps to create disorientation in the mind of the male ex.'

Hmmm. An echo of how Laurie felt when Dan presented in his shiny green Barbour.

Laurie
Well that's a ringing endorsement of my fashion sense.

Jamie
Hahaha! I don't know what you usually wear on a Saturday night, do I? The point is it looks different to Dan. WOMEN ☺

Laurie gave a grudging small smile.

Everyone was talking about her anyway. She'd give them something to talk about.

17

Laurie stepped into a very modern hair salon with retro beehive 1950s dryers, playing Carly Rae Jepsen very loudly, and knew she was trespassing. A lumpen interloper from the ordinary world in the universe of the naturally sexual, at ease with themselves and on trend.

There were about fifteen staff milling around the front desk, most of them with experimental hairstyles and tiny BMIs, clad in spray-on PVC leggings. The look was Ziggy Stardust meets Warren Beatty in *Shampoo*, and no one here was alive when either was released.

Every pair of kohled eyes was momentarily on her, and she was asked if she 'had an appointment' with an air of magnificent disbelief and disdain. Usually you'd have to go to restaurants in Paris in muddy wellies to get this sort of hauteur.

These looks were practised to repel the insuffiently cool, the narrowed eyes conveying: *You know there are perfectly good neighbourhood places that'll give you Rachel from* Friends *layers and a cup of Yorkshire Gold?* Laurie realised it wasn't only her

Afro hair that kept her out, she was also clearly too old, too shabby and too unpierced. How dare they assume; for all they knew her labia minora could set airport metal detectors off.

The camp man with arched, pencilled eyebrows and peculiarly shiny skin said, 'You're with Honey, she's on her break. Take a seat.' *Honey*. A world where honey was a name and not a sweet viscous substance.

Honey bounced out of a door within minutes. 'Hiiiiii is it Laurie? Do you want to come over? Did you want a drink? Coffee, tea, mini prosecco?'

Laurie relaxed a degree.

'Oh . . . ooh. Mini prosecco?' Why the hell not.

'I wish I could join ya, roll on six o'clock hahahahah,' said Honey, rifling in a mini fridge and unscrewing the cap, before plonking a paper straw into it and handing it to Laurie.

Honey was short, with a very round face and eyes, spiky peroxide hair with an undercut, her petite frame clad in a Metallica T-shirt. Maybe it was the openness of her expression, but Laurie found her less scary than the other staff.

'What are we doing today then?' Honey said, after guiding her to a mirror, hands on the back of Laurie's chair, looking at her reflection.

Laurie pulled the band out of her customary ponytail and started making self-conscious British jokes about the state of her hair.

'Are you type 3C?' Honey said, digging the tips of her fingers in the sides of Laurie's hair and ploofing it, putting her hand at the crown and riffling from side to side.

Laurie near-gasped. 'You know your stuff.'

'Yeah, your hair is sort of my favourite, actually! Did Emily say? Yeah.' She proudly pointed at shelves of relevant products.

Ah, thought Laurie. Always trust Emily.

'Do you always wear it pulled back? Never loose? You're wasting it!'

'Hardly ever. I got into the habit because it's easier at work. I'm a solicitor and, you know, you want to keep it simple.'

Laurie was about to stutter further explanations then thought: Honey was about twenty-four years old, white as mozzarella and a fan of heavy metal. She was not about to pass political judgement on Laurie for not celebrating her hair, the way her mum had. (A debate that usually ended with Laurie pointing out she hadn't asked to be born, and thinking her dad would probably agree)

'Your skin tone is beautiful, wish I was like you instead of getting sunburn from the flash on my phone!' Honey laughed and Laurie laughed with her. Oh, to be unselfconscious like that again.

'Your hair is actually in really good condition,' Honey said, pulling a strand and rubbing it between finger and thumb. 'What are you thinking?'

Laurie sucked in a breath and considered equivocating about 'take some of the length off' and thought, after an empowering drag on her prosecco straw, she might as well go for it. She'd come this far.

'My long-term boyfriend has finished with me after eighteen years and I always have my hair in that ratty pony and to be honest, I just want to look really fucking good for a change.'

Honey's eyes widened. 'Eighteen years! Oh my God!'

'Yep.' *About three quarters of your lifetime.*

'This is makeover kinda territory?' Honey said, and Laurie sensed her excitement levels had shot up several notches, as she nodded.

'OK, how about this. I'm thinking a centre parting, and I'll cut you in some slightly shorter pieces that blend around the front so you can still wear it up, so it's not all one length. Then, like, play up your natural masses of curls? I think it would be really nice to put some lights in too. Natural ones, like chestnut and mocha, to break the block colour up a bit? It'll be totally sensational, like movie star hair. Like *a cloud* of curls, like boom.' Honey made a hand gesture like exploding earmuffs.

Despite the fact Laurie was sure she just got cannily upsold she agreed, infected by Honey's clear enthusiasm for the task ahead.

The next two hours were sitting around with foils on her head, reading about sex with ghosts in *Take A Break* and society weddings in Amagansett in *Vanity Fair*. She texted Emily to delay their coffee by forty-five minutes.

As the process continued, Laurie could see she had less hair, and that streaks of it were now light brown. For the big finish, Honey poured out some transparent glop, worked it through Laurie's 'do with her hands and trained an enormous dryer on it, making 'scrunching a ball of paper' movements.

Gradually, the hair of Laurie's youth emerged, but much, much better. She didn't remember it ever having this shiny softness, and Honey had somehow produced the sort of ideal curl size you itched to poke your finger into. The caramel shot through it did indeed make it glimmer and catch the light in different ways to her pure black.

Unexpectedly, Laurie was envying herself. Emily was right, this sort of admiration for her own reflection was a very rare thing. She'd spent so long being low maintenance she'd forgotten the kick to be had in high.

'How's that?' Honey said, standing back, with the smugly delighted intonation of someone who knows they've absolutely smashed it and can't wait to collect the reviews.

'I love it! Oh my God, I love it,' Laurie said, turning her head and making it swish around her shoulders. 'I love it so much.'

'Right?' Honey said, and started talking her through the products and processes for best maintenance, during which Laurie mumbled 'hmmmm mmm' as if she was taking it all deathly seriously when in fact she was giddy. Such a small thing, a nice hairdo, but it was nice to know she could still appreciate small joys. Laurie paid a three-figure sum, tipped hard and she and Honey giggled delightedly at their successful collaboration throughout.

'He's gonna ask you to get back with him!' Honey called, as Laurie stepped out into the chill and felt her new curls blow about in the breeze.

'Hah. Maybe,' Laurie said, smiling, trying not to let the dagger of thinking about that right now break her skin.

'No doubt!' Honey said, waving. 'Call me psychic! Psychic Honey!'

Laurie nearly said 'Sounds very prog rock,' before considering that despite the number of vintage band tees being sported in the salon, no one would have the faintest clue what she meant.

While Laurie guessed the response she'd get from Emily would be positive, she didn't bank on what actually happened; Emily not recognising her for a moment. She passed, stopped, tracked back two steps and let out a small startled cry.

'You look absolutely AMAZING,' Emily said, clutching her chest. 'Seriously, Laurie. You look like you're a famous person trying to go unrecognised and failing. My heart's going like a broken clock here! I fancy you!'

'I thought you fancied me anyway?' Laurie said. 'It's alright, isn't it?'

Emily plopped into a seat and set her latte mug down.

'It's not alright, it's utterly fucking fabulous. You are fabulous. I wish my hair could do that. It's so good to see you like this. Fighting back.'

Laurie wasn't sure she bought in as fully as Emily to a L'Oreal vision of womanhood where bouncy hair signalled being mentally robust. But she thought there's a time and a place to be a naysayer, and now and here wasn't it. She looked different so she felt better, that'd do.

'Aw thanks, it's only a 'do I won't be able to do myself. I like it though. Feels odd,' Laurie said.

'I didn't even know your hair could do this! Can I touch?'

'I'd forgotten too, to be honest. 'Course you can!'

Emily prodded a ringlet.

When they'd drained their coffees, Emily pulled Laurie out

into the blue-dusk and up to the department stores of the Printworks for cosmetics.

'I have make-up,' Laurie said.

'Evening out make-up.'

'I wear my make-up on evenings out.'

'Not the same thing. Stop filibustering, feminazi.'

Emily could always make Laurie laugh.

Laurie found herself perched nervously on a stool at Emily's favourite concession, MAC, while R'n'B thundered at nightclub volume. Emily tapped a photo of a Naomi Campbell lookalike in Studio 54 quantities of glittery slap above the counter, and said: 'All out, Tess, go all out.'

Tess the assistant had a tool belt full of brushes, as if she was a facial mechanic who might need to contour a cheekbone in an emergency. She set to work on Laurie's eyes with serious intent.

'Maybe keep it natural on the lips,' Laurie said, nervously, as Tess snapped open the third shadow palette.

'Really, a nude lip? Because you could really carry a red,' she said.

Tess had a glint not unlike Honey's, which said: *I am about to make a right bundle on this one.*

Emily nodded furiously and said: 'Red. Let's not fuck about here. We're not here to play.'

Laurie quailed a little. The last time she wore showy make-up was at indie clubs in her twenties when she rolled glitter up her cheekbones and had a penchant for neon eye shadows. In her thirties, she was happy in her *mid-range mascara and tinted balm* rut.

When she was shown her face in an oval hand mirror, she let go a small 'ahhh!'

This woman looked like her, but had roadsweeper lashes above large, defined sooty eyes with silver sparkles. There were iridescent, light reflecting angles to her complexion, and a bold crimson mouth. Laurie tried to fit this brash vamp with Real Laurie, cowering inside. She was now projecting a person she didn't feel. She didn't entirely mind it, though. It was another mask, like the one she wore at work.

'Incredible. Really gorgeous, Laurie,' Emily breathed. 'If I could look like that, I would look like that all the bloody time.'

Laurie grinned at her. 'Instead, sadly you are a plain, pious, devout sort of woman.'

Emily was flushed, triumphant, and snuck off and paid for the haul before Laurie could protest. She then dragged her up two flights of escalators and forced Laurie to try on a black maxi dress with wisps of lace for sleeves. Laurie fully expected to refuse exhortations to buy it, yet when the zip flew straight up her misery-diminished frame and Laurie saw an elegant, Audrey Hepburnish creature of the night looking back at her, she needed no convincing.

If nothing else, it'd solve the whole 'what to wear to first date Jamie Carter' conundrum. That sort of thing was tricky enough when you were hopeful your date would be knocked out; when you didn't care and it was a performance for someone not present, it was yet more admin.

'Could I happen to run into you?' Emily said, as Laurie paid and Emily practically bounced up and down. 'No intrusion, a drive-by eyeballing. Where is it?'

'The Ivy in Spinningfields. I guess so? Remember, on pain of death, you're not supposed to know what we're up to. Act like you've caught me out and ask who he is. Etc.'

'Ten four, Red Leader.'

Jamie had inquired if it was the kind of place Laurie went, had she been before? When Laurie answered in the negative, Jamie replied with the gnomic:

That's no bad thing tbh

She didn't ask if it was a Jamie Carter sort of haunt, but he added:

It'll probably be nouveau riche AF, but.

Laurie vaguely wondered why they were going somewhere Jamie didn't go or rate much either. As she tapped her fingers waiting for the taxi, a few hours later, the answer came to her: so he doesn't see anyone he knows, stupid.

18

The good thing about this fashion for very long dresses, Laurie told herself, as she felt her ankles snugly circled by thick fabric in the footwell of the cab, is there was very little of you on show, considering it was a special occasion look.

She knew why she was jittering: she was either going to feel woefully underdone or dollied up mutton for this date, and she'd firmly landed in the second category. The chances of hitting the sweet spot of 'herself, enhanced' was always minimal and she'd overshot the runway by some distance.

Hair by Honey, face by Tess, dress by Self Portrait: the sort of label that would pass muster with Suzanne from Emily's firm, anyway.

The twin constrictions of the dress and heels necessitated a Marilyn Monroe-ish totter out to the Toyota Avensis that was her Cinderella pumpkin chariot.

Her driver Jabal looked at her curiously in the rear-view mirror and said: 'Are you going to awards?'

Laurie winced.

Yes, Mad Bint of the Year.

She could've badly done without her Shirley Basseyness pointed out and muttered: 'Nope' with a fierce enough intonation that he didn't inquire further.

Jabal said nothing, obviously thinking: *these award-attending divas.*

Laurie's stomach fizzed and rolled as she walked into the ground-floor brasserie and scanned for Jamie. Heads turned and Laurie felt she should be wearing a sandwich board saying *I am not anyone from Corrie or with a footballer, go back to your Manhattans.*

She thought of Emily saying: 'a huge part of getting attention is signalling you're up for attention' and felt the truth of it. Her clothes and make-up commanded: *look at me.* Inside she howled: *don't.*

She saw Jamie, treacle-dark head down, looking at his phone, sitting on a chair at the other side of the circular bar. It was a small island of glass and light, the staff working away within it, noisily rattling ice in shakers above their shoulders. Laurie realised the location might also have been chosen for its scene-setting potential.

Laurie picked her way carefully towards him, the prospect of going arse over tit too awful to contemplate. Jamie glanced up as she approached and did what seemed to be a genuine double-take, eyes widening, mouth open an inch, phone immediately abandoned.

Laurie was too uncomfortable to feel any compliment. It was hard to separate out making an effort for the caper, from simply making an effort for him, and the thought he'd suspect the latter was mortifying.

She reached Jamie and said: 'Hello.' There was a pause. 'Well. Getting on that chair is going to be interesting.'

'. . . He left you for *who*, again?'

Laurie rolled her heavily made-up eyes. 'I was going to say "It's not a competition" but if it isn't, why am I here? Moral high ground was in short supply, huh.'

'Well, seriously, morality aside, you look incredible.'

'Haha. Thanks.'

He stood down from his seat so it was easier for Laurie to heave up into hers. Jamie was wearing a black shirt and slim-cut grey wool trousers, the angles and planes of his face set off wonderfully by the low lighting, and Laurie relaxed a notch, thinking, at least I look like I'm supposed to be here. It was a close-run thing, but feeling too scruffy for the company and clientele would've been worse. Inspecting the room, it was indeed the sort of place for beefy men, still glowing pink from their early evening power shower, their rail-thin wives in Kurt Geiger stilettos and everyone flashing American Express cards.

'Right so, here's your resolve stiffener,' Jamie said, and motioned to the waitress who had appeared by them, holding a martini out for Laurie.

Laurie had never been ordered for in her life.

'Sorry, you drink martinis? It's vodka, dirty, olives,' Jamie said, seeing her expression.

Who did he think he was, some ASDA Whoops! aisle James Bond?

'Yes,' Laurie said, wondering if she should've said no, show me the cocktail menu please, on principle. Who ordered drinks *for* people? Was she a gangster's moll already?

Compromised, that's what she was. She'd confided in one man that another man had damaged her.

Laurie sipped it gingerly, recoiling slightly at its salt and strength, as well as the feeling of being taken for granted. Her lips numbed.

'It'll be a little easier to play-act this picture if not stone-cold sober,' Jamie said.

'What have you got in mind? Is it going to be posed like Charles and Diana's engagement photo?' Laurie said as she sipped again.

'Haha. *Whatever love means*,' he quoted, 'My kind of guy.' Laurie was quite impressed at him knowing that given he was only thirty-one, though she didn't say so.

Her phone vibrated with a message and she pulled it out of her bag. Jamie. Uh?

The bartender is a trainee and my drink took a lifetime to make! Shall I order for you? Is a martini OK? Tell you what, I'll get you that and then if you don't have it, I will. Jx

'Oh. Just got your message!' she said, glancing up from the screen, guiltily. 'Bloody EE coverage.'

'Hah. No worries.'

Assuming had made an ass of Laurie, he was being thoughtful. And it occurred to her that if he'd got her something full of passionfruit juice and Malibu, she'd have objected that, in fact, she was the kind of woman who liked proper navy strength drinks. 0/5 to the romantically scalded, grumpy Laurie Watkinson.

'OK, so, time for a little game theory, as those Twitter analysts of American politics like to say,' Jamie said, and Laurie smiled into her third sip. Dammit, it was so violent, and yet so drinkable.

'The impression we want to give with this photo is not: "Here we are getting heavy, guys!" It's far more of a "question mark" kind of thing than that, for our debut. It's a "here's an outtake from what was obviously a very good evening, draw your own conclusions." Essentially, we want to spark a guessing game. Appeal to the part of the brain that lights up during an Agatha Christie.'

'Yes . . . I suppose so?' Laurie said, hesitantly. She was allowing herself to wonder, at last, exactly how febrile the guessing game might be over this, and she didn't much like the answer. She was trying to bottle lightning, without much of a bottle.

'What were you thinking?' Jamie said, eyebrows drawing together. Typical lawyer. Turning the tables on her attitude: *have you got any better ideas? Well then.*

'I had no idea. Go on.'

'I'm also thinking we want to get our photo early so you can get away and have your real Saturday night.'

Hah, he meant *his*, but she appreciated the good manners.

'I thought I could post the photo tomorrow morning, and tag you. Then you've perhaps not fully intended everyone you're friends with to see it, but: "Oh no! Everyone sees it." Including your ex. Are you set up to show tagged photos?'

'I think so . . .?'

'The way it works is you have to opt out. So if you haven't, it'll be there.'

Laurie nodded. He was *so much* younger than her. So much. This was campaign strategy.

'You're on Instagram?' Jamie said.

'Ah. No.'

'DOH. We need you to be on Instagram. Let's set up an account and we'll do it linked to Facebook, so that you draw lots of contacts from there over to Instagram. If we leave it public then your ex only needs to know it's there, and he'll be likely to check it.'

Laurie thought: huh. She'd given up the 'predicting Dan' game.

'Do you have something handy in your photos on your phone you can sling on as an Instagram profile picture?' Jamie said.

'Uh . . .' Laurie chewed her lip and opened her iPhone.

'Actually, do you know what,' Jamie said, giving her an appraising look. 'Let's leave you off Instagram, for now. Launching one tonight looks suspicious. You can appear on mine.'

'OK. What's your Instagram like?'

Jamie tapped at his phone and handed it over.

Laurie peered at the black and white profile photo, Jamie laughing at some unseen person, half in profile, looking predictably devastating. She read his bio aloud – '*Call me when you realise none of this matters*' – and burst out laughing.

She glanced up at Jamie and to her surprise, he blushed. He'd seemed unembarrassable, and her opinion shouldn't matter. Although that might still be true, the two things weren't that closely linked.

'Alright, it's only humour, you snipe.'

He screwed his face up in a mock sulk which could've been nauseating, but his boyish charm carried it clear out of nause and right into almost cute. Laurie could see why lesser women than herself succumbed so easily.

'It's a bit . . . *I'm no good for you, baby. I'm married to the sea*,' Laurie said. She feared she might be pushing her luck, but she liked the more light-hearted, larky side of her nature he seemed to unlock. Lad Banter Laurie, as Dan used to call it, not approvingly. It chased some of the ghosts away, albeit temporarily.

'Hahahaha, married to the sea,' Jamie said. 'Right, hang on. I'm changing my bio to that now, it's excellent.'

He fiddled with his iPhone and Laurie said: 'You're not really, are you? I was taking the piss.'

'I know. And it was funny. There . . .' he flashed the screen up at her. He had, as well.

'Is there anything you won't ironise? Do you ever have genuine feelings towards women?'

'Yes of course I do! They're very genuine for the two or three hours I feel them.'

Laurie groaned.

'You're an actual womaniser, snaring the unwary by doing a comic parody of a womaniser. Modern men.'

Jamie curled his lip at the word 'womaniser'. Laurie recognised it as the same expression as when defendants who dealt drugs heard themselves described as drug dealers.

'. . . I think calling them "unwary" is a bit much. As is "snaring". I'm not The Hooded Claw.'

'Plenty of them, even if they accept it's casual, must think you only need to meet the right "them", though.'

Jamie clinked ice in his glass.

'I think you underrate how many women out there are perfectly fine with casual. You see it as my interests versus women's, and it isn't like that. Sex comes under the category heading of General Interest. I'm not exploiting anyone.'

This hurt, more than she betted it was meant to. Following Dan's departure, Laurie was sensitive to accusations of being vanilla.

'Works in theory. But Eve wasn't hoping for more than career advice tips, for example? She didn't think maybe you might bed and boyfriend her?' Backhand low volley.

'Nope,' Jamie said, though he looked discomfited. 'Not at all. Despite her uncle's prejudices about the dangers of consorting with unattached members of the opposite sex, sharing dinners with them. God who is he, Mike Pence?'

The temperature between them had cooled considerably.

As much as lotharios were anathema to Laurie, it was hardly fair of her to object tonight. If you wanted plumbing done, you hired a plumber. If you wanted your roof fixed you hired a roofer.

If you wanted everyone to erroneously believe you were at it like knives, you recruited Jamie Carter.

When discomfort meets strong liquor, at first the spirits seem wondrous panacea for it, Laurie observed – then they start extracting a heavy price. Like a Wonga Dot Com deposit on payday.

She ordered a second martini, despite an unguarded wooz-iness setting in, and despite remembering the adage that they were like breasts: one wasn't enough, three too many.

'I'm glad you're having another, when I saw your face when it arrived I worried I'd messed up,' Jamie said, pleasantly, clearly happy to move the conversation away from his love life.

'Oh no, really my thing, thanks.'

She winced inside: she'd been snippy with him to an unwarranted degree. She had a low opinion of this man, for no real reason other than the boys at work hated him and women pashed on him. Boys being the operative word. She'd accepted a second-hand version of Jamie, one largely shaped by spite, and ought to make up her own mind.

'Shall we transfer to a table? I have constant premonitions of falling off these things, while balancing on terrified clenched cheeks.' Jamie sucked the cheeks on his face in.

'Oh my God, same!' Laurie laughed, with the over emphasis of the getting-drunk-fast person.

Installed at a table, the drinks arrived on paper doily coasters and Jamie slid onto the banquette beside her, close enough that she felt the warmth of him through her lace sleeves, and chided herself for the goosebumps which rippled down her arm.

'Now,' he said. 'To business.'

He turned his camera on its side as Laurie lifted the glass to her lips and he leaned his head into the frame, tapping rapidly at the circle at the bottom of the screen. He took reams of photos, which, Emily had informed Laurie, was the insider's secret to getting a great one.

'Hmm,' he said, unconvinced, swiping through his camera roll.

Laurie peered at them: 'Snuggling up with my alcoholic wife. Hashtag blissville.'

'I am very happy to hand you the controls,' Jamie said.

'No! It's fine. It's just, you know. Seeing how the sausage is made.'

'Hey, you still have no idea how my sausage is made, baby.'

Laurie hooted with laughter and Jamie quickly pulled her towards him and into the crook of his arm, holding his phone aloft, clicking away. He smelled expensively citrus and masculine, and Laurie thought how much more presentation work singlehood involved. Dan was perfumed only by double underarm swipes of Sure For Men.

'What's your . . . scent?'

'Acqua di Parma and success.'

Jamie examined his work.

'Yes! There,' he said. 'That's it, that's the one. Oh, record time, Carter. The master at work, etc. The Samsung Galaxy Da Vinci.'

He turned the screen towards Laurie. The picture showed Jamie smiling up conspiratorially straight into the camera, all strong jawline and brow and a few dark curls on his forehead. Laurie was in profile, eyes tight shut in mirth, resting against his chest in a coquettish way. She could see he'd found a flattering angle where she looked . . . foxy? The cocktail hour dress was visible, Jamie's shirt unbuttoned the right amount. It was the kind of poseur nonsense that vain people sent out on wedding invites.

The scene looked intimate and genuine, depicting the sort of pleasure in each other's company you can't fake. Except, you clearly could.

'That's like some Harry and Meghan official photos level lenswork,' Jamie said, satisfied, flipping expertly through the filter options. 'Monochrome feels a little too studied. Let's go with a nice Mayfair.'

'Is Meghan your one handy mixed race girl reference?' Laurie said, taking the cocktail stick out of her fat olives and putting it in the corner of her mouth, grinning.

'You're a waspish character at times, aren't you?' Jamie said, but reasonably warmly. 'Should I . . . is mixed race the right term nowadays?'

'Doesn't bother me if it's not meant badly. Dual heritage is the official one for Government forms, but no one really uses that. The one I hated as a kid was half caste.'

'Ugh. Yes. All noted.'

The sort of sharpness that works in court but not in a marriage. Laurie cringed. Though that was typical Claire, suggesting being good at her job made her a bad partner.

'I was kidding, sorry!' Laurie amended. 'The name Megan comes with a trigger warning for me.'

'Ah God, sorry, yeah.'

The killer portrait achieved, it let the air out of the balloon somewhat. Chat now felt stilted, while Laurie tried to second guess how much Jamie wanted to be gone and, she suspected, Jamie laboured to conceal he wanted to be gone.

Laurie felt considerable relief when a shimmering vision of Emily in salmon satin squealed: 'Laurie! What are you doing here?!' and swooped in for a media person double air kiss.

'Oh, Emily this is Jamie, from work. Jamie, Emily,' Laurie said, 'We're out for a drink.'

'Right,' Emily said, hand on slinky hip, looking from one to the other and, Laurie thought, doing a good job of appearing to take this in, in real time.

'I'm with Suzanne from work and a few others, you know Suzanne?' and Laurie said 'Yep' and made a covert UGH face. Emily laughed and so did Jamie.

After a few minutes of Getting To Know Yous, Emily's diminutive, shinily clad behind perching on the end of their banquette, she excused herself to her companions and said, 'Really nice to meet you,' extending a hand to Jamie.

If Laurie had thought about it prior, she'd have predicted that Jamie and Emily meeting would be fireworks and chemistry and delightedly trading the kind of romcom barbs that end with them in the sack. They had a lot of similarities in disposition, and were both knockouts. If Jamie Carter had ever said 'Set me up with a friend of yours,' Laurie would've without second thought provided Emily's number and said *thank me later.*

She didn't sense much static crackle, but perhaps that was heavy expectation in a ten-minute encounter when Jamie was notionally on a date with her best friend. In fact, she felt Jamie was uncharacteristically subdued.

'Let's go,' Laurie said, under her breath to Jamie, after Emily departed, 'I'm not having the Suzanne experience twice.'

Laurie waved across the room to Emily, and Emily, leaning

in to check Jamie wasn't looking, made a forefinger to thumb circle. Suzanne boggled. Hah, *have that.*

As much as she'd enjoyed moonlighting as Pennines Beyoncé, she couldn't wait to take the bra, Spanx and the heels off. Glamour was agony.

Outside, Jamie handed her into her Uber, reiterating his intentions regarding their photo. 'Essentially a *did they or didn't they* tease. And an *are they or aren't they*. No smut, obviously.'

As he leaned down to close the door, he said, 'Can't believe you did a girl buddy "safety check-in" set-up on me, by the way.'

Ouch.

'I didn't! Pure coincidence,' Laurie said, but she knew she looked guilty.

'Hah. Don't bullshit the bullshitter, Watkinson,' he said, and slammed the door before she could protest further.

Laurie was uncomfortable, as nightscape Manchester flew past the car window, and now in more than one way. If that set-up had been so obvious to Jamie, what else might she misjudge?

She feared Emily's prediction, that lying had unforeseen complications, was already coming true.

19

You Were Tagged In A Photo By Jamie Carter.

Through her blurred senses, Laurie squinted at her handset. They'd gone live, hence the confetti of notifications. She opened Facebook and saw Jamie had captioned it:

Great night @Laurie. Though not sure if I should be thanking you or hating you for this hangover 😊

With morning bedhead, in an old T-shirt and with a light cranial throbbing from the martinis, Laurie appreciated the staged glamour of the picture all the more. They did look like a pair of celebrities, of their own invention. Jamie's post production tinkering had given it a sheen, an Oscars after party atmosphere. Laurie didn't really look like that creature who was standing in for her, she wasn't living that life. But what mattered was everyone else thought she was. One big game of bluff.

She scanned the comments, forgetting that it being Jamie's post meant most of them were strangers to her.

Looking good, sir

Wow great shot. Like an Armani advert.
Where is this?

You look like the Stark who had his throat cut in the Red
Wedding in Game of Thrones. *And she looks like the*
Dragon woman's handmaiden Missandei. i.e. both fit

♥ *She's beautiful, who's this Jamie?*

Well played, woof 👆

The name's Carter, Jamie Carter

Woah! Exotic totty!

Jamie had replied to the last saying: 'Laurie is from Hebden Bridge, surely even you've been to Yorkshire, Dave.' Since his not being sure of her name, she noticed Jamie had been very attentive to any detail she offered, and it was a neat way to point up the micro-aggression without going full attack dog.

There were tons of Likes, eighty-five in total, Bharat among them, and Dan's sister Ruth had commented:

Great to see you looking so well, Laurie!
Wowsers x

Laurie didn't see that coming. She hit reply and typed a thank you. She'd always liked Ruth, but since Dan's mum took Dan's side, she'd assumed Ruth had done the same and their obligatory 'sorry to hear' 'I'm fine thanks for asking' text exchange had been friendly but fairly economical on both sides.

What did Dan think? Had he seen it?

From her busy WhatsApp to the half dozen texts, she could see the required splash had been made. And the shamelessness of these inquiries: people she never spoke to who hadn't got in touch to say *sorry to hear about you and Dan*, now eagerly fishing.

Laurie only replied to two people directly: Jamie, to reassure him the wording was fine, and Bharat.

Bharat
WTAF YOU DARK HORSE WHAT THE HELL AM I SEEING?!
Jamie Carter?!

Laurie
He asked me out and I thought: why the hell not 😊

Bharat
This guy is a stealth bomber, I'll give him that. I'm probably
going to catch him with my mum next time I go home

Laurie
THANKS BHAZ I'm the second to last woman on earth you'd
expect him to show an interest in

Bharat
NO NO NO NO. I didn't know you were ready, that's all. Glad you're having fun. You look TOTAL FIRE. WTF THE HAIR?? Gossip tomorrow please xxx

Laurie couldn't deal with the agitation caused by the constant ping-ping-ping of new comments and likes and queries. Jamie inhabited a different online world to her, a busy, interactive one, in fact the man seemed to be a social hub, and Laurie found it overwhelming.

As the thread underneath wore on, friends outright asked if he and Laurie were 'an item', and Jamie replied 'early days', with a smiley emoji, and 'if I'm lucky' to another. He and Laurie agreed in hasty further messages, finessing their approach, that vague, non-committal positivity was the best bluster. Goodness, it felt odd.

He was right about the mixed messaging stimulating more fuss, as everyone tried to figure out if what seemed like an announcement, actually was one.

After a twitchy morning, Laurie found herself irresistibly drawn to putting on her tracksuit trousers, finding an old Couch To 5k app on her phone, and plodding round the streets, warily at first.

She could only tolerate so much of the female voice instructing her to now walk briskly for TWO MINUTES before she switched the app off, turned her music up and ran for herself, until the pace and the pounding of blood and the impact of her feet on the pavement was the only thing that existed.

Laurie ignored shouts from a car full of lads, dodged round pushchairs and urged herself onwards, and as she arrived back home, feeling exultant, thought: this is why Dan used it as springboard for leaving her. She felt ready to fight a polar bear. Unfortunately it also put Laurie in mind of what it readied Dan for. She got a flash image of grunting and pumping and wanted to die.

Was he going to ruin everything for her? It was hard to feel anywhere was her space when they were colleagues.

Laurie peeled off her clothes to shower, watching herself in the mirror, and thought of Jamie's lairy mate calling her *exotic totty*. What a sham, a long con job made of shapewear and filters. She didn't feel either exotic or like totty, she felt like a woman from Yorkshire in her late thirties with soft, malleable, untended parts, some of which were silvered with stretchmarks, and with unruly hair down there that definitely wasn't sculpted into a martini glass shape.

She'd never put her naked form to any particular objective test of desirability because she was desired by Dan. She put her hands over her breasts and hoiked them up an inch: was that where they should be? Was that where they used to be? Laurie honestly couldn't remember. If she asked Dan this sort of thing, as erotic memory keeper, he'd make a joke and then usually lunge and grapple with her.

Laurie hadn't considered herself as being defined by what any man thought of her and yet there was no denying that her body, unwanted by her lifelong partner, felt like a body she had to reassess, and own for herself again.

The thought of being exposed in front of someone else of

the opposite sex provoked abject terror, yet it was that or lifelong celibacy.

Last time Emily had shown her Tinder it was full of men called things like Kev and Daz sitting naked in hotel bidets, swigging from bottles of Peroni, declaring their 'massive love for the sesh'.

Maybe Keanu Reeves films and a vibrator would be preferable, Laurie thought, turning the water on.

20

'Morning!' Laurie said, cheerfully, power-walking up the stairs on Monday, as the two receptionists present, Jan and Katy, both detained by phone calls, almost screeched with disappointment that they couldn't bang down the receivers fast enough to commence interrogation.

It was also possible their round eyes and look of fascination was due to Laurie's change of image. She'd pulled Honey's curly hairdo up into a ponytail but it was still far more bushy than her usual more severe style. As Laurie had fretted about being conspicuous, she wondered if her mum had a point, back at school, that she could allow. Laurie's afro curls weren't a crass bid for attention, they were genetics, and yet she flattened them to move less observed in a mostly white world. To fit in. How much of her existence had been about trying – with varied success – to fit in? To keep her head down?

'Morning, team,' Laurie said heartily to Bharat and Di, and Bharat said, 'Oh here she is, whoring her way to her desk as if she's not Manchester's most notorious slut. Careful she doesn't try to shag you on her way past, Di!'

'Things have come to a pretty pass when a woman can't go for five mojitos, two toots of coke, a bump of ket and a game of strip Boggle in The Britannia Hotel without being called loose any more,' Laurie said as Bharat chortled. 'Honestly, you make one sex tape with a girthy dildo . . .'

'Bit harsh to call Jamie Carter a girthy dildo but you know him best I guess,' Bharat said.

Laurie and Bharat honked, and Di looked stunned. How many years had she sat opposite Laurie, and the biggest scandal Laurie had ever offered was admitting she'd never seen *X Factor*.

All three of them started at the sudden sight of Dan in the doorway. He was wearing that pale pink shirt of his she always liked. Laurie felt oddly pleased with the optics of him interrupting at that moment, because she'd been doing proper corpsing laughter. Dan shot Laurie a direct, purposeful look she couldn't decipher.

'Uh, do you have Mick's sixtieth collection?'

'Oh, yeah . . .' Bharat rifled through his trays in a tense silence and handed over an A4 brown envelope, baggy at one end with coins. Laurie's heart pounded.

'Ta.' Dan promptly departed and they all did a 'hmm mm' throat clearing at one another, as a way of communicating *not sure what that was* without saying so, in so many words.

It was a condition check, Laurie decided, a way of letting her know he'd seen the picture and wasn't going to react.

But, this was the first time since they broke up that he'd found a pretext to visit her desk, so given actions spoke louder than (barely any) words, it had backfired.

Having run the gauntlet and survived, Laurie was feeling almost smug, until the first loo break of the morning ran her slap-bang into Kerry as she exited the cubicle. A one-woman gauntlet.

'Oh, hello you. Belle of the ball. Apple of daddy's eye.' Laurie had long suspected Mr Salter's fondness for her made her especially problematic to Kerry. Kerry's snaky, wry tone always implied she'd caught you up to something, and was deciding whether or not to dob you in for it. It was very Lauren Bacall, the same delivery as: *You know how to whistle, don't you, Steve?*

'Your selfie with Jamie Carter is the talk of the office. Are you seeing each other?'

'Haaah,' Laurie washed her hands, 'Thought it might be. He asked me out and I thought it'd be fun.'

'Out for a drink, then? Nothing more happen?' Kerry said, running a lipstick round her mouth, eyes moving to the side to catch Laurie's expression.

'Bit personal!' Laurie said, in what she hoped was a jolly way. 'How was your weekend?'

'Hmm,' Kerry said, capping the tube as if she'd not heard, or the question was rhetorical.

Laurie wished she'd rehearsed this more, had her tactics more finely worked out. She'd been reckless. The plan went 1. Post Photo 2. Bullshit that she and Jamie were involved.

There was a lot of grey area, and now she'd made an enemy of Kerry by not preparing a fob off when directly asked if they'd slept together. It was utterly outrageous Kerry felt entitled to know this of course, but these were the unofficial rules of Salter & Rowson. Kerry either got what she wanted from you or she spin-doctored her way around and made life a misery. She Peter Mandelson-ed you the fuck up.

At lunchtime, Laurie received a WhatsApp from Bharat to meet her at Starbucks, and she suspected if he wouldn't risk saying it on premises, it was nothing to be pleased about.

Laurie was right.

As they queued, Bharat said:

'Kerry's telling everyone that this was clearly a totally contrived stunt to make Dan jealous and you and Jamie Carter can't possibly be seeing each other.' This tacit support from Bharat was a kindness; it was always accepted that you needed to know what line Kerry was pushing about you, to push back on it.

Laurie gulped.

'What a cow! Why on earth wouldn't it be true?'

Laurie knew Bharat would accept Laurie's word over Kerry's as a point of honour, and felt both glad and guilty. Laurie had already spun him the line that she was deliberately doing things that felt out of character – broadly true – and threw the bonding-in-lift incident in, relieved that wasn't an invention.

'Timing too quick, and that you dodged saying if you'd gone home with him. *She doesn't want to lie, but she wants to make us all think something happened. Laurie is not a natural liar.*'

'As if I'm going to tell her!'

'I know. She said it's totally out of character for you, you're too "straight-edged" to go for a man like Carter, and we all know you're still in bits over Dan. I quote: "one hundred per cent set up, including the Toni & Guy, Sasha Fierce do."'

Laurie flinched.

'Anyway, she's stirred the cauldron good and proper and even taken it upon herself to tell Dan he obviously provoked this, and that you must be in a real state to go this far.'

Laurie cringed again, and cursed Kerry.

'What an ultra bitch.'

She was badly needled, like everyone was laughing at her. That she couldn't see herself the way others so plainly did.

Kerry could find anyone's weak spot; it was her superpower. Somehow she'd immediately identified that the worst things for Laurie would be pointing up the implausibility of her as Jamie's paramour, and the humiliation of her ex thinking it was for his benefit.

'How dare she,' Laurie said, as they left, holding cups bearing the names LORI and BAWAT. 'And my hair wasn't Toni & Guy!'

'That was the biggest burn of all,' Bharat agreed. 'My friend Jessie you met was given the worst time there, she came out looking like Rod Stewart. Not even Faces Rod, Nana Hair Rod.'

'I don't think I've met Jessie?'

'Yeah you did. Her sister was the practice nurse in Alderley Edge who gave one of the Spice Girls her abnormal smear test remember? Forget which one. It was fine, she only needed some pre-cancerous cells lasered.'

Laurie guffawed, 'What a bio!' and then, 'Thank you, Bharat, somehow you always lighten the mood.'

'Like the NYPD, I protect and serve.'

★

Laurie had seen a case on the whiteboard for this afternoon, with the initials JC next to it. She'd heard Michael and others mutter that because he shared them with Jesus Christ, he thought he was the Second Coming.

If she got to the mags court before the hour, she could possibly intercept Jamie outside without anyone seeing. This conversation was too involved for WhatsApp. She timed it right as he was ten paces ahead of her on the pavement the whole way, talking into his phone for much of it.

'Jamie,' she said, pouncing on him as he put his phone in his pocket.

Laurie glanced around to check they weren't being observed and motioned for him to duck round the side of the building with her.

Laurie was slightly out of breath, skin still warm with not only the exertion of tracking him, but prickling shame at Kerry's cruelties.

'It's over,' she said, urgently, under her breath. 'Kerry is going round saying it's obviously fake and a ploy to get back at Dan.'

Jamie shrugged. 'And?'

'And, we've been made. Or I have. They're not going to buy the idea we're together.'

'This is to be expected, as they get their heads round it.'

'Why would they change their minds?'

'You keep saying they, plural. This is Kerry. Kerry gonna Kerry. Why do you care what she thinks?'

'Uh, I thought *what people think* was the whole point of this? Why else are we doing it?'

'Kerry is one person, and someone everyone knows is about as reliable a news source as the *Daily Star*,' Jamie said. 'Let her say what she wants. It's more fuel thrown onto the fire, which we have set.'

'But if it's out there, the idea that it's not real and it's for Dan's sake, from now on I look stupid!'

'Will you calm down?' Jamie said. 'You don't look stupid. We carry on. The plan is the plan.'

Being told to calm down made Laurie feel even more foolish.

'This has fallen at the first hurdle. It's simply not plausible. God, the last thing I wanted was for people to think I am in such a mess over Dan I'd do this.'

'Your sensitivity over his reaction is clouding your judgement,' Jamie said, frowning. 'Absolutely nothing's changed. See it from the outside, beyond Salter & Rowson's microclimate. The idea it's impossible two single people in their thirties who work in the same office might be dating – it's not "out there", is it? It's not "persuading people that 9/11 was an inside job" level of buy in?'

Laurie could see how exasperated Jamie was with her. Someone so ambitious and confident probably had low tolerance for what he perceived as weak nerves and cowardice.

'You only want to press on because it might get you a juicy promotion!'

'No shit, that's why I'm doing this? Not much of a gotcha, is it? It doesn't make my analysis wrong.'

Laurie was silent.

'OK, look,' Jamie rubbed the bridge of his nose, moving

his Clark Kent glasses upwards, and Laurie suspected he was regretting it too, whatever he said, 'If you drop it now, Kerry has won, because if it stays a one-off then it *will* look like a stunt. Carry on, and she looks more and more wrong. Which'll it be?'

Laurie had no comeback. He was right.

'. . . OK,' she shrugged, in defeat.

There was a pause as they prepared to part.

'Do you wear glasses?' Laurie adjusted the files she was carrying.

'Uh?' Jamie pointed at them, on his face.

'I mean sometimes you're in them and sometimes you're not.'

'Have you heard of long sighted and short sightedness?'

'Yes, but I can't work out which you have.'

'Is this relevant in some way I'm not grasping?' Jamie said, testily.

'It's not relevant. I'm being nosy.' Laurie smiled. 'I'm meant to know stuff about you, now we're going out.'

'They're clear,' he said, through gritted teeth.

'Clear? As in no lenses?'

'Yes.'

'So why wear them?'

Jamie turned his head up to the heavens briefly. 'When I first started going to court I looked young, OK, and I noticed I got treated differently when I wore them. They're a . . . prop.'

'OK.'

'*Don't* tell anyone at the office please. I will get roasted for it.'

'I will definitely not tell anyone at the office.'

'Thank you.'

'. . . That you do Atticus Finch cosplay! Hahahahoohoo.'

Jamie glowered as Laurie doubled over. She had a feeling no one had ever sent him up like this. Certainly no female. Laurie didn't know why she dared with Jamie, she just knew she did.

'Oh up yours. Great. Right, I've got a murder committal in court nine, going to do that before I do one myself. Catch you later.'

He stalked off, leaving Laurie wiping her eyes, not sure if she should regret her mockery.

When Laurie's WhatsApp pinged at five p.m., she expected Jamie to be saying *you know what, maybe you're right, let's leave it.*

Jamie
Big guns: why don't we do dinner at The French? The French is spendy, it would say: we mean this. If we go at an awkward time like 6 or 9.30, I bet we could get a last-minute booking. Our photos wouldn't need to point that out of course. Thoughts? J

She noticed she'd forfeited the kiss, however.

Although she'd been the one wanting to can it all, she was relieved he was on board, and being constructive. If she wanted this to work, maybe she should ditch her passivity in the process. If the next move was a candle-lit meal . . .?

Laurie

Yes, except . . . The French is more for anniversaries and occasions, I think. Second date, too much pressure, it's not quite plausible. Hawksmoor, perhaps? Steak, cocktails, moody interiors. You can even ask for date night tables when you book.

Thank you, Emily, for that intel. Laurie felt clued up and relevant for a change.

Jamie

YES. Good thinking. I will book for Friday? x

Laurie replied in the affirmative. The kiss was back, the game was once more afoot and Laurie realised, Jamie was right (albeit probably for the wrong reasons). Time to screw her courage to the sticking place, and stick it to everyone.

21

Laurie had been to Hawksmoor a year back for Dan's birthday, and if anyone had told her the circumstances under which she'd return, she'd have said: are you high on hallucinogens? Is that not a vision of my future, but an episode of *Black Mirror*?

She really took to Hawksmoor, it was her kind of place: the dark Victorian tiles and white lanterns, the gloaming, felt like starring in a bloodthirsty period piece with Tom Hardy in a Bill Sykes hat. And nothing sorted out imbibing to excess like a steak the size of a mattress. 'The cow gets the hangover, not you, it's brilliant,' she'd told Dan, who'd said 'ewwwww'.

She'd dug out a respectable if two-year-old navy pencil dress, put up her hair, done her own make-up this time – if she and Jamie were doing weekly dates, she wasn't going to make Ivy levels of effort on the regular.

Laurie was seated in the bar with something strong and marmalade-flavoured, tapping her foot to New Order's 'True Faith', when Jamie messaged to say he'd been detained by a domestic crisis. He wasn't a man who one pictured having either domesticity or crises. She snickered to herself, lifting

197

the glass to her lips, imagining one of the torches had puttered out in his BDSM dungeon.

He arrived twenty minutes later, pale face wind chilled, in a flurry of apologies and Acqua Di Parma and a Paul Smith scarf.

'No worries,' Laurie said, 'The waitress has been over to say they cocked up and had us down for an hour later, so we're in the bar for the meantime anyway.'

Jamie kept apologising and Laurie said, 'It's no issue to sit here with a drink on my own for half an hour. It's quite nice in fact.'

He looked faintly quizzical at her serenity, so she asked, 'Do the women you usually see get very upset at being on their own somewhere?'

Jamie muttered something.

What a very old-fashioned dynamic for a modern swinger. It might not hurt Jamie to spend time with other grown-ups.

Laurie was going to politely avoid the nature of the domestic crisis, but Jamie volunteered a washing machine overflow.

'You live in the city centre?'

'No, out towards Salford.'

'I totally pictured you in a central flat,' Laurie said, not wanting to say, a shag pad with sheepskin rugs.

'Unfortunately my tyrannical lodger Margaret has her needs, and they include a bedroom of her own, and a garden,' Jamie swiped to open his phone and showed Laurie a picture of a giantly plump tortie with a near-human frown.

'Haha! Oh. I didn't think of you as a cat person at all.'

'I'm not really, I'm a Margaret person. A colleague in

Liverpool found her in a hedge as a kitten and she was living in the office store room until I volunteered. She was the only one in the office I got on with, by the end.'

Laurie thought: *persona non grata in two workplaces, Jamie, I might start to look at the common factor.*

'Yeah Miss Eyebrow Raise, I know you're thinking "oh he pisses everyone off" but it wasn't like that. My ex decided to turn it into Israel and Palestine in terms of who took which side, and eventually pretty much everyone decided the quieter life was on hers.'

'So I guess you could say she did bring peace and unity to the West Bank eventually?'

Jamie almost spat his 'Shaky Pete's Ginger Brew'.

'I'd have preferred a two state solution. You do make me laugh – slash – say the strangest things.'

They beamed at each other, a moment of unadulterated mutual appreciation, the sort of brush with excitement Laurie had forgotten how to feel. Was this some sort of chemistry? Or the marmalade-flavoured intoxicator? She looked away first, taking another sip.

'It's so novel to me to be the talk of the office and have a drama with an ex . . .' Even calling Dan her ex still sounded weird. 'What with us having been going steady since eighteen. He's my only serious boyfriend.'

She presumed Jamie picked up on the implication of serious, she wasn't going to spell it out.

'Wow. Yeah. Can imagine.'

'Can you though? You probably think I should be stuffed and in a museum,' Laurie said, grinning.

'I definitely think you should be stuffed,' Jamie said and then, 'No no no no come on,' as Laurie did a shock-shriek of laughter. 'You made that too easy, rude not for me to take the punchline when offered up. And I don't know why you have this idea that I find different choices to my own so repulsive. They're different choices, that's all.'

'To be fair, you made getting married sound like a Russian prison without the sex, so you're not that accepting.'

God, was he a younger version of her dad? Is this how the oldest swinger in town started out? Ugh, and there was still the wedding reception she'd been trying not to think about to get through. Horrors.

'Haha, sorry yes, I overdid the cynicism that evening. That's spending hours in Salter & Rowson's lift for you. There are long-term relationships I think are great. My mum and dad's. My best mate Hattie and her husband Padraig. But they're few and far between. I'm over thirty, I'm not so arrogant or as optimistic as to think I'm ever going to meet the person I could have that with.'

Laurie nodded. 'Yeah I probably won't again.'

'You will. But I already feel sorry for him, you and your steel-trap mind.'

She laughed. Jamie shook his head.

'You know, the whole romantic comedy staple of The One Who Comes Into Your Life Unexpectedly And Changes Everything. Setting aside that no one's capable of that if you're a grown adult who knows their own mind, why is that a good thing? I don't want to be changed. I like myself as I am.'

'That comes across,' Laurie grinned and he rolled his eyes.

'Another?'

'It's table service.'

'Well I'm running a drink behind and can't wait.'

Chin propped on palm, Laurie watched him lean on the bar, and pondered if she could save up to redecorate her house in the style of Hawksmoor.

A platinum blonde with a bob, in an oyster silk spaghetti strap dress, slid over to Jamie's side. She looked like Michelle Pfeiffer in *Scarface* and had a similar aversion to wearing a bra. Laurie couldn't stop staring. Was she hitting on Jamie . . .?

My God, she *was*, arm draped around his shoulder, speaking closely into his ear, the way her body was angled, Jamie looking simultaneously gratified and vaguely startled. Laurie watched with amused curiosity: would he weasel out of this one, given the contract stipulations?

There was some *sotto voce* chat between them and the woman glanced over. There was some more chat, and the woman did a 'Wow what', jaw drop, and this time really scrutinised Laurie. It was hard to know how to feel when she had no idea what had sparked her interest.

Jamie broke free and came back, set their drinks down.

'Did you get propositioned at the bar?' Laurie said, quietly, awestruck.

'Er. Yeah,' Jamie said, bashful and maybe a little bit proud.

'Oh my God.' Laurie didn't want to inflate an already healthy ego but this felt like going on safari to her.

'But . . . how do . . . creatures of the night know each other? How do you tell each other is one, like the Freemasons? You could've been here with your wife; I could be your wife.

201

I could be barrelling over there, handbag flying. Or you could be gay.'

Jamie laughed.

'For the most part, especially if you're a woman approaching a man, you're pretty sure even if you get rebuffed that the person will be flattered. Also, I can't let you go on thinking I'm a God. While I have had a cold approach in my time, that wasn't one. That's Kirsten, I know her from a while back. She was dating a friend of mine at the time.'

'What did you say just now?'

'That I was here on a date.'

'That was enough to put her off?'

'Yup. Well. Apart from . . .' Jamie leaned in and whispered, 'She offered for you to join in.'

Laurie sucked in her breath and looked over. 'And when she was dating your friend, you . . .?!'

Jamie shook his head rapidly: 'My male friend! Male. No thank you.'

'She looks like normal people. All the while. Soliciting threesomes.'

Laurie thought for a moment. 'But you said something else to her? Something that made her go "Oh my!" and look at me like I was an extra terrestrial.'

'Did she?' Jamie said, blandly: this was a fob off if ever there was.

'Yes. You said I was a Mormon, or didn't have good hygiene, or something, didn't you?'

'I didn't! I made it clear you wouldn't be interested, and that was that.'

'You said, *she's not a Sex Person*, you know.'

'Sex Person, hahahaha. But no, I didn't.'

'You didn't tell her we weren't really dating?'

'No! That's verboten. We agreed?'

'Absolutely.' Laurie nodded, feeling a twinge of hypocrisy, though what risk was Emily?

'If it isn't bad, why don't you tell me?'

'Argh! You're in the right job you know that? The witness requests a glass of water.'

'Denied, the witness can have a drink of water, Your Honour, when he answers the question as clearly stated.'

'I told her . . .' Jamie paused. 'I said I don't want to share you. That's what I said.'

'Oh,' Laurie said.

A look passed between them and Laurie felt . . . unusual. Despite knowing it was fiction created for a purpose, she felt a flicker in her stomach. Then returned herself to reality:

'She was that shocked at the idea you might be dabbling in fidelity?'

Jamie shrugged and changed the subject.

Something tweaked at Laurie about it, something she still didn't understand, and as they were being shown to their table, she realised what it was.

If what Jamie said was merely created to brush Kirsten off, why was he reluctant to tell her?

After Dan and Laurie got together, they used to blow student loan cash on dinners à deux. What Laurie remembered was going wild at the Pizza Hut as-much-as-you-can-eat salad bar, and being so smitten and full of chemicals, her stomach like a balloon knot, she could only pick at it. A twelve-inch stuffed crust pepperoni would appear to be the size of the Isle of Wight and anyway, she didn't want to do something as unsexy as masticate it in front of her new obsession. There were a lot of doggy bags in her halls of residence fridge. Dan thought that Laurie had a birdlike appetite for the first year they were together. (His scoffing ability was unaffected, however.)

By contrast, the benefit of not being on a real second date with Jamie Carter, or high on the natural drug of infatuation, was that Laurie was more than able to do justice to a shared T-bone steak, bone marrow gravy, dripping fries, cheesy mash and creamed spinach, after Jamie had taken the obligatory photographs. This was the squarest meal she'd had since the break-up, and she'd returned to the fray with gusto.

'I can't look at another chip without crying,' Jamie said, after twenty-five minutes.

'Quitter. Wouldn't want you fighting alongside me in any war.' She shovelled them over on to her plate.

'I'm trying to work out what evidence we produce from this evening,' Jamie said. 'As a stern critic of my own work, I think The Ivy was a trifle obvious, a bit on the nose. I shouldn't have gone Facebook, I never do Facebook, really. This one will be strictly for Instagram.'

Laurie nodded. 'You know best.'

'But, I'm still worried that another selfie is a bit . . . meh. And labouring the point. It doesn't feel genuine. You know?'

Laurie rubbed her hands on her napkin. 'Not really, being a grandma with all this.'

'You'd be so good at it though. You're photogenic, and witty.'

Laurie beamed. She'd take it.

He found no further inspiration by the time the bill came, and said in dismay, 'I'll put our posh Harvester dinner on an Instagram story but other than that, I got nothing. I can't tag you in it as you're not on Instagram, but I will hint you were there in the caption.'

'Imagine if we'd known this would be adulthood.'

As they walked away from the restaurant, two girls in front of them were giggling and holding a phone up, shivering bare legs going knock-kneed in the cold.

'Hang on . . . hang on. I've got it, I've got the idea,' Jamie said, in a low voice. 'I'm pretty sure we're in the background of their photos.'

He drew Laurie a few steps forward and discreetly checked where the girls were again. 'OK, put your hand over my hand.'

Jamie placed it on Laurie's cheekbone, pulling her in and cupping her face as if in adoration or about to kiss, lowering his gaze as he did so. Laurie almost snorted but Jamie hissed: 'Hand, now!' Laurie put her palm over his, feeling distinctly foolish.

Seconds later and Jamie was being unspeakably charming to the two girls – who he thought might've inadvertently snapped him and his girlfriend, would they mind if . . .?

They were delighted to AirDrop him the photos and Jamie was as pleased with the results as they were to send them. Laurie squinted. Two happy twenty-somethings, mouths jammy with lipgloss, pouting in the front of the frame. To their rear, Jamie and Laurie, looking to be indeed in what the tabloids would term a clinch.

Props to his artistic direction – it was a very Richard Curtis pose, like Bridget Jones with Mark Darcy in the snow. It invited you to imagine what might have been said seconds before, and what might happen seconds after.

Laurie remembered a film and director guy they'd met at a party of Upwardly Mobiles in Chorlton who said that 'what works on screen can be too much in the room' and that 'Michael Caine is like a ship's foghorn!'– the same seemed to apply here. The face clasping had seemed very 'swelling strings' and purple in real life, but on the phone screen, it looked like an authentic private moment. Jamie's look of passion, Laurie's hand over his, so affectionate and natural. Laurie made a note to never, ever trust photographs posted online. They could be as designed and stage-managed as much as any political poster.

'No need to praise me to the skies for this gonzo BRILLIANCE,' Jamie said, almost hugging himself with glee. He skimmed through filter options, turned the light up on it so Jamie and Laurie were more distinct, and posted it to his Instagram. He flashed his screen at Laurie. She read the caption.

'When you accidentally photo-bomb someone's birthday but they're nice enough to give you the evidence. Happy twenty-first, Madeleine!'

Jamie was fizzing.

'It's perfect. No one's going to guess we saw them taking the selfies and manoeuvred ourselves into it, even if they were sceptical of The Ivy shot. It's too high concept. They'll apply the simplest explanation, and for once, Occam's Razor is wrong.'

'You call me a natural lawyer but you're no slouch yourself.' When Laurie got in, her phone blipped.

Jamie
You know how you thought this was a washout and no one would believe we were seeing each other?

Laurie
Yes

Jamie
A recently joined Instagram user, with no photos posted yet, who doesn't follow me - one 'Dan Price Mcr' - watched my story with the Hawksmoor food. So you officially have his attention. Enough to set up a stalking account.

Laurie
OMG. But . . . why did he use his real name, if he knew you'd see his name?

Jamie
If he's new to Insta my guess is he doesn't realise Stories aren't like posts on your general profile, you can see who's looked at them. It won't be his finest minutes on Earth when he realises . . . x

Laurie went to bed with an increased heart rate, mind whirring. She had been scared she could no longer win Dan's attention, so much so she'd not forecast how she'd feel, knowing for sure she had it. It was unexpectedly daunting.

Lying in bed, she wondered once more how they'd got to this point.

She and Dan had had a good origins story, and they were often prompted to tell it for new arrivals at any Chorlton parties they went to.

It was Fresher's Week at Liverpool, and Laurie was so homesick she'd cried herself to sleep every night, pasting on bravado every day, along with her Rimmel Lasting Finish in Mauve Max.

She could remember with total clarity how it felt, as if everyone else had been introduced on some other occasion and were right in the flow of it, while she ached with insecurity and inadequacy. No one else, she was sure, felt the way she did. And what *were* they doing?

Laurie was a virgin, she'd never taken drugs unless you counted weed, which came to an abrupt end after a terrible whitey at Dean Pollock's house when she was sixteen. She secretly didn't really like how beer tasted, or want to get paralytic, or swallow pills: she was sure she'd end up the cautionary misadventure story with her inquest reported in the *Daily Mail*.

She had been Saffy to her mum's Eddy in *Ab Fab*, what did a Saffy do as a student?

That Friday night, Laurie was in the eye of the storm in a rowdy barn called Bar CaVa. It catered exotically foul flavoured shots to the undergraduate population, and was the place you went to pre load before getting even more steaming at second or third locations.

She was in a Pixies T-shirt and jeans, hair in ironic school-girl plaits (she was in the student mode of immediately glomming on to the things she would have scorned and rejected back home, including hankering after the batty flavour combinations in her mum's vegetarian cooking). She was with a bunch of girls she met in halls who seemed quite loud, posh and not much her thing: two of them were discussing joining the hockey club.

Laurie was vaguely aware of a group of lads in fancy dress for some Rag Week stunt in the corner of the room but didn't pay them any heed until a girl with long straight brown hair tumbled to the floor, dramatically pissed. The lads dashed over to help her up.

'She needs to be taken home,' said an Austin Powers, through false teeth. 'Where are you staying?'

The petite girl, like a rag doll, looked to be mumbling, indistinctly.

Laurie's ears pricked up at 'be taken home'. There was no way she was letting someone who'd lost her motor functions be carried out of here by a load of men who Laurie would be unable to identify in an ID parade. She had not started her law degree, and yet with her innate fiery sense of right and wrong and moral duty, she suspected she might be a good fit for it.

'She's spannered, leave her,' said a Zorro, after they propped the girl upright in a seat. You could just about imagine she was OK if you didn't notice her eyes were closed, like the corpse in *Weekend At Bernie's*.

'We can't leave her like this,' said a Hot Dog. 'Where are her friends?'

They gingerly poked around in a purse that was attached to the drunk girl's wrist by a small loop of leather, and found a halls of residence card.

'Here's her room number,' said Zorro.

At this, Laurie swigged the last of her drink and approached. 'Hi. I don't know her, but might be better for me to take her home?'

'Hell-LOH!' said Austin Powers, truly inhabiting the role. 'I can't speak for her but I wouldn't mind you taking me home.'

'Hi,' said Hot Dog. 'And thank you.'

'I'm Laurie,' she said, feeling uncharacteristically confident.

'Lorry? As in haulage?' said Zorro.

'L-A-U-R-I-E.'

'What a great name,' Hot Dog said. 'It would be much, much better if you'd take her, thank you so much.'

'No problem.' Laurie squatted down to level of Drunk Girl. Drunk Girl appeared to briefly focus on her and gave her a sloppy little grin.

'Harro,' she slurred. 'You look nice.'

'Thank you.' Laurie grinned back. 'Let's get you home, eh? More fun to be sick in your own bed than here.' She hoisted her up, wrapping her arm around her tiny frame, and prepared to exit Bar CaVa.

'Here's her halls card,' Hot Dog said, handing it over. 'Thank you.'

Laurie read the name on the card. EMILY CLARKE.

She noticed Hot Dog had kind eyes. In fact, he had eyes with so much personality, they could blaze out of a hot dog costume. They focused on her intently. You didn't see that every day. You didn't expect to get sex looks from a foam sausage.

'Thank you, really,' Hot Dog said. Can I get in touch with you? Find out if she's OK?'

Even though his concern was supposedly for Drunk Girl, Laurie knew it wasn't her he was chiefly interested in.

Laurie found a lip liner pencil in her bag and wrote her room number and halls on Hot Dog's proffered hand. Swapping mobile numbers would've made more sense, but they were away from home, playing roles in a realm where normal rules didn't apply. Laurie was almost self-consciously acting a filmic moment, to be quirky, to be a manic Pixies-liking black girl. And Dan later admitted: 'Can I have your phone number?' was too obviously hitting on her.

It was so easy, that was what Laurie remembered. This funny, cute Welsh lad with a slight lisp and a dry wit was everything she didn't know she wanted until that moment. They couldn't stop smiling at each other because it was so right, and they both knew it.

Over the next month, Laurie lost her virginity, discovering sex wasn't that big a deal when you found someone you wanted to do it with; who liked you as much as you liked them, who was exhilarated and terrified about passing that milestone as you were.

And she'd made a fast friend in Emily, the drunken wraith she'd rescued.

It was all good things turning up at once, and Laurie felt her life had finally taken off.

One day, lolling on her bed in the Amsterdam-window red light cast by the thick orange curtains in her halls room, a lovestruck Dan was discussing infidelity. They both recoiled from the idea, that they would ever break the sacred covenant between them. It was unthinkable. They were Romeo and Juliet without the balcony, the warring dynasties or the suicide misunderstanding. They'd had whispered conversations in the dark about the future, they both *knew* this was it.

'Let's promise each other, here and now,' Dan said, putting out his hand for Laurie to shake. 'Let's pledge that if either of us even *thinks* about being unfaithful, we tell the other one, before it can start. That way neither of us ever have to worry. Complete and total honesty.'

The improbability they were ever going to do it made the sweetness of explicitly pledging all the greater. Laurie shook his hand, and they kissed.

She felt like laughing, remembering that now. The way life was so simple to kids in love. Find the right person, promise not to cheat on them. It's not difficult! They were never going to make the strange, tawdry messes their parents' generation had. The idea their parents had once felt the way they did, hadn't occurred to them. Eugh.

Dan stalking Jamie's online presence: it was a tiny glimmer of being wanted by him again, and Laurie craved it like a drug.

22

'How can you think it's real when you're not a toothless crone in the Middle Ages? I'm reading from Wikipedia here *it has no scientific validity or explanatory power,*' Bharat said.

'See, they can't explain it!' Di said.

'No you div, it means astrology can't explain anything.'

'Then how do you explain star signs describing people perfectly? My sister is a completely typical Pisces, dreamy and creative. I am a classic Virgo.'

'Credulous?'

They were doing an old favourite, running through a Bharat and Di greatest hit. In its familiarity, Laurie was finding it as relaxing as pan pipes in a birthing suite, although perhaps the analogy was unwise and a bout of unmedicated searing pain was also on the way.

The mood on Monday at Salter & Rowson Towers was decidedly different, Laurie noticed. Lots of lines of sight resting upon her, more frantic whispering, conversations that happened to end as she neared them. There was a noticeable tension, like the hush of expectation when you walk into a room prior to public speaking.

Jamie was correct: if the Ivy photo had set everyone wondering, the Hawksmoor shot had convinced them. Now the gossip wasn't *if* she and Jamie were sleeping together, it was that they were.

As Laurie grabbed some paperwork from the criminal office, Michael intercepted her.

'Can I have a quick word?' he said, briskly leading Laurie to a store cupboard which was known colloquially as Churchill's War Rooms, given it was solely used for hatching plots, strategic planning, and arguments too vicious or sensitive for the shop floor. And storage. It smelled of cardboard, and a newly fitted carpet.

After the door clicked shut, Michael turned to her. 'You're hanging out with Jamie Carter, I hear?' putting an emphasis on *hanging out* that made it sound impossibly obscene.

'Yes . . .?'

He exhaled in disbelief and disgust at the confirmation, hands on hips, shaking his head. Laurie got the feeling he had to get himself steady before he could speak.

'This is a very poor judgement call, and the last thing I expected from you. I know Dan has hurt you, but this is . . .' Michael trailed off. 'Jesus, really? Him?'

Laurie shrugged. 'It's only a casual thing.'

'I would've asked you for a drink if I thought you were ready. I'm sure a lot of guys here would've. But it was what, first come first served?'

Laurie's eyes widened and she took a sharp breath at this

insult: the entitlement, the sense of ownership. The idea she had no right to have sex with someone else, when Michael had been on the waiting list longer.

'You *what*?'

'I'm struggling to see why else you'd choose Carter.'

'Er . . . Because he's fit?'

'He's *fit*? Are you seventeen? And without moral compass? C'mon, Loz! Who body-swapped you?'

Laurie snorted.

If Michael was in All Bar One, if this was a fair fight, she'd give him verbals that would stop short of a knee in the crotch. But this wasn't quite so easy. Michael was tacitly wielding the only power over Laurie that he had – the threat of becoming an enemy who would do her unspecified harms within Salter & Rowson. As with Kerry, she had to tread carefully, swallowing down the urge to tell him to fuck off.

'I wasn't aware I needed your sign-off before I could start seeing someone,' Laurie said, calmly.

'This isn't *someone*, Lozza, this is Jamie fucking Carter. He's a rattlesnake. He's ricin. He's the kind of enemy you only get rid of by pushing him over the Reichenbach Falls. Do you know what the lads are saying? They're saying they don't want to discuss cases with you in case it turns into pillow talk. You know everyone's always liked you and trusted you, but that's going to change if you don't wise up. Fast.'

Laurie folded her arms and looked at the floor. Some part of her had known this was coming. She'd always been aware Salter & Rowson was a toxically sexist environment. She only needed to hear the way the men in the criminal department discussed the people they represented, or look at the gender of who answered phones and made coffee, and who got the bonuses and departmental headships.

Laurie had been protected. The counterpart to a senior man; A Nice Girl. But as a single woman, she was fair game for the rough and tumble of such politics. She was – apparently – daring to have carnal relations with a male the testosterone club didn't like, and that had to be punished.

'What exactly is Jamie supposed to have done to you lot be so hated?'

Michael spluttered, as if this was like asking why Mexicans didn't rate Donald Trump.

'Tell me,' Laurie said. 'All I hear is bitching about his suits being too flash and expensive.'

'I assume we're speaking in confidence,' Michael said, eyes blazing.

'Yes of course,' Laurie snapped. 'I'm still capable of independent thought.'

'When he first turned up and wanted to make his mark, he was a total tosser. He poached loads of Ant's caseload and then badmouthed his work.'

'I thought he was given Ant's caseload, because Ant was off with his Crohn's?'

'Yeah, Ant was off sick and came back to find Jamie Carter's all but taken his job. There's big trials that Ant has prepped for, like the drugs four-hander, and Carter waltzes in, gets two suspended sentences and takes the credit with Statler and Waldorf. Swaggering around like a cock.'

Laurie saw how the trick was worked: the alleged villainy

was entirely subjective, a matter of taste not substance: *waltzing* and *swaggering*. She increasingly suspected Jamie's offence was his refusal to play the popularity game.

'So, essentially, his big misdemeanour is that he efficiently took care of the work he'd been asked to cover?'

Michael's eyes bulged.

'He's really done a number on you, hasn't he? There's a theory, it's a rumour, but – rumblings that he might be going for a partnership. Can you imagine? He's been here five minutes, and tries to get made our boss. The nerve of the little twat.'

'Surely not? He's too young for that.'

Michael appeared to simmer down by a degree, with this remark. Possibly as it implied it was an unfounded rumour, if Laurie wasn't corroborating it.

'Young, dumb and full of . . .' He shot her a revolted, pained look.

Laurie had been vaguely aware that Michael had a soft spot for her, but she had no idea she'd spark this sort of possessiveness.

Unless . . . He had harboured notions. That Laurie might not be interested in him wasn't a factor in his accounting. If she was seeing Jamie, then she must have also been available to Michael, because Michael was the better man. Laurie was property and Michael was an honest broker, who had been sexually gazumped. It was revolting, discovering the antediluvian attitudes and values that lurked just beneath the surface.

'. . . And that's before we get on to him fucking Salter's niece who he was specifically warned not to fuck. Someone saw him in the Principal Hotel with her, so I think we all know how that ended. She was practically a teenager, for God's sake. *That's* who you're dealing with, someone who'll take what he wants, no matter the cost to others.'

Hmmm. Laurie saw them in the bar of this hotel. Had he been seen elsewhere in the building too? Brandishing their key cards? It was hard to tell, as Michael would naturally exaggerate to make it sound more damning.

'I don't think he did anything with her, did he?' Laurie said. It helped she had no real skin in this game – Michael wasn't in control of his emotions, she was.

'Get real, Laurie. Seriously. Of course he did. You think a man like that passes when it's on offer, on a plate, from a young pouting innocent? She was following him around like a schnauzer. And he immediately discards her when he's got what he wanted. Bastard.'

Laurie said nothing. Innocent schnauzer wasn't how Jamie had characterised Eve, but then she might be dealing with two unreliable narrators here. She had a feeling that the less she said, the sooner Michael would run out of steam.

'You're very highly thought of here, you know,' Michael said.

Ah, Laurie thought, now the manipulation changes tack to Good Cop. It was as if she'd never been in a custody suite.

'Thanks.'

'I'm unclear why you'd risk tearing so much down for so little. Carter will have fucked off to some practice in London by next summer and you'll be left picking up the pieces, in more than one way.'

'I thought he was trying to be made partner?'

'You know what I mean. His sort rape and pillage the village, then move on to the next one. He's a plunderer. Why would a smart woman like you want to be another of his meaningless trophies?'

'OK. First of all, no one's raping or pillaging anyone. Secondly, I think you might be way over the line in telling me who I can and can't spend time with, out of work.'

Michael scowled. Laurie had never been into Michael's *vicious archduke in BBC costume drama* type of good looks, and right now she was very glad. She had a suspicion that Michael hated Jamie because he reminded him too much of himself.

'OK, I've tried to warn you, Loz. What can I say. Ditch him now, while you can still repair this. We all know you've been through a tough time and we'd be prepared to chalk it up as an indiscretion, if it stopped now.'

'The Royal we? The whole criminal department gets a veto on my love life?'

'It's not love and it's no life. You heard.'

He threw the door open and stalked off. Laurie spotted the tactics: the flourish of a dramatic exit gave him the upper hand. A 'do as I say or else,' when you didn't want to spell out the 'else'.

Laurie's chest was heaving with indignation, and the things she still wanted to say. Her fingers clenched and unclenched into fists.

Whenever she and Jamie decided to end this, she'd have learned things about other men that she couldn't un-know.

★

Laurie hoped the day would pick up after Michael's counselling session, but in vain.

A district judge in an extremely foul mood gave her city centre bin arsonist a three-month custodial sentence, out in six weeks, after Laurie argued for a suspended one due to it being a first offence for criminal damage and the pigeon not being harmed. He added tartly that 'his counsel would have better spent their time engaging with plausible outcomes than trying to achieve extraordinary things at the expense of reality.'

The prosecutors smirked.

Her client didn't quite follow the language or the argument but he could tell the judge was saying Laurie had fucked up, and he flipped her the finger while the cuffs were being put on. *Yes, yes, it's my fault you tried to 'send a message' with a 'cleansing fire' to the 'consumerist chimpanzees' of the Arndale.*

Laurie messaged Jamie on her way back to tell him about Michael's hostility and didn't expect anything other than a few sympathetically chosen emojis of bells and clowns, so tossed her phone into her bag after sending.

Seconds after she took her seat at her desk, Jamie appeared in the doorway of their office, filling the frame, a hand braced on the door jamb.

'Laurie, you got a minute?'

Bharat and Di both gawped. Not only was he bonking Laurie, he was prepared to approach her desk and speak to her, asking for private audiences! Absolute libertine.

Laurie had already forgotten how ludicrously pretty he was: dark hair against snow white skin, expensive ink blue suit jacket gaping open to a slim midriff, clad in narrow cut, pale blue designer shirt. You could whip out a Nikon and snap him, standing there as he was, and probably win an award.

'Let's not risk the lift, eh,' he said, and they took the stairs, the receptionists watching them pass through the lobby as if Elvis was leaving the building.

When they were at safe distance, Jamie said: 'Michael's been aggro with you?'

'Yes. Pretty much promising me pariah status if I keep seeing you.'

Jamie exhaled. 'This is beyond shit, isn't it? What business is it of his?'

'It's truly warped. Like I should've put myself up for bids in a fair and open democratic process and not selfishly decided who I wanted to date myself. He painted you as borderline sex offender.'

Laurie knew she was being slightly indiscreet but she was rattled, and she wanted Jamie's support. And Michael despising him was hardly unknown to Jamie.

'What a creep.' Jamie shook his head. 'Imagine bullying and intimidating a woman about her choices in her private life and thinking you're the one respecting her. I did warn you he had a thing for you.'

'I didn't think it would turn so *nasty*. He and I have always got on, he knows I'm sound. We've worked together for six or seven years. One photo of me – well, two – looking cosy with you, and boom, all gone.'

'Mmm. Welcome to being outside the circle of trust in this place. It's like *The Revenant* without the snow.'

Laurie smiled. Jamie liked his film references.

'Why does Michael despise you so much?' she asked. Might as well get Jamie's side, which she didn't trust either.

'Oh he's loathed me from the word go. His big mate Anthony Barratt was off, I got given his caseload, and there was loads of stuff missing. I had to ask for documents from the CPS and get an adjournment. I mean he was sick, there's no shame that he dropped the odd ball, but what was I supposed to do? Fuck the cases up and get marks against my name, five minutes after I joined, to spare Ant's dignity?'

'It says too much about this place that I think the answer is "yes". You are describing what they call a team player.'

'Huh. More like a fall guy for their macho bullshit.'

Subservience, that was the word, that was what they demanded from Laurie, from women, but also from Jamie. Maybe he wasn't disgracefully cocky, maybe he'd simply not felt the need to tone down his self-assurance in order to be liked. Which was quite likeable in itself – to thine own self be true.

Laurie combed her memory for any example of Jamie's arrogance and could only come up with instances of him being hard working, and unapologetic about the fact. Which irked people, and to Laurie's chagrin, had irked her too.

The culture here depended so much on playing the game, they'd all ceased to notice that they *were* playing it.

'Shall I have a word?' he added.

'How? I mean . . . Why?'

'In this alt-verse,' Jamie lowered his voice, 'you're my girl-friend, and if a colleague was having a go at my girlfriend, I'd stick up for her. I'm minded to as a mate, anyway.'

'Thanks, but that would send Michael up like a Roman candle. I think we have to tough it out saying as little as we can.'

Jamie nodded.

'Also, the idea Michael has a right to an opinion here full stop, makes me fume.'

'Erm . . .' Jamie looked at the ground and scratched his neck.

'What?'

Seconds later, Dan walked past with another colleague from civil. Catching sight of Laurie and Jamie, Dan boggled, wide-eyed in shock, and looked away.

'Hi,' Jamie said, with a small, polite smile. Neither Dan, or the man he was with, spoke. Full blanking. Laurie didn't acknowledge them, so she wasn't sure she could legally claim blanking.

'If looks could kill, I'd be in the ICU at Manchester Royal right now,' Jamie said.

Laurie gave Jamie a wan smile, heart thumping.

This time, Laurie faced the fact there was no putting the genie back in the lamp. Even if she said SURPRISE, EARLY APRIL FOOL GUYS WE WEREN'T DATING! it wouldn't help matters now.

She'd had a 'fling' with the office scoundrel and that was on her record forever. Dan was perturbed. But not enough to say anything to her. Had she achieved her goal? Was this what she wanted?

'You're OK, though?' Jamie said. 'You're not going to let Michael get to you?'

'Nah,' Laurie said, with a rueful smile.

'Right. Here if you need me,' Jamie said, and squeezed her shoulder. It felt good to have an ally. Then they broke eye contact as it visibly crossed both their minds that this was a moment a real couple might quick-kiss on parting, and Jamie beat a hasty retreat back into the building.

An uncomfortable thought occurred to Laurie, as she returned to her desk – this might benefit Jamie a lot more than her. Jamie's reputation wasn't taking any hit for his liaison with Laurie and he might yet get his name above the door. Laurie, meanwhile, hadn't priced the effect on hers into the policy of upsetting Dan.

What did she have to lose, she'd asked, in devil may care manner. The answer: her good name.

And when she'd said she craved making Dan jealous, she'd omitted a crucial question, one Emily told her she used with her clients: what would success look and feel like to you? ('Expectation management is crucial or they shoot the messenger, every time,' she said. 'That is rule number one. Get them to define it, so the result is provably what they ordered. You'd be amazed how many people aren't careful what they wish for.')

What did she need from this revenge campaign? Laurie knew. She absolutely knew, but because it was so silly, so ugly – given a blameless baby was involved – so desperate and beneath her, she had pushed the thought away. And yet. There it was.

She had to face it directly.

She wanted Dan to want her back.

23

It was half an hour until home time, and Laurie longed for 5.30 p.m. like a long lost lover. She used to routinely work late, but she'd started to honour her official clocking off, to the minute. Who or what was going to stop her?

'She had a *funeral,* for her *cat*?' Bharat said.

'Noodle was twenty!' Di said. Laurie was Team Bharat on matters involving Di's sister Kim, who did appear to be somewhat detached from reality, as a healing crystal proponent and anti vaxxer.

'It doesn't get less ridiculous with each passing year.'

'Noodle was known in the area, she wanted to give people a chance to pay their respects.'

'Were there . . . readings?'

Di pursed her lips. 'A couple of short ones.'

'Hahahaha! Oh my life! Imagine if the neighbours looked over the fence. Oh here I am, having a totally normal one, reciting a passage from Corinthians, over the burial site of a Persian cat.'

The details of the passing of Noodle were interrupted by Kerry.

'Laurie. Mr Salter wants to see you,' she said, wearing malignity and triumph like a heady perfume. 'Are you free now?'

'Oh? Yeah.'

Laurie hard gulped and got up. This was . . . not good. The timing suggested that he'd either heard about Jamie or the arsonist or both, and she was about to face a reckoning. Kerry was animated by an expectant energy that certainly suggested so.

'Go straight through,' Kerry said, with a moue of her mouth, smoothing her pleated skirt under her behind as she sat back down at her desk.

Laurie knocked softly and waited for 'Come in', because Kerry was more than capable of sending Laurie in unannounced like that, to make her look bad.

Mr Salter's office was a strange separate realm, like being in Dumbledore's.

You only ever saw this interior on hiring, firing, promotions or significant bollockings, so it was impossible to disassociate it with quaking fear.

It probably looked a lot like many a provincial law partner's lair – bookcases with deeply boring tomes on Tort, a crystal water decanter, framed photos of privately schooled progeny. Mr Salter had two upright twenty-something identical twin sons, known among the workers as the Winklevosses. Mr Salter himself was a ringer for Bernie Sanders.

'Ah, Laurie, hello,' he said, looking up from papers on his desk, putting down a pricey-looking pen. It remained a status symbol of fully private office space. If Laurie had a solid silver ballpoint, it'd mysteriously go missing within hours. He didn't sound enraged. But then Salter never raised his voice; why would he, when his carefully chosen words could slice you into slivers like sashimi.

'You wanted to see me?'

He gestured for her to sit. Jesus, had Michael been in to see him?

'Yes.' He leaned forward on his desk, arms folded. Mr Salter was about five foot five, so he had a chair that must've been jacked to the highest level so that he could try for a vague looming when you sat opposite.

'Now I want you to understand that everything we are about to say to each other is both entirely confidential and entirely of a voluntary nature. You are not in any trouble.'

'Oh,' Laurie said.

'You sound surprised?' he smiled.

'Hah, well . . . you worry, don't you.'

'What goes on outside these offices is by and large, none of mine or Mr Rowson's business. It only becomes our business if it has any significant bearing on the company's operational ability or reputation.'

'Yes.' *Not quite tallying with what Jamie said, but go on.*

'Yet we also feel we have a duty of pastoral care towards long-standing employees of great value to us. Such as yourself.'

'Thank you.'

'In the spirit of that care, not in feeling we are owed an account – I'm told that you and my head of civil Daniel Price are no longer in a relationship?' He waved at Laurie not to speak yet as she opened her mouth, 'And that yourself and Jamie Carter are now involved. As a boss who would also like to think of himself as a friend . . .'

Woah. Laurie had known she had a 'favourite' status but Salter getting so gooey as to claim himself her friend was, as Bharat would say, some next level shit.

'I'd like to think that you feel you're being treated well by young Mr Carter. I think he's very fortunate if he has secured your affections.'

'Thank you. Yes, very well. He's great and we have a lot in common.' Laurie blathered this off the top of her head as she'd rather die a thousand deaths than say anything to Salter that could be construed as code for rampant boffing.

'Do you?' he said, with a tone that was a real question, not courtesy.

'Yes, we're both very serious about our work . . .' Laurie smiled. 'And equally serious about eating and drinking well at the weekend.'

'Haha! Amen to that.'

Laurie's main point of bonding with Mr Salter when they had to make Christmas party small talk was always his wine cellar, and botched attempts at cooking.

'OK, good. Good. I'd never have put you two together, but if it's working well for both of you, good. You're attending the Christmas party, I hope?'

'Oh yes, absolutely,' Laurie said. Gah.

'Good, good. Well, that was all. Marvellous stuff with the Brandon case.'

'Oh, thank you!' That was a Found Innocent Of All Charges of weeks back.

Laurie beamed as she passed Kerry on her way out, who glared back with barely concealed disappointment and irritation. Hah, Kerry wasn't as clued up as she liked to pretend, then, if she hadn't known that was going to be benign.

Laurie waited until she was leaving for the day to WhatsApp Jamie and say she might've just given him a major boost to his hopes of promotion.

Jamie
Seriously? YOU BEAUTY. Thanks L. Jx

Still glowing, she was stopped in the lobby by the office junior, Jasmine, their trainee legal clerk.

'Are you seeing Jamie Carter?' she said, pushing strands of her long, thin hair out of her moon-like face. She had hunted eyes and a tremulous demeanour that made Laurie worry for her.

'I'm not quite sure you've got the right to ask me that, Jasmine?' Laurie said, taken aback.

'No, sorry. Everyone is talking about that photo of you . . . together.' Jasmine somehow managed to make it sound like it was worthy of Pornhub.

'Well . . . yes,' Laurie said, shrugging.

'I didn't think you liked him?'

'Hah, why?'

'You said he was, uh, untrustworthy. You said he could never be trusted. You said he was like a tom cat that had not been neutered.'

Jasmine sounded as if she was reading a translation from

the original Turkish and Laurie bit back the impulse to shrug: *did I, so what?* as this clearly mattered to Jasmine.

'Ah. Snap judgement I suppose? Don't pay too much attention to me.'

Jasmine's expression spelled confusion and betrayal and she searched Laurie's face intently for something. Oh, no. Laurie realised what Jasmine was searching for – nothing about Laurie, per se, but what specifically Jamie Carter had fallen for. Thanks to Laurie verbalising her antipathy to Jamie, Jasmine's fevered imaginings had never gauged her as a threat, and yet there Laurie was, suddenly by his side.

Poor Jasmine. She had the strained look on her face of the stricken boyband groupie who was about to let out a primordial howl of longing and be wrestled away by burly security.

'He's nice . . . but it's very new,' Laurie said. 'Who knows where it'll go. If anywhere.'

'Oh?' Jasmine said, at first in surprise, and her look of horror deepened. Laurie was messing with Jasmine's future husband and captain of her heart for *nothing serious*, the facetious whore!

What was left to Laurie to say, as comfort?

'I'm sure he'd say the same,' Laurie said.

'Actually, he told Jemma you were the funniest, cleverest person he'd ever met.'

'Aw, did he?' Laurie said, genuinely touched.

'Don't hurt him!' Jasmine said, in a sudden impassioned cry, and rushed out, apparently with 'something in her eye'.

She left a bemused Laurie staring at three receptionists, for whom Christmas had come early.

24

'Strike one, he had empty champagne bottles used as décor in his room,' Emily said. 'Strike two, he has seen Mumford & Sons' – she paused – '*live.*'

'He was unlikely to have seen them dead,' Laurie said, shifting the glacé cherry on the cocktail stick out of the way to drink from her glass of rum and crushed ice.

'More respect if he had, and was holding a dripping cutlass when the police arrived. Strike three, had a tattoo of the Coca-Cola logo. I asked him why and he said it was a private joke about his love of coke. I fucking mean. Rock and roll. Shine on, you crazy diamond. Farewell, Josh. It was like the "financial advisor has it large" starter pack.'

Emily was holding court on her latest Tinder calamity, having organised a night at The Liars Club, a subterranean tiki bar and 'tropical hideaway' of kitsch. It was all uplighters and down-lighters and murals of palm trees on brickwork, and Laurie was sure she was meant to scorn it as naff, but she loved it.

Emily had invited Nadia, her radical feminist, medieval history lecturer friend who always wore a cloche hat and a scowl.

Emily was like this, an effortless collector of people, though not in a status-led or meretricious way. Just as an enthusiast. People seemed to attach themselves to her, as if she was Velcro. Emily had worked on an account at the university and come away with friends in academia.

Dan had met Nadia once and wasn't a fan. 'Like walking directly behind a gritter,' was his view.

'She's a lot,' Emily had said when making this plan. 'Can you cope with her "kill all men" stance at the moment?'

'Cope with it? I welcome it,' Laurie said.

'This is my view,' Nadia said now, after further crimes of Josh being selfish in bed had been enumerated. 'Involvement with a man in our patriarchal society is like expecting homeopathic medicine to cure you. You're not going to get better by taking a tiny dose of the thing that made you sick in the first place.'

Nadia was 'self-loathing straight' according to Emily and tried to resist entanglements on the basis of it conflicting with her politics. Some people – OK, most – would call Nadia a demented fundamentalist, but Laurie rather liked the courage of her conviction.

When Nadia was in the loo, Laurie explained the latest on Project Revenge and that so far, she had not got the twisted pleasure from it that she was supposed to.

'I did try to warn you. You're the wrong fit for this, because you're over-burdened with conscience,' Emily said. 'I'd be cackling while looking into my Disney queen mirror, whispering to my albino pet about it, but that's not you.'

'It's made me wonder if . . .' Laurie paused. 'If I'd still take

Dan back.' It was hard and debasing to admit. Not least as that would now affect an innocent child. Laurie never had a dad around, was she really going to pay that forward?

'Would you?' Emily said.

'I don't know.'

'The point when it's a definite no, that's when you're cured.'

Laurie nodded. She knew that day would come, but she was sure it would feel like pissed-on sizzling ashes and defeat, not closure or jubilation.

'Be honest with me. Was this all written when I didn't chuck him over the one-night stand? Is this my payback for being a walkover?'

'He said it was a horrible mistake and asked for forgiveness and you trusted him. That was a big thing to do. You have to have trust in a relationship, or what's the point?'

Laurie nodded. 'I'm never going to trust on that scale again. One strike, out.' She sounded as vehement as she felt.

It was highly secret, that detail of their past. It was so long buried and unspoken about it, Laurie occasionally forgot it had ever happened at all. Only Emily, and the lads of Hugo's stag do from twelve years ago, knew about it. Well, and Alexandra from Totnes, who had spent a quarter of an hour atop him. It was in a castle in Ireland, and a cadaverous looking Dan had crashed back through the door on Sunday night, wailing to Laurie that he had done something so so so awful. Laurie assumed he'd put a round of aged malts on his credit card. He told her, then promptly ran to the kitchen and vomited in the sink.

Laurie was aghast, hurt, confused. But faced with his abject contrition, his protestations that he'd rather never drink again than do anything like that, it didn't cross her mind it would be the end of them.

Nadia rejoined them.

'Nads I feel as if we are always doing intimate details about my life at the moment, like . . . emotional gynaecology,' Laurie said, high on running, solidarity and Captain Morgan. 'I was asking Emily if I was a massive idiot to forgive Dan a one-night stand on a stag do, ten years ago.'

'Yes,' Nadia said.

Emily gasp-laughed and Laurie just laughed.

Nadia gave a small bewildered smile. Laurie suspected she was used to other women being upset by her, and it was a novelty to be taken straight, in good faith.

'I love your clarity!' Laurie said.

'Would he have forgiven you the same?' Nadia said.

'No. He said he wouldn't have.'

'There's your answer then. Why should you have done?'

Laurie wasn't often stunned into contemplative silence. Dan had played this aspect as hugely romantic – *I couldn't bear it! Ugh, the thought! Kill me now rather than make me think this thought* – and Laurie had taken it as proof that their relationship should be saved. His misstep wasn't the start of: *hey yeah we'll fall off the wagon from time to time, maybe we should make things open*; it reaffirmed they wanted to protect it.

And yet . . . How had Laurie, living in such an outwardly modern, feminist and equal partnership, actually been quite unequal? Dan got his way, pretty much all the time. He didn't give to Laurie what Laurie gave to him. She'd never noticed. She'd thought sassy humour, sharing the chores and her own salary was the whole story.

But they developed roles, and it was Dan as cosseted and indulged tearaway kid to Laurie's doting, responsible adult. She never got to be delinquent.

In this moment, she made herself a promise: in the very unlikely event she found herself in love with anyone again, she'd assert herself. She'd say what she wanted, not endlessly accommodate his needs. If that made her a bitch at any point, so be it. There were no rewards to being a walkover.

'I'm Ubering,' Emily said, outside, phone in hand. 'Donal is one minute away. Ah, here he is!' she said, as the car drew up alongside her. 'Thanks for a great night out, girls. We can't go back to that bar for the time being by the way.'

'What? Why?' Laurie said. 'I liked it there.'

'I've swapped numbers with the barman, Rob, so we need to see how that plays out.' She looked at her phone. 'Sweet Lord, he's messaging me pictures already. Keeno.' Emily made a face. 'Ooh. Filth.'

'What? His . . . thing?' Nadia said.

Emily peered at her screen and swiped. 'Bit of thing, some of the other.'

'Bumhole?' Laurie asked, cheerfully. She was never dating again, simple as that.

'Not bumhole, I mean clothed ones too!'

'How has he taken that during service? He better not have touched my drinks!' Nadia said.

Emily started screeching: 'He's not taken it NOW, has he?!

He's not made off to the men's.' Emily mimed sticking a phone down her leggings.

Laurie held on to the car roof, shaking with laughter.

'I don't know how it works, do I!' Nadia said.

'You are being charged for this time,' Donal the driver said, out of the open window.

25

Jamie

Can I talk to you privately? Vegetarian Pret at 10? It needs to be somewhere we won't be overheard (and no one here's vegetarian, right?) Jx

Laurie

Can't believe you've escaped hearing about Kerry's adventures in veganism with pulled jackfruit burritos, you lucky bastard ☹ Sure, see you there x

An otherwise boring Wednesday, the following week, and Laurie was happy to oblige. Bail application paperwork could wait. When she approached, Jamie was loitering outside in a long coat, looking as if he might pull a bunch of flowers from behind his back. But he wasn't smiling, brow furrowed.

'Alright?'

'I've been better, to be honest,' he said.

'Oh?'

Jamie put a palm to his forehead.

'Oh God, so. This is so awkward.'

'Hah, I've got a pretty thick skin these days. Try me.'

'This is something that puts you on the spot, though,' Jamie said, hands thrust in his pockets, staring at his feet.

'If we need to call the deal off, it's OK, you know. I'm sure between us we can work out a decent excuse that saves both our faces.'

A thought occurred to her: has he been caught with someone else? In a way that everyone will hear about? She really didn't fancy facing the peculiar repercussions that would involve, pretending they were polyamorous.

'The thing is. I've had some bad news.' Jamie looked at her directly. She could see the real pain and difficulty, then, and that it was nothing to do with her. Or not yet.

'My dad called last night. He's got cancer. Gallbladder. It's not curable.'

Jamie's face was stricken, his eyes flat and empty.

'Shit, Jamie, I'm so sorry.'

He nodded and there was a moment they didn't speak.

'He's got a year, maybe eighteen months . . . He doesn't want chemo.'

There was an elastic band tautness to his voice that made it clear the last four words had in fact been a volatile debate, and that was the conclusion.

Laurie nodded and put her hand on Jamie's arm. Then moved it away again.

'It's his sixty-fifth birthday this weekend, back home. He's still having the party. He said: "I can use it to say goodbye to everyone now",' Jamie said, and as he said it, his voice cracked, and Laurie winced slightly for him that he was being forced to show this emotion in front of her, when he clearly didn't want to. Jamie glanced away as he composed himself.

She patted his arm supportively again and Jamie said thickly, 'It's not sunk in, to be honest. I'm walking around that office in a daze.'

'I don't blame you.'

He cleared his throat.

'But my best friend Hattie has helpfully told them about you . . .'

'Ah.'

As with his owning a cat seeming off brand, Laurie didn't see Jamie as a man with a female best friend, somehow; though given his popularity rankings with women versus men she guessed it made sense.

'Yeah. I mean obviously if I throw myself round social media saying I am madly in love, I have to expect some inquiries. She wasn't meant to tell my bloody parents. She's shown them the pictures.' Jamie gritted his teeth. 'Having heard you exist, now they – my mum and dad – are guns blazing that I have to bring you to his do.'

Laurie smiled. '*Ah . . .*'

'My dad's argument was that without his diagnosis, I'd have brought you to meet them sooner or later. He wants this party to be celebratory and sociable and not at all sad, and they're dying to meet you. He actually used those words and said "no pun".' Jamie tried to roll his eyes, swallowing hard with the effort of acting casual, and Laurie's heart went out to him. 'Honestly, I tried to argue against it, but I was floored with the news he'd given me. He even pulled "what if it's my only chance to meet her." What do I say to that?'

Jamie's eyes glittered with the threat of tears, and he blinked. There was a steadying pause.

'You see the quandary,' Jamie said.

'Do you want me to go?'

'Ah God. I'm not sure I could ask you to do that? I'm more setting out the problem. To a smart and sensitive person, who might know what to say to them.'

Laurie was touched.

'If you want me to go, that's cool,' Laurie said, evenly. 'But do you want me to? If you find this too weird then I don't mind figuring something else out.'

Jamie raised his eyebrows, face suffused with surprise.

'I'd *love* you to go, Laurie, and I'd be forever grateful. But are you sure? My parents, a whole weekend? A sixty-fifth birthday, with sausage rolls and "Come On Eileen"?'

'I like sausage rolls and coming on Eileen,' Laurie said, and she hadn't meant to be bawdy but accepted Jamie's laughter as if she had intended it.

'This is so kind. I'd be forever in your debt, to be honest,' Jamie said.

'Don't worry about it,' Laurie said. '. . . If they've seen photos, they know I'm black? They're fine with that?'

Jamie did a small double-take. 'Yeah. They're not racist?'

'Sorry, not saying they are, but still worth checking. I've had some funny moments in job interviews and meeting friends' parents in my time. "But your name sounds English," and so on.'

'God,' Jamie said. 'No, it's fine. Obviously.'

Laurie nodded. He meant well, but it wasn't an 'obviously': she had learned not to take acceptance for granted, but now wasn't the time to get into that.

'And . . . they're not going to let us stay at a hotel,' Jamie said. 'But, what I could do is sleep on the floor? The spare room is big enough.'

Laurie hooted. 'Oh God, I'd not thought of that! Yeah, sure.'

Jamie looked many degrees less anxious than when they'd met. 'Thanks, Laurie. Really.'

She liked being this unflappable Laurie again. Go with the flow and handle it, Laurie. Not the stifling presence, who made life feel like a tunnel. She might have stumbled into a moment of liking herself.

'No worries,' Laurie adjusted her bag on her shoulder. 'Friday to Sunday?'

'Yeah. I'll get the train tickets and text you the time, say seven ish, we can meet at Piccadilly?'

'See you then. I'm going in for a coffee, want one?'

'I'm already awash with adrenaline, going to leave the caffeine alone.'

She nodded.

'Oh, Jamie?'

He abruptly turned on his heel. Laurie's heart gave a little squeeze that she could see he looked less stricken, and a weight – if not the greater one – had clearly been lifted. Why had he been so worried about asking her? Perhaps he had a slightly skewed version of Laurie, as she'd had of him: angry ballbuster who in the face of his anguish, would still say *aw hell no*.

'Duh, just thought! Where do they live?'

'Oh! Lincoln. I'm from Lincoln. It's a wild west kind of a town, brace yourself.' He grinned that heartbreaker's grin.

Laurie nodded and held a palm up as farewell.

Inside the shop, Laurie felt pensive, and the feel-good factor of helping Jamie faded further as she walked back to the office, gripping the paper cup.

It was one thing to pantomime a relationship to the audience of Salter & Rowson solicitors. They were now going to pretend to be a couple in front of his dying father, and soon-to-be-widowed mother?

What if they found out that she'd lied to them, and in effect made a mockery of their kindness, hospitality and interest in her? What if they couldn't stand her and she let Jamie down, and he wished he'd never asked her? What if they fell for her so hard, they expected to see her throughout Jamie's father's illness? Once you started a charade, it was tricky to work out the optimum time to end it.

It had felt so rewarding to say *hey, I'd love to,* to Jamie, but she now felt the size of what she'd promised. However, Laurie reasoned with herself, you didn't have a choice. If you'd made up an excuse, they'd have invited you the following weekend. She had to do it; this was the least worst option.

You've told lies. The law of unintended consequences.

Laurie wheeled her trolley case across the concourse at Piccadilly in early evening and immediately spotted Jamie amid the crowd, his expression mirroring her own suppressed discomfort.

Going away for the weekend together, sharing sleeping

arrangements – it was a huge gear shift up from steak dinners and silly photo ops, occasions when they amicably parted ways at quarter past nine. Laurie was about to intrude on a family in a key moment of crisis, under false pretences. A trespasser, pranking them. She couldn't think of it without her stomach somersaulting, so if she could help it, she would try not to think about it.

Damn Emily for being so right, to the point of being a prophet (of doom). Intensely intelligent people were expected to wear it heavily, to present as polysyllabic, and with a bibliography. Emily was every bit as sharp in her understanding of human nature, but because she knew her way round MAC, you weren't primed to expect it in the same way.

Jamie, off duty, was a different kind of showy: a dark pea coat with the collar turned up (Laurie could not have done that without feeling a fool), a cable sweater and dark jeans, and lace up, artfully scuffed chestnut brown shoes which had definitely been sold-as-scuffed by a fashionable brand. Laurie was in her duffle jacket and opaque navy tights, and felt her inadequacy as companion to this off-duty member of Take That, with the chiselled jaw.

'Hi!' Jamie said. 'We're on the 19.42, change at Sheffield.'

'Right you are.'

'Want me to carry that?' he gestured at her trolley case.

Laurie smiled. 'No, no thank you.'

'I might get a Greggs pasty, and then we'll find the platform?'

Laurie grinned. Not that posh. Jamie hoisted a brown

leather duffle bag onto his shoulder and they navigated the post rush hour crush as polite companions, like colleagues attending an out of town conference.

On the train, they got a table, window seats facing each other. They were hemmed in by two corpulent men who fell asleep as soon as they were at Manchester Oxford Road, snoring like warthogs.

'Are any brothers or sisters heading back too? This journey is the Mr & Mrs opportunity for me to get some girlfriend crib notes. Revision for any tests,' Laurie said.

'No, just me,' Jamie said.

'Are you an only child, like me?'

'You're an only? Pictured you having older brothers. You're so feisty and resilient in dealing with twats in our office,' Jamie said. 'And clients too, I'm sure.'

'No. I wish. I'd have liked siblings a lot. Whenever friends talk about fights over remote controls, I'm green eyed. You have someone else who shared your upbringing. There's nothing that can replace that. I'd love a protective older brother to deal with some of the shit.'

Jamie splayed his hands, palms down on the train table, expensive metal watch face clinking on the moulded plastic.

'Laurie . . . There's something I should tell you. It might come up.'

'OK . . .?'

'I had a brother. Joe. He died when we were kids. He was hit by a car.'

'Oh! Jamie, I'm so sorry.'

'I was nine and he was eleven. Feels wrong to say I'm an

only child. Like I'm erasing him from existence. I have a brother. He's not here.'

'Yes, I see that,' Laurie said, not knowing what else to say.

Jamie looked out the window at the scenery rushing past, muscles tensed in his jaw.

'I'm sorry,' Laurie said again, and Jamie nodded.

Even mentioning his name had caused grief to rise to the surface in an instant. As with her mother and her father's behaviour, some things you were never past, the way others expected or wanted you to be. Instead you lived with it.

She didn't know what to say other than, eventually, 'Want some biog for me?'

'Yes. Very much so,' Jamie said, smiling and relaxing slightly.

'My mum and dad had a fling when they were twenty. My mum knew my dad was a scoundrel, and decided the way to get him to stay was to get up the duff with me. She told him she was on the pill, and wasn't. Then she's like "Butterfingers, we're going to be parents!" and my dad says: "No, you are, see ya." And leaves her.'

'Christ alive!'

'Yep. Then, Mum has a terrible labour with me and there are complications that mean she can't have any more children. There she is, coming to terms with that, single parent, now twenty-one, relationship over, her parents back in Martinique. Hellish.'

Laurie wondered if her mum had experienced the emotions that Laurie had, on Dan's departure. Peggy had been in love with her father, she'd never doubted that. It was clear from the wedding announcement, she felt something. Would Laurie feel anything when she heard Dan was marrying, as he probably would? It felt somewhat lesser compared to fatherhood. Yeah: it'd still hurt. She couldn't bear to think she'd now carry this cross for the rest of her life.

'Oh God! And you've never seen your dad since?'

Laurie raised and dropped her shoulders. 'I see him every year or so, he has a fancy loft he rents out in Manchester and a place in Ibiza. It's not a relationship as such, though. It's like he has a recurring cameo in my life. Austin Watkinson, if you've heard of him?'

Jamie's mouth opened slightly and he said: 'Haaaang on, not Austin Watkinson? Producer – DJ guy? Madchester, etc?'

'Yep, him. Dancing around in the background of the Happy Mondays "Kinky Afro" video, hanging out with Tony Wilson. That's my pops.' Laurie made the scathing intonation clear.

Jamie's mouth was now fully open. 'That's crazy! Austin Watkinson is *your dad* . . . Why doesn't anyone at work know this? Or do they, and they dislike me enough not to tell me the interesting stuff?'

'No, they don't know. Bharat knows, and obviously Dan knew, but I said not to mention. It's not a dread secret or anything, but I have so little to do with him, it's pretty irrelevant. It's not a conversation I want to have.'

'You're so insanely cool,' Jamie said, and she could see he meant it, that he'd blurted it and was now going pink at having gushed. 'Not that . . . not because of your dad, but because you don't show off. You are all substance, not image.'

'Hah, I am definitely not image.'

He blushed harder. 'I didn't . . . you know what I mean.'

Laurie's heart swelled. *Silly girl, because the good-looking younger man called you cool?!* Then: *no, I'm allowed this. Ever since Dan left me, I've seen myself as a frumpy millstone. Adjusting my self-image, it's welcome.*

Laurie rescued him by adding: 'It's an extra mind blower because of the ethnicity.' She pointed at her face. 'As much as you logically know there was a white parent involved, it's somehow still unexpected, right?'

Jamie smiled and nodded.

'How did your mum cope, after your dad dropped her in it?'

She was impressed Jamie asked a thoughtful, considerate question, rather than carrying on asking her about her notorious dad's pills and raves.

'Up and down. She's a singer and that didn't pay the bills, so she had admin temp work and things.'

'Your dad didn't help?'

'Only when he was flush. Every once in a while he'd dump a thousand or even two into my mum's current account and that night we'd have a chippy tea and I got a can of Fanta. But you never knew when the next instalment might arrive. You couldn't rely on it. Or him.'

'Jesus. I mean. If you don't support your kid, you've failed at the most basic test of adulthood haven't you?'

'Yep. Mum had a lot of boyfriends, and when one of those was around they tended to help out. She's a hippy free spirit type. Free love, no rules . . .'

'She must be so proud of how well you've done in life, though?'

'Um . . . not . . . as such. The problem for my mum is I'm the kid who trashed her relationship and ruined her womb. I think she's . . .'

One of the large men awoke with a snort and it provided humorous punctuation to a speech where Laurie's voice was growing thick.

'I think she's struggled not to blame me. If you want me to be honest. I was the reason he left.'

Laurie hadn't meant for things to turn profound, and Jamie was staring at her with a look so full of concern it was almost too heavy to receive.

'Laurie,' he said, quietly. Not a question, or an opening to saying anything else. A full sentence in itself.

'He used to promise to come to see me as a kid and take me on a trip back to Manchester, I'd get ready, bag packed – I remembered I had this rucksack with a rabbit on it – and wait and wait. He'd call . . . oh he'd forgotten. Was next week OK, sweetheart? As if kids work on that sort of timetable or delayed gratification.'

'As if anyone does,' Jamie said.

'Yes. Still. Not as big a crime as his albums of incredibly lucrative "chillout anthems",' Laurie said, and Jamie laughed. She could see he was vaguely bedazzled. That his view of her had shifted.

While Laurie was pleased, it felt cheap, as these were things that had happened to her, not things she'd chosen to do. Someone who'd behaved as badly as her dad didn't deserve this aura, bestowing his civilian daughter with a frisson of rascally excitement. It was one of the things that had frustrated her most about Dan, that despite his being on her side in most things, all her dad had to do was crack a joke and Dan would be badgering her to let bygones be bygones.

'You're going to find my family soooo conventional, after this . . .' Jamie said.

'Fine by me.'

Laurie paused. 'I know the obvious psychoanalysis is I settled down with my first boyfriend as a direct result. But I wouldn't have grabbed onto anyone. I was happy with Dan. Or we were.'

'You're a survivor,' Jamie said. 'Of some difficult things. What needs explaining or apologising for about that?'

Laurie had never thought of it that way before. She'd never been called a survivor. She turned the word over her in mind: she liked how it sounded, applied to her. It wasn't victimhood and it wasn't self-aggrandising, it was about coping. And she had definitely done that. Her spirits rose. Jamie was an unlikely champion. They shared a look of new understanding, as the refreshments trolley rattled into view.

Not all unintended consequences were bad.

26

'There he is,' Jamie gestured with the crook of his arm, hand stuffed in coat pocket, at a tall beaming man, a few yards away.

Jamie's dad, Eric, was waiting for them on the platform in a Millets cagoule, jangling car keys in his hand. He doesn't look ill, Laurie thought. He was balding, with rounded features and spectacles, no trace of Jamie whatsoever, to Laurie's eyes. Jamie had told her he was a retired law lecturer and that was exactly what he looked like. He had the right bearing.

'They're very British, I wouldn't expect too much cancer talk,' Jamie had said during the journey. 'My dad sees self-pity as a vice.'

They did hearty introductions, Jamie giving his dad a hug. She stepped back while there was some clapping of shoulders and second round hugging, then Jamie's dad leaned down and pecked her on the cheek with a hello. He took her case from her without asking.

'Easy drive here?' Jamie said, and they made the obligatory small talk about traffic on the way to the car, over the noise of luggage wheels on concrete.

Laurie could almost see the Jamie Carter of myth and legend dissolve on contact. No one, not even Prince at the height of his fame, Laurie reckoned, could maintain their adulthood persona around their parents. Your closest family returned you to whence you'd came, when you were still a work in progress. They weren't fooled for a second. Older you was a construct.

He drove them home in his Volvo, Laurie having to insist to be allowed to sit in the back, saying Jamie should be upfront with his dad.

'Now it's too late for a proper dinner obviously but we thought you might be peckish, so your mother's got a lump of Stilton and some pork pies.'

'Do you like pork pies, Laurie?' Jamie said, turning in his seat.

'Love them. Especially with pickle and mustard.'

'I'm sure Mary will have some. Or we can send Jamie to the shop!'

'Good for you, Jamie,' Laurie said, and Jamie mock huffed.

They arrived at the house, and Laurie thought: had anyone asked her, a few short weeks ago, what Jamie Carter's background was, she'd have said, he's definitely from money. Possibly privately schooled. You didn't get his sort of confidence from nowhere.

Yet here they were, in a very pleasant but ordinary three-bed semi-detached in a suburb of Lincoln.

Jamie's mum was who he took after physically, dark – presumably dyed her original colour – hair in a bob, slender frame, high cheekbones, the same neat nose, dark blue eyes.

She was a retired R.E. teacher and reminded Laurie of Joan Bakewell.

They poured lots of red wine and they sat round a table in a dining room stacked with bookshelves, and insisted Laurie eat, *eat*.

Laurie wolfed down cheese on crackers and grapes and slices of pie and discussed the law, crime in Manchester, politics. Her twitchiness disappeared in small increments, until she was having a thoroughly nice time. She was less ashamed of the false pretences that brought her here. Yes, she might not be what they thought she was, but her pleasure in their company was sincere, and she hoped vice versa.

The Carters appeared delighted she had plenty of opinions and insights. Dan's parents were nice people, but they were principally interested in things immediately around them, the neighbour's intrusive extension, the weather, their own children.

Jamie's parents wanted Laurie's take on world affairs, they wanted to know where she was from (but in a: 'You sound Northern . . .?' kind of way), what motivated her. When Jamie had said they badly wanted her to visit, she thought that it was excitement or relief their wayward son was settling down. While it might still be that, she could see they simply enjoyed meeting people.

'I'm very impressed at your commitment to legal aid cases,' his mother said, when Laurie described why she first wanted to study criminal law, and that everyone deserved a defence, 'My son wants to make the world a better place, but only for himself.'

They all laughed.

'Nothing wrong with starting with the man in the mirror, as Michael Jackson said,' Jamie said.

'I think at some point you're supposed to *stop* looking in the mirror,' Laurie said, and his parents hooted, slapped their thighs.

'Oh, I like her, Jamie, I really like her,' his mum said, putting her hand on Laurie's wrist. Laurie squeezed her hand in return and met Jamie's awestruck gaze of gratitude, and it was in some ways, the most unexpectedly rewarding split second of Laurie's life.

They asked how Jamie and Laurie met, and Jamie told the lift story with much light wit. Laurie was glad to let him take over there, still prickling at the falsehood.

'We sparked, you know, and that was that.'

Laurie gave a forced smile.

Jamie had been right that the cancer wasn't present. They obviously wanted normality, to still meet the girlfriend and talk interestedly with her, without the Sword of Damocles hanging over them.

When it came time to turn in, Laurie went ahead and Jamie hung back, tacit agreement it'd be easier for her to change without him.

It had been peculiar, when packing, to plan around the hitherto unexplored social occasion of 'sharing a bedroom with a straight man you were not intimate with.' She had a Lycra vest top to stand in for the support of a bra overnight, and on top of that, baggy grandad pyjamas. She'd brought a silk pillowcase because she was too self-conscious to wear her usual turban to protect her hair from breaking against cotton.

Eesh, she'd thought this would be easier because they weren't sleeping together but in some ways, it was harder.

'I'll sleep on the floor,' Jamie said, in hoarse whisper, tiptoeing in quietly when Laurie was in bed.

'Jamie,' Laurie hoarse whispered back, 'Don't, it'll be crazy uncomfortable for you and if your mum comes in with a cup of tea and sees you it's going to be a disaster. You'll have to start making up lies: I'm a True Love Waitser. We can put this big pillow between us like this,' she flumped it onto the bed, 'As a breakwater.'

'Are you sure?' Jamie hissed.

'Yeah.'

'OK, thanks.'

'I'll shut my eyes while you get changed,' Laurie whispered and they started giggling, stupid uncontrollable giggling, as if they were naughty kids at a sleepover.

'This is so fucking bizarre,' Jamie whispered, and Laurie said: 'Telling me!'

She twisted round and buried her face in the pillow.

Moments later, Jamie got into bed beside her.

'Am I safe to look?' Laurie said, in stagey whisper.

'No, I am doing a naked dance, it's a nightly ritual of mine,' Jamie replied.

Laurie was shaking with laughter. It was welcome and necessary, this puncturing of the tension.

'Your parents are fantastic,' Laurie said.

'Aw, thanks. They liked you too. You look like a "young Marsha Hunt" apparently. I'm not sure who she is.'

'She was bedded by Mick Jagger.'

'That doesn't narrow it down really, does it?'

'Says you!'

'Oh, for fu— I'm sick of this perception of me as the greatest man slag of the North West,' he said.

'Then be less man slag. Be the unslaggy man you want to see in the world.'

'Pffft. I'm selective.'

'Then select fewer of them.'

'This country. It'll soon be illegal to be a human man.'

Laurie heaved with laughter.

They whispered 'n'night' to each other and Laurie felt grateful that she didn't, to the best of her knowledge, snore.

The next thing Laurie knew, it was dawn, and she had an extremely disorientating moment when she awoke, remembering she was in the East Midlands, not Chorlton, and that the sleeping male form next to her wasn't Dan. She couldn't help wondering what would happen if she moved the pillow away, slipped her arms round him. Would he respond?

How did I get here? she wondered dozily, then it occurred to her that was a bloody good question.

27

Jamie decreed a Full Tourist Day was in order to Laurie, and pointed out that it would yield some killer content for the 'Gram.

Laurie was increasingly unsure she wanted to be killer content for the 'Gram, but agreed. It was obvious they could sell it as *look how serious I am, I've taken her to meet the folks* and yet neither of them said so, because it was exploiting the real reason they were compelled to be here, his father's illness.

They started with a trip to Lincoln Cathedral, and Jamie showed Laurie the Lincoln Imp, a little stone grotesque with sticky outy ears, nestled in the eaves.

'First, he and his mates went to Chesterfield and twisted the church spire, a proper Imp ruckus. Probably all had cans on the train, you know the sort of thing. In a medieval justice version of a life term, this one's behaviour was so bad, he got turned to stone,' Jamie said. 'Very punitive, considering he was a youth offender.'

'Brutal,' Laurie agreed, taking a photo. 'Obviously Satan wanted to send a message to the other Imps.'

'The lesson we take from this is, keep your demonic children under close supervision. Something anyone who's eaten in a Nando's during half-term can fully agree with.'

Laurie laughed. 'Do you want kids?'

Jamie shuddered. 'One hundred per cent no, no thank you. Do you?'

'I'm more fifty-fifty.'

Laurie got a mental flash image, pulled straight from Boden Kids catalogue, of she and Jamie bumping a winter-bundled toddler up steps, holding one tiny hand each. She never fantasised her children with Dan, this must be happening because she was entirely safe from its possibility. She tested her emotions on this for the umpteenth time. It still felt like Item 5(ii) on the great agenda of life questions, and couldn't be answered without 5(i) – If I Find Appropriate and Willing Father.

They walked Steep Hill, Laurie had a nosy around the florists and the gift shops. She admired a silver necklace, a leaf on a chain. 'Can't justify it, I have so much trinketry already.'

They walked on.

'Hey, Laurie!' she turned and Jamie snapped a photo of her above him on the street, turning to smile down at him. 'Great for Christmas shopping, round here,' he said, 'Entre nous.'

'Are you inviting me back?' Laurie said, grinning over the bundle of her scarf.

'My parents would have you back in a heartbeat.'

'Unlike you,' Laurie said, and Jamie rolled his eyes in an impression of a truculent pubescent.

'OK, I would too. Whatever yeah. Girls are stupid.'

It was so easy, this platonic romance. She and Jamie could communicate their liking of and respect for each other without any fear of it shading into *and I want to jump your bones*. Here was why she didn't believe the caricature of Jamie at Salter & Rowson – he was so much a comfortable, easy joy to be around. A genuinely terrible person couldn't mimic warmth like this, surely.

Laurie thought on something she'd not faced fully until now – she was very likely going to be alone on Christmas Day. Emily went somewhere long haul and hot, the day before Christmas Eve, having always declared herself 'racist against Christmas'. Laurie would be welcome to join, except she neither had the money nor the inclination for Bali, and Salter & Rowson wouldn't give her the days off to make the travel worth it.

Laurie's mum didn't celebrate it and went to her friend, Wanda's, in Hebden where they made a whole seabass and everyone got their instruments out after lunch for a singalong. She would most likely be happy to have Laurie, but the place was crammed to the rafters with randoms and she didn't feel comfortable imposing herself. Also singalongs? Shudder forever.

Her dad, hah. God only knows where he spent the twenty-fifth. Face down in a pile of substances. She wouldn't be surprised if he didn't keep track of the calendar well enough to know it was Christ's birthday.

She and Dan had always either gone to Cardiff or hosted his parents, his sister and her boyfriend. She supposed it would be Megan's debut, meeting the family.

Oh well. Laurie would shop and plan for a complete single woman bacchanal. And she fancied adopting a kitten, sod society's sexist stereotypes.

They had lunch at the Wig & Mitre, a pub that had leapt straight from a magazine shoot of the cosiest and most picturesque in the country.

Jamie had posted the photo of Laurie – '*Showing Laurie the historic birthplace of a legend etc*' – and his phone was the usual cascade of Likes and comments.

Then something else pinged, a different colour notification that wasn't Instagram, and in a smooth practised move Jamie palmed his phone and turned it over, screen facing down. Laurie knew it was something she wasn't meant to see and that it must be female interest, and yet wondered why he was hiding it from her. Did he imagine she'd object?

They both ploughed through lamb shanks and mounds of mashed potato. Well, Laurie did, Jamie declared himself short on appetite.

'I'm stressed about my dad's speech to everyone at the party tonight,' he said. 'I don't know if he's going to tell them about the diagnosis.'

'You don't want him to?'

'I don't . . . know. I want him to if he wants to, but I'll find it overwhelming. I haven't started to work through how I feel, so having tons of his mates from college and my mum's sewing club all coming up to me tearful, expecting me to discuss it . . .'

'I see that.'

'But if he doesn't mention it . . . it'll still be exceptionally emotional, knowing something everyone else doesn't.'

Laurie put her hand on Jamie's shoulder and said: 'It'll be OK. You'll be OK.'

'How do you know that?' Jamie said, but with a smile.

'Because you're you and he's him and everyone coming tonight cares.'

'Thank you,' Jamie said, brightening. 'How do you do that?'

'What?'

'Say the right thing.'

'Oh . . .' Laurie blushed. 'Well . . . You're pretty good at that too. Hey, look at us. Becoming *actual sort of maybe almost friends*.'

Jamie's grateful smile faded, just a little. Oddly, Laurie suddenly had a sense she'd said the wrong thing. Maybe he didn't like the responsibility towards each other that might imply.

The party was in a function room at a pub near the cathedral called the Adam & Eve Tavern, and Jamie's parents went on ahead to do some prep.

Laurie had brought a trusty favourite with her to wear, a cream dress with bracelet-length sleeves and a full skirt that Dan used to say looked 'proper swit swoo' in. It was nicely modest for a family do, she thought, dressy up but not loud, and no excess tits or leg.

Laurie could hear Jamie bumping around downstairs and risked changing without warning him. She was holding it against her front, pulling her arms through the sleeves, when

Jamie walked into the bedroom and said, 'Shit, sorry!' backing out fast.

'No, it's fine! I'm decent! Could you zip me up?'

She knew this dress to be a proper fiddle, it was one that Dan always did for her, putting down the console for *Call of Duty Black Ops 4* on request, as long as the game wasn't at a critical juncture.

'Er . . . sure.'

She sensed Jamie's reluctance. Odd, she thought, that someone whose principal hobby involved removing clothes with people he didn't know very well, would get discomposed by a woman he didn't fancy, almost wholly wearing an L.K. Bennett prom dress. Maybe it was the *not fancying* that made it tricky.

Laurie turned her back and held her hair clear, and Jamie fumbled with the zipper. It snagged at bra level and he said: 'Oh . . . arse it. No wait, I'll undo it and redo it again, some of the fabric's got caught.'

Was she imagining his jitters? Was he already antsy about his dad's speech?

He pulled it back down to the base of her spine and suddenly Laurie felt a frisson at the physical contact, the warmth of Jamie's hands on her skin and the air on her exposed back. He pulled again and this time it sailed past her bra, up to the back of her neck. She let go of her hair.

'Do I look OK?' Laurie said, upon turning round, an automatic reflex in a relationship. Jamie looked awkward once more and said: 'More than OK. Lovely. What's the famous Eric Clapton song?'

'"Layla"?'

Jamie laughed.

'Not the one about diddling George Harrison's wife, no. I meant, "Wonderful Tonight".'

She'd forever be a big city rather than a town or village person, and Lincoln wasn't a *city*-city by Laurie's reckoning, but she was thoroughly charmed by it. The Adam & Eve was a gable-roofed, white-bricked eighteenth-century tavern with low exposed beams and that whiff of characterful mustiness that elderly ale houses always had.

In the Lounge Bar, a banner hung across a buffet table of sausage rolls, scotch eggs and crisps, declared HAPPY 65th ERIC!!!!

Jamie was immediately claimed by the mostly pensionable-age throng, people declaring 'Last time I saw you, you were that high!' – gesturing a diminutive height with an open palm – discussing bike rides, the whereabouts of long lost friends, asking where he worked now.

Nevertheless, Jamie barely left her side, his hand often lightly on her lower back, fetching her a drink as soon as her glass was empty, making introductions. Laurie felt looked after. She was being better looked after by a pretend boyfriend than she had been by her real one. The dynamic with Dan at parties was that he was loud, drunk and funny and she scooped him up at the end, when he'd be slurring how much he *lubbed* her.

As Laurie sipped her wine, she realised this was what had slipped away, in the last few years with Dan – his seeing her.

She became scenery, a prop. In the grim ordeal that was Tom and Pri's wedding, perhaps what he hated about dancing to 'Someone Like You' was that for three minutes, Laurie had a full claim on his attention.

Laurie wished she had this sort of family, she thought, as she saw Jamie's dad call him over, dragging him to his side in a rough embrace in front of ruddy-faced men of a similar age, talking animatedly. Her soul ached somewhat. You could miss so much and not notice or mind, until the 'here's what you could've won' comparison was right in front of you.

Imagine a proud dad, who was there for you. The solidity of it.

'Hello! You must be Laurie? I'm Hattie!'

Laurie turned. A pale, plump girl with enormous eyes, in a low cut 1950s style dress with fruit on it, smiled at her.

'Oh, you're Jamie's best friend!' Laurie shook her hand. She'd said the right thing, as Hattie lit up.

'Do you mind if I hang with you; virtually everyone here is someone who last saw me naked as a kid, apart from red wellies, playing in the sprinkler in Jamie's garden.'

'Not at all. I don't know anyone either. But thankfully absolutely no one here has seen me naked.'

'Apart from Jamie,' Hattie said.

'Ah, yeah.' *Nice one, Laurie.*

They were distracted by the banging of a fork on a glass and in a moment, Jamie was back by Laurie's side, pausing to give Hattie a kiss on the cheek and a hug.

Maybe it was the emotion or the sauvignon blanc, but Laurie sensed Jamie had moved back to be near her for the speech, not for appearances' sake, but as she alone here knew he found it hard.

She slid her arm around Jamie supportively, without pausing to think if this was a trifle gropey. They were somewhat off the map, in terms of what was and wasn't appropriate contact. She noticed she'd never once feared Jamie taking advantage of that. He might have nihilistic views on monogamy but he was no letch, or so far, opportunist.

Jamie moved her arm away from his body and for a heart-stopping moment, Laurie thought he was rejecting the gesture. Instead, he swung her round to directly in front of him, and linked his arms around her waist, the stance beloved of annoyingly touchy-feely couples at gigs. She put her hands over his.

This felt . . . good. Surprisingly good. Laurie hadn't realised how much she missed being held close like this.

'Thank you for coming here tonight everyone. Sixty-five, how did that happen! Maurice and Ken here will confirm it when I say that we were at school ten years ago, so there's been some awful accounting error.' He paused. 'I don't want to drone on self-importantly and this is keeping you from the buffet and the bar, so merely a quick thank you for being here. You don't know what it means to me, especially tonight. You get to an age in life where what really matters, becomes obvious. And it's family and friends. Look after each other, be kind to each other. I can't abide old bore pub philosophers who think age confers wisdom upon them, I'm sure there are twenty-year-olds here who are wiser than me . . .'

'My son isn't!' shouted a voice, and everyone laughed.

'But there's something about getting to the final furlong that allows you to see clearly what mattered, and what didn't.'

Laurie squeezed Jamie's hands. He gripped hers more tightly in response.

'Money didn't matter. Promotions didn't matter. Feuds and competitions and arguments, they didn't matter. Being soundly beaten at golf . . . OK that still matters,' – loud whoops from the golf contingent – 'But I tell you what I know for sure. You all matter, very much. Time with the ones you love. That's all that matters.'

Applause.

'With the power vested in me as the birthday boy, I now declare the buffet open,' Eric concluded. More applause.

She and Jamie disentangled to join in, and once the clapping subsided, Hattie grabbed a paper plate and announced she was going to hammer the egg sandwiches. The stampede for the de-clingfilmed food pushed Jamie and Laurie into a corner.

They looked at each other, expectantly, both waiting for the other to speak, but neither did. Laurie felt her stomach do a slow lazy flop forward as looking at each other turned into Looking At Each Other. Their being tactile, it had affected her. She couldn't stop staring at Jamie's mouth. He was gazing at her equally intently and she thought, are we . . . going to kiss . . .?

Their heads moved closer. Her hands were on his lower arms and he moved them around her waist. Oh God, this was genuinely on. There was no other reason for them to be entangled, this was explicit.

Laurie didn't know what this meant, or why she suddenly wanted to do it, she only knew she wanted to kiss him, badly. She even felt an anticipatory throb, somewhere in the region of her groin. She didn't expect lust to make a surprise re-appearance in her life, so soon.

For fuck's sake, she was meant to be immune to him! She was Penn & Tellering his act, remember? *Yeah yeah*, said her libido, emerging from its long winter. Laurie didn't know what status they would have, on the other side of the kiss.

'Are you Eric's son?' said a somewhat booze-amplified, mature female voice right by them, causing them to abruptly step back.

'Uhm, yeah?' said Jamie, turning to the short woman who looked like a Tory peer, in the huge pearl choker necklace.

'You must be the new girlfriend.'

'Laurie,' Laurie affirmed.

'You can't keep your hands off her, can you?' she said to Jamie, nudging him, and both Laurie and Jamie laughed awkwardly, and could no longer meet each other's eyes at all.

28

As the party entered its last gasp, Hattie was a port in a storm for Laurie, and possibly vice versa. As Jamie did farewells that involved working the room for an hour, Hattie had pulled chairs together and fetched Laurie a nightcap of a very sticky plum-flavoured vodka.

She'd known Jamie since childhood when their parents lived next door to each other. She worked at the university, putting its magazine together. Her husband Padraig was home with their two-year-old, Roger.

'I know, Roger,' she said, though Laurie had hoped her reaction was neutral-positive. 'I was on the gas and air when Padraig got me to agree to it, it was his favourite uncle's name, he died eating poisonous mushrooms. I've warmed to it. Poor little bastard, hope he's OK at school. And never goes mushroom foraging.'

She was disarming, unpretentious and humorous and Laurie really took to her.

'You're nothing like I expected,' Hattie said, and Hattie

wasn't like anyone Laurie would have pegged as a Jamie Carter BFF, either, expecting someone flashier, more conspicuous. Not someone who'd stayed in their childhood town, content with her lot.

She'd not believed Jamie about not adversely judging other choices to his own, and yet Laurie was forced to admit here was a powerful corroboration.

And it was obvious they were honest to goodness, best mates, from the sibling-like shorthand between them, and Hattie's casually worn and yet contemporaneous knowledge of the inner workings of Salter's.

'Oh, why's that?' Laurie said, thinking: 1. Black 2. Too old 3. Not glamorous enough.

Hattie slopped her drink from side to side. 'Don't be offended, as I'm clearly saying you're *not* like this, but I expected a trophy girl who'd spend the night studying her gel manicure and messaging her friends about how basic we all were. The sort who posts those Boomerangs of clinking flutes with her Mean Girls.'

Hattie mimed a repetitive backwards and forwards motion with her glass and a strained Miss World full teeth smile, and Laurie hooted.

'Haha! I'm not a trophy, agreed,' Laurie grinned.

'No, you are. But one with real value. I thought Mrs Jamie would be a princessy madam, that's all.'

'Is that because you think Jamie is a princessy madam?' Laurie said, but with a conspiratorial smile to make it clear she wasn't laying traps.

'Hah! Nooo, well, he has that side to him, for sure,' Hattie said, and Laurie could see by how slow her blinking was, and the slight fuzz of the edges of her speech, that she was considerably drunker than Laurie. She would probably cringe at having said this in the morning. 'He's always had this other, much better side to him. More serious, more reserved. Almost fiercely moral, actually. You fit with that.'

'Has he not brought girlfriends home before?'

Hattie looked gobsmacked. 'He's not told you this? No, never. To the point where Eric and Mary were told he must be a *comfort to his mother, lifelong bachelor,* if you know what I mean. No. That's why I couldn't believe my eyes when he was posting photos with you. I mean, that is like posting wedding banns, for Jamie.'

'Wow!' Laurie said, fraudulently, thinking Hattie must have heard his views on settling down, but was tactfully skirting round them with his new love.

'He was terrified of commitment,' Hattie said. 'But clearly he's got over it.'

'Ah well. I'm not . . . you know. Putting too much pressure on it.'

'But you're in love with him, right?'

'Uhm . . . yes.'

'He's madly in love with you. I can see it in the way he looks at you, the way he's so affectionate with you. I've never seen him like this before. He's transformed.'

Laurie grit-smiled, frowned and necked the rest of her vodka in one.

'I fell in love with him when we were twelve, you know,' Hattie said. 'Then right through our teenage years.'

Laurie thought, *hoo boy*. She's wrecked. She might not even remember saying this. 'Really?!'

'Yeah. Nothing ever happened, I should say,' Hattie waved a hand emphatically, 'Or we'd not be such good mates now. But yeah, I was in love, and he let me down gently. He could've so easily exploited it, and he didn't. *That* is the side of himself he keeps under wraps. When you're his friend, he will go to the ends of the earth for you, and he won't tolerate anyone being damaging towards you. Whatsoever.'

'Right.'

'Maybe that's why he doesn't make many friends, looking after people that much is a burden.'

Laurie nodded. So, she'd been right, earlier, when she saw worry flit across Jamie's face. He didn't want there to be any obligations, after this was finished. This was strictly business, not pleasure, however intimate it might feel at times.

'And,' Hattie continued, 'of course, you know what happened with his bro—'

Jamie approached them.

'I like her, can we keep her,' Hattie said, grabbing Laurie and planting a sloppy vodka kiss on her cheek.

'Uh oh. Have you been dropping me in it, as per Hats?'

'Would I.'

He ruffled her hair.

'In a strange inversion, I'm done in and having to drag my parents home,' Jamie said. 'Would you be up for heading back together?'

Laurie agreed readily, she didn't have another drink in her. Jamie had stayed away from her for the last forty-five minutes and Laurie understood why, and was grateful. The previous tension needed to dissipate.

'It was so good to meet you,' Hattie said, encircling her waist, smushing her face into Laurie and kissing Laurie's left breast, having evidently missed her intended target of 'slightly above her left breast'. 'I can tell you and I are going to be huge friends. I'm slightly psychic in that respect.'

'You and my hairdresser both.'

'Really? What did she predict that came true?' Hattie said, peering through the one eye she could still open.

'. . . Ah,' Laurie regretted this remark now. 'Nothing yet.'

'Hattie is similarly unencumbered by a track record of success,' Jamie interjected.

'I told you, it's feelings, sensations. Maybe, visions! Like, I can see you and Laurie with a toddler. A boy! Bringing him back here to visit. It's cold weather, he's in a coat . . .'

Laurie swallowed hard.

'Alright, enough from mystic you,' Jamie said, briskly. 'I can see a vision of you with a hangover tomorrow, how's that.'

29

'Your speech was really nice,' Laurie said, to Jamie's dad, as they sat with nightcap whiskies in the over-stuffed, homely front room with the wood-burning fire, then winced at the cutesome inadequacy of 'nice'.

'Thank you, Laurie. It was from the heart.'

'When are you going to tell them all?' Jamie's mum asked him. This was the first time the cancer had been directly mentioned in front of Laurie.

'I might not,' Eric said, sinking back into his chair. 'Let them read the news in the obit column of the *Lincolnshire Echo* and say: "That sneaky bastard!"'

'That's not fair on me, they'll be pestering me for the story for weeks on end,' Mary said. 'It'll take me an hour to make it across Co-op when I need a loaf of bread.'

'Yeah, you have to think of Mum here,' Jamie said.

'Oh God, even when you're dying you don't get out of the To Do list, Laurie, can you believe it!' Eric said. Laurie smiled and wished her heart didn't feel so waterlogged that she found it difficult to match his lightness, and be who they needed. She didn't want Eric to go. The world could do with more Erics, and fewer of other people.

'Ahhhh it was good to see everyone though. Mary, can you believe the mop on Ronald Turner! Bald as coot a few short months ago and now he's had plugs. Cutting about with that lounge lizard's quiff like he's Bryan Ferry. Talk about straining credulity.'

There was some discussion about the unexpectedly luxuriant hairline of Eric's former boss and then he said, 'He's an avid churchgoer, Ron. I wish I had faith. I wish I thought I was going to see Joe again.'

He glanced up at a photo on the cabinets to their right that Laurie hadn't noticed until now, a barrel-bellied kid Jamie next to an older brother with a broad toothy grin, both in grey V-neck school sweaters and ties.

Eric raised his glass to it in a toast, and Laurie found herself desperately swallowing over and over to stop herself starting to cry. She didn't look at Jamie or Mary.

A tear rolled down Eric's cheek and Laurie felt shocked, despite herself, as she thought by now the Carters weren't going to do conventional sadness. Jamie's mum poured herself more whisky and Jamie put his hand on his dad's arm and nobody spoke for a moment, because nobody could.

'Maybe I should join that religion that Tom Cruise is in, what is it, Scientology?'

'I don't think there's a Scientology church in Lincoln, Dad,' Jamie said. 'You might have a Wagamama but don't get ahead of yourself.'

'It was a delight to have you there, tonight, Laurie,' Eric

said, turning to her. 'We're very proud our son has convinced such an impressive woman to be by his side. I mean at this point we were so desperate to meet a girlfriend we'd have made our peace with Ann Widdecombe, but you're really something special.'

'Dad!' Jamie said in outrage, as Laurie laughed heartily.

They said their goodnights and Laurie found it peculiarly awkward when they got to the bedroom. More so than she had at any time throughout the visit. Was it the near kiss? *Was* that a near kiss? She thought about Emily's wisdom. *Sooner or later, one or the other of you is going to wonder if you mean it.*

She didn't wonder that, but she did wonder if the line between things they needed to do and things they wanted to do for solace, was getting blurred. Her mind kept spooling back to that moment, imagining them not being interrupted, imagining how it would've felt to kiss him and then claim it was part of the act. Laurie wanted to know what it felt like to kiss someone who wasn't Dan.

It would've been too much, she concluded, to accidentally tap off and then not be able to get away from each other.

Sex was obviously out of the question with his parents sleeping yards away, but the thought of it was too much anyway. Laurie didn't want a confused pity shag because Jamie's emotions were in a tumble dryer, and him to sorely regret asking her here, and there to be another man she was desperate to avoid at her office.

They danced around the arrangements for going to bed, Laurie changing in the bathroom.

'I thought your dad did really well,' Laurie said, quietly,

once the covers were up to her armpits. 'The atmosphere tonight was lovely.'

'Yeah.'

He was oddly clipped. Don't make the almost-kissing thing weird, she silently begged. We can get past it if we pretend it didn't nearly happen.

'You seemed to handle it well?'

'Mmm.'

She thought a further silence indicated subject closed, or Jamie nodding off, until he made a heaving noise that was, unmistakably, a sob.

'. . . Jamie?' Laurie whispered into the darkness. She stared at the pattern of street lights on the bedroom ceiling.

'Sorry, shit . . .' he said, trying to steady himself with a series of sharp gulps. Like someone trying not to hiccup by holding their breath. 'Sorry,' he said. 'You've come here to help me out, and now this . . .'

'Hey, don't be silly.'

'I'm just . . . I'm not ready to live in a world that doesn't have him in it.'

Laurie moved the pillow barrier out of the way and pushed her arms around him as he sobbed. She thought he might resist, but he wrapped himself around her.

'It's OK to be sad,' Laurie said, hotly, stroking his hair, his head resting against her chest. 'You're allowed to be really sad, and not apologise for it.'

She could feel Jamie's tears making her shoulder wet and his hand gripped her waist tightly as he sobbed near-silently, face buried her neck. She squeezed him, to let him know he wasn't expected to stop.

'There's something I've never told anyone. I thought I'd left it behind, compartmentalised it. It's been crucifying me since I got Dad's news.'

'Do you want to tell me? I won't judge you,' Laurie whispered, into the darkness. The darkness helped.

'It's about Joe. We were playing a game, a stupid game of chicken, running into the road, dodging cars. My parents know that part. What they don't know is that I was taunting him, winding him up, saying I'd won.' He had to pause, and gasp. 'Saying I'd won the game. It was my fault. It was my fault Joe ran back into the road and got hit, Laurie.'

'Shhhhh.' She held him as his body convulsed again. 'Jamie, you were a child. You could've just as easily died. You didn't mean to hurt him.'

'Should I tell him? Dad? Before he dies? He should know, right? He deserves to know.'

'No, because he won't care about that detail. He'll care that his son who he loves very much is torturing himself. What I've seen of your parents shows they want your dad's remaining time to be about love and happiness, and not anger or recriminations.'

Jamie mumbled something that sounded like agreement.

'You have survivor's guilt. I think you push yourself super hard to try to be both sons, to make them doubly proud.'

Laurie hadn't known she'd thought this until she'd said it, and yet as she said it, she knew it to be true.

'But they're already proud of you,' she added. 'You're enough as you are.'

Jamie hugged her tighter.

'I can't begin to imagine how terrible it was for you. And your parents.' God, Jamie must have been with his brother, he must have seen it . . .? The guilt he must have had to carry, as a nine-year-old.

'It changed us completely. There was life before Joe was killed and life after. I think a lot of the pulling through my parents did was for my sake. They didn't want my childhood to be a vale of tears.'

Jamie's breathing steadied.

'I try not to think about it for the most part. That's what living life is, isn't it? Coping,' Jamie said.

'Yes.' God, yes.

'Thank you for what you've said. I mean it. I'm going to think about these words and try to remember them when things get shaky. If someone as intelligent as you thinks this, it can't be completely wrong.'

He had too high an opinion of her brains, but let him find the comfort there.

'I really do.'

How had a lift breaking down ended with Laurie in a bedroom in North Hykeham, sleeping with and yet not sleeping with a colleague, consoling him about bereavements, both past and future tense?

It was so strange and yet the strangest thing of all was that it didn't feel strange. For the first time since Dan left her, Laurie hadn't thought about him much at all. If she could be helpful to Jamie in a time of need, it was therapeutic for her.

Something else dawned on Laurie. She understood Jamie, at

last. He hadn't developed his self reliant, streamlined, *take no passengers* persona because he was superficial, arrogant and selfish. He wasn't, as she'd assumed, playing life on the easy setting.

The world had dealt him an almost intolerable blow at a very early age and this constant forward motion, and refusing to care too deeply about anyone, it was his coping strategy.

'Lau . . .' Jamie said, mumbling. He wasn't awake anymore, he was drifting off, sleep-talking. 'I want . . .'

'What?' she said.

'I want to hold on to you.'

'Sure,' Laurie whispered.

Laurie wondered if he meant it literally, or as a statement of intent. She'd gently disengage right before she nodded off, she thought. Sleeping in someone else's arms was one of those things that worked in movies and was uncomfortable as piss in reality.

Next thing she knew, she was waking up wound round him, the grey-yellow light of early winter morning creeping in under the blinds. It felt reassuring, and sort of oddly healing.

Laurie listened to Jamie's heartbeat through his T-shirt and inhaled the faded scent of his aftershave, mentally reassembling where she was, what they'd done and said last night. She thought again about a traumatised nine-year-old boy, a vulnerability that reappeared now he was losing his father. Would Jamie push her away after this? Laurie had grown fond of him but she wasn't naïve, he hadn't wanted her involved, it was necessity. If the situation was reversed, she'd not want Jamie to see her like this.

He stirred and blinked and stared at her in a moment of dumb incomprehension.

'. . . Morning.'

'Morning.'

She pulled away and sat up, self-conscious, smoothing her hair and rubbing the sleep out of her eyes.

'Did we . . .?' he said, looking down at the bedclothes.

'No, we did not, how dare you!' Laurie said in an indignant, jokey half-whisper.

'No, I didn't mean that, of course not *that*. I meant . . .' Jamie gestured at their proximity. 'All night? I've never done that before. I usually hate it.'

'Haha. Why am I not surprised? Do I get to say I taught you something new in bed?' She was letting her mouth run on, in the uncertainty of what the tone between them was going to be today.

'Yeurgh,' Jamie said, rubbing his neck, doing a little shudder as he heaved himself out of bed.

Oh, so that was it. Making it clear he regretted their intimacy.

'Why are you such a prude with me? Where's the wild sex man of myth and legend, strutting around swigging Wild Turkey, in his Jim Morrison snakeskin trousers?'

Jamie turned, frowning. 'Why do you have to constantly characterise me like that? How would you feel if I was all "lol, Laurie with her one boyfriend"?'

Laurie opened her mouth, no justification came out. She felt slightly ashamed.

'Sorry,' Jamie said, 'Sorry. That was morning me and you didn't deserve that.'

He went for a shower and Laurie sat, hugging her knees. Jamie returned from the shower, dry clothes, wet hair, and said: 'Laurie. I'm an unspeakable shit for snapping at you, after everything you've done for me. I hate myself right now. Please accept my grovelling apology?'

Laurie smiled up at him. 'No, you were right.' She paused. 'The truth is, I'm terrified of The First One After Dan and it comes out as lairy bravado.'

She surprised herself by being this open. It suddenly felt better to share it than hide it. She'd seen Jamie naked, figuratively speaking, and she felt more able to expose herself.

'Why? I mean, why are you terrified?'

Laurie was embarrassed to say, but the urge to purge herself of these thoughts was greater.

'What if he thinks my body is off-putting, and the way I do sex is boring?'

Jamie laughed. 'He won't.'

'How do you know?'

'Because the last man liked the deal so much he stuck around for nearly twenty years.'

'Hah!' Laurie said. 'Thanks.'

'I don't want to disappoint you, but us men, we're not that different. There's not that much variety.'

She was intrigued Jamie would say this. It was very off brand. Wasn't variety, not same-same, his whole raison d'etre?

'That's what my best friend tells me.'

'Was she the hair-flicking girl in The Ivy?'

'Yes! Hah. Emily's not a hair-flicker, she's great.'

'That was a set-up, wasn't it? No way did she run into us.'

Laurie made a face. 'OK, yes, but not a safety check-in. She was being a voyeur as she thinks you're hot. "Yeurgh", as a man once said.'

'Imagine how foolish you're going to feel when you realise she was right all along.'

Laurie barked with laughter. 'When's that going to be?'

'About an hour, if Mum gets the photo albums out. The nineties was a very strong decade for me.' He shaped his wet hair into a boy band middle parting and pulled a dim face.

Laurie laughed like a drain. She remembered watching him holding Eve in the palm of his hand in Refuge; *the lad knows how to turn it on alright.*

'Can I ask you an embarrassing question?' he said, scuffing his hair back to normal with the heel of his hand.

'Sure.'

Jamie hesitated, and Laurie gleaned it was genuinely embarrassing to him, not some 'oh gee shucks this is awkward, can a penis be TOO big,' gambit.

'How do you know, when you've fallen for someone in a long-term, could marry, settle down forever sort of way? Please don't say 'you can't imagine life without them' or similar because I can't imagine life without Hattie but I don't want to marry her. Something that might give me real insight.'

'Oh . . . er.' This was a role reversal, Laurie feeling like the knowledgeable one. 'Hmmm. It feels like a conversation that you never want to end, I suppose. A renewable energy source. You know how with some people you can't get chatting off the ground? They're hard work? Falling in love is the extreme opposite. Endless fascination. It's effortless. A spark turns into a flame turns into a fire. That doesn't go out. Unless you meet some leggy ginger whore specialising in Contentious Trusts and Probate.' She smiled.

'Endless fascination,' Jamie said. 'OK.'

'Yeah. I mean, that makes it sound a bit like a one on one seminar with my brilliant old law tutor, Dr McGee. Obviously there's the part where you would gladly lick them like an ice cream in any place they asked. I would not lick Dr McGee anywhere he asked.'

'Funnily enough, I did,' Jamie said. 'Got a first though.'

'Ahahahaa.'

'Why are you wondering what love is like? Do you want to know what love is, like Foreigner?' Laurie said.

'I might have . . . met someone,' Jamie said, meeting her eye, looking supremely ill at ease, eyes darting away again.

'Wow,' Laurie said, feeling an odd sharp heat flare inside her.

Ah, that text. The hasty phone flip. It made sense now. 'After everything you said!'

'Yeah.' Jamie looked sheepish. 'No one's more surprised than me.'

'Hey – but you're going to wait until we've ended our pretending, right?'

'Oh, definitely,' Jamie said. 'The faking has to be over.'

As she walked to the shower, feeling stirred up, Laurie thought: well damned if I know what almost putting his tongue down my throat was about, then. Rotter. She disliked the fact she had a little ache, a pulse of envy for this unknown woman. Oh to be loved like that again.

30

'Alright, this is huge. You're no longer giving me the "just fooling around", line,' Bharat said. 'You went to his home town and met his parents?! For the weekend? What the hell? Should I buy a hat?'

Bharat insisted they buy pastries as an alibi to get a table in Starbucks and stay for a fifteen-minute catch-up. 'We'll buy Di's foul eggnog latte at the end, so she won't spot it's gone cold.'

Manchester was in full swing winter, lights on Deansgate, the bloody Slade song starting to peal from shop doorways.

'I can't go into any detail without betraying confidences but can I say, there was a purpose for the trip. It was . . . circumstances driving it, not necessarily a massive urge to take things up a notch.'

They'd left yesterday with foil packages of leftover food from the party foisted on them, extracted promises from an uneasy Laurie to return soon, and Jamie's mum indeed wailing: 'We didn't get the photo albums out! Wait wait, Laurie, you have to at least see this.' She disappeared off and returned with a photo of a stark naked toddler Jamie in a cowboy hat, on the driveway, poking his tongue out defiantly.

'Oh MUM,' Jamie said, turning scarlet, as Laurie mimed covering her eyes.

'*Nice penis*,' Laurie whispered as they got into his dad's car. 'I will hate you forever, you vile bully.'

Laurie had to fight to keep her voice level when chatting with Eric on the way to the station.

The train ride had zoomed by, as they discussed Jamie's long-range career plans – pro bono work in Chicago's ghettoes. 'You are such a clichéd hipster, don't use your pulling lines on me!' Laurie said – and listening in on the hungover students playing Cards Against Humanity on the table across the aisle. When they embraced warmly at Piccadilly, Laurie's heart had felt full and her life felt wholesome.

'Were they alright, his parents? Are you going to get engaged? Is the sex off the CHAIN?' Bharat said, sipping his cappuccino.

Laurie counted the answers off on her hand: 'Yes very, no lol, and what, staying in his parent's spare room?'

Bharat gurgled.

'It's great to see you upbeat again. After what happened with Dan it was obvious you were destroyed,' Bharat said, adding hastily: 'I mean, you didn't *make* it obvious, but I could tell. He's not who I'd have predicted putting a smile back on your face in a million years, but I'm glad he has.'

They went different ways as Laurie was due in court, a first hearing for a public order offence. For once, for the first time she could think of since the benders of her twenties where she still thought she could cane it on a Tuesday night and work a respectable Wednesday, she was winging it slightly. She had to admit, there was more preparation she could've done, but her weekend was hectic and she wasn't in the mood for her caseload on Sunday night. She'd had a long bath, red wine and thought about Jamie Carter's inviting mouth a bit too much.

So, Laurie flunked it. She didn't flunk it in a discreet way. It was a flamboyant flunking, in grand style, as she'd forgotten to follow up on an alcoholic client's alibi that he was in a boozer across town when the fighting was occurring.

'Your Honour, the pub the defendant has identified in his witness statement closed down some three weeks prior to the night in question,' said Colm McClaverty, prosecuting, nobody's fool anyway.

'Could you shed any light on this discrepancy, Ms Watkinson?' said the magistrate, over his reading glasses.

'Your Honour, I . . . was not aware that this was the case and ask for an adjournment while I . . .'

Laurie desperately shuffled papers and cringed, while there was a banging of gavel. Colm gave her a 'them's the breaks' shrug. If Laurie had done her due diligence, she could've got her to client to 1) think harder about which pub it was or 2) advised him to plead guilty, because he was likely knackered.

He'd raised that alibi in interview and Laurie had totally forgotten to follow it up. She got back to the office in a light sweat, giving silent thanks to the Lord that Salter and Rowson were out of the office for the next two days on some sort of bosses' retreat jolly.

At least if she had to pick a time to screw up, this was the one.

★

Her phone rippled with a WhatsApp from Dan wanting a chat: 'Are you free this afternoon?' and Laurie thought, *oh, piss off. I'm not having a toilet day made worse, you can wait. The scan showed it's twins or something, did it.*

Two hours later, Diana said: 'Er, PSA, Dan and Michael have marched Jamie Carter into the War Room.'

'Oh my God, FIGHT!' Bharat said. 'A duel over your honour!'

'What?' Laurie said, 'About what?'

'I don't know but . . . what are the chances?'

Laurie got up from her seat and said: 'Right, I best . . .' she couldn't immediately finish the sentence. 'Find out.'

What should she do?

As she neared the door, she could hear raised voices.

'You know exactly what I mean,' she heard Dan saying, 'And we're putting you on notice that we see you.'

'You're head of *civil,* last I checked,' Jamie's voice, 'How would you have the first clue?'

'Look you're a slippery little fucker, that is a known fact,' Michael now, 'We can't appeal to your better nature so instead we'll try self-interest, which you have in spades. If you don't stop interfering with Laurie, then we'll go in to see the bosses and tell them we think you're harming her professionally. On purpose.'

'"Interfering"?! She's not a child!'

'Yes, I mean she's older than your usual type, I'll give you that.'

Laurie swallowed hard and opened the door, to see the three of them stood in a circle, Dan and Michael bearing down like a pair of CID heavies with a prime suspect they liked for at least two manslaughters.

'Hi. Is this anything I should be involved in?'

There was a tense silence and Jamie said: 'Well? Doesn't Laurie deserve to know what you're saying about her?'

'The quality of your work's fallen off a cliff,' Michael said to Laurie. 'It's one shit-up after another, lately. Everyone's noticed.'

Laurie spluttered. 'I've had one or two results that haven't gone my way, that's all.'

'I just saw Colm and he said they'd noticed now unprepared you were,' Michael said. 'He said it's gone from "we hope we don't get her defending" to "we hope we do".'

'Oh my God, that is standard dick-swinging rubbish, the hazing they do constantly!' Laurie said, stung all the same.

'Don't you see what's going on here?' Dan said, in gentler tones. 'He's undermining you, on purpose,' he gestured at Jamie. 'He saw you were vulnerable, steamed in and now the most likely person for promotion ahead of him is . . .'

Laurie folded her arms. 'Is?'

'. . . Not operating at full capacity.'

Laurie's mouth fell open at this: 'You *what?!*'

Michael couldn't blackmail her out of dating Jamie so now he was going to shame her. She was raging: the bullying was abhorrent. She couldn't find the words because there were so many she wanted to use, volubly.

'Let me get this straight, you have an issue with Laurie and myself being involved as you think it might affect her concentration? Is what happened between the two of you, completely irrelevant to her state of mind, then?' Jamie said to Dan.

'There's a difference between the breakdown of a long-term

serious relationship and a colleague with previous for exploiting vulnerable women,' Dan said.

Laurie made a coughing noise of disbelief. 'Exploitation! Jamie's some sort of predator now and I'm a powerless victim? You make it sound like he trafficked me!'

'This is nuts,' Jamie said. 'Laurie is an adult, making her own choices.'

'Did you or did you not take advantage of Salter's niece?' Michael thundered.

'No, I didn't and what the fuck does that have to do with anything?'

'You were seen in the Principal Hotel with her, are you saying that's a lie?'

'I'm saying piss off, mainly.'

'Oh, brilliant dodge. No wonder you're a lawyer. I've got you worked out,' Michael said. 'It's not enough for you to bone your way around Greater Manchester, it has to be high value targets now. There has to be an angle.' He gestured at Laurie. 'Once she was back on the market, you moved fast, didn't you? Saw an advantage.'

There was a giant insult in this. Not only were two men she worked with, one her ex no less, appointing themselves her guardians – but they had jointly concluded that Laurie and Jamie were so unlikely a couple, she had to be the target of a scam. As if she was one of those poor older divorcees who got hoodwinked into marrying after a holiday romance with a Tunisian waiter, who got his green card and then cleaned out her current account. The way they wouldn't accord her the same powers of perception they claimed for themselves was infantilising, it made her feel ludicrous. It was like their sexism was coming in through the air con units, invisible but utterly pervasive.

'Sorry, I missed the part where I became a ward of court?' Laurie said, fully shaking with rage now. 'This place has always been chauvinistic, but this is incredible. You've decided I'm not seeing Jamie of my own free will?'

'Of course it's your choice,' Dan said. 'But both Michael and I care about you and we can see that he doesn't have your best interests at heart.'

'How dare you!' Laurie spluttered, 'You of all people, Dan, think you have *my best interests at heart?*'

'I knew you'd hate me for this, Laurie, and I am still speaking up because, yes, I do. Unlike him.'

'Ha! Incredible,' Laurie looked wide-eyed at Jamie and he shook his head.

'I mean obviously Laurie is a valuable possession, and this is about who will take more careful care when in charge,' Jamie said. 'No wonder you were trying to do this without her.'

Laurie snorted.

'I'm not making the connection between us seeing each other, and my result in court today?' Laurie said. 'It's as if you two have never cocked up?'

'When have you ever fucked up on checking an alibi before? And where were you this weekend, when you should've been prepping?' Michael said.

'What the . . . !' Jamie said. 'Who do you think you are?'

Laurie spluttered. 'You have opinions on how I spend my *weekends* now?'

'You used to work cases into the evenings, now no one can find you for dust after half five.'

'What? I have to clock in and out with you, Michael?'

'Stop being obtuse. You know what I'm getting at.'

'I actually don't.'

'Right. If you think I am going to stand by and let you try to damage mine and my girlfriend's careers because of your petty jealousies, you're badly mistaken,' Jamie said.

Dan looked horrified, plain shocked, at Jamie referring to Laurie as his girlfriend. Michael gave a nasty laugh.

'Laurie's one of the most competent, hardworking people here and you both know it. A couple of results not going her way is neither here nor there.'

A pause.

'Yeah, I've heard enough,' Laurie said. 'You can both stop right here, because I'm not having it. I had a meeting with Salter last week. He's fine with my performance. If you want to raise concerns about me then do it, but you'll harm me, not Jamie, which I presume is all that matters to you.'

A deeper sullen silence fell, as this was indisputably true.

'Michael and Jamie, can you leave me to have a word with Dan, please?' Laurie said.

They trooped out, Michael shaking his head at Laurie as he passed, Jamie frowning deeply.

'Let me get this straight,' Laurie said, fingernails digging into her palms with the effort of not shouting, 'You do what you did to me, I start seeing someone else, and you think you have the right to sabotage the relationship? As if you, of all people, think you get a say here, Dan?'

'I wasn't going to do this now but Michael practically grabbed Carter by the scruff. I was going to speak to you first. I messaged you but you didn't reply.'

'Speak to me now. I want to know how you could *possibly* be this far out of line?'

'I have no rights to comment on who you want to see . . .'

'Could stop there.'

'. . . I have no rights, but I was worried from the off when I saw you were involved with Carter. He will do you damage, and I know you're not going to want to hear that, least of all from me.'

'Based on?'

'Based on tons of stuff, Loz, the stories that followed him from Liverpool, where he gave a woman at that firm a nervous breakdown— ' Dan paused to gather Laurie's reaction. She tried to remain impassive, she badly wanted to know more. But not from Dan, and not now. '. . . Yep, bet he didn't tell you about that, from Eve, to a client he was rumoured to have hit on. He's bad news and you can bet he's seeing you with a motive.'

'Or it's exactly what it looks like? We really like each other?'

Dan grimaced.

'OK, someone who always stayed in the shadows was suddenly super keen to advertise being with you on social media, doesn't that ring any alarm bells? You've met his parents, how fast? Do you think maybe this is for the bosses' benefit, because he thought your standing would do him good in getting a promotion?'

Laurie rolled her eyes. This was a no score draw. Dan had it figured out, though not in the way he thought. Laurie hadn't succeeded in making them believe it. He was jealous, though.

She could see then how discomposed Dan was. She wanted him to feel hurt too, and now he did, she got no succour from it.

It's lying, and lying goes wrong. Lying is just bad karma.

'Him being super keen on me, is not possible?' Laurie said, while knowing it hadn't happened so it could well not be possible.

'Don't be an idiot! I think you're all that and then some, of course I do.' Dan gave her intense, hooded eyes for a second. 'Any man fancying someone as beautiful as you is natural. It's not about you, it's about who he is.'

What? Laurie couldn't shift the feeling he was . . . God, was he vaguely flirting? She felt possibly gratified, mainly appalled and weirded out.

'Here's the bottom line, Dan. I didn't get any rights when you left me for another woman, who you'd spent months having an emotional affair with behind my back, making stupid running playlists together.' She let that land, Dan looking stupid in his exposure, now making a face like Bert from *Sesame Street*. The face she used to love so much. 'I had no rights when you told me you'd impregnated her, despite doing an insulting routine about wanting freedom and no kids, five minutes prior. If Jamie Carter took another woman on the floor of the lobby, he couldn't possibly hurt me the way you have. This whole "splitting up" that you chose, means neither of us have any powers to tell each other what to do, or with whom we do it with. We're totally independent actors. Right?'

Dan, after a moment, shrug-nodded.

'So stay the fuck out of my business, Dan. I'm with Jamie, you're with Megan, no feedback or interventions allowed.'

She stormed out and slammed the door, scattering several members of staff who apparently needed to wait for the room to be free, like stamping your shoe next to a fly-covered dog turd.

Laurie got back to her desk to find Kerry had sent a global email.

5 WEEKS TO CHRISTMAS PARTY!!!!
DETAILS FINALLY REVEALED!!!
It's at Whitworth Hall!
Dress code: eveningwear please.
Submit names ASAP for your Plus Ones.

With that rousing speech, Laurie had effectively signed off Dan bringing Megan. And she was going with Jamie, except she wasn't. While he was falling for someone else.

Laurie had been avoiding admitting something to herself, and blinking at the Clip Art of a dancing elf, she finally faced it: the sham relationship had morphed into a stupid, self-defeating, corrosive mess. Dan might be jealous, but was this her victory, standing around trading jibes with men who thought she'd been taken for a ride by a chancer? Jamie had been much more astute than Laurie: his aim here was defined and clear, he either made partner or he didn't. Laurie was putting herself through all this for what, a few pained looks from an ex who nevertheless, didn't want her anymore? Did she honestly think Dan would picture her astride Jamie, and see the error of his ways?

You're not a liar, which is why you shouldn't get involved with a big bout of lying. Too late. She'd have to see it through.

31

When Laurie's phone rang on Sunday morning, she was trying and failing to make shakshuka, ending up instead with vegetable stew topped with a raw egg. Laurie squinted at her handset warily, as if she was in a clanking daytime television drama with a lot of Face Acting. Emily. But Emily didn't call, Emily messaged. If Emily was going to call, she'd message to say she was going to call. Those were the rules.

'Hi.'

'Hi. Can you come round?'

Emily didn't do *can you come rounds*, and she didn't do that tone of voice. Low, beaten.

'Of course, now?' Laurie said, gathering 'on the phone' wasn't the way Emily wanted to be asked why.

'If that's OK.'

Laurie Uber-ed to Emily's flat in the Northern Quarter with a queasiness that wasn't eased by heated seats and Capital FM and the driver singing along with '(I Just) Died In Your Arms' by Cutting Crew. It could be a bereavement, but she didn't think so. Emily wouldn't hold that sort of information back.

They'd had so many parties at Emily's place, or drunken nights out in the city that had carried on at hers. Laurie got her thousandth pang for Dan. The woozy moment she'd look round at Emily with her head on Dan's shoulder, and think of the two of them as her beloved family.

The split-level apartment had every trapping of 'young, urban, fast lifestyle, moneyed' – the oil-spill dark flooring, red Gaggia machine, the mezzanine with modern staircase up to the huge bed, the fireplace you turned on with a remote control. It would've felt too showy, too hectic to Laurie. It wasn't a place that could do 'cosy' if it tried, with its vast windows onto a Manchester cityscape of cranes and concrete. It put you on show. It was purest Emily.

She answered the door in black silk paisley pyjamas, hair fluffy from sleep, looking younger with no make-up. She nodded a greeting and led Laurie near wordlessly to the kitchen, pointing to a scattering of cherry tomatoes on the breakfast bar. Had Laurie been this worried for the sake of a split shopping bag? Was it going to be 'SOS, we need to go out for brunch'?

But as Laurie drew closer, she realised the fruit was arranged into a pattern. She squinted. It spelt out the word F A K E.

'Robert. From the tiki bar. He left before I woke up.'

Laurie paused in confusion, and thought confusion was justified. She hoiked her cross-body bag off and dumped it by the kitchen cabinets.

'I don't get it. "Fake"? He did this?'

'Yeah. He stayed last night, left before I woke up. I found it when I got up.'

'What? Had you argued?' Emily shrugged and ran her fingertips through a matted section of her hair.

'I dunno, kind of? He called my work superficial, blood-sucking and parasitical and I kept laughing it off and then we had the sort of sex where there's some pushing and pulling and mild slapping.'

Laurie inwardly shuddered at sharing bodily fluids with someone both so hostile, and largely unknown.

'What a piece of shit,' Laurie said, exhaling in shock. 'And what a PSYCHO. Who does this?!'

The tomatoes emanated a sinister force, as she looked at them again. You'd have to plan it, rifling through the salad in the fridge. Weighing up whether frozen peas would do the job.

'It scared me and then I realised, I'm supposed to be scared, aren't I?' Emily said. 'He's with his friends on WhatsApp right now, taking sick pleasure in imagining me finding it, him having the last word. *Hahahaha guess what I did to this stuck-up bitch*. Photo attached.'

Laurie's stomach churned.

Emily dropped on to the L-shaped sofa and covered her face with her hands.

'The worst thing is, he's right. He's right.'

'What? How?'

'I am a fake.'

'In what way are you fake?'

'What's not fake about me? This isn't my hair colour,' Emily yanked at a hank of what Laurie had learned was called balayage. 'These aren't my nails!' she waved Shellacs the colour of blood at her. On her pale small hands, they looked to Laurie like the Snow White spinning wheel pin-prick.

'And this?' Laurie said, gesturing at their grand surroundings. 'A figment?'

'I've got a mortgage larger than the moon, Laurie, you know that. You are looking at debt. Debt with Hague Blue walls.'

'You have a big mortgage because you have an even bigger salary because you are CEO of your own very successful business.'

'Yeah and there's not a day that goes by I don't think it might topple over.'

'That's why you work so hard. That's why you're so good. You don't take anything for granted.'

'I'm right not to. Lost two accounts last week.' Emily put bare feet on the edge of her coffee table and flexed her matching red toes. She was still every bit the over-caffeinated waif who buzzed around Laurie's halls bedroom. Laurie hated her seeming so world weary. Brought low by a total tosser.

'That's work. That's life. You'll win three next week.'

'It's not only that though, Loz! You think I'm thin because I'm thin, right? Maybe I was, once. Now, if I'm not eating with clients or eating with you or whatever, I skip meals.' She gestured over at a spotless kitchen. 'It's never seen a chopped onion. I'm not saying I have an eating disorder. I'm saying I'm thin because I work very hard at being thin and deprive myself and then pretend I don't have to work at it. Even to you. I don't know why. Why don't I say, "I am thin because

I try very hard to be"? Because my world runs on envy, you need to incite envy. Because I'm *fake*.'

'You're not fake!' Laurie said, wilting a little in sympathy.

She sat down beside Emily and put her arm around her. Emily had the musky odour of the night before and it occurred to Laurie there were very few friends you could call before the shower.

'I wouldn't get too close, I smell like a monkey's handbag,' Emily said with a sniff.

'Aye yeah you do.' They both did the kind of weak stomach-laughing that sits right on the border with tears.

'You're very real, Emily. You're dynamic and clever as hell and you never complain. Just because you don't discuss the effort it takes, doesn't make you fake. Would a man do that? What would your *twin brother* do?'

Emily smiled, wanly, at mention of an old catchphrase. At university, discussing with righteous fervour at the different treatment meted out to men, they always put it to this test – the hypothetical male twin in this man's world, who had all the masculine advantages.

'People will always need lawyers,' Emily continued, voice tremulous. 'They won't always need what I sell. Or they won't want it from some craggy fifty-something still cramming herself into her skinny jeans.'

'Right, stop. What does bar man do?'

'. . . Work in a bar?'

'Right, work in a bar. There's nothing wrong with that. But he's what, thirty?'

'Thirty-two.'

'You are four years older than him, Emily, you live here and you are a boss, and you depend on no one. Have you got any idea how threatening that is to the male ego, for women not to need them? Do you think it came from nowhere, Rob the thirty-two-year-old barman's need to put you down, to break you in some way, to humiliate you?'

Laurie thought about her own working week. You were equal with these men so long as you didn't make them feel unequal, lesser, challenged. If you stayed in your lane.

'This is pure misogyny. Those tomatoes are highly relevant to his therapist's notes, not yours.'

Emily nodded.

'Then there's the sex. What am I doing? The people I sleep with, we all have the same problem. The moment we find something is there for the taking, we don't want it anymore. How fucked up is that?'

'Is that what it is? You go off someone once they fancy you back?'

Emily nodded. 'Kind of, yeah. I choose things that I know will short circuit. There must be some psychological blockage or self-loathing, else why do I hate myself so much to sleep with someone like him?'

They both glanced back at the tomato art.

'You've had a scare,' Laurie said. 'But some of this is bad luck, playing the odds. Sooner or later you were going to encounter a nutter.'

'Guess so. With my incredible numbers.'

'I didn't mean that!'

'I know.'

'Can I ask something? Do you think the thing with men is, you're frightened of needing someone, of relying on them?'

Jamie had given her an insight.

'Yeah, maybe?' Emily said, pulling her hair off her face.

'You always got the horror at your mum being so reliant.'

Emily had the most suburban, timid parents Laurie had ever met, and her mum used to have her housekeeping cash for the week put in a biscuit tin by her dad. In a way, no wonder Emily came blazing out of it like a comet. Her older sister had moved herself to Toronto, aged nineteen.

Emily sniffed. 'I met a man through work recently and he asked me out and I said no, as I could tell he wanted a girl-friend. I liked him, but I thought, I'll only mess it up. And better I reject him and he carries on thinking I'm unattainable and great, than finds out the bitter truth. That's wildly messed up, isn't it?'

'I think that's something a lot of people do. What is the bitter truth?'

'That I'm fake. That I'm dull. That sometimes, when I go to do a wee I do an unexpected fart instead that sounds like a bear complaining.'

Laurie rolled onto her side with the force of the laughter.

'I'm serious!' Emily said, through her own laughter. 'If he gets to know me, he won't love me.'

'Or, he'll love you even more?'

'High stakes,' Emily said.

'That's the deal, I think, with love,' Laurie said. 'But I got to know you, and only loved you more.'

'Oh, you.'

They embraced.

'Can I suggest something?' Laurie said. 'Can I suggest we spend a day in together, watching films, eating takeaway food, and completely erasing the lunatic tomato creep from memory?'

Emily nodded. 'We could ask Nadia over, too.'

'Yes!'

They put on music and Laurie made coffee and they did the kind of low key, chatting and pottering you could only really do with a very close, very long-term friend. Laurie felt there was a secret of how to live life buried in this unusual Sunday: they had turned a negative into a positive reason to spend time together, to remind themselves of how valuable they were to each other. Laurie had thought Dan was the source of the unconditional love in her life, but actually it was Emily: she wasn't going to turn round and say sorry, she'd found a new Laurie.

It just happened. We shared Spotify playlists. She's who I confide in now.

Nadia arrived half an hour later, in trademark hat. 'Show me the crime scene,' she said.

They pointed her to the counter.

'Oh my God! Report him to the police, at once!' Nadia bellowed.

'What for, GROCERY REARRANGEMENT?!' Emily shrieked.

When they'd finished laughing, Laurie said: 'Did you get 'em?'

'Oh yeah,' said Nadia, disgorging three packets of cherry tomatoes from her backpack.

Laurie tore a packet open and started building an 'R'.

'What are you doing?' Emily said.

'I'm writing ROB HATES WOMEN in tomatoes, which you are then going to take a photo of, send to him, and block him before he can reply. Nadia, you work on "women",' Laurie said.

Laurie thought Emily might argue but she observed their quiet industry in awe.

'This is . . .' Emily teared up. 'Everything.'

32

Dad

Darling just seen this, sorry to hear – his loss!! 🙁 *The wedding piss-up is at Cloud 23 a week this Friday, we've hired the place out so give them your name on the door. Bring a friend if you want. Can't wait to see you! Nic's gone completely fucking bridezilla by the way, she's absolutely spanked the plastic. She'll probably look like something out of the Moulin Rouge with fuckin' ostrich feathers. So get your gladrags on. Love you darling. Austin. Xxx PS no gifts ta, we're drowning in towels*

A wedding reception, notice given, 'a week Friday.' On a Wednesday. So what, nine days? Her dad had outdone himself.

And Laurie wasn't going to tell him that the way modern messaging services worked, 'just seen this' no longer cut it as a fob off. It had never cut it anyway. 'His loss' and a sad face emoticon, after eighteen years, wow.

Laurie wanted to get through this party as fast as possible, merely showing her face, without the encumbrance of a plus one.

She and Jamie had no dates in the diary other than the Christmas party now, and she felt them both giving each other breathing space as they geared up for it. Was he finding it hard to keep himself away from whoever he was falling in love with?

Laurie bumped into Jamie, in the middle of the following week, as he was leaving court and she was on her way in. She hadn't seen him in the Atticus Finch glasses for a while, maybe her teasing had put him off.

After an awkward hello where neither of them knew quite how to greet each other physically, and ended up settling for a chaste cheek-kiss, Jamie asked after her weekend plans.

'Oh it's a doozy, this one. My dad's got married, and the party is at Beetham Tower bar this Friday night. In case anyone asks about it, now you know, but don't worry about coming along.'

'Uhm, if it's your dad's wedding reception, shouldn't I go?' Jamie said.

'Oh, nah. No one here's going to know it's happening. You're safe to swerve it.'

'There's still a chance it could get out that I wasn't with you. I'm not doing anything on Friday and I'm only going to need a cover story for not being there, and one good enough that if anyone asks me, it fits with whatever's been on social media if they check up.'

Laurie kept forgetting that asking some people to keep a low profile online for a weekend was akin to requesting them spending it locked in a cupboard.

'Coming along seems easier. Unless you really don't want me to?' Jamie said.

'No, sure, come!' Laurie said. She finally saw Jamie was looking slightly hurt. 'It'd be good to have the company, actually.'

Why hadn't she asked Jamie from the off? Having expected him to put a distance after Lincoln, was she doing that herself, rejecting him before he could reject her? Maybe.

It could also be because fake boyfriend and forever-faking-it father was too much fake, for one event. And yet Emily thought Emily was the fake?

But when she was with Dan, he'd have felt like an anchor. Jamie Carter was like holding on to a balloon.

And yet . . . which one of the two, recently, had been completely attentive in a room where she didn't know anyone? And had heard her story of her childhood, and treated it like proper testimony, not a little bit of a sob story she should get over?

'Hmmm. I feel like I am forcing myself on you now,' Jamie said, and Laurie sensed he was hinting, *I will do this, but you need to make up for not inviting me from the start.*

'No, seriously Jamie, please come,' Laurie said, more imploring and certain now. She put her hand on his arm. 'My reluctance was nothing to do with not wanting you there, my dad is just . . . a basket of snakes for me, I guess, and I thought it was simpler to deal with it alone rather than put someone else through it.'

'After what you did for me in Lincoln, don't you think I want to repay you?'

Laurie beamed. 'Yeah of course. But I didn't do that so I could hand you a bill afterwards. It didn't come with any strings.'

'I know,' Jamie said, and gave her a quick hard hug that shocked the air out of her lungs.

On Friday night, she met Jamie at a rowdy pub on Deansgate for a resolve stiffener and they walked to Beetham Tower together. Jamie was in a blue suit that matched his eyes – that flash wardrobe of his was coming in handy – and Laurie, a black jumpsuit and red lipstick. She'd consulted her feelings and gone with strong-defiant rather than a flouncy dress, plus the Ivy-date maxi dress now felt too special to want to waste on her father, wedding or no.

'It's the whole bar? Hiring this must've cost a fortune,' Jamie said, squinting at the skyscraper slab of glass, slicing upwards into the Manchester evening sky.

'Yeah, my dad's always liked to spend money. Nicola's not short of a few bob either.'

After a soaring, seasick lift ride, they were welcomed into Cloud 23, trumpeted as 'the highest point in Manchester'.

'This works, because my dad is usually the highest in Manchester,' Laurie whispered, and Jamie laughed, looking the way he did at her on the train. As if she was . . . what did his mate call her? Exotic. Don't admire me for this, she thought. None of it is about me.

Stevie Wonder's 'Superstition' was on loud, the room a hubbub of dressed up people, pretty much none of whom Laurie knew.

They handed their coats over. Floor to ceiling windows displayed the city beyond at dusk, inside, it was mink velvet modern sofas and white leather chairs, vertical tombstones of mirror breaking up the space. It was like a VIP airport lounge. A waitress with a tray of lowball glasses full of amber liquid and orange peel appeared, Laurie and Jamie lifted one each, sipped. It tasted to Laurie like three fingers of Cointreau.

'There she is! My little girl!'

Laurie heard her father's familiar buoyant tones and allowed herself to be pulled into a hug, mumbling 'congratulations, congratulations' on repeat as substitute for anything more meaningful to say. You didn't need to be told Austin Watkinson made his money in a creative field: a very well preserved late fifties in immaculate designer labels, the mod hair, trim figure, violently expensive chestnut brogues.

She did the same with Nicola, who tottered over in a cloud of fruity perfume, clad in a rainbow sequin dress, volumised hair fanning out like a lion's mane.

'God, you're a bit of alright, who are you?' she said to Jamie, who smiled and shook hands with her. Laurie noticed Nicola was wearing an engagement diamond next to a wedding band, the size of a grape.

'I'm with Laurie,' he said.

'Ahhhh so you found someone!' her dad said. 'I was ready to set you up with Harry over there, after you said you were going to be on the hunt tonight.'

Laurie blinked and realised what he was referring to – a remark on WhatsApp months ago, 'maybe I'll meet someone at your tear-up.' Tactful of him to repeat it in front of her date. Laurie scratched her neck and tried to avoid Jamie's pointed *oh well whaddya know* look.

'Good to meet you, son,' Austin pumped Jamie's hand. 'Hammer that bar, it's free all night. Heeeeeeyyyy!' her dad's attention was pulled away by someone else behind them.

'I guess that solves the mystery of why I wasn't needed for manoeuvres, then,' Jamie said.

'Hardly! My dad talks a lot of rubbish.'

'Mmmm. Harry best not try anything.'

Laurie laughed.

Having been sceptical at first, Cloud 23 actually came into its own when there were no clouds, and the scene beyond the glass was a winter's night. The streets were long sweeps of yellow, bluer lights from buildings, a jewel box of illuminations amid soft black. It made the city look so full of potential, so exciting.

'Wow,' Laurie said, nose almost to pane. 'The view is really something. Like a Michael Mann film, huh.'

She turned to see if Jamie enjoyed the reference, and he was looking intently at her, not the great outdoors.

'Did you really not want me to come tonight? Have I clipped your wings?'

'No! That thing my dad said, he was repeating a message I sent before you and I had even . . .' she waved her hand. 'You know. Started doing this.'

'Yeah but given we're not "doing this" . . . I don't like to think I'm closing off avenues to you.'

Was Jamie worrying he'd taken on a project with Laurie,

one that wouldn't end when the dating scam did? That they'd have to go through the motions of still socialising? That he was already trying to gently detach? She'd sort of known all along this was how it would feel when it came to an end, and yet it still made her feel empty.

'Jamie, I'm not your responsibility. You know that don't you? You don't have to worry.'

Jamie frowned. Now safely through the door, she'd briefly thought they might have fun tonight, watching the Hogarthian gin hall scenes and squalid tableaus of her father's life unfold. Looking at Jamie and his taut expression, she knew it was one of those nights when communication doesn't flow and drink sits heavy.

'Are you regretting this? The showmance,' Jamie said, taking a swig of his welcome cocktail.

Laurie paused, before the glib automatic denial sprang to her lips. 'Yes. A bit. But that's nothing to do with you. It's the situation at work, Dan and Michael's paltry attacks.'

'You know they're both in love with you, right?'

'What?' Laurie said, screwing up her face. 'Nah. A fifty per cent hard "nah", given what Dan did.'

Jamie was undeterred. 'Don't let them make you think that their problems are your problems. They are trying to do a head-wrecking number on you, to undermine you, and you have to resist.'

'Hah. I told my best friend something very similar the other day.'

'Were you right?'

'Yes.'

'So am I.'

Laurie had plans to slink out of the party in full swing and go for a late drink with Jamie elsewhere, but the lure of 'just one more here' after they'd seen off two welcome cocktails was too strong. It was a long way down.

Laurie was at the bar when a late middle aged man at her elbow turned towards her. She felt she recognised him, and he said: 'Hello you,' as if he knew her.

Laurie didn't reply.

It wasn't often in life that a revelation came in an instant. They were usually delivered in stages, sometimes across years, and you had to do some self-assembly to make sense of them. But this man's features, a ghost from Christmas past – he in a split second summed up why she had been so reluctant to come tonight. He encapsulated what was wrong with spending time in her father's world.

Looking him in the face, she realised there was something she'd not looked at directly in a long, long time. Since it happened, in fact.

'What're are you having?' said the barman and Laurie couldn't remember a thing. 'Gin . . . and tonic and lager.'

'Which one?'

'Whichever,' Laurie said, dully.

'Let me get these,' the man said.

'Are you . . . Pete?' Laurie said dumbly.

'Yeah! Crikey, how do you know that? Are you? Hang on, you're not Austin's girl, are you?'

It had downloaded from nowhere. He was called Pete. The sensation of looking at him was that of the bogeyman threat appearing in a nightmare, a leering ghostly visage between the bedstead posts. You tried to scream for help, but nothing came out.

A voice inside her said: *You don't have to stay here, you know.* So she walked away.

33

Laurie found her way back to where Jamie stood, on legs that felt like the bones in them had dissolved.

'We have to go,' Laurie said. 'Now.'

'OK,' Jamie said. 'You're very pale, are you OK?'

'If we go, I will be,' Laurie said.

'Understood.'

Unfortunately, leaving involved collecting their coats, which attracted the attention of Laurie's new stepmother.

'You're not leaving?!' Nicola shrieked.

Laurie didn't know what to do, as she had momentarily lost the power of normal speech.

'Going to get some fresh air, then we'll come back up,' Jamie said, swiftly. 'Too cold to go without coats. Laurie's had a lot very fast.' He gestured a tipping glass motion at Nicola, as Laurie stood mute.

'Oh right!' Nicola said, squinting her eyes in sympathy. 'Do a tactical barf, darling, then have a Smint. See you both in a bit.'

★

'Thank you,' Laurie said in a small voice to Jamie, as they otherwise descended in silence in the lift.

At ground level, Laurie calmed somewhat. She'd felt trapped up there, as though her skin was two sizes too small.

'Do you want to tell me what's going on, or do you just want to go home?' Jamie said.

Laurie breathed out.

'Yes, but not here.' She took Jamie by the hand to lead him somewhere on the street they wouldn't be jostled by the Friday night crowds, and Jamie squeezed her hand back reassuringly. She felt relief from him somehow, despite the unnatural interruption, and wasn't sure why.

Once they were in St Peter's Square, she turned to face him, tucking her hands deep into her pockets and hunching her shoulders against the chill. She was suddenly very cold.

'There was a man, at the bar,' she said. 'One of my dad's friends. He brought a memory back.' Laurie shook her head. 'Until ten minutes ago, if you'd said, did I repress any memories from my childhood I'd say "Haha, I wish." But I had. I'm kind of . . . *stupefied*, to be honest. It's like I knew it was there, but I'd never looked at it. Like having something in your loft storage.'

She wasn't just cold, she realised she was shaking. Actual physical shaking, like she'd been plunged into sub-zero temperature water.

'You don't have to tell me,' Jamie said, and Laurie nodded, then shook her head again: *I can, I will be OK*.

She breathed and steadied herself. 'I want to. Ummm. When I was about eight, I went to visit my dad for the weekend.

One of the few times he did turn up. He took me to his old flat,' Laurie paused. 'His mates came round. They got wankered. My dad disappeared off somewhere, "to see a man about a dog". He does that a lot. He left Pete and another guy to watch me. I knew I wasn't safe, I knew . . .'

Laurie steadied herself so she could continue. Jamie put his hand on her shoulder. That was the worst of it: before she knew, she *knew*.

'Pete said . . . oh God. I haven't told anyone this, or thought about it, for so long.'

'Not even Dan?'

'No. Not that I was consciously keeping it from him. I was keeping it from myself.'

Jamie nodded.

'That guy Pete said to me: "Come sit on my lap and show me what colour knickers you're wearing."'

Jamie's face changed. 'What the . . . To an eight-year-old?'

Laurie nodded.

'Fuuuu—'

'I don't know if he was joking, trying to frighten me. What would've happened. I said I needed the loo, and I went and let myself out of the flat. This would be about eleven at night. I walked through the city until I found Piccadilly station . . .'

'On your own? Aged eight?'

'Yes.'

'You must've been petrified.'

'I was. I think it was fireworks night, you know. Explains why I hate fireworks. And drunken people who didn't mean any harm were shouting "Where are you going?!" and trying to talk to this little kid wandering through the streets, and I was hyperventilating.'

Laurie was as still as a statue as she recounted this. Jamie looked stricken.

'. . . I made it to Piccadilly, I asked them to sell me a ticket to go home to my mum. Of course, they flagged me as a lost child. The transport police turned up, they found a number for my mum and called her. I had to spend a night in a room at the station until she could get the first train in the morning to pick me up.'

'Oh, Laurie.'

'She was furious with me, Jamie.' Laurie welled up now, 'She thought I'd wandered off. I mean, she was more furious with my dad, but he made up some story about how he only went to the corner shop for five minutes and I had no reason for what I'd done.'

'Why didn't you tell her?'

Laurie wiped away tears. 'She'd have never let me see my dad again. I might've been eight, but that much I knew. He wasn't coming back from having left me with a paedophile, was he?'

Jamie blew his cheeks out. If nothing else, Laurie had succeeded in taking the shine off the largesse and larging it upstairs. This was the unattractive reality, the dysfunction. Her dad didn't care about her, or care for her, at all. That was why she hung back from him, she didn't want the contagion of the pretence. She didn't want to be suckered in by the money and the connections and then hate herself for it. She didn't want to *become him*. She had to hold onto the truth.

'Fuck, Jamie. Seeing Pete. It's summed up so much for me. I feel like . . . this is where I've been stuck, my whole life. Between my mum's anger and his indifference. The crossfire. I've got this vivid memory of sitting in McDonald's with a hash brown in a little paper sleeve, and an orange juice, and her saying *Why did you do it, why did you run away, how can you expect me to trust you won't do it again,* to me, over and over. I couldn't tell her. Should I have told her?'

It felt oddly incredibly freeing to simply *ask* someone this. She didn't know the answer, and she had beaten herself up for not knowing it, without even realising, for so long.

Jamie held her by the shoulders: 'Laurie. You had to escape someone threatening to assault you, get yourself to safety and then decide if you wanted your relationship with your dad to rest on reporting it? Do you know how many thirty-eight-year-olds wouldn't know what to do, let alone an eight-year-old?'

'When you put it like that . . .'

'There was no right or wrong answer. Whatever you did had a cost. There was only survival.'

Jamie hugged her and said: 'Also, remember this. You're safe now.'

Laurie buried her face in the wool of his coat and leaned on him and said: 'Betcha wish you didn't come now eh, Jamie Carter. I did warn you.'

He leaned down and said, close to her ear: 'No, now I couldn't be more glad that I did.'

Laurie's heart gave a squeeze and she couldn't immediately look at him.

When they separated again, she said, 'No point ever telling

my dad, anyway. He'd minimise it, say *oh Pete's got a sick sense of humour, sorry you were startled by him, princess. And I was just round the corner buying some fags.* Even if he wasn't. He'd never join the dots and be like "I left my child with a nonce, I am a disgraceful person!" That would mean some reflection and taking responsibility, and that can't happen to him.'

'Can I make a suggestion? Tell your mum.'

'Now? It'd only upset her. She can't do anything about it.'

'You're upset. You've never told her: let her in. Give her a chance to help you. Stop making it your responsibility alone.'

Laurie gave a morbid laugh.

'When did you get so wise?!'

Jamie sighed. 'I had counselling. At university. I was living in reckless ways, trying to hurt myself. Which I came to realise was about punishing myself.'

Laurie stared. 'Oh.'

'One of the things those sessions taught me is, you need to speak up, ask for help. If you don't tell people why you're suffering, or even that you're suffering, they can't help you.'

'I'm not suffering!' Laurie said. 'Missing the end of that party sure ain't suffering.'

'Yes, you are,' Jamie said. 'You are standing here crying, frightened, about something that happened that was so bad, you blocked it out. You're suffering.'

Laurie nodded and sniffed and wiped her nose on her coat sleeve.

He hailed her a taxi.

'Look. You were there for me. Do you want me to come back to yours?' Jamie said, and Laurie's mouth opened in surprise.

'Not like that!' Jamie said, hastily, at her widened eyes. 'If you don't want to be alone, I mean.'

'Thanks. I'll be OK.'

Afterwards, lying in bed, she thought about how that would've worked, and how it would've felt, and whether she wanted him to. Did he mean a drink? Did he mean he'd hold her all night like she did for him? She sensed the latter. Was it any kind of good idea to have someone play-act that depth of feeling for you, wasn't it the kind of innocent sweetness that could turn into a slow-acting poison?

She didn't want him to do things like this: for her to come to feel he was there for her when she wanted, and then for it to be abruptly revoked in the New Year, when he'd got things going with the new love.

But as she admonished herself about how it wouldn't have been at all sensible, Laurie knew she was rationalising, because she wished she'd said yes.

34

The conversation with her mum on the phone the next morning was peculiar. Finally telling her the full story after twenty-eight years, and explaining seeing the man at her dad's wedding reception had triggered it, did not go as Laurie had expected.

She expected lots of fulminating about her father, but her mum was quiet, asking questions but not audibly reacting. The subject change wasn't surprising but still hurtful.

'Is it still alright if me and Wanda come to see the Whitworth Gallery next week? Do you want to meet up?'

'Oh. Yes. I'll come for the culture, and we can have lunch at mine afterwards.' She knew from experience that Wanda and her mother wouldn't accept her treating them if they went out, as they were both on tight budgets.

'Sounds lovely, love. See you then.'

Well – shoulder shrug – that was something and nothing, why bother opening old wounds like that, in return for nowt? She stopped herself: this was the cynic in her, the lawyer in her, the impatient child. Laurie had pushed this away for three

319

decades; what if listening to it was the most her mum could manage, right now?

Laurie met them outside the building the following Saturday (after a week of seeing little of Jamie due to busy work schedules, but it turned out a sympathetic, knowing smile as you passed in the corridor could do much for a feeling of someone quietly being there for you), both looking splendidly eccentric in their own ways. Her mum still favoured her stage wear – over the knee suede boots, long dramatic coat, ensemble set off by a now-silvered close-cut afro. Wanda was about six foot, in crushed velvet smock, moonstone rings on every finger, thin white straggle of hair. Dan used to say she resembled Rick Wakeman.

'I was worried you'd be too thin but you look well,' Peggy said, after kissing her on each cheek. This was a compliment; her mum thought women should be 'bountiful', not 'hungry'.

Wanda had been babysitter to Laurie throughout her early years, and fostered many children – her house effectively doubled as the local youth centre. She gathered Laurie in a crushing embrace that brought a Proustian rush of the sweet peppery perfume she always wore. It was an essential oil, which came in a tiny blue glass bottle with a rubber teat atop.

Laurie was ashamed to admit in childhood, she'd thoroughly nosied Wanda's bathroom cupboards, a practice that was forbidden after Laurie exited it wearing Wanda's contraceptive cap as a tiny yarmulke, asking why this hat was made out of a bendy material.

Wanda went inside the Edvard Munch exhibition, and Laurie made to follow but her mum laid her hand on her arm.

'Will you walk in the park with me?'

This mother-daughter time had clearly been pre-agreed with Wanda, who didn't look back.

They walked through the gates of Whitworth Park, and Peggy linked her arm through Laurie's as they strolled down dappled paths. It was a brisk, bright morning, cold enough that their breath misted but sunny enough that they were both squinting slightly.

They reached a quiet corner and Peggy guided Laurie till they were sitting down on a bench.

'I want to thank you for telling me about what happened,' she said, after a long pause. 'I've done much thinking about it. I think I understand things I never did before. Not about that incident, but in general.'

'Oh?'

'I . . . I've been very short-sighted, Laurie. I never thought that because your father did me harm, he did you harm too. I know he wasn't around very much, that he could be negligent, but apart from that . . . You seemed to take him so much in your stride. I thought you enjoyed visiting him, more than you liked being at home. When you came to live in this city, I thought it proved that,' she continued. 'Your father always had the cash, he was fun dad. He didn't partake in the drudgery, tell you to do your homework. He let you stay up late, watch anything, eat fried chicken and sweet things.'

Laurie grinned in spite of herself. 'The KFC and butterscotch Angel Delight was amazing, Mum, I won't lie.'

'I didn't want to let you go to his home for weekends, I didn't trust him to take proper care. But you wanted to

go and he accused me of ruining you having any relationship with him, when I resisted. I kept thinking, am I trying
to take him away from her, because I couldn't have him?'
Her mum's eyes sparkled with tears and Laurie opened her
mouth to contradict her and her mum shook her head: *let
me finish*. 'I kept going against my instincts as a mother,
Laurie. It's my fault what happened. I knew something
untoward had happened the night you ran to the station,
but you wouldn't tell me what it was. Then I let the
fact you were protecting him make me angry. I took it out
on you. That was wrong.'

'Dad is an abuser,' Laurie said, quietly but clearly. 'Of drugs
of various kinds, which don't help his judgement, but also an
emotional abuser. One of the reasons I never face Dad down
is I know it wouldn't go well if I did. I'd have to see a different
side to him. You live within the lines he draws or you don't
have a relationship with him at all. So I chose to live inside
the lines. I wanted to have a dad.'

Peggy nodded. 'Yes. I remember when you were born. I
was in intensive care afterwards and he wouldn't come and
take you. He said he wouldn't know what to do. I was going
to tell him then he could never see you again, or not until
you were old enough it was your choice. My parents told me
not to do that. That you needed a father.' She gulped, blinking
rapidly in the grey-white sunshine. Laurie took her hand.
'Then you were always such a determined, smart girl. Knew
your own mind, made good choices. Not like me at twenty,
I was a child. I had childish expectations of love.'

'It isn't your fault that Dad is the way he is,' Laurie said.

'While we're on the offloading, I should tell you something else too, Mum: it turns out Dan lied. He left me for someone, he was having an affair, and the someone is now pregnant.'

'No?'

'Yes. I think women spend a lot of time beating themselves up about how they caused or deserved male behaviour, and it doesn't happen anything like the same way in reverse. They get on with doing what they wanna do.'

'Dan always seemed such a pleasant and devoted boy.'

'Yep. Didn't he just. That's the part that destroys me. How will I ever spot the signs?'

They leaned their heads against each other, looking out over the grass.

'You're not angry at me?' Peggy said, eventually.

'What for?'

'For not protecting you from your father. I knew what he was. I knew what he was from the moment I told him I was pregnant, and he said, "What did you do that for?"'

Laurie gasped, despite herself. 'No. I feel like we may have spent quite a lot of time putting feelings on each other that belonged with Dad. He kept marking those parcels Not Known At This Address, didn't he? Sending them back.'

'You are a very clever, very emotional girl.'

'Emotional!' Laurie said ruefully, with a smile, wiping her eyes.

'Emotionally wise, I mean. You have been since you were a little girl, with those watchful eyes. You take it all in. I'm sorry if you should've taken less in.'

Peggy started sobbing, to Laurie's shock and she said: 'Hey don't do that, come on. I'm OK!'

She held her mum tightly. Laurie hadn't realised that in asking for help, she was also offering it.

Laurie seated Peggy and Wanda with a glass of red in the front room while she put the spinach and feta filo pie in the oven, enjoying looking after them.

Over the meal, Wanda said, 'You were always a good cook, Laurie. Remember when you made cheese toasties for about eleven people?'

'Oh yes! I used to love doing that. Worcestershire sauce was my secret weapon.'

'You know who I found the other day, Dundee the badger!' Peggy said.

'Dundee!'

'Dundee?' Wanda said.

'I saw the name on a map and I loved it. I used to say I was going to call my son Dundee,' Laurie said. 'My daughter was going to be Fife.'

Laurie noticed she could say this, without loss. Maybe she would have kids. Maybe she'd have them, with someone less selfish than Dan. Think big.

'She couldn't ever be apart from that badger, Wanda. Years and years and it went everywhere with her. Your father would send you those huge teddies and toys. When you did tea parties, Dundee had to have the highest chair at the head of the table and get his tea first, in case he thought you were favouring the new arrivals.'

'Haaah. I'd forgotten that!'

'You are a loyal person. When someone has your loyalty, it's for life.'

'Yes well, you keep Dundee safe for me,' Laurie said, topping her mum up, feeling self-conscious at the praise.

Laurie had earlier explained the pudding, vanilla ice cream, espresso and liqueur: 'It's an Italian dessert, affogato.' Wanda had looked enraptured at the idea.

'Shall we have the ice cream? Let's have ice cream!' she said now, as if this was the most transgressive thing that three adults could do. 'Let me get it!'

Wanda also insisted on clearing the plates. Laurie knew it was fruitless to stop her, Wanda was one of those kinetic people with need to always be doing.

During the noises offstage, her mum looked around and said, 'Keeping this beautiful place on your salary. What a successful woman you are.'

'Thanks. I don't feel very successful at the moment.'

'You miss him?'

Laurie nodded. There was a pause full of Miles Davis, which Laurie had put on to please Wanda.

'I still don't know exactly what went wrong. I know I'm bright, Mum. Why can't I figure out what went wrong with Dan?'

This was as open and raw as Laurie had been about the situation with anyone, and she hadn't predicted it would come tumbling out with her mum. Yet she knew why it had, even without their confidential in Whitworth Park.

Whatever miscommunications, whatever differences, your

mum was your mum. She was the earthing cable in your circuitry. There were still things you could say to her you couldn't say to anyone else. The connection with someone who had changed your nappies and was trusted with Dundee the badger went deep. You couldn't deny the power of history, and genetics.

'I think I know what happened, but do you want to hear it? You won't get cross with me?'

This surprised Laurie, that her mum had thought about it.

'I definitely want to hear it.'

'Daniel was able to flourish in your partnership, because you gave him the confidence, and because of that, he used you as base camp for his adventures. Your father used to do the same to me.'

'Oh . . . I guess . . .?'

Laurie didn't immediately recognise this as true, and yet when she thought on, she remembered numerous times she had urged Dan to aim high or to have times. The headship promotion at work. The fateful stag do; she'd encouraged him to go. She'd still been pro lads weekends away afterwards, in part to make it clear she trusted him. Nights out. Seeing his parents, visiting his sister in London. The running.

She worried the life she'd built for them had become a cage to Dan, she'd missed the part where she'd supported his every interest and freedom. It was, as her mum said, a base camp.

'Sooner or later, Daniel stopped realising it was you who gave him the strength, the foundation,' Peggy continued. 'He thought life could be only adventure, without you. When he realises what he has done, he will regret it very much. But first he'll need to recognise the value of what he had, in order to mourn it.'

Laurie nodded. She wasn't at all sure this would ever come to pass, but it matched up so neatly with Emily's take, and that alone was satisfying. If their perspectives only meant that they both saw what Laurie had done for Dan, that was enough.

'What do I do now?' Laurie said. Another question she would only ask her mum, this bluntly.

'Have your own adventures.'

Peggy leaned across the table, patted Laurie's face and Laurie suddenly felt six years old in the school playground, with frizzy pigtails and her rabbit backpack.

'Don't wait for him, even though he is on his way back to you. In that way, he is nothing like your father.'

'Ta dah! Now then, Laurie, do you want to pour?'

Wanda was filling the doorway, a coffee pot in one hand and a bottle of amaretto in the other.

Laurie fetched the bowls of Häagen Dazs and they slopped it together, Wanda demonstrating a heavy hand with the liqueur.

'Thank you for letting me crash your mother-daughter time,' Wanda said, ice cream on her chin.

'You're welcome, Wanda, and you're not crashing anything,' Laurie said.

'You're a second mother to Laurie,' Peggy said, patting her hand.

'I'm more like your husband by this point, Peggy! You would've electrocuted yourself by now if I let you do your DIY,' Wanda said and they both roared.

Laurie smiled at them. Her mum might not have had settled relationships, but she had rock-solid friendships. Laurie hoped she could say the same.

35

Since Baby Shower Gate, after which had ensued the longest, stoniest silence imaginable, on both sides, Laurie had been in danger of believing she could avoid the Chorlton set forever. She was getting a loaf of bread in the local deli, and too late, spotted Stepford Claire by the luxury spreads.

Claire put down a jar of organic orange curd and made a swift beeline. Laurie inwardly slumped in dismay. Where was Claire's sense of good old-fashioned burning shame, couldn't she simply pretend she didn't see her? But that wasn't Claire's style, of course. Nothing about Claire's style was Laurie's style.

'Hi! Wow. OK. This isn't easy . . .'

Why bother then? Laurie said nothing. Claire didn't sound uneasy, she sounded slightly breathless and gleeful. In her place, Laurie would've been shrivelling into smoke.

'Reeeeeaaalllly sorry about the WhatsApp thing. We were all still getting our heads round it but there's no excuse. Please accept my apology?'

'Sure. I'd forgotten it, to be honest,' Laurie said.

Claire narrowed her eyes. 'So how are you doing?'

'Great,' Laurie said.

'Oh, great. Pleased for you.' Claire tipped her head to the side, *so that's how we're playing it*.

This wasn't a friendly exchange; it was like fencing.

'I hear you're seeing someone?' Claire said, picking a stray strand of her neatly scissored, blunt blonde bob out of her lip balm. Dan always said she had Lego hair.

Naturally, whether Laurie had another man was the most important thing. Especially with it being foretold that she'd never be able to find one.

'Yeah,' Laurie had forgotten the three witches of WhatsApp would be seeing Facebook, same as everyone else. 'Jamie.'

'You work with him?'

Oh God, of course. She'd have then been straight on to Dan.

'Yes, Jamie is at Salter's.'

'I didn't know if . . . you're, you know. At the stage of meeting each other's friends, or if it's that serious, but I wondered if you'd like to bring him to Phil's fortieth this Saturday coming? It's nothing much, open house, barbecue. Dan's invited. He'll be on his own, I should add . . . she's, erm . . . his new girlfriend is away.'

Hah, so Dan and preg Meg got an invite straight out of the traps. Claire, on spec, decided it might make for a spicy spectacle to throw Laurie and toyboy into it too. Ugh.

'Thanks, I'll have to see. Socialising with Dan isn't among my favourite hobbies now, you can probably imagine.' *Seeing Pri and Erica and their husbands appeals as much as getting the runs on a choppy ferry crossing, too.* 'And I'll have to ask Jamie if he's free,' Laurie added.

'Yes, Dan said he didn't think your fella would come.'

This was lightly, rather than deliberately, thrown. Claire could be extraordinarily insensitive, Laurie had forgotten that. It wasn't only about what she inflicted on purpose, she was perfectly capable of doing it by mistake. She was hugely indiscreet.

'Oh. Why not?'

'Erm . . .' Claire looked flustered, for the first time during their conversation.

'He said . . . well, implied, really. That it was more of a fling than a relationship. That coupled-up stuff wasn't the page you guys were on. Said Jamie's kind of known for casual, not commitment.'

Laurie *seethed*. She was loath to give Claire the satisfaction of knowing she'd got to her, but she had. Dan had said disparaging things about Jamie, and possibly even about his purported misuse of Laurie. Meanwhile, Laurie had spread nothing about stupid Spotify playlists.

She'd not done the Wounded Woman tour, made them feel bad about picking his side, made it a female solidarity issue. She'd never be so crass. But Dan's stupid, wounded, pathetic male pride, after all he'd done, drove him to call Jamie trivial, a distraction. *Don't embarrass her by asking her to produce him at an event full of responsible adults, he's not up to that sort of scrutiny. Bit of a jack the lad, if you know what I mean. For display purposes only.* Well. Two could play that game.

'What time does it start? Half six. OK, I'll let you know.' This was obviously British code for 'I'm as likely to attend as self-immolate,' and Claire said, tartly: 'Sure, well, you're welcome.'

When she got in, Laurie called Jamie, more to rant than anything. Expecting him to make polite noises of sympathy while saying he was very sorry, he had something on that night, and her saying *oh sure, sure I was only venting.* Instead, he offered to pick her up at six.

'It's walking distance from yours, right?'

'What? You want to go?'

'"Want" is overselling it but fuck them, if Dan's been running me down, running us down, then this is essential labour.'

'The rivalry of men,' Laurie said, and Jamie laughed.

'I don't know if you noticed, my interests in this and your interests bled into each other a while back. Never mind the promotion, since Dan accused me of trying to ruin you professionally, this became wholly personal.'

Laurie internally repeated *my interests in this and your interests bled into each other a while back*, after ending the call. Ostensibly a fairly trivial remark, but that was precisely how Laurie felt and didn't dare say. They started as accomplices, now they were a team.

Jamie squinted in the low evening sun on Laurie's doorstep, all facial geometry and good tailoring and lightly worn masculine confidence, holding a bottle of red wine, and Laurie thought anew: *God you're so beautiful, you're nonsensical.*

You wouldn't ever want to be that beautiful because becoming less beautiful as you aged would be so hard. How would he cope when that incredible jaw sagged, when those full lips thinned, when the dark blue eyes became pouchy?

Would he mind, would he notice the difference in how the opposite sex treated him, as his powers dimmed? In Lincoln and after her dad's party, he'd started to be a boyish funny friend; in Manchester, this evening, he was returned to being an intimidating semi-stranger.

'You alright? You look like you're doing very long addition in your head or something,' Jamie said.

Laurie gave a startled laugh. 'Yes, no, fine, sorry. Haha. Shall we head off?'

Jamie gave her a quizzical look as if to say *Ey up, have you started on the wine already.*

They walked to Claire and Phil's at Corkland Road and Laurie said: 'Brace yourself for a major lump of property. Their home is ridiculous.'

'Belfast sinks with boiling water taps? Heated tiled floors? Quartz worktops? Am I warm?'

'Oh my God, you're burning up!'

A five-bedroom, bay-fronted Edwardian semi-detached, Laurie had wondered how much of Claire and Phil having loads of friends was because they had loads of money. They were both quite brittle people, really, but presided as king and queen over Chorlton's thirty-somethings and parents party circuit because they had the castle.

'Laurie! You came!' Claire said as she threw the heavy front door open to the Minton tiled hallway, in genuine astonishment.

'Phil's only forty once!' Laurie said, feeling grimy at the insincerity.

Claire openly stared at Jamie until Laurie intervened with the introductions, passing over coats, bottles and gifts.

Their ocean liner sized kitchen was fairly busy but the fall-quiet-and-stare when Laurie and Jamie entered was perceptible.

In a corner, she saw Dan turn, the emotion pass across his face. He turned back, quickly.

Claire fussed over getting them both drinks and then they stood in splendid isolation, as Claire as hostess was fast claimed by someone else.

A conversation right by them involved a man in an ecru polo neck saying: 'It's only worth doing if the courgettes are properly ripe, and sadly we're in south Manchester, not Sicily, hahahaha.'

They'd been there ten minutes when Pri and Erica, both looking mortified, made an approach.

'Hi, Laurie.'

'Hi! This Is Jamie.' They cooed hellos. Neither Pri or Erica were truly malign, of course, they were just in Claire's gang, playing by her rules. They weren't as egregious in the Baby Shower roast. But some people never really leave school, and more fool them, given how horrible living by school rules was.

Neither of them had the front that Claire did and didn't reference the WhatsApp, looking pink around the edges, and gulping wine like it was water after a marathon.

When they did steal looks at Laurie, it was with a nervous incredulousness. How was this possible, that she could survive being thrown over by Dan for a woman now bearing his child, and consent to come to the same party, and have a dashing younger man in tow? Had she made a pact with an old washerwoman that would see her teeth fall out on the stroke of a fairytale midnight?

Laurie remembered coming to dinner parties here and she and Dan putting effort into being a funny, charming double act. It was an aspect of being in a couple you never talked about, the way you developed a you–wash–and–I'll–dry persona for public consumption.

That's why the schadenfreude had been so strong when they split. There were couples here that got gossiped about after they left, speculation on why he spoke so harshly to her, why she drank so hard, whether the au pair was too pretty to be a good idea.

But Dan and Laurie were being groomed to join the upper ranks, as proven by Dan being asked to man the barbecue of a weekend with Phil, or Laurie making it into baby shower WhatsApp groups, despite having no baby to contribute.

'They like the quota filling of having another ethnic face in the gang, you and Pri are great for the photos,' Dan used to guffaw, while Laurie bashed him with a cushion in mock outrage.

But you know, he might not be totally wrong. There was a really nice woman called Maya who ran a local vegan café who was a single mother, and very large, and Claire had made disparaging remarks about *I know I shouldn't say this, but what can she eat that puts weight on?!* And Maya never scored invites.

'How did you two meet?' Erica was asking, and Jamie was deftly retelling the lift story.

When he excused himself to the toilet, both Erica and Pri breathed: 'Oh my God, Laurie. What a catch.'

'Ah, he's alright.'

'He's gorgeous,' Pri sighed, reverentially.

Laurie should be feeling some ignoble glory but her over-riding feeling was, this is bollocks. It's ALL bollocks. Not purely because Jamie was a stunt man, an actor, but she saw it for what it was. When she had Dan, she fitted, she was accepted. He left her, and she was unclean, cast out, othered.

Now she sashayed back with another presentable member of the opposite sex, and her status had shot up again. None of it was to do with who Laurie was, anything she had to say for herself.

If your value was dependent on these things, you had none.

'I'm so so sorry about the WhatsApp group,' Erica said, having possibly had enough alcohol now to broach it. Both she and Pri looked at their shoes.

'I don't mind. Talking about people you know is natural, isn't it,' Laurie said. Then, in case they thought she was going to be nothing but magnanimous, added, 'Claire doesn't like other women though, from what I can tell. So good luck with her continued friendship if either of your partners leave you.'

Their heads snapped up and their mouths fell open.

'If you'll excuse me, I think Jamie needs some rescuing over there.'

Had walking away ever felt this good? As Laurie crossed the kitchen to join Jamie in another group, she knew this was probably the last time she'd spend time with these people, and realised that it finally felt OK. She was more than these people said she was – if breaking up with Dan was the catalyst for giving fewer fucks about other people's opinions and reminding herself who she was without him, well, perhaps it had almost been worth it.

Perhaps, in their relationship, she had lost herself a little bit.

Jamie was politely discussing the merits of turning forty with Ecru Poloneck Courgette Guy (and Laurie was counting the minutes until it was safe to politely leave), when a chilling scream went up from the direction of the Belfast sink with the boiling water tap. Laurie spent a second wondering why red wine was spurting out of Phil's arm like a geyser, before realising it was his blood. A jagged shard of wine bottle stuck proud out of the sink, like a shark's fin.

While everyone else was frozen, Jamie grabbed a tea towel, Laurie glancing at him in surprise.

'Here, mate. You're going to be fine.' Calmly, authoritatively and with great speed, Jamie tied it round Phil's arm as a tourniquet, the blood instantly staining it rich crimson. Phil slumped forward and Jamie caught him, with some effort, as Phil was north of six foot.

'Oh my God oh my God he's passed out?!' Claire wailed. 'Due to blood loss?!'

'He's fainted at the sight of the blood, and who can blame him, to be fair,' Jamie said, lowering Phil to the ground and carefully manoeuvring his head forward, both hands smeared with the overflow. Claire crouched down, putting an arm round her husband, whimpering.

'Phil! Phil? Can you hear me?'

'He needs to go to hospital, I think he might've cut an artery. It's Saturday night and I don't know how fast the ambulance will be, versus taking him there ourselves. You got a car I could drive?' Jamie said. 'I've only had half a beer.'

A sheet-white Claire nodded and fumbled keys out of her handbag.

'Thanks. Can I get some help putting him into it?'

It was a confronting situation, and only a minute or two had elapsed, but Laurie still couldn't help notice that their closest mates were spectating and letting unknown plus-one guy Jamie do the heavy lifting, literally and figuratively.

Dan darted over to the semi-conscious Phil's side and helped heave him to his feet. Laurie had an ungenerous moment of wondering if it was an authentic urge to help or if he'd had enough of Jamie being first responder.

'Are you a doctor?' said a posh, thin man in spectacles, to Jamie, in a tone of challenge as much as any admiration.

'No, I did a first-aid course at cub scouts,' Jamie said, and Laurie couldn't tell if he was being funny or not.

Outside, Dan helped heft the bloodied Phil into the back-seat of a BMW, next to Claire, while Jamie in the front jammed the key in the ignition and adjusted the mirror. Laurie got in the passenger side.

'I didn't think you were coming today,' Dan said to her, as he closed the back passenger side door and peered in at her, as they prepared to drive off.

'Yeah, I heard – you didn't think Jamie would be up to it, or something?'

Dan had no comeback but to stare blankly, and she slammed

the door. They pulled out of the drive and into the evening traffic.

'We'll be at the Royal in no time,' Jamie said, 'How's he doing back there?' Claire had reached the tearful stage and merely whimpered.

'Hey, hey,' Jamie soothed. 'This is a few stitches and good as new. It's frightening to see blood, that's all.'

Claire nodded. Phil was a sickly beige colour and not fully with it, which Laurie judged may be a good thing. She wouldn't want to be there when they unwound the tea towel.

At A&E he got rushed straight through and Laurie and Jamie were left in their party clothes, under bright lights, surrounded by people with sections of their anatomy leaking or bandaged, a baby crying on the other side of the room.

'Fresh air?' Jamie said, and Laurie nodded. 'Let me wash this off and I'll meet you out front.'

'Well, that was the most dramatic way to get out of cooking fifty burgers I've ever seen,' Jamie said, joining her five minutes later, a few rusty specks on his sleeves and a massive Nike swoosh across the front as trophy of the evening's unexpected turn.

'Your shirt,' Laurie said, gesturing at its ruin.

'TM Lewin,' Jamie inspected it, pulling it away from his abdomen, 'RIP.'

Laurie had a split second of imagining unbuttoning it before a shower, and wondered if there was something in the adrenaline of emergency that made you randy, because she really wanted to.

Minutes later, Claire found them, looking considerably more composed.

'They're giving him a transfusion and they might keep him in overnight for observation, but he's going to be fine.'

'See, told you. Let us know how he gets on, won't you,' Jamie said, kindly.

'I can't thank you enough,' Claire said, to the Hammer Horror splattered Jamie.

'No thanks necessary,' he said, returning her car keys.

'You were an uncompromising man of action and a general hero tonight,' Laurie said, as they waited for their taxis.

It was only when Laurie hugged him goodbye, she felt how hard he was trembling. He drew back and could see in her expression, she'd felt it.

'You OK?'

'I . . . I find stuff like this difficult, after my brother.'

Of course. Laurie hadn't thought of that until this moment, how was that possible? Of course Jamie might have learned what to do, that he'd want some basic skills.

'But you helped anyway?' she said. 'There were tons of people who knew Phil, there, one of them would have stepped in eventually.'

Jamie looked slightly baffled. 'My dad always says if you can help someone, you should help someone.'

'I love your dad,' Laurie said, on reflex.

'Thank you,' Jamie said.

'Can I . . . will you let me write to them, when we go our separate ways? To tell them how much it meant to me, meeting them? I couldn't bear for them to think I flitted in and flitted out without a backward glance.'

'Yes,' Jamie said, looking drawn. 'Sorry I've put you in that position.'

'I would rather be in that position than have not met them. That's the truth.'

Jamie stared at her heavily for a second. 'There's something I said. That weekend away. I think I suggested that . . .'

A car horn interrupted them and a cab driver waved at Laurie.

'Suggested what?'

'Ah. It'll keep,' Jamie said.

36

As Christmas drew ever closer, Laurie was back on form at work, and it highlighted how unfair it had been to accuse her of falling standards. She'd known this, but it was reassuring to have it confirmed.

She saw Colm McClaverty on the court steps, after her Disturbance of the Peace client had got off with a mere knuckle rap.

'Thanks for the hatchet job reviews you've been giving me,' she said.

'It's just Chinatown, Jake!'

'Pranny.'

'Oh God, if one of Arsenal's strikers is off form, Man U don't let them win to be nice.'

'Yeah, but winning or losing happens in court, there's no need to garbage talk me outside afterwards.'

'All I said was you didn't seem like yourself, and that – Malcolm is it? Michael, yeah, took it and ran with it. Like you had other things going on.' He raised his eyebrows.

Laurie wasn't going to bite.

341

'Next time, can you not?'

'You have my word.'

Colm ducked down, grabbed her hand and kissed the back of it, while Laurie said: 'UGH GERROFF.'

Men in her profession, honestly.

'Coffee and a Pret at lunch?' Jamie had WhatsApped her. They'd done this a few times, and when Laurie today commended him on attention to detail in keeping up appearances, Jamie said, 'To be honest, it's nice to have a friend at work. Nothing more than that to it.'

'Aw God! You poor thing,' Laurie said.

'Don't worry about me, I'm used to it. "I'm married to the sea."'

Laurie snorted, digging a wooden fork into her crayfish and avocado.

'I have a question for you, and you don't have to answer. When Dan and Michael were having a go, they mentioned a woman in Liverpool who had a nervous breakdown. Was that your ex?'

'Yeah, God. Michael has people everywhere, huh?' Jamie said. 'Stephanie had time off work and said she'd had a breakdown, I'm not sure if it was true. Yes that sounds . . . unkind, but she leaned hard on how it looked unchivalrous of me to contradict her. I was screwed. Stay silent and tacitly accept her version, or speak up and be the bastard adding to her pain. By the end I had no friends, a whack reputation, and I had to leave.'

Laurie had a funny twinge at 'Stephanie'. Nothing like the same magnitude as hearing of a 'Megan', but that thud when an abstract concept of a person becomes flesh and blood specific. Names mattered more than you realised.

'What happened?'

'We had a thing, for maybe two months. I broke a rule by getting involved with someone in the same office which I will never, ever . . .' he looked at Laurie and stopped. 'Except when it's deeply civilised, like us.'

Laurie nodded.

'I thought we'd been clear it was casual. She was not happy when I decided it had run its course, felt I'd wronged her and misled her. Tale as old as time.'

'Tale usually told by men, as old as time,' Laurie smiled.

'Yes, alright, no need to go all Emmeline Pankhurst on me,' Jamie smiled. 'Anyway, from then on it was warfare: psychological, biochemical. I had to block her on every place online, she dragged my emails from the work server, she said . . .' Jamie grimaced, and brushed a piece of rocket from his jacket sleeve.

'You don't have to tell me.'

He lowered his voice: 'She went round saying I'd roughed her up in bed. That there'd been some choking, I'd gone too far and had violent tendencies.'

'Ugh,' Laurie blanched, immediately wondering if he was into choking.

'Yeah, ugh, you have a visceral reaction to that. Afterwards, though, the doubt sets in that maybe, *maybe*, I did do it. Her whispering campaign was pretty effective, they started calling me the Boston Lincolnshire Strangler.'

'Oof.'

'Eventually it wasn't possible for me to stay, and I started looking for jobs here. So Michael and Dan are right, my name's mud at that firm. I would point out two things though: one, my work was fine, and two, it all relies on the testimony of one person, who I was forced to conclude isn't very stable.'

Laurie knew that as much as Michael and Dan were biased as hell in wanting to think the worst of Jamie, she was biased in wanting to believe the best. She'd heard men do the *oh her, she's crazy* spiel to discredit women before and she instinctively didn't like it. But unless she'd been very blessed or Jamie was exceptionally cunning, she'd not seen a whisper of this villainy herself.

'Anyway, enough of my grisly past. What's on my not-girl-friend's weekend schedule?'

'Oh. Sunday lunch at Albert's Schloss with my dad. Before he goes back to the Balearics for the winter.'

She told Jamie how his advice to tell her mother had been spot on. 'I thought you were a new soul but you might be an old soul. As my mother says,' Laurie said.

'Being strictly accurate you thought I was an arsehole,' Jamie said, laughing. He paused and she thought he might be ruminating on her paternal relationship, except he said, 'Mind if I copy that venue idea? I'm meant to be organising something lunch-like myself.'

'Sure.'

As they arrived back at the office, a slender, striking young woman, with slicked-back hair and co-ordinated belted coat and spike-heeled shoes, reached the door at the same time as them.

'Eve!' Jamie said, more of an exclamation than a greeting. 'Oh, hey you.'

She swung in for a wholly nothing-like-a-former-intern kiss on his cheek. Her eyes flickered to Laurie and back again.

'I'm here for lunch with my uncle,' she said.

She was clearly lingering to say more to Jamie, and Laurie muttered polite excuses and left them to it.

Jamie's relief at her absenting herself was palpable, his nerves crackling and swooping in the dead air, like a radio trying to find a signal.

Suddenly, as much as she wanted to believe that nothing untoward had happened between them, she didn't. They were birds of a feather: sly, stunning, up to Machiavellian shenanigans that remained mysterious to plodding mortals like Laurie.

Wait, *wait*: Eve was the woman he'd fallen for? Of course! It was forehead slap obvious. No wonder Jamie had seemed so discomfited just now, no wonder he'd been edgy in Lincoln. What a quandary! He was going to get his partnership, then figure out how to broach it with Salter? Woo hoo.

How life surprised you: not so long ago, she'd have thought, *ideal match, those two can sit on thrones side by side in hell together.* Now, frankly, it seemed more like heaven.

She'd grown so fond of Jamie, and just like that, he was returned to the magical realm he was from. This would be true even without Eve – Jamie wasn't going to stay doing his job long. If he didn't get made partner, as Michael correctly predicted, he'd be off to London, no doubt.

Back at her desk, Laurie had a feeling of missing him, before he'd left her life.

37

Laurie liked to go to noisy, busy venues with her father. It plugged any gaps in conversation or understanding between them like insulation foam.

Albert's Schloss was everything Laurie expected: a barn-like space heaving with people who saw themselves as part of the city's scene, fire pits dotted around the room, a live jazz band on acoustics. The festive season reflected in some additional red-green napery and strings of gold bells.

'Is Nic joining us?' Laurie had texted, when making the booking.

'Nah, she's got business to do in Liverpool.'

She'd never been asked about her premature exit from the wedding party, which she put down to 1. Her dispensability and 2. Neither of them being able to remember much the next day.

Laurie was glad she'd gone for a low key showy offy Sunday outfit, a floral dress with a biker jacket over the top, as the clientele here were very much sporting the Woke Up Like This look that took an hour to create.

She got seated bang on time at half twelve, asked for a mulled cider. It was soon quarter to one: her dad was late, of course he was. Laurie relaxed into people-watching instead. She thought back to doing the same in Refuge in the summer, spying Jamie on his date with Eve. God, that felt like a lifetime ago.

It was one o'clock now. Her dad wasn't only going to be late, he was going to be flamboyantly late. Laurie pushed down the rising querulousness inside her, the outrage of: *how is forty-five minutes late, when we hardly ever see each other, OK? How is it not a massive indication of indifference?* Because whenever she got a height up, as Dan liked to call it, her dad would sweep in with bonhomie and fulsome apologies and a stupidly indulgent present of some sort, and in a finger snap, she had to convert her mutinous mood into a welcoming one.

How did you fall out with a parent you barely saw from the end of one year to the next? Arguments needed to be something out of the ordinary from generally getting on. If you had a row, then that was it for another year: the row defined the relationship. At some level her dad knew this, of course. He depended upon it. No wonder her mum hated him.

Laurie asked for another cider ('Did you want to order food?' 'No, I'll wait, thank you.'), then another. The third was a poor decision but it was now quarter to two and Laurie was half-pissed and entertaining the possibility she had been stood up. By her own dad.

There should be a clever word, a German word, for that feeling when someone lets you down and it's not remotely surprising and yet still shocking. She drained her glass. A fourth was probably crazy, though she could really fancy one. Because drunk.

'Excuse me?'

Laurie looked up at the Belfast-accented waitress with the cheekbones, through her slightly cider-fogged gaze.

'I'm really sorry. We need the table back?' She held her slender arm out and twisted the strap on her wristwatch so the clock face was visible to Laurie, to underline her point.

Of course, Laurie had forgotten the harsh table turning in popular places like this. She couldn't squat here and get smashed even if she wanted to.

The waitress did indeed look really sorry for Laurie and Laurie was aflame with the heat of the room's fire pits for what her father had put her through. She left cash with a big tip for the beers and tore out of Albert's Schloss without making eye contact with anyone.

Outside, Laurie checked her phone to see if her dad had messaged – *lol of course he hadn't* – and called him. It rang out, unanswered. *Hi this is Austin! I know we all hate talking into these things but speak after the beep if you can bear it.* She could leave a stinging rebuke on answerphone but what would be the point?

When she glanced up, she started at Jamie walking towards her, looking like the essence of young gorgeous Manchester wanker in a black sweater, dark jeans and black trainers. Jacket thrown over the crook of his arm, even though it was minty-fresh cold. Vanity, always.

He was with another heavyset young man in a red jacket and two girls, one with short dark hair and another with a ballet dancer's bun. They were both, it was evident from a distance, gorgeous.

'Hi!' Laurie and Jamie both said, in unison.

They mutually exchanged an alarmed look that said: *If we are meant to be dating then this should be handled a certain way but we've not really thought what that might involve.*

'You go ahead, I'll have the house beer,' Jamie said, fixing it hastily, gesturing his friends inside.

When they'd safely trooped through the door, he said, 'That's a mate from my Liverpool days and some other friends. Somehow I didn't think when you said you were coming here, it'd be Sunday. You waiting for your dad?'

'Well I *was*.'

Laurie explained to Jamie why she was leaving, and Jamie grimaced and said: 'That's completely shit. And he's not picking up? Wow.'

'Yep. Also, don't turn round and look, but be aware they've given your friends seats in the window, and they have a direct line of sight to us right now.'

'I've never felt as guilty in my life as I do, doing absolutely nothing wrong with you.' Jamie grinned and Laurie tried to smile, but she couldn't manage much of one.

It was good to see him, if in excruciating circumstances. Was he on a double date . . .?

'Are you OK?' he said.

Being asked if she was OK, a friend seeing her not OK-ness, tipped the balance. Laurie's eyes stung in the bright winter sunlight and she said, morose with alcohol on an empty stomach: 'Was there something in Dan that was like my dad, that I unconsciously homed in on? I feel like I wore a *please kick my arse some more* sign. Without knowing it. Should I have treated them both differently?'

'*No*. Listen,' Jamie put his hand on her side and moved Laurie further out of the way of the door, as more customers arrived. 'Listen to me on this, I know what I'm talking about. It's got fuck all to do with you. I've let down some great people in my time and it was never, ever anything to do with them. In fact, sometimes the fact they were great sent me spinning off even harder in the opposite direction.'

Laurie gulped. She was right on the precipice of tears and this sort of kindness could push her right over.

'*They* are messing up. This is *their* inadequacy. Don't put it on yourself. That your dad can't be a father and Dan can't not be a treacherous dickhead are faults in their own stars. You're over here.' Jamie gestured a circle around Laurie. 'Doing you. And you are completely fucking great.'

'Thank you,' Laurie said, tightly.

'If you ever believe that you'll be completely unstoppable. I kind of hope you don't.'

He smiled and Laurie smiled back, weakly.

'Jamie . . .?' The ballet bun hair girl hung off the door, in an insouciant way, like a child playing. In skinny jeans, she had a pelvis the size of a banjo. Laurie wondered if Jamie was playing it. She felt a pang of insecurity.

'We need to order food?'

'Get me the roast dinner thing. Do they have that? OK, one of those please.'

The girl lingered, looking to Laurie, then Jamie, then back to Laurie again, disconcerted.

'Can I have a moment with Laurie, please?' Jamie said to her, and her eyes widened.

The door slapped shut as she scuttled off inside. The girl watched them with bug eyes, from beyond a pane of glass, her mouth moving rapidly as she no doubt updated her tablemates.

'Are you seeing her?' Laurie said, blurting, slightly taken aback at the idea. What a tangled web this was: what about his fake girlfriend, and what about Eve?

'No,' Jamie said, frowning. 'I thought we agreed we wouldn't do that, while this was going on. Are you seeing anyone?'

Laurie shook her head, thinking, I should've thought that was obvious. Who'd date this gibbering wreck. She can't get a date with her own dad.

'I'd not say what I just did to her, if I was, would I?' Jamie looked perplexed, even faintly annoyed, and Laurie couldn't entirely read why.

'Sweetheart!'

They both turned at the male voice behind them.

Worse than her dad not turning up, was her dad turning up now. So of course that's what he'd done.

'We did say half two, didn't we? Hello there, Jamie, was it?'

Slovenly. That's what her father was. It was an odd word nowadays, you only ever heard it when detective sergeants read from their notebooks in court to describe the defendant.

Not in appearance, quite the opposite: another immaculate checked shirt, a bauble of a watch and spotless Harrington jacket. Austin Watkinson was slovenly in his habits, in his attitude, his care for others. Slapdash. Blew one way and then the other.

'No. We said half twelve.'

'Oh.'

Her dad looked at Jamie, who was staring at him.

'Shall we go in?' he said.

'We can't. Our reservation was for half twelve, until half two. They've thrown me out after I sat waiting for you for the entire time,' Laurie said.

'Oh. Right. Whoops. Sorry, love. Let's think about where else we can go, then. It's on me!'

Her dad rummaged in his coat pocket, produced a carton of Marlboro Lights. He tapped one out of the packet and lit it behind a cupped hand. After he blew the smoke out sideways, he said, 'Why are you both so glum and why are you looking at me like that?' He addressed Jamie, then Laurie. 'Why is he looking at me like that?'

'Because you're two hours late and short of one decent excuse?' Jamie was perfectly direct and steady and Laurie was quite impressed at him deciding to stay put, and stay in character.

'Oh dear!' her dad clapped his shoulder in a faux matey manner. 'Very chivalrous defence, young man. You have my approval.'

Jamie looked at Laurie in disbelief and Laurie almost winced at how cheap and glib her father was. When she was younger, she briefly thought the devil may care routine was impressive. It had aged badly.

'Do you think after I've sat staring into a beer for two hours, without you having had the basic courtesy to use your phone, I want to go to lunch like nothing happened?' Laurie said.

'I'm sorry! I wasn't sure what time we said and then Linus

called me and we were on the blower for an age and when I got off I thought it made more sense to race here than . . .'

'Translation, you didn't give enough of a shit to check, or it didn't suit you to be here at half twelve and you thought messing me around was a price worth paying for that convenience.'

'Oh, it was hardly that considered, it's an honest mistake. Do we have to do this in front of him? I feel like I'm going to be finishing this conversation being tape recorded in the nick. What *is* your problem?' He half laughed at Jamie. He didn't like Laurie having support, she could tell, probably used to Dan smoothing over any gaps in realities in the past. And his manipulation had always worked better on her alone; he didn't like a witness.

'My problem is wondering what you did to deserve a daughter like this, when you treat her like this,' Jamie said, simply.

'Christ alive, I think you might be extrapolating hard based on one cock-up, don't you? Hello, I'm Austin, we met a minute ago. Let's start again, shall we?'

'We met at the wedding reception,' Jamie said.

'Oh? Look, that was a busy room, I met a lot of people. Bet you liked the free bar though.'

Laurie took a deep breath. Somehow, she'd known this was coming, if maybe not this soon. She couldn't face the Pete memory, and not know this would be the consequence. 'I don't want to go for lunch with you.'

'Suit yourself. Let's do this when you've calmed down. I'm in town for a couple of days next month, I think.'

'I don't want to do it ever. What's the point of pretending, when this sort of selfish bullshit is the total of our relationship? Let's let this go. I don't know what you get out of it, I certainly don't get anything but humiliation and disappointment.'

Around them, happy carefree dressy people streamed past and into Albert's Schloss to eat sausages and get ratted, in a hedonistic millennial version of the Sabbath.

Meanwhile, Laurie was terminating her relationship with her father, standing next to the man she was only pretending to be romantically entangled with, in order to hurt the man who had hurt her. Hashtag blissville.

Her dad finished his cigarette, threw the stub on the floor and ground it underfoot. 'This wild overreaction based on one foot wrong is strongly reminiscent of your mother in her heyday, I'm sorry to say.'

Invoking her mum, thinking Laurie would hate the comparison with a woman he'd rejected. What an utter arsehole.

Those who said family mattered above all else were wrong. People you love, who love you back, matter above all. Crap people you happen to be related to: you need to stop thinking you owe them a limitless number of chances to hurt you.

Laurie inhaled deeply, tasting the freedom from expectation like the first tang of salt air at the seaside.

'I was a mistake, I know that. You didn't want me. When I was a baby, you walked away and left Mum to deal with everything alone. Well, now I'm the one calling you a mistake, and walking away.'

Her dad said nothing for a moment, his eyes flicking from Laurie to Jamie and back again.

'Jeez Louise. OK. I'm going to have a pint in there,' he jerked his head towards Brewdog. 'When you've calmed down, feel free to join me. If and when you and laughing boy detach yourselves from each other.'

Laurie belatedly noticed Jamie had his arm around her waist. It made her straighten her back.

Her dad thrust his hands in his jean pockets and slouched off to the pub, with very much a careworn air of: *the things I have to put up with.*

Jamie turned round and hugged Laurie to him. It felt like he absorbed her anxiety, defused it.

'That can't have been easy. But I think you did the right thing,' he said, while Laurie breathed hotly into his jumper.

She got herself back under control as quickly as possible, not wanting to be street theatre for Jamie's gang. She'd stopped looking to see if they were looking.

'Do you want me to stay with you? That lot will understand. Or they'll be told to understand it,' Jamie said, with a winning smile. Those smiles were hitting Laurie harder, lately.

'Ah. No,' Laurie said, fully disentangling, wiping her eyes. 'Thanks but no, I'm fine. Walk home will do me good.'

'OK.'

Jamie leaned down and kissed her on her cheek, gave her shoulder a supportive squeeze, turned and went into the restaurant.

Laurie walked down the road, past Brewdog where her dad was sinking Estrella, past The Midland where she and Dan once spent a hedonistic forty-eight hours, and drew her coat together against the cold. Why had she been in denial about her dad for so long, and accommodated so much? It was strange, but she realised, partly because Dan would've disapproved of her getting shot. Whenever her dad took the bare piss, Dan made the case for Not Making A Scene or Not Blowing It Up Into Something or You Know What He's Like, Though.

If he'd been here this time, he would've undercut Laurie, said: *Not here, not now, let it go. Let's have a pint. Come on, you two hardly ever see each other.* Her dad would've divided and conquered.

Afterwards whenever Laurie fumed: *But, Dan, he deserved it*, he'd have said *oh true.* But the moment had always gone.

Dan came from his lovely, safe middle-class parents, and Laurie's dad was the rogue who offered Dan lines in the toilet, the first time they met. Dan couldn't take him seriously, in every sense.

When they still spoke in theory of a wedding, Laurie always said to Dan, 'I'm not having my dad give me away, nope, no way.'

And Dan always protested, quite vociferously. 'Come on, Lolly,' (she was only ever babied as Lolly when he wanted to shut down a debate) 'he's your dad. Your dad gives you away. It wouldn't be a day for grudges.'

No matter how many times she explained it, Dan didn't get it.

Jamie got it. She could hear his voice in her head now, clear as a bell. *Fuck him, why should he, why couldn't it be your mum? She raised you. If it's for any parent to 'give you away', it's her.* His lack of sentimentality about tradition had its uses. She smiled at the thought.

When this was over, she wanted to stay friends with Jamie. She'd been wrong about him – she suspected in part because Jamie had been wrong about himself. They might be chalk and cheese but he was a whole person, a grown-up, the real deal. She valued him, his perspective on things. She felt like he valued her.

Laurie felt her phone go *brrrrp* in her pocket and yanked it out. It'd be her dad saying: *'Where have you got to? Come on let's make up. Got some champagne in here and a pint for your fella.'*

The way he spent money was to guilt you, to indebt you, to bewitch and befuddle you. Only later you'd realise you'd been bought.

Jamie

If you're a mistake you're the greatest one ever made. I'm really proud to know you. xx

Laurie's eyes pricked with tears and her heart soared and she remonstrated with herself, as cartoon stars started to dance around her head: this is a warm friendship. He cares. And you're vulnerable, and cider isn't meant to be hot.

He got two kisses after her thank you, though.

A small voice inside her head whispered to her, and she hissed at it to shut up. The voice insisted. *Jamie was there on purpose, to see you. He wanted to be there. He knew you were going for Sunday lunch. You said Sunday. Definitely.*

Oh, shut up, Laurie nearly said out loud.

I'm not wrong, said the voice.

38

There was a certain type of celebration thrown by people who didn't do parties and they were significantly worse than those organised by people who liked parties.

The difficulty with Salter & Rowson's annual Christmas bash was that it was conceived by two men in their sixties who never socialised beyond their golf clubs, trying to imagine what people in their thirties might do for a knees-up. It resulted in Greek restaurants with traditional dancing and taramasalata the colour of bubblegum and baskets of dry pitta corners. Or deafening volume wine bars trying to moonlight as mass caterers, serving forty-five turkey risottos with a cranberry jus and parsnip tuile.

This year was at the university, and with its wood panelling and organ and chandeliers, it looked pleasingly like the Hogwarts banqueting hall. The plus, no karaoke. The drawback was that in order to make it profitable, it accommodated multiple companies and hundreds of people.

For all the elegance of the surroundings, it would've been tons nicer to have a lesser place to themselves. Hey ho.

Or HO HO HO, as the giant illuminated letters on stage had it.

However, it wouldn't have mattered if they threw tonight's shebang in the Palace of Versailles, it only mattered to Laurie that Dan was taking Megan. This was confirmed by a message shortly after the company email, asking if it was OK. Wanker. Bastard. One of the worst things about you, Laurie decided, is I thought I was a good judge of character.

But Laurie, so soon after announcing them free agents, could hardly object, and it was face loss to care, anyway. The chutzpah of this woman, too; Laurie couldn't make the imaginative leap where she thought it was acceptable, let alone desirable, to sit at a table in the same room as Laurie.

'She'll have rationalised: we didn't do anything until they were over, if they were right they wouldn't be over, and I'm the one with the baby, which is a complete and final answer to what matters here, so stand aside,' Emily said. 'None of which makes her any less of a bitch.'

'Telling me.'

Laurie spent a small fortune on a fire engine red, one-shouldered dress, that pulled in tight at the waist and had a chiffon skirt that flared out in soft folds, in a *Strictly Come Dancing* sort of way. Laurie felt as if she should be raised overhead in it by a ripped Eastern European hunk, to a big band reinterpretation of a Lady Gaga song. She wore her hair out and big, having gone for a blow-dry. And utilised the siren lipstick that Emily got her. The look was almost comically 'Thank U, Next' defiant to an ex, and yet Laurie had no qualms about making an effort, not like her apprehension before The Ivy. Anything less than a pyrotechnical show of strength, when faced with your ex and his pregnant mistress, was unconscionable.

When she removed her outerwear at the coat check, Jamie said: 'You look utterly, completely hot,' and seemed to mean it. Laurie could only give him a tense smile.

Jamie was in a black suit, white shirt, black tie. ('I look like a waiter or a Reservoir Dog but I'm not wearing a tuxedo. Unless you get one made, they never fit, and I'm not wearing a baggy hired one and feeling like I'm in Boyz II Men.')

'It's going to be OK,' he said quietly, taking her hand, as they entered the main hall.

'But we split up after tonight!' Laurie hissed at him, with a smile. They'd reaffirmed that post-Christmas do, it was time to draw things to a close.

'True. This is so meta,' Jamie said.

They studied the seating plan and located their table, seeing they'd been put directly next to Michael and his date for the night, a nervy vape smoker called Sam.

Given the bile that Michael had sprayed at Jamie previously, Jamie was extremely gracious and solicitous to both him and Sam, while Michael looked stormy and murderous throughout.

Sam took to Jamie, the way most women did. Laurie noted that as soon as it was in danger of becoming obvious, Jamie found a way to refer back to Laurie and bring her into the conversation, so there was no danger of Michael claiming Jamie had flirted. Except, Laurie was sure that Michael would claim that anyway. Once you despised someone with that sort of Old Testament fervour, you could always find the material.

They were cheek by jowl with lads from Experian, and a six-foot-something giant in a kilt called Angus insisted that, as he and Laurie were back to back, they had to introduce themselves to each other. She shook his hand and felt glad of the merry goodwill all around. However tempting, it would've been so wrong to stay away tonight.

Angus angled his chair towards Laurie and made conversation with her until the salmon mousse appeared.

As the starters were being swept away and the right combination of people were out of their seats at the same time to provide a direct line of sight, Laurie saw them.

Dan was in an old suit she remembered helping him choose, Megan, a small but prominent bump visible, was in a pale blue strappy dress, a shiny curtain of poker straight red hair tucked behind her ears. Laurie gazed at the bump. Now it was in front of her, as simple fact, its power was considerably dispelled. It was nothing to do with her.

Megan didn't appear to be interacting much with anyone, inclining her head to say something to Dan every so often. Then someone spoke to them, and she saw Megan place her hand on Dan's knee in a proprietorial fashion. Laurie flinched, but after a moment's analysis, realised it was a flinch at the strangeness of seeing this, not Megan's rights over Dan. It felt disorientating and peculiar, like selling a piece of family furniture and seeing it in someone else's house. But you knew it didn't fit in your place anymore.

Megan leaned in, doing a cutesome and stagey head tilt, as if someone was taking a photograph of them, before bursting into peals of girlish giggles and petting at his face.

Dan received this with tolerance but slight embarrassment, Laurie detected.

And in another moment of observation, Laurie got it – she finally figured it out. The clear difference that Megan offered, compared to her: uncomplicated adoration. Dan was running the show and being made to feel in charge and manly.

She recalled that moment in the spare room, Dan saying resentfully: 'You're so bloody clever, you are.'

Laurie had thought she and Dan being a match was a good thing, that she kept him on his toes. They sparred. But a woman had come along offering to play-act the supplicant, do the *You Tarzan Me Jane*, and he couldn't resist. He'd started to find Laurie wearing, by comparison.

She never thought she'd have an explanation, or closure, and now she did. Huh. It felt relieving and slightly flat, like finding out whodunnit in a murder mystery and realising the question was more intriguing than the answer. Megan looked over at Laurie, and Laurie fought her inclination to glance away and returned Megan's gaze, steadily. After a long moment, Megan dropped her eyes and fussed with the napkin on her lap.

'Yep,' Laurie said, to no one but herself, picking up a bottle of wine and refilling herself.

'You OK?' Jamie asked again, in her ear, arm round the back of her banqueting chair with the broad festive red and green sash ribbon round it.

'Yes,' Laurie said. 'I'm more OK than I've been in a long while, and I have no idea how or why.'

'I do,' Jamie said, with a smile.

'Oh?'

'I told you when you started to believe in yourself, you'd be unstoppable.'

Jamie Carter, what an unlikely hero. In that second, she wondered if she loved him.

39

'The Idiocy Hours are well underway.'

Laurie and Bharat were leaning against the bar on a leg stretch, and Bharat was looking around the room with a curl to his lip. The dancefloor had appeared after a third of the tables were whisked out of sight, replaced by stretch of parquet floor, scattered with disco ball fragments of light. 'This'll be a scene of horrifying carnage pretty soon. A few will have to be Medi Vacced out by helicopter.'

Laurie laughed. Bharat strongly believed that anything that happened after 9.30 p.m. at the Christmas do was best heard about rather than participated in, and was preparing to make good his departure.

'Let me know if anything scintillating kicks off? Di's had three Babychams so she'll not remember.'

Laurie faithfully promised Bharat she'd be his surveillance detail.

People were stood up now, ties loosened, bottles of beer in hand, covert snogging in the darker recesses of the room. The night time sky was visible through the vast stained-glass windows and as she walked back to the table, Laurie thought about how she'd go home alone, but wasn't really lonely any more. Or if she was, it was only in passing, not as a constant state. Her powers were returning. She'd met Dan when she was eighteen, when she had the confidence to stride up to a bunch of lads in Fresher's Week and tell them she'd sort the problem out. That girl wasn't created by him, she existed already.

Dan had chosen a future without her, and as sad and harrowing and unexpected as that had been, now she got to choose a future for herself. It was exhilarating.

'Dance with me?' Jamie said, as she reached him, pushing his chair out and taking Laurie's hand.

'Is this for their eyes?' Laurie said, behind the back of her hand, and gestured towards Misters Salter and Rowson. Rowson looked like an angry schoolmaster in a Dickens adaptation, wiry with a square set face, a thatch of brown hair that looked as if it was made from wire wool, beetling eyebrows and black-rimmed glasses. ''Cos I think you're alright, they've clocked us together.'

'No it isn't,' Jamie said, affronted. 'Sometimes I think your opinion of me is as bad as everyone else at this company.'

Laurie exhaled and long-suffering-smiled and let herself be led on to the floor, feeling the many eyes following them.

Prince's 'Purple Rain' was starting.

'Are you good at slow dancing?' Laurie said, with difficulty over the music. 'I'm never quite sure what to do.'

'I think it works like this.'

Jamie put one arm round her waist, and placed her hand on his shoulder. With their free hands, they held hands. The moment her fingers closed round his, she felt a jolt of something, an aliveness where she was acutely conscious of every point of contact between their bodies. His palm slipping towards her hip bone, the fabric of his shirt and his shoulder muscle underneath her fingertips. The light pressure of her corseted chest pressed against his – it was completely U Rated, Family Friendly and yet somehow, the sexiest thing Laurie had ever experienced.

She couldn't look him in the eyes, and laid her head against his chest, breathing their closeness in. Laurie had been in proximity to Jamie numerous times yet there was something in this moment, this sustained embrace, it forced her to face chemistry she'd been assiduously avoiding.

They were consciously creating the closing credits to their story, the one that started in a broken lift. How should it end? Should she turn her head upwards, tilt it slightly, and finally kiss him, before the stage curtain fell?

But how would she know he had genuinely wanted to kiss her? Did she want someone to pretend to want to kiss her, however well he did it?

I only wanted to be some kind of friend

Even the song seemed to be speaking to them, a sense of something spinning off its axis, going awry. She couldn't see Jamie's face, or judge if he was feeling anything like what she felt.

When they broke apart at the end of the song, she looked up at him in wonder to see if his face held any clue, and he was looking back at her with a completely intent, lovestruck expression she knew she'd try to hold on to in her mind's eye until her dying day. You didn't get many of those looks, in a lifetime.

'I need the loo,' she mumbled, breaking away before Jamie could say anything, picking her way through the increasing Christmas party carnage to the ladies.

On her way, she passed Dan, who looked like the time on the caravan holiday when he'd found rat droppings in his Coco Pops box after eating them for four days.

'Hi!' Laurie said, and swept onwards before he could reply.

Slow dancing with Jamie, and it hadn't even occurred to her whether Dan was witnessing it.

What would success feel like to you? She could finally answer that: self-respect.

It felt like not caring anymore.

She washed her hands in cold water and looked at her face in the mirror and tried to make sense of why three minutes of clinging to Jamie Carter like a koala had left her in this state. Alcohol, Prince, him looking great in a black suit, these were factors. They didn't add up to the full answer. She balled a paper towel in her hands.

A toilet flushed and Megan came out of a cubicle, looking as dumbstruck to see Laurie as Laurie was to see her. She stood perfectly still for a second.

The only noise was the burble of the music beyond a thick wall, and the dripping of a tap.

'I didn't think I'd ever be this person,' Megan said, eventually.

'Neither did I,' Laurie said. 'And I didn't have a choice about it.'

She threw the paper towel into the bin, and left Megan standing there.

When she returned to the main hall, she could see Jamie at a distance, chatting with a good-looking girl from another table, and wanted to wolf howl with possessiveness. She felt a wash of confusion, yearning and rivalry.

He *thought* he was falling for Eve, but no one would hold him back for long, would they? He was no doubt constitutionally incapable of monogamy.

Laurie wouldn't do this, she *refused* to do this. She wouldn't break her own heart, in the style of a raving idiot. Jamie Carter was sold as seen, she had no cause to criticise him for being who he was, and she was glad of that. She wanted to keep liking him.

She backed out of the door and through an ante room and she was in blessed fresh air, albeit blessed fresh air that was going to feel Arctic within seconds.

'Hello, again,' said a friendly giant in a kilt.

'Hello, Angus from Experian,' Laurie said.

'Hello, Laurie the lawyer. What are you doing out here?'

'It got too much. Briefly.'

'I know what you mean. The lass I was seeing until November is tonguing Duncan from Complaints. I wonder if he'll listen to my complaint. How about you? What got too much?'

'Ah, tricky. My ex of eighteen years is here with his pregnant girlfriend. Always going to be challenging.'

'Woah,' Angus said. 'That's some deep water. You're single?'

'Single,' Laurie said. It now felt natural to say it. Even positive.

'That won't last long. You're crazy pretty,' Angus said. 'You look like the girl out of Corrie. Or was it *Emmerdale*?'

'Angela Griffin,' Laurie supplied.

'Oh my . . .! How on earth did you get there that quick?'

Laurie laughed. 'Because when you're half black, black-ish, everyone has the same five reference points for you. I'm collecting them. I've had Missandei from *Game of Thrones,* and Marsha Hunt already this year. What's funny is none of them look remotely like each other.'

'Shit, sorry,' Angus said, and she winced: he was obviously a benevolent character.

'No no, I'm flattered!'

'Better than who I get. Alex Salmond, usually.'

Laurie hooted. 'Not true.' She paused. 'Singlehood. I'm quite nervous about the idea of being with someone new.'

'It'll be grand. Like riding a bicycle.'

He had a friendly face, a kind face. *Was Jamie going to go home with that girl?*

'You're so pretty,' Angus repeated.

'Thanks.'

Angus leaned down and put his mouth on hers, and Laurie only processed she was about to be kissed, once the kiss had begun. She responded at a delay, feeling as if she was standing outside herself and observing what it was like with someone unfamiliar, who moved their mouth differently. It was neither unpleasant nor that great, she decided. One milestone passed though. The first kiss after Dan.

A coughing, right by them, and they moved apart. Jamie was watching them, holding Laurie's coat.

'Shall I get you your taxi? Looks like you've had enough,' Jamie said, and with his tone of voice, Angus said, 'Right ho,' and made himself very scarce, very fast.

Jamie whisked Laurie round the corner, propelling rather than holding her, and when he was sure they were alone, said: 'What the actual fuck? Remember the whole thing about no cheating during our dating? It being a humiliation for the other person? And the Christmas party being kind of important?'

He looked utterly furious and Laurie found herself stuttering apologies.

'Seriously, outside the *Christmas party*? Are you for fucking real?'

'Sorry,' Laurie said hanging her head like a naughty schoolgirl. 'I'm really sorry. I didn't think.'

Jamie stared at her, as much it seemed in disbelief as fury.

'Thank God it was only me who saw, I guess. And I don't matter.'

'Well. Neither do I.'

'What does that mean?'

'I don't know.'

'You're drunk,' Jamie said, but she wasn't, and he knew she wasn't, and it was merely a welcome way out for both of them.

40

Torrential rain, the emphatic Manchester sort, the size of stair rods and sounding strong enough to break glass, bucketed down. It was as if the weather had reacted to what she'd done. The sky had exploded, the way Jamie did.

At home, Laurie lay down on the sofa, kicking her shoes off, feet hooked over the arm. She should take the dress off but she couldn't bring herself to de-Cinderella yet, it might be years before she wore this again. Then she got up, lit some candles and put a Prince compilation on.

He was completely within his rights to let fly at her, she'd been reckless and selfish. She was trying to escape from herself, and everyone's expectations, and their deal was collateral in testing what it felt like to tart about.

She couldn't shift the sense she and Jamie were broadcasting on multiple frequencies now, that things were no longer necessarily about what they were about. Emily's prophecies kept on coming true.

Ding-dong.

Laurie's heart went bang and she sat up straight. She knew

who it was at the door; knew, and yet pretended to herself she didn't. If it was anyone else, her dismay would swallow her. In that split second, she'd learned something about herself.

'It's Jamie.'

She slid the bolt. THANK GOD, and, OH NO.

She opened the door: he was drenched, water running from hairline down his face, coat wrapped round himself like a dressing gown. The clematis over the porch had a small water-fall pouring from it.

'Hello,' he said.

'Hi.'

A short pause, Laurie's pulse still thundering in her ears.

'Do you want to come in?'

'It'd be better than being out here.'

She stood back as he brushed past, soaked enough that he left a wet streak on her dress.

'Do you want a towel or something?' Laurie followed him into the front room trying to keep her voice even, trying to conceal how jittery she was.

'Yeah, if I can?'

Laurie ran upstairs and grabbed one from the bathroom rail. She handed it to Jamie, who patted his face and hair ineffectually.

'Take the coat off and I'll stick it on the radiator,' Laurie said, trying not to notice the wet white shirt underneath.

'Lovely house,' he said, glancing round.

'Thank you, I'm still paying for it,' Laurie said, smiling. 'Maybe in more than one way.'

'It looks exactly like the one on that Oasis album cover.'

'Ha. Yep. Not entirely unintentional. Maybe I have some of my father in me after all.'

They smiled at each other. Laurie took the towel back and held it over her arms, a small barrier. There was an excruciating silence.

'Did you know they wanted cans of Red Stripe on that album cover, instead of the red wine, but they weren't allowed the product placement?'

Stop wittering, Laurie! And he's turned up on your doorstep, it's for him to announce his business and fill awkward pauses. I am scared about what he's going to say.

'I didn't know that. Are you some sort of an Oasis superfan?'

'No! I liked that . . . décor.'

Jamie gazed at the floor.

'I'm sorry to turn up like this. I'm sorry I shouted at you. Only, I've been turning it over and over in my head. I need to know why you kissed that bloke. I can't work it out at all.'

Laurie took a shaky breath.

'Can't I have kissed him for the reason anyone kisses someone, when knee deep in cheap plonk at a Christmas party?'

'Number one, he was a right dozy twat. Number two, if it was to make your ex jealous, he wasn't witnessing it. Number three, it contravened the agreement we made, so you were taking a risk. Number four, fucking kilt. There are four compelling reasons for not kissing Angus from Experian.'

'. . . You know when you want to do something totally out of character? The fact I'd never kiss someone like that or do something like that. That was why. It was spontaneous stupidity. That was all.'

Jamie looked at her from under his brow, the muscles in his jaw visibly clenching.

'OK. I didn't ask exactly what I wanted to ask. What I really meant is: why did you kiss him, and not me? It seems to me that if you take a Fake Boyfriend to a party, and you're going to do some meaningless copping off, you probably would do it with the Fake Boyfriend. I know we're in an unusual situation and a lawyer should be able to cite precedent, and I can't, but, you know . . .'

Laurie folded her arms, play-acting insouciance when she was in a state of excited terror.

'Jamie, do you think you're so irresistible it's against the laws of physics for a woman to kiss another man, instead of you?'

'Objection: deviation. I knew you'd say that and in the words of District Judge Tomkins, it's a fallacious argument.'

She saw that look again in Jamie's eyes. That look of star-struck fondness she wanted to see so much, and didn't trust.

'What's Angus got, except a stupid kilt, the goofy tartan wearing nationalist?'

'It would've been . . . weird to kiss you. We're friends.'

'Friends,' he repeated.

Laurie nodded.

'When we were dancing together, it felt like two people who are much more than friends.' He paused. 'It's the closest I've felt to anyone in my entire life.'

That, in a nutshell, was what Laurie felt.

A silence developed. Laurie didn't trust her voice.

'When the song finished, you gave me this look, this look like we were . . . actually *in bed together*, or something, this total intimacy that I felt too, and then you bolted. Next I know? ANGUS.'

Laurie sucked in air and wished she'd not lit candles or put Prince on.

'Please, don't do this. Don't turn one of the best friendships I've had into the shock twist that we sleep with each other for a while, and then fall out when one of us, who, shock twist, will *be you*, doesn't want to keep doing it anymore. It would turn gold into scrap metal. I don't want to be your millionth fling. This is bigger and better than that.'

'I agree with all of this.'

'Then what are you doing here?'

'To tell you that . . .' Jamie paused. 'I don't want to pretend anymore. I want to be together. Somewhere along the line this stopped being a pretence for me.'

A beat of blood in her ears; time seemed to slow. Should she try to stop this?

'What about what you said about thinking you were falling in love with someone? What happened to her?'

'In Lincoln?'

'Yes.'

'I was talking about you.'

Laurie's jaw dropped. 'No, you weren't, because you said . . .'

'I made a dick of myself by blathering about *how I'd know* and not thinking you'd ask "why" and then I had to do that lame mislead. I thought you guessed?!'

'No,' Laurie said, replaying it in her head. Her? *She* was Eve?

'Take anything I've said as part of this performance art from, oh, I don't know. At least from Lincoln onwards. Possibly at fancy steak restaurants. I meant everything I said. I felt what I felt before I knew what I felt, you know what I mean?'

She remembered how reluctant he'd been to tell her how he rebuffed that girl at Hawksmoor: *I don't want to share you.* He'd spooked himself because as he'd said it, he knew it was true?

Laurie laughed, in nerves and shock and disbelief, and yes, even if she didn't admit it, joy. 'You said love was a temporary manic state, like a debilitating psychosis!'

'Yes, and I was wrong. I was ignorant, and arrogant. I thought because I'd never experienced it, it didn't exist. It's not being out of your mind. It's being in it, it's complete certainty. When I'm with you, I know I'm where I belong. I want this to be real, Laurie. I want you to be mine. I want to be yours.'

Prince started on 'I Wish U Heaven': his music should be regulated, as a Class A intoxicating substance.

'And,' Jamie said. 'I think you feel the same way, but you won't trust it, or me, because of who I was when you met me.'

Laurie sucked in a breath that went to the bottom of her ribcage.

'It's true that I haven't got the strength for another rejection, after you try out being a one-woman man and find it's not for you.'

376

'That's not going to happen.'

'How do you know that?'

'I just do.'

'Bit risky . . .'

'What if I'm right?' His hair was so dark when it was wet. Laurie felt this sort of detail was unhelpful, in coming to a reasoned decision. 'The risk isn't worth it? I'd risk anything for what I felt between us tonight.'

'I've only recently mended myself. I don't feel so brave,' she said, a small wobble in her words.

'OK. I'll be brave for both of us. Kiss me. Afterwards you can tell me that there's not enough here worth taking a chance on, and we should leave it as mates.'

'I don't owe you a snog, Jamie Carter!' Laurie said, laughing.

'No, you don't.'

Jamie moved in and Laurie almost sprang back with the shock of finally being at the point of something she'd thought about doing, so many times.

'But that doesn't mean I want to kiss you any less.'

He inclined his head, ducked down and when his lips met hers, he was right: Laurie forgot every single objection she had.

She put her hands on the back of his head and her arm round his body and finally gave in to longing she had no idea she could still feel – no, that she could *ever* feel; this was something a few leagues above her and Dan's most intense early years. She and Dan hadn't known each other when their lips had first met, she and Jamie were finally expressing something that had built and built.

Time slowed, the rain thundered down outside.

After minutes of kissing passionately, he pulled back slightly.

'Why didn't we do that ages ago?' Jamie said, his eyes blue-black.

'Because we'd have known how we felt about each other straight away? The cat would've been right out of the bag, and we'd have had to deal with the cat parading around.' Laurie grinned. 'I don't think I could've carried off kissing you like that as just a contractual obligation.'

'Yes. That's true.' He smiled.

'Jamie. The reason I kissed Angus is . . . after we danced together, I came back into the room, you were talking to some beautiful girl. That's what I know being in love with you is going to be like. Like trying to keep running water in a sieve. I know this – we – are new right now, so it's exciting. It won't always be new.'

Jamie frowned. 'Katya? From Barker's? She's gay.'

'OK. You still see my greater point.'

'An hour ago I had to physically detach you from another man, and your take away is that *I* might cheat?'

Laurie laughed. 'Come on, though. You're asking me to accept a major change in your outlook, here.'

'I get why you want guarantees,' Jamie said. 'I can only make you a promise.'

'Which is?'

'Whatever happens next . . . you're my soulmate.'

41

'Oh no, fuck that! You don't get to do: "We kissed, woo, wavy lines screen fade". We need details.'

Jamie had spent Friday and Saturday nights at Laurie's, and by Sunday, they agreed it was time for him to give some quality time to Margaret the cat, so Laurie went for a walk in Etherow Country Park with Emily and Nadia.

She decided to drop the 'I have been having sex with Jamie Carter all weekend' bombshell when they were half an hour in, having some water. She was worried they'd spot it from the way she was walking.

Naturally, Emily spat her Evian in a huge arc.

Nadia straightened her cloche hat. Laurie wondered if she'd wear it in summer.

'We do, we need details,' Nadia agreed.

'It was . . . good,' Laurie said, knowing she was involuntarily doing a smug, dazzle eyed, faraway face. 'It was better than good. He said . . .'

'Yes?!' Emily said, primed for porn.

'He said I'd knackered him out by the time he left.'

'Haha oh my God! Was it face holding *I ruv you*, or virile mean pounding?'

'Kind of a combination?'

'Oof. Potent.'

The First One After Dan experience had been a strange combination of quite overwhelming and completely straightforward. Laurie had built it up to be a seismic shift in the universe, some kind of nude *Krypton Factor* challenge where she'd be marked out of ten for adventurousness. When in fact, rolling around unclothed with someone else was, it turned out, rolling around unclothed with someone else. It all worked on instinct, really. Knowing what to do next. Once she realised she was neither offputting, nor remotely boring to him, she was, as Jamie said, unstoppable.

'He looks very nice without his clothes. He didn't suggest we do anything athletic or freaky or involving ropes, so that was a relief. *And he was very good at it and it was bloody nice and I'd like to do it again soon, that's all, ARGH.*'

'OK, not exactly an excerpt from Anaïs Nin but we can work with that,' Emily said. 'Going forward, please take more notes.'

Emily was, as to be expected, overjoyed Laurie had taken her advice. Except with her usual ratlike cunning, had deduced Laurie had done more than that.

'You've fallen for him, haven't you? I can see the milk-drunk baby look. You tool.'

'He says he's fallen for me too.'

'No doubt. Just bear in mind you're still recovering and don't go too fast. No solitaires from Boodles. No surprise calls to me while I'm away this Christmas to announce rash engagements, and impending mad flits down the aisle, because you got egg nogged up and stupid.'

'Haha! Hardly. It's a helluva drug, egg nog.'

When Laurie looked at her phone when she got back, she had a text from Dan.

I'd like to get some photos copied. Is 5pm OK to come round?

Hah, a very late arriving realisation.

Laurie
Yeah, fine.

When he knocked on the door, she was still in her running gear.

'Not like you?' he said.

'All kinds of changes round here,' Laurie said. 'I've got the boxes of photos out from under the spare room bed, take the ones you want. I trust you to bring them back.'

Dan darted upstairs and reappeared after ten minutes, holding thirty-five or so pictures: holidays, the house in its embryonic stages, friends' weddings, beer gardens. Christmases in Cardiff.

'Fucking hell, remember the kitchen? Those Irish builders straight out of *Fawlty Towers? Lick o' paint lick o' paint.'*

Laurie smiled, thinly.

'Do you want to check which ones I've got, so you can count them out and count them back in?' he added.

They sat on the sofa while Laurie riffled through, and Laurie marvelled at how these months had transformed Dan from the person she knew best in the world to this person, sitting a short distance and yet a whole continent away. A thought occurred: this is a pretext. If he really wanted pictures, he'd have taken them by now. He has something else to say.

She handed them back. Dan's eyes came to rest on something thrown on the floor, down by the sofa that Laurie was sat on. It was one of Jamie's shirts, removed sometime on Saturday after they'd tried and failed to go out for dinner and decided they preferred staying in. It hadn't been the sort of weekend where she did much tidying up.

'Oh,' Laurie said, gathering it up, and stuffing the bundle next to her. It had not been done as any sort of taunt and yet it was difficult to think of a way she could've made the frenzied state of her relationship, clearer.

'It's really on, with him then?' Dan said, and swallowed hard.

Laurie nodded.

'I know how this makes me sound, but I convinced myself maybe you were pretending, to rub my face in it. That it was a deal between the two of you, to get him ahead at work and for you to get back at me.'

Laurie sighed. She had no reason to dissemble, now she and Jamie were the truth. 'Look, being honest, that's how it started. Then we got involved for real.'

To Laurie's complete amazement, Dan teared up, then started properly weeping.

'I want you to know something. I want you to know that I know I've fucked up. Every time I see you. When I see you with him. It's like being turned inside out.'

He wiped his face, nose running. Laurie sat, hands in lap, slightly stunned and mostly aghast.

'It was an affair, Laurie, you were right. It was a stupid self-indulgent *oh God I'm going to turn forty soon* affair because she flattered me and came on to me and I started to let myself believe there was this other life I should be having. I was bored and dissatisfied with myself. It was so much easier to tell myself I was bored and dissatisfied with you, that you were holding me back. That someone else was the fix.'

Laurie nodded, staring at her hands, twisting them together.

'I would've tried to come back, asked to come back. It was a fad, a phase and you and I are forever. Or we were. And then she . . . Not she, we. We got pregnant. *So.*'

Dan looked hollow. Laurie felt nothing but pity for Megan. To the victor, the spoils.

'Why didn't you tell me on the day you broke up with me, that you had feelings for her? Why the lies about needing yoga or to find yourself or whatever?' Laurie said.

'I thought it would hurt you less if I left it weeks or months for you to find out about Megan. If I'd said: "Right now I want her more than you," it would've been the most terrible thing.'

This was a category error that too many people made, Laurie thought – thinking untruths that didn't add up, were better than a hard truth.

'The thing is, Dan, it would've been terrible but I would've coped. I could've started the process of coping straight away, instead of having to turn into Sherlock Holmes, trying to crack the puzzle. It's the lies that killed me. Feeling I wasn't important enough or worth enough after these years to be let inside your head, to be told what was happening.'

He nodded and took a shuddering breath.

'Do you love him?'

'Yes,' she said quietly. 'It's grown into something neither of us expected.'

Dan made the sort of inhalation when you're trying to stifle a hiccup.

'Well, good. I want you to be happy. Seeing you lately has reminded me of who I fell in love with, but ten times over. You are,' Dan cleared his throat, 'a force to be reckoned with.'

'I'm sorry it took this, to remind you of who you fell in love with,' Laurie said.

'So am I,' Dan said, and she had a feeling they were sorry in different ways.

'Would you have said any of this if you weren't torn up by me being with a younger stud?' Laurie said, and Dan said, 'Yes,' as reflex response and she almost cynic-laughed as she thought, *no*.

She gave him a brief tight hug in the hallway, shut the door on him, slid to the floor, cupped her hands over her face and howled.

Not because she loved Dan, or wanted him back. She'd thought this was her ultimate goal, but there wasn't a shred of gloating or will to hurt him left in her. Only intense sadness that two decades of their life had ended the way it did, that a chapter of her life, a chapter she'd thought would be the full story, had closed.

She hoped Dan made Megan happy, and she hoped he was a good father. She meant that from the bottom of her bruised and battered heart.

This epiphany took her by such force she had to pick up her mobile and make a call, still sat on freezing cold floor tiles.

'Emily? I've realised something. Ever since Dan and I split up, there was something I couldn't make sense of. You said Dan and I were hit by lightning, in Bar CaVa, that it was fate, that it was a once in a lifetime chance and it changed everything forever. I knew it was true, I could feel in my water that it was true, so I couldn't reconcile it with Dan having gone. Well, I've figured it out. I did meet the love of my life that day. Only it wasn't Dan. *You* are the love of my life. Are you still there?'

'Yes, I'm crying, you soft shite.'

Laurie's mum had once said to her, keep a close eye on the worst things that happened to you, they could turn out to be a doorway, a route to someplace else entirely, a map you couldn't yet read. Laurie, as a cynical youth, had rolled her eyes at this. Uncle Ray's broken bones again. Hippy talk.

'Look at the disaster with your father – I got you,' Peggy had said, and Laurie had responded with sulky, ungrateful disbelief.

Well, her mother was right. Daniel Price deciding he was done? It was the best thing that could've happened to her.

42

As the days between the party and the Christmas break ticked down, Jamie remained as popular in the criminal department as a drugs dog in a college dorm, but now his relationship with Laurie was realer than real, they began to spend more time together in the office, and he was gladly welcomed into the inner circle with Bharat and Diana.

'Bharat's hilarious, isn't he?' he said, over an afterwork dinner with Amaretto Sours at Rudy's Pizza on the Thursday before Christmas. 'Really witty. Wasted in med neg, he should be doing Graham Norton's job. Though to be fair he's stunningly good at the lawyering.'

'It's his incisive arguments, absolutely nothing gets past him,' Laurie agreed, wiping the dough dust from her hands. 'He sharpens his teeth daily on Di. He should be fictionalised in a series starring Aziz Ansari.'

'I was wondering,' Jamie said. 'Would you declare it the naffest thing in the world if I changed my profile on Facebook to the one of us in The Ivy? I know it was a construct and all that at the time, but it's still a lovely one of you.'

Laurie laughed. 'We spent forty-eight hours with each other last weekend during which time I think the only thing we wore was a smile, and you're politely inquiring if I'll find a picture too much?'

'Look, grandma, where I come from, a joint profile photo is a big step, OK. I might even caption it with a heart emoticon. That makes us legally married on social media.'

'Do it,' Laurie said. 'I am happy to be social media married to you.' Jamie tinkered with his phone and held it up.

'I don't want you to think it's anything to do with my promotion meeting tomorrow!' he said.

'Hah! I'd forgotten about it.'

'Would you believe it that I'm not that bothered if I get it anymore?' Jamie said.

'Not really,' Laurie said, making a mischievous, tongue-lol face.

'Hey, it'd still be amazing. But it turned out this wasn't about finding the treasure; it was about the friends I made along the way.'

The following morning, Laurie returned from a decent sized win at court, checking her watch. Jamie would be in with them now.

This was the final shitstorm they'd have to weather, if he got it – Michael, for one, would be apoplectic. She'd do it, for Jamie. She was proud to know him, too.

Bharat met her in the doorway of their office, and looked so upset that Laurie feared there'd been bad family news. Di looked no less concerned.

'What is it? Who died?'

'Here, look.'

Bharat swung his mouse from side to side to wake the screen.

The email, cc all staff, was titled: 'FYI: It Was All Bullshit, From The Start.'

To: all

From: jamieryancarter@gmail.com

Hi!

As discussed here's how I thought the arrangement might work. Obviously feel very free to say either, no, these are the ravings of a lunatic, or suggest any guidelines of your own.

As said, we'd start next weekend (how you fixed to take a photo in a bar, early doors Saturday?) and then run it up until Christmas . . .

'Right,' Laurie said, taking a deep breath, in shock and a light sweat. 'So what happened was . . .'

Who sent this? And today?

Kerry put her head round the door.

'Laurie, Mr Salter wants to see you. This minute, please.'

Laurie hard-gulped and followed her across the landing, past the lifts to his office. After she knocked and was told ENTER, she saw that Jamie was already standing there. He gave her the merest glance and looked away again.

'Hello, Ms Watkinson,' Salter said. 'Sit please. An email chain has been brought to my attention between yourself and Mr Carter that suggests that the pair of you have been pretending a romantic liaison for effect, is that correct?'

'Yes,' Laurie said. She didn't think lying was a remotely good idea at this point, and even if she did, she'd had no time to think of any.

'Can you explain to me, why you did this?'

'I . . .' Laurie threw a look at Jamie and Salter bellowed 'DON'T LOOK AT HIM PLEASE, I AM ASKING *YOU!*' making Laurie jump out of her skin. She'd never seen him this angry.

'I'd been left by Dan Price, for another woman, who he'd got pregnant. I was in the situation of still having to work with him here. I wanted to make him jealous, to get my own back.'

It sounded as tawdry and ridiculous as it was, repeated in this room.

'Why was Mr Carter moved to help you?'

'He . . .' God, she couldn't think of how to cover this up, 'he wanted to apply for a promotion and felt it would better his chances if you thought he had a girlfriend.'

Laurie really hoped Jamie had already come clean. It was his only hope.

'The fact you work in law, and this was a deception. That gave you no qualms?'

Laurie thought her only way to survive was self-lacerating honesty.

'I told myself that it was my private life, nothing to do with my work and therefore had no bearing on my job. I am pretty appalled and ashamed at this now I stand back and look at it from a distance, but the break-up had put me in a hyper state, I think. I wasn't eating and I wasn't sleeping much either. I was consumed by the pain of what had happened.'

'Yet you knew Mr Carter was doing it for professional advantage?'

'Yes.'

'I don't think the hygiene of this being personal and not professional existed quite in the way you think it does. If you were involved in Mr Carter's pretences, and you knew he wanted to be made partner as a result, you are an accessory to what he was doing. Are you not?'

'Yes.'

A heavy silence.

'Mr Salter. I have no idea if I am making things better or worse by saying this, but I don't want to be involved in any more lies—'

'A rather late arriving fit of conscience,' he spat. She was going to be sacked. Surely.

'Jamie and I are together. We became involved for real, some weeks back.'

'You're in a relationship now?'

Laurie said, 'Yes,' at the exact same time that Jamie said, 'No.'

This was the first he'd spoken. Laurie stared in shock at Jamie.

'Which is it?' Mr Salter said.

'We're not,' Jamie said, firmly, glancing at Laurie. 'We had

. . . crossed a line or two for authenticity's sake, got a bit carried away. But we certainly aren't together.'

Jamie barely met Laurie's eyes, set his jaw and stared straight ahead.

Mr Salter saw all of this, she realised, as she turned back and his rheumy gaze came to rest on Laurie.

'Alright, I've heard enough, Ms Watkinson. I feel severely let down by you, and by this. We had spoken in this office, on trust, which I believed was mutual. Consider this a verbal warning and if you do anything to piss me off in the foreseeable future, I might skip the written stage. Close the door on your way out.'

Laurie was desperate to speak to Jamie, to find what had happened, and she didn't have to wait long.

A junior from the criminal department called Matt appeared in the doorway, and said, breathlessly: 'Jamie Carter's been sacked. Immediate effect.'

Laurie, Bharat and Di almost comically scrambled to get past one another and out to see what was happening.

A Roman amphitheatre of spectators had gathered on the second floor as Jamie exited the criminal office, holding a briefcase, his coat, and the umbrella that Laurie once remembered him jamming lift doors with.

A very sad-faced Mick, the security guard, was guiding Jamie towards the stairs. Laurie made to go after him.

'I wouldn't follow him out,' Michael said, arms folded. 'Or they might just lock the door after you. You don't want any more of his reputation smeared over you.'

'He's my boyfriend, so I'll see him out, thanks,' Laurie said, to an audible 'ooh!' from the crowd, presumably both at the declaration and the insubordination. She glimpsed Dan, looking pig sick at the back. At least her honesty with him had stopped this being any gotcha.

'You can stop the show now, we've all seen the email,' Kerry snapped.

Laurie turned.

'You know what, I couldn't care less what you do or don't think, Kerry. You're not the policewoman of my private life. Or anyone else's here for that matter.'

'Can I get an Amen!' Bharat shouted, from the back of the crowd, and incredibly, a reasonably hearty 'AMEN' went up. Kerry scowled, looking green as a parrot.

Laurie walked down the stairs with Jamie and out through the lobby, Mick holding the door for them, beckoning for Jamie to hand over his security pass and pulling the door shut behind them.

Once they were outside in the street, Jamie turned and said: 'I hate to say it, but Michael's right. Go back in, now. Salter's temper's on a hair trigger. If he hears you're out here with me you could get sacked too.'

'I can't believe they sacked you and not me?!' Laurie said.

'Laurie, now I'm gone, blame the whole idea of the phony relationship on me,' Jamie said. 'When Salter's calmed down, he won't want to fall out with his best defence lawyer.'

'But this is unfair! And probably illegal, getting rid of you but not me for the same offence.'

'Hah. They know every loophole and can safely get rid of

anyone. I've struck a deal where they say it was my decision and I get some gardening leave. Word will get round, of course, so I have to be quicker than the word before the pay runs out. He knows I couldn't stay, Laurie, not when they loathe me. It was untenable.' He paused. 'They didn't only sack me for our relationship.'

'What then?'

He didn't speak for a few seconds. 'They think I was involved with Eve.'

'You said . . . you didn't . . .?' Laurie said, and trailed off. *Oh, no.*

'Yeah, I wasn't. But I haven't told you the whole story of that night.'

Laurie swallowed hard. 'OK.'

'It was dinner, nothing more. But Eve had booked a room at the hotel. She made a play for me at the end of the evening and I said no, stakes are too high here, thanks. She was not impressed. She had a point. I shouldn't have been seeing her out of hours. It was mixed messages and it was undignified to have to put her straight. For both of us.'

'Right . . .'

'I told you I was networking, but quite specifically, I wanted to know if Salter was thinking of retiring. I thought she might have information, as family, that'd help me with the timing of my pitch for partner. Short version, I used her. She's whip smart. She figured that out.'

Jamie continued: 'Then the photos of you and I started going up, and Eve got in touch and said, I see what you're doing and I know what was said in your promotion meeting

– she'd fished with her uncle. She said, you're using another woman to get ahead. I told her you were happily in on it but she didn't believe me. This sounds strange, but she didn't want you to feel used in the same way that she had done. She thought I was playing you and wanted to find a way to make you see sense – she'd clearly worked out that if she said anything to you directly, she'd sound jealous.'

The text, in Lincoln, that Laurie wasn't allowed to see.

'What was the lunch time visit about?'

'To unsettle me, and it worked. More pertinently, to give Michael my phone passcode. She asked me to find something on my phone, moments after you'd gone upstairs, and she leaned right in as I did it. I think Michael reached out to her to see if we'd slept together, they discovered a common cause. She had the idea of unmasking me to "save" you and Michael probably laid it on thick about how vulnerable you were. But Michael probably spotted that to be absolutely sure I got the heave overboard, she needed to tell her uncle I had form.'

They stood in silence for a moment. Laurie felt numb.

'How did Michael get your phone?'

'I leave it on my desk plenty. It's locked, so I don't think anything of it. I guess he'd have gone in, searched for your name for incriminating material, and bingo. There's no other emails between us.'

Laurie absorbed this. 'He sent it global, for maximum damage.'

'Oh yes. No one's asked how he got hold of it, from what I can tell. Fuck this place, it's a clique and it's rotten. I'm glad to go.'

'But I should stay?'

Jamie looked discomfited. 'Unless you have any other irons in the fire. The bosses love you.'

'Correction. They used to.'

She'd been in denial, but this was it. Jamie was off, into the horizon, and Laurie's standing at her workplace was irreparably soiled. Much as she hated Dan and Michael's intervention, their premonitions had come to pass.

'Did you split up with me in there, when Salter asked us point blank?'

'No. I knew I was fucked and I thought any more idea from Salter that we were a couple, and you would be too.'

'What if he'd not sacked you? How would we have managed that? We start keeping a real romance secret?'

Jamie shrugged. 'I suppose so?'

'Or, or. You would've split up with me to keep them happy?'

This felt eminently possible, despite everything. She believed in Jamie's feelings for her but she'd never seen a second's self-sacrifice regards his career, for anyone. All this time worrying about another woman coming between him, but was his job the thing she could never compete with?

'No,' Jamie said, frowning. 'I never wanted the promotion that much. Wow.'

'You sure? It seems to be all that's driven you since I've known you.'

'I've changed since I've known you.'

People don't change. Do they?

Laurie couldn't let this go.

'It was pretty mortifying, me saying yes when you said no.'

'Well, sorry. It didn't mean anything.'

'If you've changed, why still lie? Why not say, hey Mr Salter, yeah I shouldn't have done it but now here is the situation and yes I am with Laurie.'

'The truth wasn't what was needed, here, or what was going to help.' He clenched his jaw and jutted his chin slightly and they were clearly skirting the territory of their first big fight. Or, the last one?

'Jamie, the truth is sometimes of value in itself. Not working out what it'll get you.'

'Oh Laurie, of all the times to go all "inspirational meme over a sunset" on me.' Jamie smiled, weakly, and it felt so much like Dan's brush-offs that her hair stood on end.

'Of all the times for you to go lying triangulating lawyer bastard on me!' she snapped.

'This is the way the world IS, Laurie!' Jamie's temper broke. 'I know you're honest and decent and I love you for it, but this is how it actually works. It's shit and cruel and unjust and you do what you need to do to survive. I learned that young. So did you.'

'Don't do that, don't try to make me feel bad for being upset about this.'

'What exactly are you angry with me for, here, please? Not standing there pledging my undying devotion to you, to someone who'd sack us both for it?'

'Ah . . .' Laurie turned her eyes to the sky. 'Right now? Everything. For not telling me about Eve, so this ambushed me.'

'Yeah, sorry.' Jamie adjusted the weight of his briefcase. 'I'd hoped I wouldn't have to. There it is.'

She didn't feel much apology coming from him, however.

'How will you get another job in Manchester? With the rules on practising elsewhere?' Laurie said.

'I don't know, I might have to look at other cities.'

'London?' Laurie said. Jamie did a double-take. 'Uhm yeah maybe, I don't know? There are a lot of law firms there. Give me a second, given I got my P45, five minutes ago?'

'That's us done then, isn't it?'

'Is it? There's this thing called a train . . .'

'Remember what Michael and Dan said? That you'd lie to me, that you'd leave my professional standing in tatters when you moved on to pastures new? No part of that prediction was in fact wrong, was it?'

'What? You're agreeing with their view of me? That's pretty disloyal and weak.'

He glowered in disgust, nose wrinkled. She'd never felt this defensive hostility from him before. She had to come out fighting, to stop it frightening her. Attack as a form of defence.

'*I've* been disloyal and weak?! You manipulating another woman has brought the whole house of cards crashing down on both of us, but I'm supposed to carry on thinking you won't treat me badly, because you've changed, or it's different with me? All those lines that have been used by bad men since the dawn of time.'

'"Bad man"! Stop acting like this was all my idea, something I've tricked you into for my nefarious ends. We both did it because we both wanted something from it. Sorry it went wrong, but then I'm the one who lost my job.'

'It *was* your idea.'

Jamie rolled his eyes in genuine contempt. 'Nice. So under pressure, I tried to think about what's best for both of us. You revert to shit old stereotypes of me, start insinuating I'm using you. This is how deep it runs, your good opinion of me.'

'Did you sleep with Eve?'

'You honestly have to ask me that, when I just said I didn't?'

'Yes. It's the one thing you've been accused of that isn't true, according to you. It's something of an anomaly.'

'It doesn't sound like you're going to believe me, whatever I say.'

Laurie's chest hurt. It was one of those rare times when you can feel something being torn down, the something intangible that exists between you.

A moment whistled between them, in the frostbitten Manchester wind. It was one of those moments that decided how everything was going to be afterwards.

'I'm not sure I know who you are,' Laurie said, simply. Persuade me, she thought. Talk me round. Please. She didn't want to push this hard but she had to, or she wouldn't trust him from now on.

'In that case, you're not who I thought you were either,' Jamie said.

Chattering people spilled out of the doors behind them and Jamie gave her a weary, hard glance, adjusted his briefcase again, and turned, walked off. Laurie sucked in air and let it out and said 'oh', to herself. She thought he'd fight harder. Apparently not.

As she trod back up the stairs, empty as a husk, Michael was stood at the top, jangling change in his pocket.

'I did try to warn you. We tried to protect you from him, but you wouldn't have it.'

'Get bent, Michael,' she said.

'Let me guess, he's announced that you're not together as of round about now? Given that he has no need for you anymore?'

'Incorrect, sorry.'

He'd hear eventually, but no way was she adding to his jubilation this afternoon.

'Oh, right. I look forward to the announcement of your wedding, at which point I will bike naked around Piccadilly Gardens singing "Life Is a Rollercoaster".'

'Get yourself some saddle rub in then.'

'Haha! Good one. Don't cry over him darling, he's not, and has never been, worth it.'

'I wish I was as interested in your life as you are in mine.'

'So do I,' Michael said, as a very sudden, spiky way of declaring himself, a No Score Draw sensation. Laurie said nothing, marching past, leaving him standing, startled, by himself.

'Bharat, Di,' Laurie said, back at her desk, 'I'm so sorry I lied to you. It had to be a strict policy of telling no one or it wouldn't have worked. I was telling the truth later on; Jamie and I did end up together for real.'

'Oh darling, I don't care, I think it's genius!' Bharat said. 'So bloody cool. You're my wife from another life. And that *Jerry Maguire* shit you just pulled was BALLSY AS FUCK.'

Laurie flopped into her chair. At least she only had Monday and the morning of Christmas Eve to get through before the office closed at lunchtime for ten days for Christmas, and she'd not have to see any of the rest of her colleagues until the new year.

She hadn't begun to mentally pick through the wreckage of what happened with Jamie.

How had it all gone wrong, so fast?

Bharat leaned over and patted her hand. 'Don't sweat it, Lozza. Some days you're the dog, and other days you're the bone.'

43

'Lobster tacos,' Emily said, studying the menu and speaking over a remix of Ed Sheeran: '*Lobster tacos*. Sometimes you feel we've strayed far from God's light, don't you? Why would you put lobster in a taco?' She glanced around her. 'Also making club versions of Ed Sheeran is like putting my dad in cargo shorts.'

They were in a bar–nightclub–restaurant that as per, Emily had nominated. There was neon squiggly writing above them declaring *If The Music Is Too Loud You Are Too Old* and bright leather banquettes and a framed Marilyn Monroe Warhol, and the kind of 'graffiti is a valid artform' murals that looked as if they'd let troubled teenagers design as part of a community rehabilitation project. Emily had proposed a last meet-up, to celebrate Monday being Christmas-Eve-Eve, with the caveat: 'No fucking walking involved like last time, don't even try.'

'I am more upset at "Lil Chick Burgers" and "Lil Hot Links",' Laurie said. 'I would rather forego sausages than ask for "Lil Hot Links", and I don't forego sausage lightly.'

'We're on to the Jamie situation already!' Emily said.

'Har har,' Laurie said, rolling her eyes, with the tense, clenched up feeling she got when thinking about him.

He'd not contacted her since the fight, so that was clearly that. It confirmed her suspicions that he would now laser focus on re-employment, probably in the capital. She'd not contacted him, either, of course, so this was hypocritical. But what would she say?

She hadn't thought she'd be another scorned woman left in Jamie Carter's wake, but equally, no scorned women left in his wake thought that was who they'd become. That was how it happened.

Who was he, in the end? Had he been totally himself in the dark, when they were alone? The man who wore glasses and didn't need glasses, who could be so generous and open and then so cold and hard, in that moment outside the office.

But mostly, Laurie had been studiously not thinking about Jamie. Doubt lingered, but doubt only caused more trauma. Better to forcibly banish doubt, and get on with the rest of her life.

Laurie explained the situation with Jamie, as much as she could. Referring back to Liverpool, and to her doubts over Eve. 'I was at the quacks like a duck, walks like a duck point,' Laurie said, sipping her wine. 'He's a duck. I'm OK, though. It's OK.'

She wasn't OK, obviously, but Emily was a good enough friend to know that it meant Laurie wanted to be treated as OK.

'You think he *did* sleep with this boss's niece? I mean she was clearly pissed at being used by him, to do what she did?' Emily said and Laurie winced anew.

'. . . I don't know. Maybe?' She played it as not caring much, while it turned her intestines into a reef knot.

'Mmm,' Emily tapped her paper straw against her mouth thoughtfully. 'Although, although . . .'

'Oh God, what!' Laurie said.

'No, I think you did the right thing. One strike, out. It's just . . .'

'*What*?'

'It's not mutually exclusive, is it? He could have been a person who did those things, and then fallen for you for real, later? I don't know.'

Laurie shook her head.

'It's like you said. This isn't what I need. Also no one can change anyone's character. No love of a good woman can fix a bad man. It's you who told me this!'

Despite saying this, Laurie couldn't accept Jamie was a bad man, not yet. But that was due to attachment hormones still swirling through the body. She imagined that final realisation would arrive with a jolt, when a tale of his misdeeds got filtered back to her via the usual channels at Salter's. Like reconciling herself to Dan and his affair: your mind has to start the process, and your heart will follow.

'I know, I know. It's a shame but at least you got a sensational rumping out of it. By the way, warning, Nadia may be what I believe she calls "ornery",' Emily said. 'She's been thrown out of her sister's book group. Ah, here she is now.'

'Why?' Laurie said under her breath.

'Because Nadia is the epitome of herself,' Emily raised her

voice. 'Laurie wants to know why you got banned from the book group?'

Nadia was in her usual cloche hat, today a pleasing salmon shade.

'Firstly, I rejected the central tenets of *Eat, Pray, Love,*' Nadia said, as Emily pushed a glass of wine towards her, and she wriggled her duffle coat off. 'Then we were required to produce "Gratitude Lists" to discuss what we were thankful for.'

'Oh really?' Emily said, swinging a *and how did that go look* at Laurie, who tried not to laugh.

'I said I was not grateful for my life, I had worked for it, and my sister's friend Amy said I was "too centred" in my own privilege and I told her to fuck off and then my sister said I had to go.'

'We won't ask you to be grateful for anything this evening, Nads,' Emily said, handing the menu over. 'Not even lobster tacos. Can I tell her your latest news?' she looked to Laurie.

'Knock yourself out,' Laurie said.

'She's no longer with the hot lad she was pretending to date. It turns out that messing women around and then saying he hadn't was kind of his thing, he got sacked for it.' Emily gave Laurie a 'fair?' questioning look and Laurie nodded.

'Ugh,' Nadia said. 'I'm sorry. I mean I am sorry for any pain. While not being sorry you gave him his marching orders, if he is a shit.'

'Thank you,' Laurie said. 'I'm not in pain. Well, I'm in some pain over it, but I know that it will pass and I'll feel happier again, at some point. That will do for now.'

'Like that poem "to the girl crying in the next toilet stall." *Listen I love you, joy is coming*,' Emily said.

'Yes. Joy is coming. If maybe not here,' Laurie said, glancing around. It was the kind of poseur's bear pit that would've scared Laurie, pre-Dan's bombshell, but not now. Her fling with Jamie had given her that confidence back, at least. *Sigh. Who would ever measure up to . . .* STOPPIT.

'Can I propose a toast,' Laurie said. 'To what happiness looks like, to us.'

'Yes,' Emily said, picking her glass up so fast she spilled some. 'To deciding what *our* happiness is, and being happy that way. Rather than having some bunch of bastards tell us what it is.'

They clinked glasses and drank.

'Are you girls ready to order?' said a waiter with a goatee, appearing at their side with a touch screen pad. 'Need me to explain anything?'

'We're not girls,' Nadia said. 'So you can explain your mode of address.'

'Hey y'all look pretty young to me,' he said, chewing gum and grinning in what he thought was a flirtily winning manner.

Emily said: 'Oh, you dear sweet fool, she will now verbally decapitate you.'

Laurie felt it was a poorly advertised part of kitten owning, that they were absolute sodding hooligans. If her new twelve-week-old black longhair mix breed with white whiskers, Colin Fur, was in the magistrates court, Laurie would be advising the short sharp shock of a custodial sentence for sure.

'Only language he understands, sadly,' she'd tell the bench, while removing another shredded pair of Wolford tights from the little beggar's jaws.

She'd impulsively picked him up from the PDSA at lunchtime, on her way home from work, Christmas Eve of all days, thinking how nice it would be to have a tiny friend around on her solo Christmas Day. She was now realising it would mean spending the whole time extracting said tiny friend from re-enacting *Touching The Void* on the curtain rails.

Laurie wasn't daunted by Christmas Day alone, not one bit. She was going to dress up, only for herself, make a giant lunch, only for herself, and share some smoked salmon with Colin Fur. Finding out she could manage on her own was great.

She didn't mind the time off work, either. It had been wild lately. After Jamie's sacking on Friday, Monday had felt like a peculiar limbo period where she had no idea what her status was. In the end, she took the initiative and asked to see Mr Salter, late on Monday afternoon. He said yes, he *and* Mr Rowson would see her, suggesting an unprecedented both-partner bollocking designed to strike fear into her heart.

Laurie went in with armour, however. She knew how strong she was. She'd lost Dan, and coped, she'd lost Jamie, and coped. She'd drawn a final line with her dad, and coped. And if she lost her job, she'd cope.

So much of her life had been about being scared of not being wanted by people. If the news was that this law firm no longer wanted her, well fine. Plenty of others would.

She'd spoken honestly about the manner of Dan's leaving,

the devastation she'd been in, and how seriously she took her responsibilities.

'In conclusion, I badly regret the "relationship"' – she made air quote marks. She still couldn't believe the way it had been fake, real, then fake again, – 'with Jamie Carter, but I was not my usual or best self when I made that decision. Given he didn't get the partnership and has left, it seems sensible to put it behind us. I feel as if I'm on the back foot now. I like working here and will look elsewhere for employment if you think it's necessary, but I'd rather stay.'

Salter and Rowson boggled at her confidence.

'We don't want you to leave, Ms Watkinson,' Salter said, though from Rowson's expression she thought he might've considered it. 'I would like to know this, however. Why were you helping Jamie Carter to a partnership, rather than applying for it yourself?'

'Oh . . .' Laurie was stunned. 'I suppose I'm content doing what I am. I didn't think I was partner material to be honest.'

'That's a shame, as I would like you to apply for it in the New Year,' Mr Salter said. 'I was thinking of asking you to put yourself forward anyway. The sangfroid with which you've dealt with this, despite your mistakes, has convinced me. We don't only divine character in how people handle wins. You see more in the disasters.'

Ain't that the truth.

'Oh . . . OK.' She was getting a promotion out of this?! 'Thank you.' She paused, and blurted: 'You think the criminal department lads will cope with a female boss?'

'No,' said Mr Salter, and they shared an unexpected bout of conspiratorial laughter.

Laurie's phone went with an unrecognised mobile number on Christmas Eve afternoon and despite her conviction that those were always best to leave to ring out, she picked up.

'Hello, sweetie! It's Hattie! Jamie's best mate. We met at Eric's sixty-fifth. In Lincoln. I was drunk. I made you ingest plum vodka.'

'Oh, hi!' Laurie said, smiling at the number of descriptors Hattie felt necessary, to identify her among all the Hatties that Laurie had met at sixty-fifth birthdays in Lincoln recently.

'I will get to the point as you probably have presents to wrap and shit. I know everything, Jamie told me. And I mean everything. Well, I don't know *everything*, like not how many positions in a night.'

Laurie laughed, despite herself.

'I know about the deal you two made. I've known for a while.'

'Did you know before Lincoln?!'

'. . . Yeah. Dread secret. Only at the last minute after I'd blabbed to his parents that I knew he was seeing you. Jamie said I had to stop getting their hopes up and explained why.'

Hah, he'd told his best friend too. Wait – so when Hattie said Jamie was besotted, it wasn't based on any fibs they'd told?

'You asked me if I was in love with him?!'

'Ha. Jamie said you were sharp! How do you remember that? I was bladdered! You were more like a couple than anyone else in that room and I couldn't resist stirring.'

'Hah,' Laurie said, but the atmosphere of that night was now roaring back in her memory.

'From the way he was talking about you constantly I thought it must be more complicated than he was saying, and then I saw you both together, and I knew for sure.'

'Right.'

'I know why he lost his job.'

'Yeah. Not been a few weeks I'll forget in a hurry!' Laurie said, with fake jollity.

'Your decisions are your decisions, for your reasons, but if it was because you thought Jamie was some lying manipulator, I want you to know that Jamie really, really loved you. I've known him since we were small, and yes, he's broken some hearts but only in the way anyone as beautiful as him does; he's not nasty. It's beyond unfortunate that Past Him bit him on his arse when it did. For what it's worth, he told me about the Eve thing at the time. He told me the same thing he told you: he knocked her back. And Laurie, look: he had no reason to lie to me.'

'This is really kind of you, and you're a great mate to him,' Laurie said. 'I think Jamie and I are just not meant to be.'

This was said off the top of her head, given Laurie wasn't otherwise one for fate, and mystical catechisms.

'Fuck "meant to be"!' Hattie said, heartily, '*Meant to be* is too passive, in a crisis. He's talking about moving to London. I know he'd stay in Manchester if he thought you wanted him. Part of the reason he's going is to avoid seeing you around. He said it's not even about seeing you with other men, just that simply *seeing you* would hurt too much.'

'He said that, did he,' Laurie said, with a doubtful tone.

'Yes, he did.' *But*, said that little voice, *he'd hardly tell his best gal pal, he was up to no good.*

'He's right, he probably needs to go,' Laurie said. At least she'd be spared seeing him draped over someone from Office Angels in that tiki bar.

'Laurie, seriously, I am going to back my claims up. I'm going to show receipts. He and I always stay in touch over email. Massive long Gmails about all sorts of things you know, and it's quite personal. Things we wouldn't tell anyone else.'

'. . . OK?'

'He sent me one the Sunday after you got together. Let me read it to you . . .'

'Hattie . . .' Laurie said, but she obviously wasn't going to be diverted.

'Hats, big news: I finally told Laurie how I feel. I was absolutely bricking it, but seeing her with another man, briefly (explain another time) (God I am still fuming, I knew that beefy beta mope was going to crack on to her from the start) put me into the kind of state where a man listens to Nick Cave albums at top volume and smashes back bottles of whisky, while primitive roaring. It spurred me into action, and I turned up on her doorstep at midnight and declared myself. She said she felt the same way, but, understandably was very wary of me after the times I'd bragged about being Poundshop Errol Flynn.

This, despite the fact I was a quivering mess at the sight of her bra strap, or had been trying to hold her hand all the time, like we were fifteen. It didn't apparently clue her in to the fact I hadn't been that person since almost the moment we met. She has no ego in that way whatsoever, I don't think. So that's something I can definitely bring to our relationship, haha!

We're so similar, Hats. That's the wonderful, strange, incredible thing that we would never have found out, if it weren't for Salter & Rowson solicitors off Deansgate being skinflints in building maintenance. We help each other, in a way that I didn't know was possible. We're a little way off the heavier conversations regards marriage and kids but there's pretty much nothing I wouldn't feel I could tackle if we did it together. I keep thinking: if I'd never met her, how different things would be. I scoffed at the idea anyone could make you see your life through new eyes and I'm so, so glad to be wrong.

Anyway, sorry for the heated prose. At least you're spared hearing the sex was amazing eh! (The sex was amazing.) (I know how terrible and juvenile this sounds, but I didn't know what it could be like with someone you're actually in love with.)

She's so gorgeous, I get slightly out of breath thinking about her. I can't wait to bring Laurie back to Lincoln and for you and Padraig to meet her properly. I want everyone to love her as much as I do, though Mum and Dad are there already I think.

Hey how's the infection, did it clear up?

'Wait, discount that last part, that wasn't directly relevant content,' Hattie said.

Tears streamed down Laurie's face as Colin Fur let go a guttural howl from somewhere above her head.

'Did you . . . wail?' Hattie said, hesitantly.

'No, that was the kitten.'

'Jamie's getting the four p.m. train to Lincoln, so he'll be at Piccadilly in half an hour,' Hattie said. 'I'll just leave that there.'

44

Where was he where was he where was he?

Laurie scoured the concourse for Jamie to no avail, but looking at the Departures board, he *had* to be here, somewhere.

She'd locked the kitten in the kitchen and dragged on any old things on top of her 'it's Christmas Eve, time to let go' outfit of baggy joggers and sloppy, shapeless wide-neck jumper. The Uber had been painfully slow to arrive but once she was in, they'd flown through the streets, past boozy office workers spilling out of the bars and up the ramp of the station, where Laurie had practically fallen out before the car came to a complete stop.

He must've gone through the barrier by now. At a ticket machine, Laurie endured an agonising wait behind the world's slowest stoner gap year boys, wearing flip flops with socks in December, then bought the cheapest she could find, a single to Stockport, and dashed through to the other side.

When she got to the platform, she looked right, left, right, left. He wasn't here. Had Hattie got the time wrong?

Her eyes came to rest on a man in a navy coat with short

curly dark hair and exceptional cheekbones, standing by the Coke machine, staring at her.

There.

In her haste, Laurie half skipped to him, apprehension at what she had to say briefly cancelled out by the elation of finding him.

'Hi,' she said.

'Hello?' Jamie said, looking at her curiously.

'Going home for Christmas?'

'Er . . . yeah. And you? Getting a train too?'

'No, I've come to find you.'

'OK?'

'To tell you that I'm sorry. I doubted you and I freaked out. I trusted Dan and he let me down and I wasn't ready to go through that again.'

A silence, where she wondered if she would get the Jamie who'd been so scornful last time they met, or the tender Jamie of the messages to his best friend.

'I know. I get that. I think it was too big an ask, to be honest.'

'You do?'

'Yeah.' He got his phone out of his pocket. 'You can have my pass code; I can show you texts from Eve that back up everything I've told you. I should've offered that before but I was in too big a state, thinking I'd lost my job and you on the same day. I lashed out.'

'Thank you but I don't need to see them.' Laurie paused. 'I trust you. Hattie shared the email you wrote about me, with me . . .'

'Oh, *did* she now?'

413

'She did. I shouldn't have needed to hear you'd said those things. I knew them anyway, because it's how I feel too,' Laurie drew breath. 'That's what's special about us. It's funny given I thought we were chalk and cheese but it's like we have some sort of telepathy. I purposely turned that intuition off, and surrendered to what everyone else thought of you. I didn't want to rely on my own judgement because it let me down so badly where Dan was concerned.'

Jamie said nothing.

'So I didn't think about the person I spent time with in Lincoln, or at barbecues that turned into slasher flicks, or having nervos in skyscrapers with. Because him, I trust, and I am madly in love with.' She paused. 'Why haven't you been in touch with me?'

'You haven't been in touch with me. Checkmate.' Jamie smiled.

'I know. I was worried you'd say, after some thought, you were definitely sure it was over.'

'That's exactly why I didn't call you. I thought, let the silence speak for itself and you can avoid those crushing few seconds of certainty.'

The Manchester icy wind howled around them and Laurie pushed her hair out of her face.

'What I'm saying is, do you want to try again?' she said.

'No, not really, what's done is done,' Jamie said. 'And I've had a promising inquiry from a member of Little Mix.'

Laurie was stunned for a moment and then Jamie's frown cracked, and he started laughing. 'Your face, hahaha.'

'You bad bollock!'

Jamie stooped and rifled in his bag.

'Open this. I was going to post it from Lincoln.'

Laurie fumbled it open with cold hands and found a short note, wrapped around a small cardboard box. She opened it. It was the necklace she'd admired on Steep Hill.

'I'd got my mum to buy it and send it,' Jamie said.

She opened the note:

Dear Laurie,

If there's any chance whatsoever you might change your mind, I want that chance more than anything in the world. I wouldn't waste that chance. I'd use it for the rest of our lives, in fact.

All my love, Jamie x

Laurie looked up, tears in her eyes.

'Come here.' Jamie dropped his bag and grabbed her in a hug. 'I'm so sorry for what I put you through,' he said, muttering into her hair. 'I should've told you upfront what had gone on with Eve. Keeping my cards close to my chest became second nature.'

'You lost your job. You paid enough for it.'

The train pulled into the station.

'What are you doing for Christmas?' Jamie said. 'Do you want to come to Lincoln? I'd not steeled myself to tell my parents we were no more yet. We could get a later train, after you've packed a bag?'

'I could, except I've got a wrecker of a kitten that can't be left.'

'I've got a house sitter for Margaret. We could add your kitten into the deal, pay her extra?'

'Oh God. It'll be like Clouseau and Cato!'

'I'll tell her to charge me for some pruning gauntlets and sedatives. For her.'

'Looks like we have a plan, then,' Laurie said.

Jamie hugged her again and they walked out of the station, hand in hand, only to find Laurie couldn't get back through the ticket barrier until she'd bought another single.

'You know, this reunion was written by fate. Hattie said she knew we had a future, as she's psychic,' Laurie said, once they'd extricated themselves from the admin.

'If Hattie's psychic, why did she date the lad in our twenties who pretended to be an heir to the Farmfoods fortune, and ended up rinsing her savings and disappearing to Worcester, until the fraud squad caught up with him, watching scat porn in a Premier Inn?'

'Maybe she had to date him, to find her way to Padraig?'

'Too heavy a price. And I like Padraig.'

Laurie put her hand in Jamie's free one and pulled him to a stop.

'Do you know. I've had the maddest, craziest idea, and you'll say LOL NO but hear me out on it seeming hasty. Particularly as I'd like your parents to be there. Do you fancy getting married?'

'LOL NO!' Jamie said. 'Uhm. Kidding. But shouldn't I propose?'

'Not necessarily in this day and age.'

'You're seriously proposing to me? We've only been a proper couple for a weekend!'

'I'm less respectful of what you're *supposed* to do, these days, if you get me. If we discover we're horrendously ill-suited after two years of bickering about overspending on the food shop and picking up wet towels, think of the fun we'll have had before we realise? If this is a mistake, think how much fun we'll have making it?'

'The speech is writing itself!'

'And you know, if it's a no, I will cope fine. It struck me as a thing I'd really enjoy doing.' She grinned up at him. He had the same look on his face as he did at the final chords of 'Purple Rain'. There, they had the first dance sorted already. 'I appreciate I'm asking you to go from someone who despised marriage, to someone charging into one. But that's me, now. I ask for a lot.'

Jamie reached up and tucked a piece of hair behind her ear. Laurie felt loved, and, more than that, she'd remembered how to love herself. She wanted his answer to be yes, but a no wouldn't change either of those things.

'Yes. My answer is yes. I will marry you. Can I ask you back? Feels proper. Laurie Watkinson, will you marry me?'

'Yes!'

They stopped, embraced and kissed, the Christmas Eve crowds flowing around them, Jamie's bag at their feet, while they stayed a fixed point, a moment in time. An irritable commuter tutted, in a broad Manc drawl. 'Get a fuckin' room.' And they laughed and carried on kissing.

Many ages of Lauries had walked through Piccadilly, since she was a little girl in fact. She liked this one best. Whatever happened in the future, Laurie would never forget the lessons

IF I NEVER MET YOU

of these months. She was a survivor of some difficult things, and she was happy.

They walked down the hill, hand in hand.

'My best friend Emily can give me away.'

'And Hattie can be my best man.'

'I like making up our own rules. Let's keep doing that.'

Minutes later, over engagement champagnes in Refuge, under tiles that declared THE GLAMOUR OF MANCHESTER, Laurie managed to make a phone ring in a province of Indonesia.

'Emily. You know how we said we had to define what happiness looks like, for ourselves? Without fear of judgement? Now there's been no egg nog, but. Please remain as calm as possible.'

Acknowledgements

Something I'm learning on my sixth (sixth!) outing is that each book is its own unique beast and the process works differently each time. *If I Never Met You* was unusual because 1. I somehow managed to never hate it, even when it was giving me serious gyp; and 2. It very much came together in the editing, which is a posh way of saying it needed a fair bit of work. On the latter point, huge thanks must go to my dedicated editor Martha Ashby, who never lets me nap on the job and gives each book her one hundred per cent. I really appreciate it and the end result is so much better for her tireless efforts. There you go, M, read that back to me next time I am howling NOOOOO about a note.

Once again, big up to brilliant copy editor Keshini Naidoo whose thoughtfulness and humour makes her pass through the manuscript a pleasure.

My sincerest thanks to the whole HarperCollins family – the positivity and encouragement I get is truly special, please know you have a grateful author here. (I'd start naming individuals but let's be honest, that's an etiquette minefield. But if you think I mean you then I definitely mean you.)

On the agenting side, I benefit from not only the capability but the friendship of Doug Kean at Gunn Media – here's to you, sir!

Particular thanks to poet and novelist, Kim Addonizio, for generous permission to quote a line from her work 'To the Woman Crying Uncontrollably in the Next Stall'.

If I Never Met You required me to describe some aspects of being a solicitor, and my dear friend Serena Mandair helped me plenty, even as she was rushing around actually being a lawyer while I asked dumb questions. Thanks, Serry – any mistakes are mine!

Also, finally, a correction: in my last book, in some sort of Prosecco-clouded fugue state, I forgot to thank Sarah Brown who gave me tons of help when I stole the idea of her cool show 'Cringe'. So sorry, Sarah, whenever you're next in the UK, the drinks are definitely on me.

'What would your twin brother do?' came from conversations with the relentlessly inspirational Sally Thorne, an author who I was lucky enough to share events with in Toronto – thank you for your company and your wisdom.

Gratitude as always to my first draft readers: Tara, Sean, Ewan, Katie, Kristy Berry – I'd find this SO much harder without you, and that's the truth.

Thank you to my friends and family who cheer me on, and especially to Alex, who lives the highs and lows of the creative process with the 'temperamental artist', heh heh, oh dear.

And thank you to readers who keep buying my books. I don't want to end on a note that makes it sound like I think I'm Taylor Swift but my God, I feel so lucky: bless you all.

A Q&A with
Mhairi McFarlane

What inspired *If I Never Met You*?

I'd been wanting to write the Fake Romance trope for ages. Then, inevitably, a friend said 'hey Mhairi, you have to see this great new Netflix film *To All The Boys I've Loved Before*!' and not only did it have the 'we're only pretending we're dating' plot, there was a scene where they set the rules for it! Argh! Curse my luck! But, I reasoned a high school passion has major thematic differences to two colleagues in their thirties. The social media age is such a rich time to write the wholly performative love affair because there's so much highlights-reel-showing-off going on already. To counterpoint the high concept romance, I wanted the pain that spurred the protagonist into doing it to feel very real: thus the awful separation and 'emotional ghosting' Laurie gets, right on the cusp of starting a family and in sight of middle age. And of course at the heart of it all is that romantic comedy mainstay: two people who imagine they're chalk and cheese and turn out to be uniquely suited. That twist always thrills me.

One thing your readers always say about your novels is how real the characters feel. Did you have any IRL inspiration for Laurie, Jamie, Emily and Dan?

That is an incredible compliment, thank you! The truth of character inspiration is a little prosaic – there's always parts of people you know, but never all of someone you know. (For some reason, ripping off anyone wholesale tends to fall a little flat on the page, probably because you're not doing your job of *fiction* writing.) My longtime university friend Serena is a brilliantly capable lawyer at a large firm so she's the closest I had to Laurie inspo (and she gave me tips on the legal side of things) but otherwise, her life is not Laurie's! My super successful PR friend Julia in Manchester was the initial inspiration for Emily, but again, two-thirds of Emily is definitely not Ju. As for Jamie and Dan, damn, I *wish* I knew Jamie. Both Dan and Jamie started as archetypes – Dan is the ultra-solid guy you're supposed to seek when you want marriage and kids and stability, and of course turns out not to be that. Laurie's revelation that they had an outwardly modern relationship but in fact she was tolerating some traditionally unequal crap is very much the Author's Message of that pairing. (Not that I write to educate! But I think rom coms can explore modern lives in interesting ways.) And obviously, Jamie's the fly-by-night ambitious heartbreaker who'd leave you for dead if you were going to slow him down. I love mining the potential of appearances being misleading – I think even those of us who pride ourselves on judging on non-superficial traits, are way more suckered in by image and assumption than we'd ever like to admit. Me included.

When you're not beavering away on the next book, what do you do with your time?

Hahaha! This is like that terrible moment in CVs when you get to the section that says HOBBIES and you realise you're supposed to be some sort of respectable person when you're not doing your full-time job, what the hell is that about? 'The cinema and socialising with friends.' What do I like, hmm being honest I like dramas like *Mindhunter* on Netflix, Prosecco, quality time with my cat and going for a curry. There's sod all paragliding, ceramics, choir practice or wiffle ball, soz.

You were an early adopter on Twitter and have a really active presence there. How do you think it's evolved over the last few years and what do you like/dislike about it as opposed to Facebook or Instagram?

Ahhhh terrible addictive evil mistress Twitter. Yes, I've been on there since 2009, when I was a lonely working-from-home freelancer and it became my virtual office space. Evolved, hmm, I wish I could say it's developed in good ways, but being honest, about six years ago or so it became a village square full of mobs doing hangings and floggings, and I doubt it's brought anyone the same innocent joy since. What I like about it is that Facebook & Insta can often depend on having things in your life you want to show off about, and Twitter's non visual nature means it's far more about debate, ideas, conversations and jokes than the others. I've made firm friends on there and it can be very generous in terms of sharing and amplifying each other's wit, wisdom and good news. Dislike – well, the aforementioned cruelty. Something I learned a while back is that social media is a mood mirror – if you wake up grumpy and fire out anger into it, you'll very likely get the same back. If you'd rather have a lighthearted time, share the cat picture.

What's next?

The next book! I am SO excited, slash scared, as per. I think it would probably be a bad sign not to be scared. Every time though it's such a joyous challenge and a privilege to be able to ask yourself: what would I find interesting? And write about it.

Keep up to date with *Mhairi* online and get the latest news on her books, life and cat

 @MhairiMcF

/MhairiMcFarlaneAuthor

If you enjoyed
If I Never Met You,
you'll love
Don't You Forget About Me

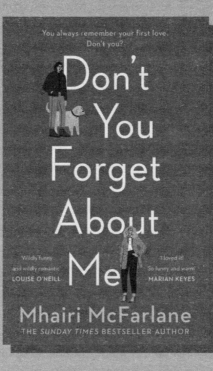

Available in **ebook, audio**
and **paperback!**

Or discover
Mhairi's backlist

Available in **ebook, audio**
and **paperback**